TODAY'S HOTTEST READS
ARE TOMORROW'S SUPERSTARS

VICTORY'S WOMAN   (4484, $4.50)
by Gretchen Genet
Andrew—the carefree soldier who sought glory on the battlefield,
and returned a shattered man . . . Niall—the legendary frontiers-
man and a former Shawnee captive, tormented by his past . . .
Roger—the troubled youth, who would rise up to claim a shocking legacy . . . and Clarice—the passionate beauty bound by one
man, and hopelessly in love with another. Set against the back-
drop of the American revolution, three men fight for their
heritage—and one woman is destined to change all their lives forever!

FORBIDDEN   (4488, $4.99)
by Jo Beverley
While fleeing from her brothers, who are attempting to sell her
into a loveless marriage, Serena Riverton accepts a carriage ride
from a stranger—who is the handsomest man she has ever seen.
Lord Middlethorpe, himself, is actually contemplating marriage
to a dull daughter of the aristocracy, when he encounters the
breathtaking Serena. She arouses him as no woman ever has. And
after a night of thrilling intimacy—a forbidden liaison—Serena
must choose between a lady's place and a woman's passion!

WINDS OF DESTINY   (4489, $4.99)
by Victoria Thompson
Becky Tate is a half-breed outcast—branded by her Comanche
heritage. Then she meets a rugged stranger who awakens her
heart to the magic and mystery of passion. Hiding a desperate
past, Texas Ranger Clint Masterson has ridden into cattle country
to bring peace to a divided land. But a greater battle rages inside
him when he dares to desire the beautiful Becky!

WILDEST HEART   (4456, $4.99)
by Virginia Brown
Maggie Malone had come to cattle country to forge her future as
a healer. Now she was faced by Devon Conrad, an outlaw
wounded body and soul by his shadowy past . . . whose eyes
blazed with fury even as his burning caress sent her spiraling with
desire. They came together in a Texas town about to explode in sin
and scandal. Danger was their destiny—and there was nothing
they wouldn't dare for love!

*Available wherever paperbacks are sold, or order direct from the
Publisher. Send cover price plus 50¢ per copy for mailing and
handling to Penguin USA, P.O. Box 999, c/o Dept. 17109,
Bergenfield, NJ 07621. Residents of New York and Tennessee
must include sales tax. DO NOT SEND CASH.*

WINGS of MORNING

VICTORIA THOMPSON

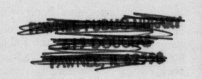

ZEBRA BOOKS
KENSINGTON PUBLISHING CORP.

ZEBRA BOOKS are published by

Kensington Publishing Corp.
850 Third Avenue
New York, NY 10022

First Printing: July, 1996
10 9 8 7 6 5 4 3 2 1

Printed in the United States of America

To my beautiful daughter Lisa and her new husband.
May you always be as happy as you are today.

One

Grayson Sinclair was the rudest man alive. Emma Winthrop was certain of it as she sat in her bedroom fuming over his latest outrage. Imagine, summoning her to a meeting in her own house, a house in which he was nothing more than a guest! And summoning her to a meeting to discuss *business* when he knew perfectly well she was still prostrate with grief over losing her dear Charles!

Widowed a mere two months ago . . . Well, almost three, now, but surely that was still much too soon to expect her to turn her mind toward such things as *business!* And to send her very own maid to fetch her down to her very own parlor, as if he had the right to order her about! Sometimes Emma couldn't believe he was really dear Charles's brother.

Of course, they weren't *really* brothers, only stepbrothers. And they hadn't even met until six years ago, when Grayson's mother had married dear Charles's father. But still, Emma was sure Grayson should behave like a gentleman toward her even if he and her dear Charles weren't actually related by blood. After all, he'd suffered himself, losing his own wife so tragically, so he knew what she was going through. Or at least he should have.

Emma had tried to excuse him, reminding herself that Grayson and his mother had traveled a very long way to be with her. But it wasn't *her* fault that they lived all the way in Texas, which, she remembered from her geography lessons a few years ago at Miss Farnsworth's Academy for Young Ladies, was more than a thousand miles from Philadelphia. And it *also* wasn't her fault they'd had to come in the first place! *She* hadn't sent for them and never would have dreamed of imposing on them. Charles's *attorneys* had sent for them, and Emma hadn't known a thing about it until she'd received word of when they'd be arriving.

Emma still couldn't understand why they'd had to come in the first place, either. If there was some kind of problem with dear Charles's estate, why hadn't Charles's attorneys discussed the matter with *her?* But when she'd questioned them, they'd only clucked their tongues and told her not to worry her head about it, that Grayson would take care of everything when he came.

She was sorry now that she'd told them about Grayson at all, but when they'd asked her who her closest male relative was, what else could she have said? Her parents were gone and dear Charles's father was gone and there was no other family except some cousins she didn't even know who lived in New York someplace, she wasn't exactly sure where. So they had sent for Grayson because it was Grayson's *duty* to help her. That's what families did, even families as tenuously connected as hers and Grayson's.

When she thought about it, Emma wanted to scream with frustration, but of course ladies didn't scream, no matter how great the provocation might be. So she swallowed the urge, the way she had been swallowing similar urges for practically every one of her twenty-three years, and resigned herself to the coming meeting with her impossibly rude stepbrother-in-law.

With a sigh, she rose from the red velvet chaise where she had been spending most of her afternoons of late and straightened her clothes. The black silk still looked presentable, she judged after smoothing her bodice over her bosom—a bosom she had always felt was much too large for fashion—and checking her appearance in the cheval mirror. A few pats and her thick, chestnut hair was in order again, too. She looked awfully pale, but a young widow *should* look pale, she thought, and did not pinch her cheeks or bite her lips. Let Grayson feel a twinge of guilt at her haggard appearance.

Her dress, while beautiful and exquisitely made, was awfully plain and could have done with some ornamentation, she noticed. She glanced longingly at her jewel box and thought of the beautiful pieces inside, most of which dear Charles had bought for her. But women in mourning did not wear jewelry, and Emma would be in mourning for a long time. The rest of her life, in fact, because she knew that no man on earth could ever replace dear Charles in her heart. Heaving another sigh, she started for the door.

Moving slowly, as befitted a lady in mourning, Emma took the time to admire her home as she descended the massive staircase into the front hallway of the town house. Charles's father had built the house for his first wife decades ago and furnished it with only the best of everything. Then the old man, after being widowed for many years, had met and married Grayson's mother, Virginia, during a visit to the shore which was the first holiday he had ever taken in his life. Virginia had added a few touches of her own during the four years before Charles's father had died. But Emma, who had come here almost three years ago as a bride, was the one who had truly finished the house, replacing many of the dated pieces with things she and Charles had found in their travels in Europe. A vase here, a sculpture there, some tables and chairs, new carpets and draperies of the finest fabrics, all of those things had served to turn a once beautiful home into a showplace. Emma allowed herself a small measure of pride that did nothing to ease the deep sorrow of losing the beloved husband with whom she had shared it all.

Downstairs, the parlor pocket doors stood open, and Higgins, the butler, waited in the hallway to close them behind her. And to eavesdrop, she thought in annoyance. If she had to submit to Grayson's summons, she did not have to let the servants know why he had summoned her.

"Thank you, Higgins," she told him sharply. "You may go."

A flicker of disappointment crossed his usually impassive features, but when she waited outside the parlor door, he had no choice but to withdraw. When he was gone, Emma stepped into the room and pulled the doors closed behind her.

Virginia was sitting on the rosewood sofa. She wore a lace cap over her graying hair, and her small, plump figure was encased in the required black for mourning. Her usually bright eyes were clouded now, and she half-rose when Emma turned to face her.

"Emma, dear, we're so glad you could come down."

Emma favored her with a smile. Virginia wasn't to blame for this. "I was a little surprised at the request," she said with just the slightest hint of censure, glancing about to find Grayson who was standing across the room, in front of the sideboard from which he had helped himself to dear Charles's whiskey. Grayson was, she noted, much too tall. Men had enough advantages without being so tall, and he was also entirely too good-looking. Her smile to him was less than pleasant. "I can't imagine what was so important that it couldn't wait until supper."

Grayson returned her smile with one as equally insincere. "Perhaps you will when you hear what I have to say," he said, holding up his glass in salute.

"Grayson, please," his mother cautioned. "Emma, why don't you sit here with me?" Virginia patted the sofa seat invitingly.

Emma glared at Grayson, hating his male smugness and being annoyed all over again at how handsome he was. How dare he be so handsome? "Beauty is as beauty does," her mother had always told her, but if that were really true, Grayson Sinclair would be a hunchbacked troll instead of a raven-haired Adonis. Without comment, Emma took the seat Virginia had indicated.

"I see Mary laid tea for us," Emma observed, more annoyed than ever. *She* hadn't ordered tea.

"Let me pour you some, dear," Virginia offered, "before you hear what Gray has to tell you."

For the first time, Emma felt uneasy. She'd been so concerned with her wounded sense of propriety, she hadn't given a thought as to *why* Grayson had called her down. She'd known, of course, that it must have something to do with Charles's estate, but the only thing he should have to *tell* her was that everything was in order once again.

But when she glanced at him, she saw him drinking deeply of dear Charles's whiskey. How odd, she'd never seen Grayson drinking hard liquor so early in the day, she realized with a frisson of alarm as Virginia handed her a cup of tea.

The china was from the hand-painted set she and dear Charles had brought back from their trip to England last year, she noted absently. Mary had used the best, as if sensing the importance of this meeting. The cup rattled slightly in its saucer as Emma's hand trembled.

"Careful, dear," Virginia cautioned, steadying the cup, but when Emma tried to meet her gaze, seeking comfort or at least some assurance that things weren't as bad as she was imagining, Virginia refused to look her in the eye.

"Emma, Gray has some things he must explain to you," Virginia went on, busily refilling her own cup. "About Charles's business."

"I'm afraid I know very little about his business," Emma said in a last effort to shield herself.

"You don't have to know very much at all to understand this," Grayson said coldly. "Charles's business is bankrupt."

"What?" Emma cried, almost dropping her cup as Virginia gasped in dismay.

"You heard me," Grayson insisted, and Emma could easily have hated him in that moment. "The business is *out* of business. There's barely enough left in the coffers of Winthrop Shipping to pay his employees the wages they have coming, and nothing at all to pay his creditors. I closed the offices down today."

"You had no right!" Emma cried.

"Your attorneys gave me the right," he said. His dark gaze betrayed no hint of sympathy.

"But I thought they called you here to straighten things out, not destroy them!"

"I didn't *have* to destroy them. Charles had already taken care of that himself."

Emma gaped at him as Virginia made little scolding noises at her son.

"This is impossible!" Emma said. "Winthrop Shipping is one of the most successful companies in Philadelphia!"

"It was when Charles's father retired and put him in charge," Grayson confirmed, apparently oblivious to Virginia's remonstrances, "and it was successful for several years afterward, until . . ."

"Until when?" Emma demanded when he hesitated.

For an instant, Grayson looked uneasy, or perhaps she only imagined that. In the next instant, his gaze hardened again relentlessly. "Until he married *you*. It seems that Charles was much more interested in his bride than in his business, which he neglected shamefully."

"That is a bold-faced lie!" Emma informed him indignantly. "Charles was *devoted* to his business! He always spent at least two mornings a week at the office, and sometimes three!"

"Now, now," Virginia soothed, taking the rattling cup from Emma before she spilled the whole thing in her lap. "Try not to upset yourself."

"I'm not upsetting myself!" Emma pointed out acidly.

"Emma," Grayson said sharply, commanding her full attention again, "running a company like Winthrop Shipping requires more than just a few mornings a week. Before he married you, Charles used to spend ten or twelve hours a day at the office, five or six days a week."

"Good heavens," was all Emma could think to say. Whatever could he have found to do for all those hours? Emma was certain her own father had never worked so much. In fact, she could hardly remember him working at all.

"Without Charles's guiding hand," Grayson went on impatiently, "the business gradually slipped away, one customer after another, until there simply was no longer a business at all."

Was *that* what Grayson had considered so terrible? "Well, then, you'll just have to get the business back," Emma said, certain her reasoning was sound. "That's why you came, isn't it? To straighten out Charles's affairs?"

Grayson glared at her. "I'm a farmer, Emma. I don't know the first thing about running a shipping business, and even if I did, I have no intention of moving to Philadelphia and taking over Winthrop. I have a home and a family of my own fifteen hundred miles away."

Of all the preposterous things to say! Grayson wasn't a *farmer*. He was a *planter*. He owned thousands of acres of Texas bottomland (whatever that was) and over a hundred slaves. If he could run a plantation like that, surely he could run a little shipping company. And as for having a family . . .

"Emma, dear, you know what this means, don't you?" Virginia was asking. She'd taken one of Emma's hands in hers, making Emma aware of how icy her own had become. "This means you don't have any money left."

Emma blinked in surprise. That was the most preposterous thing she'd heard yet. "Of course I have money," she reminded Virginia. Or maybe she wasn't really reminding her. Maybe Virginia—and Grayson—didn't know. "My parents left me . . . uh, quite well provided for," she hedged. Ladies simply didn't speak of such things. Emma had been surprised when her parents had encouraged her to marry Charles, a friend of her father's and eighteen years her senior, whom she had known all her life. She had planned to remain single and care for her parents as long as they lived. But when her parents had both died within a year of her wedding, she had understood that they had seen this coming and had provided a protector for her. "Even if Charles's business is . . . is *bankrupt*," she said, casting Grayson a venomous look, "I still have my inheritance."

Virginia's kindly face fell, and for the first time Emma thought she looked every one of her fifty years. "Emma, dear, I don't know how to . . . to tell you this . . . but . . ." She cast Grayson a beseeching glance.

"Charles spent your inheritance, too," he explained coldly.

Emma stared at him in horror. "He couldn't have! He *wouldn't* have! There's been some mistake!"

"There's no mistake," Grayson assured her. "The attorneys have checked all of Charles's accounts. The money is gone, squandered on trips to Europe and new furniture for the house and clothes and jewelry and—"

"But Charles was a wealthy man!" Emma insisted. "He used his *own* money for all those things!"

"He *was* a wealthy man, at first," Grayson said, finally having the grace to look uncomfortable. "But after his business began to fail, instead of economizing, he started to use your money. As your husband, he had every right," he added unnecessarily. Emma understood perfectly that when she'd married Charles, all her property had become his. She'd been only too happy for him to manage her affairs, especially when her parents' deaths had given her so much to manage. How could Charles have done such a thing to her?

"To give Charles his due, I doubt he realized how bad things were until about a week before his death," Grayson went on, oblivious to Emma's distress. "His accountant explained it to him at that time, and I think it must have been the . . . the distress of discovering his true situation that caused his heart to fail so suddenly."

Emma stared at him, numb with shock. Of course. Now everything made sense. Charles had been so strange those last few days, preoccupied and not himself at all. He'd tried to pretend otherwise, but Emma had known something was troubling him. She'd even tried to get him to tell her what, but he'd only patted her hand and told her not to worry, just like the lawyers had told her not to worry and just like other men had been telling her throughout her whole life not to worry because *they* would take care of her.

But he should have told her, should have *warned* her, because now he wasn't here to take care of her anymore and no one else could take care of her either! How could he have left her like this? How could he have left her penniless and alone, without a single word of warning? Emma had to swallow down another urge to scream out her fury and frustration.

"I've met with Charles's accountant," Grayson was saying. "If we sell what's left of the business, his ships, and the house—"

"The *house?*" Emma cried incredulously.

"—and the furniture and most of your jewelry—"

"My *jewelry!*" Emma's hand went instinctively to her throat to protect the jewels she wasn't wearing.

"Then we'll have enough to pay off Charles's creditors with a sum left over to invest for you so you'll have an income of about . . . about three hundred a year." He said the last so softly, Emma almost didn't hear, and for some reason he had dropped his gaze and seemed to be intently studying something in the bottom of his glass.

"Three hundred *dollars* a year?" she asked to clarify.

Grayson did not look up. "Yes."

Emma glanced at Virginia who was inordinately concerned with stirring her tea, then back at Grayson who still would not meet her eye. "Charles always handled our finances, of course, so I don't know a lot about . . . but that . . . that doesn't seem like very much," she ventured.

"It's not," Grayson confirmed, finally meeting her gaze. His eyes shone like black glass. "I daresay the dress you're wearing cost more than that."

Emma gasped, and this time her hand went to her bosom, as if she could hide the delicate, handmade tucks adorning it. "Then how am I supposed to run the house and pay the servants and—"

"You're not," Grayson said brutally. "I told you, you'll have to sell the house and everything in it."

Of course he had, but Emma hadn't understood, hadn't allowed herself to understand. But now she did, and she could only stare, numb with the horror of it all.

Virginia took her hand again. "Emma, dear, I know this must be a shock," she said gently, trying vainly to smooth things over.

Indeed, Grayson had to admit, Emma looked shocked and then some. He couldn't blame her. He was feeling pretty shocked himself. He hadn't been able to believe the amount of money Charles Winthrop had squandered on her in less than three years. Nothing could explain such irresponsible behavior, but looking at Emma now, Grayson could understand it. If any woman could compel a man to destruction, Emma Winthrop was that woman.

Grayson remembered only too well standing at the altar beside Charles the day his stepbrother took her as wife and watching her walk down the aisle toward them, radiant in her innocent beauty. He couldn't ever recall wanting a woman the way he'd wanted Emma that day and every day since when he'd been foolish enough to let himself think of her. It was only, he'd told himself then and many times since, because he'd lost Lilly so recently. When his wife was alive, he'd never allowed himself to look at another woman.

But Lilly was dead, damn her soul, and Gray had been only too glad to flee back to Texas where fifteen hundred miles would separate him from his stepbrother's wife. He would need that much and more, he had reckoned, and he had resolved never to set eyes on Emma again.

For years he'd had no trouble at all keeping that resolve, and then Charles had died. There had been no question of them coming for the funeral. The distance was simply too great. But when Charles's lawyers had written, asking him to come and settle the estate, what choice had he had? Duty demanded he respond, and Virginia had, too. Unwilling to explain to his mother why he should not go near Philadelphia and Emma Winthrop, he had come.

"But where will I live if I sell the house?" Emma was asking his mother. Her beautiful blue eyes glistened with unshed tears and her ivory cheeks were stained crimson with her distress. And her breasts, those magnificent breasts, quivered ever so slightly beneath the delicate silk of her gown. The urge to take her in his arms and crush those trembling breasts against his chest was almost overwhelming, and in desperation, he drained his glass.

"You must have some family," Virginia was saying. "They could take you in, couldn't they?"

"No one on my mother's side at all," Emma replied, her voice—in spite of that hideous Yankee accent—like the tinkle of fine crystal as she bravely fought the tears. He took the liberty of refilling his glass. "I have some cousins on my father's side, but . . . Well, there was an argument a long time ago. They haven't spoken to us in years, and I've never met them."

"There's no one else?" Virginia pressed. "No one at all?"

Please, God, Grayson prayed silently, taking another long swallow of Charles's very fine whiskey.

"Not a soul," Emma said, dashing all his hopes. "That's why my parents were so anxious to see me settled before they . . . they passed on. They chose Charles because he could take care of me and . . ." Her voice broke, and she pulled a lace handkerchief from her sleeve and pressed it to her lips.

Charles had taken care of her, all right, Grayson thought bitterly. If the man hadn't already been dead, Gray would have gladly shot him on the spot. What had Charles been thinking?

But Gray knew perfectly well what he had been thinking, and his concerns would have had nothing whatsoever to do with his bank balance. He had been obsessed with his new bride and with keeping her happy and grateful so she would show that happiness and gratitude between the sheets. Long ago, Gray's concerns had been exactly the same, back in the early days with Lilly, but he had been much younger then. Young and foolish.

But Charles had not had the excuse of youth. Older than Gray by more than a decade and never married, Charles had seemed an unlikely victim for unbridled passion until Gray had seen Emma. The first time Gray had met Charles, at the wedding of their respective parents, Charles had been a stolid, even dull, businessman. The second time Gray had met him, on the eve of his marriage to Emma, he had been as excited as a school-boy waiting for Father Christmas to fill his stocking.

Gray imagined that Emma had filled that stocking admirably.

"Isn't that right, Gray?" his mother asked.

"I'm sorry?" he said, mortified to have been caught in his lascivious thoughts.

"I said, then Emma must come to live with us."

Gray and his mother had discussed this as a last resort, but he'd never really let himself believe it would be necessary. "I'm sure she'd much rather stay here, where she has friends," he tried, desperate now.

"Of course she would," his mother said, smiling reassuringly at Emma. Gray knew that smile. She always used it when she was going to solve a particularly vexing problem in the only possible and very best way. Except this time, the very best way wouldn't be good at all, at least not for Gray. "But she can't stay here, can you, dear?"

Emma sobbed delicately into her handkerchief, and Gray almost groaned.

"I know you think Texas is the ends of the earth," Virginia continued, "but we're really quite civilized. Why, Gray's home is almost as elegant as yours, and our way of living is just as gracious. You'll have parties and balls to attend, and books to read. We even have a literary society. You won't even know you've left Philadelphia."

But Gray would know. He would know only too well. Dear

God, she would be living in his house, *sleeping* in his house, separated from him by only a few walls and doors and . . .

"I couldn't," Emma protested weakly. "I'd be a burden to you!"

She really had no idea how *big* a burden, either, Gray thought.

"Not at all," Virginia assured her. "You could help me run Fairview. That job could keep a dozen women busy, and of course there's little Alice," she added, naming Grayson's daughter. "She would certainly benefit from the training you could give her."

Gray cringed at the thought of Emma Winthrop having any influence at all over his only child. Alice's mother had been only a helpless, empty-headed child herself, with little to recommend her except her beauty, and Emma was, if anything, worse. The kind of woman who never had a thought in her head except to wonder what dress she was going to wear. The kind of woman his life with Lilly had taught him to loathe.

"But you probably won't be with us very long, in any case," Virginia was saying.

Emma's smooth white forehead wrinkled in distress. "What do you mean?"

"I mean," Virginia said brightly, "I know at least a score of planters who need a wife, and not all of them are as determined to remain single as my son." Gray ignored his mother's sharp glance and took another sip of the whiskey. He wasn't going to be drawn into *that* argument again. "I'd be surprised if you didn't find yourself married to one of them and settled in your own place by next year at this time."

The color drained from Emma's beautiful face. "Oh, no, I couldn't! I'll never marry again!"

Gray almost choked on his whiskey.

"I know exactly how you feel," Virginia said with that fix-it smile again. "I felt the same way when Gray's father died, but then I met Mr. Winthrop. You're much too young to think you'll never fall in love again."

"But I won't," Emma insisted. "I know I won't."

Virginia glanced up at her son and winked, silently telling him everything would work out—or at least he hoped that's what she was telling him. "Well then," she said, turning back to Emma and patting her hand, "you'll just stay with us forever."

Over Gray's dead body, he swore silently. But he shouldn't have any trouble at all getting someone to take a woman as beautiful and desirable as Emma off his hands. He would make it his all-consuming passion to see her married before the end of the year, preferably to someone who lived at least a hundred miles away from him.

"Yes, dear, you just rest now. We'll have your supper sent up to you," Virginia was saying as she escorted Emma from the room.

Emma didn't even glance at Gray, which was fine with him, and she could have *all* her meals in her room from now on, too. The less he had to see of her, the better. He might even try to find her a prospective groom on the ship they would have to take to Texas. Then she wouldn't have to spend one single night under Gray's roof.

And *he* wouldn't have to spend one single *sleepless* night thinking about her lying just on the other side of a wall. And he wouldn't be tempted to seek her out in the dark of night and soothe the burning of his lust in the sweet, lush depths of her body.

Because no matter how sweet and lush her body might be, Gray would never, not as long as he lived, tie himself to another woman like Lilly.

At first Emma was afraid she was going to die. Then she was afraid she wasn't. She'd never been seasick before, not the least little bit, not one single time of the several times she and dear Charles had crossed the Atlantic on their way to England and France and Italy and Greece. But she was sick this time as their ship wound its way down the Eastern seaboard and rounded Florida to enter the Gulf of Mexico to sail to the port of Galveston. She was so sick she wished to die.

But of course she didn't die. She merely groaned and vomited and thrashed and vomited and vowed to get hold of herself and vomited, until she was too weak even to vomit anymore and simply lay in her bunk in a fevered state of semidelirium.

And the worst part of the whole ordeal was not having her own maid to take care of her. Instead she'd had to submit to Virginia's maid, Beulah. Beulah hovering over her and lifting her and sponging her fevered body during the seemingly endless voyage.

Oh, Lord, how she missed Bridget who had been her maid for the past three years. But Bridget couldn't come to Texas and *wouldn't* have come even if Emma had had some way to pay her wages because the people in Texas didn't have white servants. They had black slaves, of whom Beulah was one.

One of many, Emma had come to understand. She hadn't even thought of such things when she'd agreed to return to Texas with Virginia and Grayson. Not that she'd had any choice, of course, but still, it seemed so odd. How was she ever going to get used to it?

At least she was beginning to feel human again for the first time in weeks. At Galveston, they'd had to carry her on a stretcher from the ship to this funny boat with the enormous paddle wheel to propel it up the river to Grayson's plantation. But now she was sitting on a deck chair, inhaling the fresh air and watching the shoreline inching past and beginning to think she might possibly survive this awful ordeal.

"How are you feeling, dear?" Virginia inquired as she came up beside her and sat down in the next chair.

"Better," Emma admitted weakly, fingering the lap robe that protected her from the nonexistent chill. Indeed, the air itself felt like a blanket, thick and heavy, just as the trees lining the shore seemed thick and heavily draped with the strange gray masses that Virginia had told her were Spanish moss. The moss made everything look as if it were perpetually shrouded in fog and lent an air of unreality to the scene passing before her.

"Beulah's brought you some tea," Virginia said, indicating the huge black woman who had come up behind her carrying a small tray with a cup of the steaming liquid.

"You should really try to drink it," Virginia advised, and Emma knew she was right.

"Thank you," she whispered, taking the cup from the tray without looking at Beulah. She was being a fool, she knew. She was going to have to become accustomed to having a different kind of servant, she knew. And she would. Just not right this moment. The fragrance of the tea wafted up deliciously, and for the first time since Emma could remember, she felt hungry.

"Try one of the crackers, too," Virginia suggested, and Emma saw several soda crackers lying on the tray.

Obediently, Emma took one and nibbled delicately.

"It won't be much longer now," Virginia was saying. "We're only a few miles from Fairview. Look, there's the McCarthy's house. That's where little Alice is staying. They have a daughter her age, and the two girls just love playing together."

Emma squinted in the bright sunlight and was able to make out a rather large home set high on a hill overlooking the river. To her surprise, she realized that house would be considered a mansion in Philadelphia. Was it possible that Grayson's home was equally as grand? Virginia had insisted she would feel perfectly at home at Fairview, but Emma had only half-believed her. How civilized could life really be so far from the Eastern centers of culture and education? If Emma had had a choice . . . but of course she hadn't.

By the time Virginia told her that they were approaching Fairview's dock a few hours later, Emma was feeling almost normal. She had been able to eat a light supper, the first real food she'd consumed since leaving Philadelphia, and the meal had revived her somewhat. She was considering trying her legs to see if she could stand by the rail when Grayson appeared on deck. She hadn't seen so much as a glimpse of him since they had boarded the riverboat, and she decided not to risk falling on her face in front of him now.

He stopped beside her chair. "You're looking better," he informed her stiffly, looking disgustingly robust himself. His cheeks were ruddy from the sun and wind of the sea voyage, and his dark eyes glittered with obvious excitement at being home again. The wind teased his raven locks and tugged at his expertly tailored suit, molding the black fabric to his muscular thighs. *Beauty is as beauty does.* Emma had to remind herself and wondered why she suddenly felt so breathless.

"I do feel more myself," Emma admitted, although she felt a strange weakness stealing over her again. "I can't imagine why I was so sick. The sea has never affected me like that before."

"And you've certainly experienced more than your share of ocean crossings," he said, his disapproval obvious.

"I had no idea of our financial condition," Emma reminded him, stung. "I never would have agreed to those trips if I had."

Grayson's square jaw tightened, as if he were holding back the words he really wanted to say. Emma wished he would say them so she could tell him . . .

"Gray, dear, look!" Virginia called from where she stood at the rail. "I can see our dock."

Grayson turned and joined his mother at the rail, robbing Emma of any chance of venting the anger that had seethed within her ever since she'd learned of Charles's betrayal.

"Can you see any of the fields yet?" Grayson asked. "Does it look like the crop is in?"

"Of course it's in," his mother assured him. "Nathan would have had it in weeks ago."

Nathan, Emma recalled as she once again swallowed her fury, was in charge of the plantation. He was some distant relative of theirs who worked for them, overseeing the farming. What was his title? Oh, yes, Overseer. How logical.

"And there's the house," Virginia exclaimed happily. Apparently, she shared her son's joy at being home again. Emma wished she could feel anything except anger and despair. Life as she had known it for her first twenty-three years was over. Her home had been sold. Her furniture and every beautiful thing she had ever possessed were gone except for a few keepsakes carefully crated up and carried with them. She would never see her friends again or any of the places she had known and loved her entire life. She would grow old and die among strangers in a strange land.

Fighting the urge to rail at the injustice—Emma could just imagine how any display of emotion would disgust Grayson—she forced herself to gaze out in the direction in which Virginia and Grayson were staring to catch a glimpse of her new home. What she saw astonished her.

Fairview sat on a hill, too, overlooking the river and surrounded by the gnarled and twisted trees that Emma had learned were called live oaks. The house itself seemed enormous. It stood three stories tall with whitewashed columns stretching from the ground to support the porches that ran the entire width of the first and second floors, and on top of the third floor was a cupola, its windows shining in the afternoon sunlight. Attached to the main section of the house were one-story wings extending to either side. An emerald-green lawn dotted with all manner of flowering bushes and trees swept down to the river. Emma was certain she had never seen a more inviting vista or a more impressive aspect.

"It's beautiful," she said aloud.

Virginia favored her with a smile, but Grayson merely arched his eyebrows at her. "You were expecting a one-room cabin with dirt floors, perhaps?"

Emma felt the heat staining her cheeks. "Of course not, but it's so . . . so huge."

"The family only uses the main part of the house," Virginia explained. "The wing on the left is where the house servants live, and the wing on the right is for guests."

"You must have a lot of company then," Emma observed. *And a lot of house servants,* she added silently.

"We've tried to keep the tradition of Southern hospitality alive, so we do entertain a lot," Virginia said. "Many of our guests have to travel a long way, so they must spend at least one night."

Or the rest of their lives, their latest visitor thought bitterly. Would she be given one of the guest rooms permanently?

Emma jumped as the ship's bell clanged.

"They're letting our people know they need to meet the boat," Virginia told her. "In a few minutes, you'll see our carriage coming down the drive."

"The captain said we've been having a lot of rain," Grayson said to his mother. "If the crops are in, they're getting a good start."

"Stop worrying," Virginia scolded. "I told you, Nathan got them in. He's worse than you are about those things."

Emma listened to them with only half an ear. She was busy peering out from under the broad brim of her hat to study her new home, learning the lay of the land and trying in vain to see where her closest neighbor might be. They'd passed the last house at least an hour ago. Didn't anyone live nearer than that? And if the closest neighbor lived an hour away, how far were those who felt they must spend the night?

In a short while, Emma saw an open carriage coming down the drive, just as Virginia had predicted.

"Look, there's Ignatius coming with the carriage," Virginia said. She turned to Emma. "Ignatius has been with us almost thirty years, and when he came, he let it be known that he had been a chiefton back in Africa and that he had no intention of serving anyone. My husband didn't know quite what to do with him for a while and even thought of selling him—if anyone would have been foolish enough to buy a slave who wouldn't work!—but then Ignatius agreed to drive our carriage and take care of the horses, a job he felt was in keeping with his dignity. To this day, I don't think he considers himself a slave at all, does he, Gray?"

Gray smiled that sardonic smile Emma was beginning to hate. "I'm sure he doesn't. If anything, he feels *he* owns *us.*"

Emma glanced away, disturbed by this talk of owning creatures that seemed so much like human beings. She knew, of course, that the Negroes were supposed to be far less intelligent than whites and in need of the kind of care and oversight they received on plantations like Grayson's. Still, she also knew, although she seldom saw them, that free Negroes lived in northern cities like her own Philadelphia and seemed to get along fine. The question of slavery bothered her a great deal when she thought about it, something she'd been doing a lot ever since she'd realized she would be living with it for the rest of her life.

If only Charles were here, she could discuss it with him. Charles had always been able to explain things to her so that she felt comfortable again. But of course, Emma now realized with a start, he had only been shielding her from the unpleasantness of life, just as her parents before him had shielded her. But all that protection had only made her ignorant and weak and helpless when the unpleasantness had reared its ugly head to knock her flat. What would she say to Charles's explanations now, she wondered, and knew that if she could see him one more time, she wouldn't swallow down the anger any more but would grab him by the lapels and shake him and demand to know how he could have done this to her!

To her horror, Emma realized she was trembling with suppressed rage and forced herself to draw in several deep breaths to calm herself before Grayson and Virginia noticed. When she had steadied herself, she glanced around, looking for a distraction to her troubling thoughts, and she saw Beulah approaching. The woman had gone below earlier to pack up their things.

"Land sakes, it's good to be home, ain't it, Miss Virginny?" Beulah exclaimed as she stopped beside Virginia at the rail.

Beulah stood a full head taller than her dainty mistress, almost as tall as Grayson, and probably outweighed Virginia by a hundred pounds. Emma remembered with dismay the ease with which Beulah had handled her when she was ill, lifting and turning her as if she were a doll.

"It certainly is," Virginia told her servant. "Ignatius is already at the dock to meet us."

"So I sees," Beulah said, her tone suddenly cool. "I also sees he got on his fancy coat."

Indeed, anybody could see it. The coat in question was scarlet, decorated in gold braid that glittered in the late afternoon sunlight. Although too far away to make out his features, Emma could tell that his skin was black as ebony above the red coat, and he carried himself like a king as he waited for the pale-skinned people who owned him.

"I made that coat for him years ago," Virginia told Emma. "I thought it would make him more . . . more resigned to his station in life, but I'm afraid it only gave him reason to be proud."

"He don't need no reason," Beulah decreed dourly. Plainly, she had no affection for the other slave.

The ship's engines groaned as the paddlewheel stopped, then reversed to deliver them safely and accurately at the dock. Emma and Virginia waited in their deck chairs while the deckhands tied off the boat and unloaded all their luggage. Grayson oversaw the procedure while Virginia sat beside Emma the whole time, chattering gaily about her home while Emma listened with only half an ear.

Then Grayson came for them.

"Mother?" he said, offering her his arm.

"I'm fine," she told him, rising from her chair and straightening her skirt. "But I'm sure Emma would appreciate someone to lean on."

"Of course," Grayson said with a polite smile, but Emma hadn't missed the flicker of reluctance that had passed over his face. If she hadn't hated him so much, she might have been insulted. She only wished she dared venture off the ship *without* his help, but her knees were still weak. They almost gave out entirely when she rose from her chair.

"Careful!" Grayson cried, grabbing her arm and slipping his own around her waist to support her.

She could feel the heat of his hand on her side right through the many layers of her clothing, and the arm supporting her seemed unbelievably strong. She'd known men were stronger than women, of course, but Grayson's power seemed overwhelming. For a second, Emma couldn't get her breath.

"Are you all right, dear?" Virginia asked, her face creased with concern. "Maybe we should get a stretcher or—"

"No!" Emma insisted. "I'll be fine. I just . . . was dizzy for a moment." She would die before she'd let them carry her ashore on a stretcher again.

She straightened and was quite shocked to discover how close she was standing to Grayson whose arm was still securely wrapped around her waist. Drawing a startled breath, she inhaled his rich, male scent, a mixture of tobacco, bay rum and masculine musk. A scent she had not realized she'd missed so much until every nerve in her body jolted to life.

She lifted her startled gaze to his and saw the strangest expression on his face.

He stiffened instantly and wiped away every trace of emotion, but not before she saw—she was *sure* she saw—that he had been looking at her breasts in a way she'd never seen any other man except Charles look at them, and then only in their most private moments.

Emma felt the heat washing over her, staining her face and her throat in what she knew was a most unattractive manner, then surging downward to scorch the breasts in question and lower still, to places she did not name even in her own thoughts. She didn't bother to explain that heat to herself except to decide that she was thoroughly embarrassed.

"Are you all right?" Grayson asked, his voice as brisk and

impersonal as a stranger's, and his touch, too, as if she had never seen the flicker of naked lust in his dark eyes.

"I said I'm fine," she reminded him, wishing her voice sounded a little less breathless and wishing her body wasn't tingling so strangely, as if she were about to be struck by lightning.

"You're flushed," Virginia observed. "Are you feverish?"

"No, it's . . . just the sun," Emma stammered, trying to move discreetly out of Grayson's embrace, but he held her fast. "I'm not used to it."

"I wouldn't want you to fall and hurt yourself," Virginia said, hovering solicitously.

"I'll be sure she doesn't fall," Grayson said, a promise that should have reassured her but which only caused her more distress.

Emma stiffened her spine and willed the strength back to her traitorous knees. "I'm not going to fall. You may unhand me," she said more sharply than she had intended.

Grayson jerked his hand away as if she had burned him, and his dark eyes registered surprise and . . . and something else that she could not name. "I beg your pardon," he murmured, his square jaw working again.

"Just take Gray's arm, and you'll be fine," Virginia instructed, and when Emma glanced at her, she was surprised to see a complacent smile on the older woman's face, almost as if she were pleased by Emma's momentary faintness.

Before Emma could begin to make sense of it, Grayson had taken her hand and tucked in into the crook of his arm. "Are you ready?" he inquired without the slightest trace of concern.

"Yes," she said, not deigning to glance at him. Lifting her heavy skirts with her free hand, she picked her way carefully across the gently rolling deck toward the gangplank while trying, unsuccessfully, to forget that Grayson Sinclair had possession of her hand and most of her arm.

Their luggage was a neat pile of trunks and crates and carpet bags on the dock. Beside them stood the ebony servant in his ridiculous scarlet livery. He held his whip up at his side as if it were a lance which he was using to guard his booty.

The captain had taken Virginia's arm, and the couple proceeded them down the sloping gangway, chatting amiably. As she and Grayson approached it, Emma instinctively tightened her grip on Grayson's arm, instantly hating herself for the automatic show of weakness. She had been leaning on men her entire life, and this was the first time she had felt any reluctance to do so.

But, she reminded herself, she really had no other choice. With a resigned sigh, she clutched at Grayson's strength and let him lead her to the relative safety of the dock.

"Welcome home, Miss Virginia," the black man in the red coat was saying to his mistress. His tone was as reserved and formal as his manner.

"It's good to *be* home, Ignatius," Virginia assured him cheerfully.

"Welcome home, Massa Gray," Ignatius said to Grayson with a slight nod and a small salute with the end of his whip.

"Thank you, Ignatius," Grayson said, stopping before the servant and forcing Emma to stop, too. "Emma, this is Ignatius. He drives our carriage." Emma blinked in surprise. She had never been introduced to a servant before. "Ignatius, my sister-in-law, Mrs. Winthrop, will be staying with us for a while."

"We's happy to have you here, Miz Winthrop," Ignatius informed her.

Emma could hardly get her breath for the shock. Having a servant presented to her was bad enough, but for one awful moment, she'd been afraid that Grayson was going to present *her* to *him,* too! Of course, she had to admit, Grayson had handled the situation well, making the two of them known to each other without technically breaching the great social gulf that lay between them. But still, Emma couldn't help wishing she didn't have to be known to any slaves at all. Dear heaven, how was she ever going to get used to the idea of owning servants?

The captain had handed Virginia up into the carriage, and Virginia was shaking his hand in farewell. "You simply must stop by on your way back down the river and have a meal with us, Captain," she was saying, her Southern drawl thicker than Emma remembered. "Our cook is the best in the county."

"So I've heard," the captain assured her. He was a middle-aged man with a drooping mustache and a pot belly who appeared to be quite taken with Virginia. Could a romance have blossomed in the short time they'd been on the riverboat? "I'll make a point of stopping whenever I can," he promised.

"I won't ever forgive you if you don't," Virginia swore coyly. Could she be flirting with the man? Emma found such a thought nearly scandalous, considering Virginia's advanced age. Emma considered *herself* far too old for such things. The very idea of a twice-widowed woman of fifty doing such things made her nearly breathless with astonishment.

"Captain, I want to think you for your kind attention to us," Grayson was saying. When he reached out to shake the captain's hand, Emma was finally able to free her own from the crook of his arm. She told herself she was glad to be released, although for a second she couldn't think what to do with her hand until she remembered to drop it to her side once more. Whatever was wrong with her?

"Mrs. Winthrop, I hope you're completely recovered," the captain said, turning to Emma after he and Grayson had finished exchanging compliments. Why did the captain's accent sound so charming while the same accent sounded harsh on Grayson?

"I'm sure I am," Emma said. "And you mustn't feel the least bit responsible for my indisposition. Indeed, I began to recover when I boarded your vessel."

"I'm happy to hear it, and I hope you enjoy your visit to Texas as much as I'm sure we will enjoy having such a lovely young woman here with us."

Emma blinked again. Was the man flirting with *her* now? And why was Grayson just standing there allowing it? And couldn't the man see she was in mourning? Did he have no respect at all?

"I think we'd better get Emma out of the sun," Grayson said at last and escorted her to the carriage.

Once more he took her arm to assist her up the folding steps into the back of the landau, and this time Emma was able to accept his touch without growing breathless. She took her place beside Virginia in the seat facing forward in a bustle of skirts and petticoats. The bulk of the two women's hoop skirts took up most of the carriage, and Emma tried not to notice the familiar way Grayson gave her own a shove to get them through the small doorway.

She busied herself with getting settled so she wouldn't have to look at Grayson again, and she raised her head only to wish the captain farewell once Grayson was in the carriage seat facing theirs and the driver had taken his place in the front. Beulah remained behind with the luggage.

The carriage started with a jolt that forced Emma to grab the side strap with one hand and her hat with the other. The wind caught the wide brim and tried to tear it from her head, but she held it fast and managed to readjust it more securely as the carriage made its way up the long, curving drive.

The sunlight seemed unnaturally bright, bathing every detail of the scene with crystal clarity, from the twisted oaks to the graceful willows to the lush flowers. Emma was sure she'd never seen such beautiful flowers growing on a private lawn. The climate here must be wonderful for growing things, which probably explained why Grayson's father had moved to Texas from South Carolina thirty years ago to plant cotton.

"Are the crops in, Ignatius?" Grayson asked, turning slightly in his seat toward the driver. Emma did not allow herself to admire the fine figure he made sitting there in his dark suit with the wind ruffling his raven hair.

"Yes, sir, they is, in and sprouted. Doing real good, or so

Massa Nathan say. He be real sorry he not here. Had to go see Mr. Phelps 'bout that boy you wants to buy."

"He hasn't closed that deal yet?" Grayson exclaimed in surprise.

Ignatius shook his dark head. "Mr. Phelps, he change his mind. He decide he want the girl on his place so's he can have her young'uns."

Grayson frowned and muttered something under his breath.

Burning with curiosity, Emma refused to ask Grayson for an explanation. She turned instead to Virginia who was also frowning.

"One of our girls wants to marry one of DeWitt Phelps's boys," Virginia said. "Mr. Phelps is Lilly's father, Gray's father-in-law. It happens a lot that a slave from one plantation will want to marry one on another plantation, and sometimes an owner will sell one of the couple so the two can be together. Owning the girl is preferable, of course, since whoever owns her, owns her children, too."

"DeWitt agreed to sell Peter before we left for Philadelphia," Grayson reminded his mother. "We'd settled on a price and everything."

"DeWitt isn't known for being a man of his word," Virginia reminded him, shocking Emma thoroughly. She had never heard Virginia utter a single harsh word about anyone. DeWitt Phelps must be a scoundrel indeed to merit such criticism from gentle Virginia. And how terrible to have such a low opinion of someone to whom Grayson was related.

The sun was *awfully* bright, Emma noticed once again, brighter than she had ever remembered seeing it in Philadelphia, and she was beginning to wilt under its heat now that they were away from the river's cooling affects. Her black dress was stifling, and her body prickled beneath it.

Up ahead Fairview loomed larger even than it had seemed from the boat, and now she could see that slaves were working the gardens. They paused as the carriage approached and began to wave, and Grayson and Virginia waved back. Soon more slaves appeared, emerging from the fields, their dark faces shiny with sweat but broken by the white slash of their grins as they shouted and cheered their returning master.

Grayson and Virginia waved at all of them while Emma simply stared. There were so many of them, so many dark faces and so few white ones. She'd never seen this many Negroes all in one place before. Hearing about the magnitude of slavery and actually seeing it were two very different things, she suddenly realized. Emma's head begin to spin and her heart began to pound beneath the burning silk of her dress.

With more gratitude than she could ever have imagined feeling, she saw that the carriage had finally reached the house. It stopped with a lurch before the massive front door.

Heavy ropes of wisteria draped the porches, their thick purple flowers hanging down in bunches and drenching the air with their rich perfume. Emma found the scent cloying and nearly gagged when she tried to draw in a full breath of air.

Inside the house, a woman was shouting, summoning all the servants, as Grayson stepped briskly out of the carriage and reached up to assist his mother. Virginia followed him, light of step and smiling her happiness at being back where she belonged.

Grayson reached up for Emma who felt as if her bones had become lead. With difficulty, she roused herself and gathered her skirts and found the uncertain footing of the carriage steps. Grayson's strong hands guided her, but she barely felt his touch, as if she were no longer quite inside her body but merely an observer of the scene.

"Welcome to Fairview, my dear," Virginia was saying, taking her arm to lead her inside. The foyer was massive, stretching up to the second floor landing and beyond and extending the entire depth of the house to another door which stood open to face the fields beyond. She was aware of rich woodwork and shining brass and crystal, but mostly she was aware of the sea of faces staring at her.

Virginia was telling her a name to go with each face, but

Emma quickly lost track. She no longer had the strength even to make the effort to remember them.

"Mrs. Winthrop will be staying with us for a while," Virginia told them, as if she considered Emma's presence here a blessing they should all cherish. "We'll put her in Miss Lilly's old room."

"But Mother . . ." Grayson protested.

"It's the most comfortable room in the house, and one of the coolest," she said.

"But . . ." he tried again.

"We'll have Uncle Sam seal off the connecting door," Virginia said. Emma had no idea what she was talking about and couldn't quite summon the energy to ask. "Where's Chloe?" Virginia asked.

A young woman stepped forward, and Emma noticed with amazement that she was lovely, full-figured and graceful beneath her homespun dress, her flawless skin the color of coffee with lots of cream.

"Emma, this is Chloe. She was Lilly's maid. We've had her doing housework since . . . since Lilly's accident, but I'm sure she'll be glad to have a lady to serve once again, won't you, Chloe?"

Chloe didn't smile, and her black eyes were guarded as she met Emma's gaze steadily. "Yes, ma'am," she agreed solemnly.

Emma felt her heart laboring in her chest, as if it could hardly find the strength to beat, and once again she couldn't seem to get her breath. She glanced around frantically, desperate for something, although she could not have said what if her life had depended upon it, and then she was very certain it *did* depend on it, because the room was growing very dark and very hot and she couldn't breathe, not at all. Virginia called her name from someplace very far away just before the darkness swallowed her up completely.

Two

When Emma opened her eyes, for a long moment she didn't know where she was. She lay in a huge cherry-wood, four-poster bed. Above her was a canopy lined with rich pink satin intricately folded and tucked into a rosette pattern. Nothing looked the least bit familiar or jogged her memory at all, but when she carefully pushed herself to a sitting position and glanced around the enormous bedchamber, she saw her trunk sitting open in a far corner. Then the memories of the past few weeks came rushing back: Grayson's awful report, Charles's betrayal, divesting herself of all her worldly goods, the nightmare trip here on the ship and then the riverboat, the carriage ride up to the house and then . . .

And then nothing. Emma recalled entering the house and being presented to at least a thousand of Grayson's one hundred slaves, but nothing after that. Somehow she had gotten from the foyer up to this bedroom and undressed—because now she was wearing only a nightdress and her hair hung loose around her shoulders—but she had no recollection of any of that or of anything at all from the moment in the foyer until now.

All she knew was that she'd been standing face to face with a girl . . . what was her name? Oh, yes, Chloe. One minute she had been standing there face to face with Chloe and the next minute she was lying in this bed. If she had felt ill or groggy, she could have understood the lapse, but she felt surprisingly well, better than she had in weeks, in fact.

Except for the lost time, her mind was completely clear, which was probably why, after she had thought about it for a few more moments, she realized with growing horror what must have happened. Dear heaven, she had *fainted!* She had walked into Fairview in front of God knew how many of Grayson's servants and had fallen to the floor in a heap like a . . . like a . . . Well, she couldn't think of any comparison except a vaporous female. How humiliating! How mortifying! And how Grayson must have sneered at her unconscious form crumpled at his feet.

She already knew he despised her. His attitude was painfully clear. He thought her stupid and weak although she couldn't see where she'd done anything to give him that impression. Certainly, she'd been ill on the sea voyage, but seasickness can happen to anyone. Ordinarily, Emma was the picture of health, and she hadn't been ill a day since she'd been a small child and had contracted the measles. And as for her intelligence, she'd been one of the best students at Miss Farnsworth's Academy. If she didn't know certain things—such as the way Charles ran his business—that wasn't because she was stupid, only ignorant. She *could* have understood if Charles had explained things to her, but he hadn't. In fact, Emma was beginning to realize, no one had ever explained anything to her at all in her entire life. Grayson was unreasonable and even cruel to despise her for things over which she had no control.

And how on earth was she going to live under his roof if he did despise her? The very thought was appalling. She would have to make her peace with him somehow and bring him to understand that she wasn't the witless, spineless ninny he thought her, although Emma felt certain that fainting on his doorstep had done nothing to further her cause. She would have groaned aloud except she didn't know who might be lurking about to hear her.

And she was sure someone *was* lurking about because she felt their eyes boring into her just the way those eyes had been boring into her in the front hall when she'd first come into the house. Over by the windows, yes, that's where they were. She could almost see them out of the corner of her eye, and when she jerked her head around, she saw . . . nothing.

The room was empty. She was completely alone.

Dear heaven, she thought with a shiver, was she losing her mind completely? She didn't know. In fact, she realized she didn't know much of anything at all, not where she was or even what time of day it was. She was remarkably hungry, though, and had an urgent need to use the chamber pot.

She glanced around again. The room in which she had determined she was completely alone was furnished with cherry-wood bureaus and dressers and wardrobes that matched the bed, and the windows—which stretched the length of one wall—were covered with the finest damask draperies, closed now against what appeared to be full daylight. Either she had only been lying here a few moments since her faint or else—a fact that was becoming painfully obvious—she had been unconscious through the entire night and into the next day!

More than humiliated now, Emma scrambled up from the bed. She would make up for lost time, she decided, and without the help of whatever servants might be available to her. The mere thought of sending for the girl at whose feet she had fainted made her cheeks burn, but fortunately, Emma was able to find what she needed herself, located behind an elaborate screen upholstered in more of the pink satin. Not a chamberpot but a commode chair and with it a bathtub waiting to be filled and a washstand with a pitcher of tepid water.

When Emma had relieved herself, she washed her face and hands with the cool water and some soap she found. She really wanted a bath and someone to help her dress and fix her hair and—she remembered when her stomach made a growling protest—get her something to eat. But she could do none of those things by herself, which meant she would have to send for help. Which meant she would have to swallow her pride and send for Chloe and face her somehow and pretend nothing had happened.

The thought made her want to groan again, but what choice did she have? She couldn't leave this room in her current condition, and she couldn't even dress herself without assistance. So she could stay locked away here and starve, or she could pull the velvet cord that hung beside her bed and summon the maid she had every reason to believe would be waiting.

Emma wrapped her arms around herself, crushing her breasts beneath her arms as if she could somehow fold into herself and disappear. But she remained just where she had been, whole and only too substantial. And her stomach growled again. Then she remembered the way Grayson had looked at her the day he had told her about Charles's business and the way he had looked at her every day since, as if she were the most worthless excuse for a human being he could imagine. If she'd made a fool of herself by fainting, she would not compound the damage by cowering in her room afraid to call a servant.

Lifting her chin, she marched over to the velvet cord and pulled. Somewhere in the depths of the house, a bell would be ringing, she knew, and soon, very soon, a maid would come, and if facing that maid made Emma uncomfortable, she would never let the girl know it. After a moment of silent debate about where she should be when the girl came in, she dove back into the bed and pulled the pink satin coverlet up and arranged the pillows behind her back so that she would seemingly be at ease.

By the time the door to her room opened, Emma had almost convinced herself she *was* at ease. The girl she remembered from the foyer came in. She carried a tray and wore a fixed smile that didn't quite reach her dark eyes.

" 'Morning, Miss Emma. I's Chloe, your maid," she informed Emma who felt more than a little chagrined to know that the girl believed she needed to be reminded.

"I remember. Mrs. Winthrop introduced us," she said, glad to hear how confident her voice sounded.

"You was kinda sickly, so I thought maybe you didn't,"

Chloe said. Her head was wrapped in a red bandana, completely concealing her hair, and Emma found herself curious as to what it might look like. "How you feeling now?"

"I'm . . . much better," Emma admitted. She would have lied if she hadn't, just to protect what was left of her dignity.

"You hungry?" Chloe asked, coming forward.

Emma realized the tray the girl carried was giving off the most delicious aromas of coffee and bread and bacon. "I'm starving," Emma confessed, pride giving way to baser instincts.

Something passed over Chloe, something that might have been relief, but Emma took no time to analyze it because the girl was beside her, setting the tray across Emma's knees, its little legs resting on either side of her thighs.

Chloe's hands looked awfully dark against the white cloth covering the tray, but then she pulled the cloth away, and Emma saw the food and forgot how different her new maid was from her old one. There were golden brown biscuits and eggs and bacon and butter and jam. Emma hardly even noticed when Chloe reached over and poured coffee from the small China pot into the delicate China cup. She was too busy slathering butter on a biscuit which was, she was certain, the lightest one she had ever seen.

"I reckon you be wanting a bath," Chloe said as Emma sank her teeth into the buttery biscuit and confirmed that it was also the most delicious one she had ever tasted. "I bring up the water in a minute."

With that, she slipped away, to Emma's great relief. At least she would be able to eat without worrying about what kind of an impression she was making. Emma couldn't ever remember being so hungry, which was probably why the food tasted so extraordinarily wonderful, she told herself. She had eaten well many times during her life, food prepared by famous chefs in restaurants all over the world, but she was sure nothing had ever tasted quite as good as this lavish breakfast.

Forgetting every lesson in manners she had ever learned—no one was around to see, after all—Emma devoured her meal and gulped down the rich, dark coffee with unseemly haste. Only when she'd picked up every last biscuit crumb with a moistened fingertip and licked it clean did she begin to think about other things.

She had neglected to learn some vital information, namely where she was and what time of what day it was. The fact that Chloe had said "Good morning" and given her breakfast gave her hope it might still be morning, at least. And she also needed to know what the reaction had been to her disastrous entrance into Fairview. And what she was expected to do with herself now that she was here. Virginia had told her she could help her run the house, but exactly what did that entail? Emma had run a house in Philadelphia, but she hadn't needed any help in giving orders to the servants. Virginia had many more servants, which should have meant even less work for her. Perhaps Virginia had been humoring her about helping. Perhaps there was really nothing at all for her to do here, and she would spend her days in blissful idleness. No prospect could have frightened Emma more.

Before she could grow truly terrified, however, the door opened and Chloe entered, carrying two buckets of steaming hot water which she took behind the screen where the tub sat. Emma heard her pouring the water into the tub, and then she emerged with the buckets.

"You done already?" she asked, seeing Emma's empty plate.

"Oh . . . yes," Emma admitted reluctantly, ashamed to have the girl know what a pig she had been.

Chloe set the buckets down and came for the tray. "Cook, she make the best biscuits in Texas," she said. "You want me to bring you some more?"

"Oh, no," Emma said too quickly. "I mean, I couldn't eat another bite."

Chloe's dark eyes were guarded as she lifted the tray from Emma's lap and set it down on the floor. "I be right back with more water. Miss Virginia give me some lavender soap to wash your hair."

"I . . . That's lovely," Emma managed, knowing the girl must think her a fool. The instant Chloe was gone, she jumped out of bed, determined to make a better impression when she came back.

Emma managed to be busy selecting her clothes when Chloe returned with more water. This time another girl came with her, and between the two of them, they filled the tub with enough hot and cold water to make it the right temperature. The other girl was giggling and staring curiously at Emma and who tried to ignore her. Finally, Chloe sent her away and closed the door behind her.

"It's ready, Miss Emma."

Emma had known this moment would come, the moment she would have to strip herself naked and put herself into the hands of this total stranger. She had known and had prepared herself, but now she wasn't so sure she could go through with it. On leaden feet, she marched over to the screen and stepped behind it.

Instantly, the scent of lavender engulfed her, sweet and inviting. Chloe had shaved some of the soap into the water and was swishing it around with her hand. "Water's getting cold," Chloe warned, then as if she had somehow sensed Emma's reluctance, she turned away, busying herself with a stack of towels so that Emma could strip off her nightdress in privacy.

Emma took advantage of the moment, tossing the gown aside and stepping into the tub so quickly she sloshed some water onto the floor. But as she settled into the warmth of the bath, she couldn't help the sigh that escaped her.

"Feels good, don't it?" Chloe asked, turning back to her.

"Uh, yes," Emma said, self-conscious of her naked and vulnerable state even while the blissful heat of the water seduced her into forgetting it.

"You miss your own maid, I reckon," Chloe guessed, handing Emma a washcloth and a piece of the lavender soap.

"She'd been with me for a long time," Emma said, unable

to meet the girl's eye as she took the cloth. She proceeded to work up a lather so she wouldn't have to look at Chloe.

"I was with Miss Lilly all my life," Chloe said. "At least, since we was real little girls."

Emma gaped at her, forgetting her own concerns. "They put you to work when you were a little girl?" she asked incredulously.

Chloe grinned, and for the first time Emma got the feeling the emotion she was expressing was genuine amusement. "Oh, no, ma'am. I was her playmate at first. We was together all the time, from morning 'til night, and then we slept in the same room, her in the big bed and me in the trundle. When we growed up, they teached me to be her maid. I come here with her when she marry Mr. Gray and then . . ."

Her voice trailed off, and so did her eyes, to some private place. Undoubtedly, the girl sincerely mourned her mistress.

"You miss her," Emma said, somehow surprised at the depth of the girl's sorrow. Would Bridget have mourned her that way?

"Yes, ma'am." With obvious effort, Chloe brightened again. "I don't mean to worry you. It's just . . . being in her room again, I reckon. Makes me think about her."

"This was her room?" Emma glanced around, seeing the place with new eyes. Of course. This was the mistress's bedroom, which explained the elegance of the furnishings. She vaguely recalled Virginia saying something about putting her in Lilly's room just before . . . Well, she wouldn't think about that now.

"Yes'm, and sometimes . . ." Chloe glanced over toward the draped windows. "Sometimes it's like if I turn my head quick enough, I'll see her standin' there, still alive."

Emma recalled her own certainty that someone was watching her from over by the windows and shivered slightly in spite of the warmth of her bath.

"But I don't expect she'd mind havin' you stay here," Chloe went on, shaking off her melancholy again. "And you don't need to worry none, we's gonna lock up that door what leads to Massa Gray's room."

"What?" Emma cried, instinctively covering herself and looking frantically around until she found the second door which was, mercifully, tightly closed. "That door leads to *Grayson's* room?"

"Yes, ma'am, but don't worry, he ain't in there. He slept down in a guest room last night. Soon as you's done in here, we have Uncle Sam—he the blacksmith—come and fix up a lock, and then everything be fine."

Emma didn't think everything would ever be fine, but she said, "Yes, of course," acutely aware that she was naked, although why she should be worried about Grayson coming into her bedroom even if there *were* just an unlocked door between them, she couldn't imagine. He had given her absolutely no reason to believe he found her at all attractive, except perhaps . . . As if remembering a dream, she recalled the way he'd looked at her in that one moment back on the riverboat just as they were getting ready to go ashore. For one brief second she had seen what she thought was lust burning in his dark eyes.

But surely, she had been mistaken. She knew only too well what he *really* thought of her, didn't she? A man wouldn't lust after a woman he despised. The very idea was ridiculous. So Emma's virtue was safe, at least from Grayson Sinclair, lock or no lock.

Emma began scrubbing herself, performing the familiar task absently as she tried not to think of Grayson, and before she knew it, she had finished.

"Lean your head back," Chloe instructed, and Emma obeyed without thinking until Chloe's hand cupped her head to steady it. She froze at the girl's touch.

Chloe didn't seem to notice her reaction, though. She simply poured some warm water through Emma's long, thick hair, making Emma shiver with pleasure. Emma closed her eyes, determined not to think about how different Chloe was from her other maids. Forcing herself to concentrate on the pleasure instead, she held herself perfectly still while Chloe worked up a lather and began to massage it over Emma's scalp and through her long tresses.

Dear heaven, the girl's fingers felt wonderful and more than wonderful as they worked their magic, and Emma relaxed in spite of herself.

"Too bad about your husband," Chloe said after a few moments.

Emma stiffened slightly, bracing herself for the onslaught of pain she always felt at the mention of dear Charles. But when it came this time, it wasn't an onslaught, only a twinge, and she realized that ever since Grayson had told her about Charles's business failing, her grief had lessened considerably. "He was only forty-one," Emma said.

"He was some older than you, then," Chloe said, using a small bowl to pour water through her hair once more. The warm suds sluicing down Emma's shoulders were like a caress that raised gooseflesh and brought her nipples to pebbled hardness. She crossed her arms over her chest self-consciously

"Yes, he . . . eighteen years," she said, having a little trouble following the conversation.

"Massa Gray, he was some older than Miss Lilly, too, but only six years."

Automatically, Emma did the math in her head. "Good heavens, she must have been a child when she married him!"

"Just turned sixteen," Chloe confirmed.

"Is that the . . . the *usual* age for girls to marry around here?"

Chloe shrugged. "For some," she confirmed. "I reckon a girl could marry at three if'n her folks would agree. Ain't nearly enough women to go around. Miss Lilly, though, she'd set her cap for Massa Gray, and she was gonna have him. And she'd promised me . . ." She stopped abruptly, and Emma opened her eyes, hoping to read something in the girl's expression that would give her a clue as to what she had been about to confess. She saw nothing at all. "Well, she wanted to get married is all," Chloe finished.

But then Chloe started soaping her hair again, and lost in the delicious sensations, Emma forgot to wonder any more.

"Water's getting cold now," Chloe said a few minutes later, when she'd finished her shampoo. "Stand up and I'll rinse you off."

Instantly, Emma snapped out of her sensual daze. The thought of standing up, exposing herself completely . . . but she'd done so a thousand times before in front of other maids in other places and never given the matter a moment's thought. Just because this maid was so different . . . Suddenly, she thought of what Grayson's opinion of her modesty would be, and Emma grasped the sides of the tub and pushed herself to her feet.

Emma squeezed her eyes shut as the water came sluicing over her head, rinsing away the last traces of soap and grime. She didn't realize they were still closed until Chloe pressed a towel into her hands.

Quickly, she unfolded it and dried her face as Chloe's deft, brown hands wrung the water from her hair. Focusing on each task so that she wouldn't remember she was standing naked in front of a stranger who was helping to dry her off, Emma quickly wrapped her head and her body and stepped out of the tub onto yet another towel Chloe had spread on the floor.

"You gots a real nice figure, Miss Emma," Chloe decreed, bringing the color to Emma's face. "Nice, big bosom. Mens, they like that."

"Uh, thank you," she stammered, mortified.

"Miss Lilly, now, she was skinny as a rail. Never did fill out, neither, not even after she had a baby. We always had to sew ruffles in her bodice so's she'd have a bosom in her dresses. I used to tell her it looked like she had two 'skeeter bites on her chest."

Emma didn't know whether to laugh or gasp, but plainly, Chloe had meant the remark to amuse her, so she smiled uncertainly. Although she knew she shouldn't be gossiping with a servant, she was also curious about Grayson's late wife. Such a thing was only natural, she reasoned, since she would be living in the woman's house and even sleeping in the woman's bed. The bed she had no doubt shared with Grayson himself . . .

Suddenly, Emma had a very clear picture of Grayson in that bed, Grayson without his tailored suit and starched shirt and holding a woman in his arms, a woman to whom he was making love and . . . She shivered violently.

"You getting cold!" Chloe determined and quickly wrapped a dry towel around her shoulders. "Quick, let's get you into a robe."

Emma gratefully slipped on the robe Chloe held up for her, only too glad to cover herself from the girl's eyes as well as from the invisible Grayson's.

"But you now," Chloe was saying as she led Emma to the dressing table and seated her before it. "Nobody gonna have to sew ruffles in *your* bodice."

Emma self-consciously grasped the lapels of her robe more tightly together over her ample bosom. "Uh, no, that's . . . never been a . . . a concern for me."

Chloe rubbed Emma's hair vigorously with the towel, squeezing out the last of the water. "Pretty woman like you won't have no trouble at all catching yourself another husband, neither."

This time Emma didn't *have* to decide whether to laugh or to gasp. She practically yelped in outrage. "I'm not *looking* for another husband!"

Startled by Emma's vehemence, Chloe froze, and Emma peered up at the girl's reflection above her in the dressing table mirror. "You ain't?" Chloe inquired incredulously.

"Certainly not! My husband is hardly cold in his grave! And besides, I can't imagine I'll ever *wish* to marry again!"

Chloe nodded wisely. "He was mean to you, I reckon."

"Of course he wasn't mean to me!" Emma exclaimed. "He

was the best husband any woman could have wanted! He treated me like a queen, and he never refused me anything and . . ." Emma caught herself. That had been the problem, hadn't it? If Charles had refused her a few things, perhaps she would still have her home and her friends and her life instead of being in Texas, living on Grayson Sinclair's charity.

"You don't think you can find another fella like him?" Chloe suggested.

Emma nodded curtly, not trusting herself to reply. The *last* thing she needed was another husband like Charles.

Having learned what she wanted to know, Chloe seemed content to devote herself to drying Emma's hair. Gently she brushed out the tangles, then alternately toweled and combed it until it was nearly dry.

"You ready to get dressed now, Miss Emma?" she asked.

There was no use in doing her hair until she had her clothes on, Emma knew. "I suppose so."

"You wanna wear something black, I expect," Chloe said. "How about the serge? The silk one needs to be aired some."

"That's fine."

Emma had laid out the undergarments she had chosen, and now she rose and accepted each piece as Chloe handed them to her, trying not to be aware of the fact that Chloe had now seen every inch of her body or to think about the fact that she would be serving Emma's most intimate needs for as long as she lived in this house. When she had put on her drawers and her chemise and fastened up her corset, Chloe pulled and tugged on the laces until the fit was tight enough. Then Emma pulled on her stockings and adjusted her garters, and by the time she was finished, Chloe was waiting to lower the heavy petticoats over her head. At least she wouldn't need a hoopskirt for a simple morning at home.

Emma ducked beneath the mountain of rustling taffeta and emerged through the waist hole as Chloe let the yards of crisp fabric settle around her. As she stepped back, Chloe's hand brushed Emma's bare arm, and Emma jumped, instinctively recoiling from her touch.

Startled, Chloe stared at Emma for an instant, her dark eyes wide with surprise, then narrowing with understanding. "Don't worry," she said coldly. "It don't rub off."

"What?" Emma asked, genuinely confused.

"The color," she said, holding up her brown hand. "It don't rub off."

Mortified, Emma could only stare for a long moment. "I know that!" she finally managed. "I just . . ." She caught herself in time to keep from making things worse. "I'm sorry, it . . . it's not that," she stammered in an agony of embarrassment. She'd never found herself in quite such a situation before. While she had been raised to consider even a serving girl's feelings important, she hadn't been raised around Negroes, so she wasn't quite sure how to soothe this girl. "I'm just not used to . . . I've never had a colored servant before. I'd never even *seen* a colored servant before until Virginia . . . Mrs. Winthrop, I mean, until she brought Beulah to Philadelphia."

Chloe's lovely face might have been carved from stone. Her dark eyes were flat as she stared back at Emma, her mouth pressed into a tight little line. She lowered the hand she'd raised for Emma's inspection and clasped it to its mate at her waist as she pulled herself up straighter, assuming all the dignity Emma had lost. She looked like a queen standing there in her butternut homespun.

"If you want, Miss Virginia can get you another girl."

"No! I mean, that wouldn't make any difference! I'd just be nervous around her, too!"

Chloe's large, dark eyes widened in amazement. "You's *scared* of me?"

Emma's cheeks were scalding with humiliation. How on earth could she have said such a thing? How on earth could she have *admitted* such a thing? She laid a hand over her pounding heart in hopes of slowing it by the sheer force of her will. "Not . . . not *scared* exactly. I mean, I don't think you're going to hurt me or anything. It's just . . . haven't you ever been afraid of something new and different? Something you've never experienced before?"

An expression passed over the girl's face, an emotion so naked and raw that for an instant Chloe was actually ugly. Then, just as quickly, it was gone, and her lovely face settled back into its grim blankness. "Yeah, I been afraid."

"Everything here is so new, I just have to get used to things," Emma hurried on, pressing the slight advantage. "It isn't you. You've been fine . . . perfect, in fact. I couldn't ask for a better maid." Emma stopped, biting back the urge to beg the girl not to leave her. She must be losing her mind.

"I reckon I gotta get used to you, too," she said after a moment.

"Yes, of course, it's always awkward at first. You've never served anyone but Lilly," Emma said, aware that she was blithering but unable to stop herself.

Chloe nodded once, and Emma took that as agreement.

"I'll do your ties," Chloe said, and Emma turned obediently so she could tie up her petticoat strings.

Next came her skirt and finally the bodice with its myriad tiny buttons. Emma began at the top and Chloe at the bottom and when their fingers brushed as they reached the middle, Emma didn't pull away.

Chloe glanced up in apparent surprise, but if she *was* surprised, she said nothing and her eyes gave nothing away.

"There now," she said, stepping back when the last button was fastened. "You look real fine. Let's get some sunshine in here," she added turning away and going for the windows. With one broad sweep of her arm, she drew back the draperies to reveal a door made of panes of glass that led to the balcony outside. Chloe opened it, allowing the sweet, warm breeze to waft inside. When she turned back to face Emma again, she was smiling. "Ain't hardly been any sunshine in here at all since Miss Lilly been gone."

Emma tried to remember what she knew about the young woman's death and realized she knew practically nothing. Virginia always referred to it simply as Lilly's "accident."

"How did she die?" she asked, then wanted to snatch back the bald question. "I mean, what happened to her?"

Chloe's smile vanished. "She fell," the girl said, oddly defensive. "She fell right off the gallery out there. And don't let nobody tell you she jumped, neither. I know that's what they say, but my Lilly, she wouldn't *never* kill herself."

Emma was still a little shaken a while later when, her hair pinned up neatly by Chloe's expert hands, she ventured out of Lilly's former bedroom. Too stunned to ask for any more details about Lilly's death, she had allowed Chloe to dress her hair and then had gratefully taken her leave while Chloe cleaned up the mess from her bath.

She still had no idea what time it was or where she was in the house, but she quickly figured out the layout of the house when she was in the hallway. The stairs came up from below into the center of the house and the bedrooms were built around it. She saw what must be the door to Grayson's room—she tried not to think about how close it was to hers or about the single door between them—and then several others. One of them would be Virginia's room and one would be Alice's nursery.

Emma smiled in spite of herself at the thought of the little girl who was Lilly and Grayson's daughter. Virginia worshiped the child, and Emma found that she was eagerly anticipating meeting her. Heaven had denied Emma children of her own, a disappointment she would always feel keenly, but she still felt a longing to mother someone. Perhaps Alice could help her satisfy that longing.

Drawing a deep breath, Emma headed for the stairs which swept down into the entryway she recalled from her ill-fated arrival yesterday. Taking the banister which had been worn smooth by many hands, she descended the stairs slowly as she studied each and every detail of the home known as Fairview.

The walls were covered with green silk, faded by the sunlight to the color of lime, and enormous portraits hung at intervals. Emma recognized a young Virginia and a man who must have been her first husband and Grayson's father. Then came a younger Grayson, looking unnaturally somber, and farther down was a lovely, willowy young girl who must have been Lilly. Emma paused, studying the picture for some clue as to what she had been like, some hint of the darkness that would cause people to gossip about her untimely death, but she saw only a pretty face, golden curls and large blue eyes. Her expression, Emma was sorry to note, did not reveal much character.

The sound of a door opening in the hallway below distracted Emma, and before she could even think to react, two men emerged into the hallway. One of them was Grayson. He looked even more robust today than she'd remembered, and he was dressed far less formally than she had ever seen him, in trousers and shirtsleeves. She was surprised and somewhat disturbed to note that his shoulders really were as broad as they appeared beneath his suit coats. The thin fabric of the collarless shirt hugged those shoulders rather faithfully, making Emma feel strangely breathless. Chloe must have laced her corset too tightly.

Mercifully, Grayson didn't see her standing there on the stairs. If she didn't have to speak with him or look into those dark eyes, she knew she could recover and breathe normally again in just a moment, and at first she thought she might, by standing perfectly still, escape notice altogether. But she wasn't to be that fortunate.

The man with Grayson happened to glance up and see her. "Well, now, this must be the beautiful Mrs. Winthrop," he said, and his smile told her nothing could have pleased him more as he crossed the hall in long strides to the bottom of the stairs and gazed up at her.

But Emma was much more concerned about Grayson's reaction to her presence, and he looked far from pleased. What could she have expected after her performance yesterday? "Good morning, Emma," he said without the slightest trace of warmth. "How are you feeling this morning?"

He did not, she noticed with some relief, make any move toward the stairs. Apparently, he was as reluctant to encounter her as she was to encounter him. "I'm much better, thank you," she said, forcing herself to resume her journey downward. She favored the other gentleman with a small smile.

He was dressed casually, too, although he wore a coat over his shirt and duck trousers, and his riding boots were decidedly dirty. This was a man who worked for a living.

"Aren't you going to present me, Gray?" he asked cheerfully.

"Emma, this is my cousin, Nathan Sinclair," Grayson said coldly as Emma reached the last step where she came face to face with Nathan Sinclair.

He was, she saw now that she really looked at him, remarkably like Grayson except that where Grayson's hair was jet black, Nathan's was dark brown, and where Grayson's eyes were nearly black, Nathan's were merely brown. And where Grayson was devastatingly handsome, Nathan was simply attractive. Like a paste copy of a diamond necklace, appealing in its way, but still somehow less than the original.

Emma gave him her hand. She noted with surprise that his fingers were rough, but he bowed over her hand quite chivalrously and, to Emma's everlasting amazement, lifted it to his lips. Although several European men had performed this ancient rite, Emma had never had an American man kiss her hand. She could not help but gape.

"We are honored indeed to have such a fair flower grace us with her presence," Nathan said when he lifted his head. Emma saw that his eyes were dancing with mischief, as if he knew perfectly well how much he had shocked her with his gesture and was delighted to have done so. "I'm afraid Gray did not prepare me for so much beauty. When he told me his widowed sister-in-law was visiting, I expected a frail and elderly lady, leaning on a cane."

"I'm . . . very pleased to meet you," Emma stammered, years of training in the social graces completely deserting her. Surely, there was a polite reply to such an outrageous comment, but if Emma had ever learned it, she could not recall it now.

"I sincerely hope you *are* pleased to meet me," Nathan replied. He had not, she realized with alarm, given her back her hand. She tugged, but he still did not release it. Desperate now, Emma glanced over at Grayson who, she was relieved to note, was finally coming toward them, although the look on his face was hardly comforting.

"I don't think Emma is quite used to Southern charm yet, Nate," he said grimly as he stopped beside his cousin at the foot of the steps.

Nathan didn't seem the least bit chastened, although he did release her hand at last. Emma snatched it back, much to Nathan's amusement.

"She'd better *get* used to it then," Nathan was saying. "She'll be exposed to a lot of it, I'm afraid. You see Miss Emma, when a Southern gentleman sees a beautiful woman, he simply cannot help being charming."

Grayson was glowering now. "I think he probably could if he *tried,*" he informed Nathan. Emma didn't know which was more disturbing, Nathan's teasing or Grayson's anger, and she was beginning to regret hoping he would rescue her.

Nathan ignored Grayson's chiding. "When are you planning a party to welcome Cousin Emma to Texas, Gray?"

Grayson's eyes were nearly black as he glared at his overseer. "I do not believe Emma is *your* cousin or any relation to you at all, come to think of it."

Emma realized she must take a hand in this while she still could. "I'm afraid a party is out of the question," she said to end the controversy. "I'm in mourning."

"I doubt that the bachelors in this county would let a little thing like that stop them from coming to call," Nathan predicted, shocking Emma all over again. "I know I wouldn't."

"Nate, you are upsetting Emma," Grayson said, which was perfectly true, although Emma was surprised that Grayson had noticed. But perhaps he just meant Nathan was upsetting *him*. He certainly looked upset, although she still didn't understand why he should be.

Nathan laid a hand over his heart and looked appropriately chagrined. "I must beg your pardon, Miss Emma. I had no intention of distressing you, and if I did forget myself, it was only because I was so distracted by your radiance. We have not seen its like here at Fairview since . . ." He glanced at Grayson and quickly caught himself. "Well, for a very long time," he concluded instead. "I hope you will forgive me."

"There is nothing to forgive," Emma assured him, also glancing at Grayson. She wanted to see some kind of approval for the way she had handled Nathan, or at least an absence of the contempt he usually showed. Instead she saw only anger. She didn't think either she or Nathan had done anything to provoke him, so probably, she thought in resignation, he was simply angry that she was here at all.

Before she could decide, a noise outside distracted them, and in the next second, a tall colored man ducked his head in the open front door.

"Miss Alice's coming!" he reported before disappearing again.

Emma's heart leaped at the prospect of seeing the child about whom she had heard so much, and she felt the same excitement spreading throughout the house. In a matter of seconds, people emerged from every possible room heading for the front door, dark faces and white, coming to greet the master's daughter. The master himself muttered, "Excuse me," and left them to go meet her.

Emma felt so much relief at being released from his scrutiny that she hardly noticed Nathan Sinclair was still scrutinizing her thoroughly.

Virginia appeared from one of the rooms toward the back of the house—Emma guessed it might be a parlor or sitting room—and she seemed happy to find Emma where she still stood on the stairs with Nathan gazing up at her with more admiration than Emma could believe was proper.

"Good morning, Emma!" Virginia exclaimed. "How are you feeling?"

"Just fine," she assured her hostess.

Virginia turned to Nathan, who towered over her just as her son did. "Nathan, dear, have you met Emma?" she asked, laying a hand on his arm affectionately.

"Yes, Gray introduced us, although I am sorry to say I had to remind him to do so. Honestly, Aunt Virginia, I don't believe he remembers a thing you taught him about manners." Nathan shook his head in mock despair.

"Perhaps he just wants to keep Emma to himself," Virginia bantered back, making Emma blush furiously.

Neither of them seemed to notice her embarrassment, however.

"If he does want to keep her to himself, he'd better marry her today, because as soon as word gets out that she's here, he won't have another chance," Nathan said.

"You know my son would never do anything quite so impetuous," Virginia replied, batting her eyes at Nathan as if she were flirting, although Emma knew that couldn't be what she was doing, not with her own nephew. "So I think we'd be safe in planning a little barbecue in about a week or so to introduce her to the neighborhood, don't you?"

"Most definitely," Nathan agreed and favored Emma with a glance that said, "I told you so!"

The sound of a carriage rolling up outside drew their attention, however, and saved Emma from having to respond to either of them.

"Alice is home," Virginia told Emma and Nathan unnecessarily, and hurried past them to the front door. Outside, they could hear the happy squeals of a child.

"Does he?" Nathan asked Emma, drawing her attention back to him again.

"Pardon me?" she asked in confusion.

"Does Gray intend to keep you for himself?"

"Certainly not!" The very idea brought the heat to Emma's cheeks, and she knew she must be blushing again.

"I'm sorry to be so blunt, Miss Emma," he assured her, although he didn't look the least bit repentant, "but many people will be wondering why you have come all the way to Texas just for a visit, and the more romantic among them will credit my cousin with drawing you."

Emma could have choked on her humiliation. "Mr. Sinclair, the only thing with which people may credit your cousin is charity. I am not merely visiting. I am a poor relation that Grayson and Virginia have taken in. I feel certain that will become common knowledge very soon and ease the minds of even the most romantic of your friends and neighbors."

Nathan Sinclair registered a slight surprise at her revelation, but she never heard whatever else he might have to say on the subject because Grayson and Virginia and all the slaves who had left the house moments ago were now reentering it. With them was perhaps the most beautiful child Emma had ever seen.

Three

Blond and blue-eyed, Alice Sinclair was seven years old, an awkward age for most children, but Emma suspected Alice would never know an awkward age. Small for her years and slightly built, she bore herself with a natural grace and with all the confidence that being the only, much loved child of a wealthy family could give her. Having been such a child herself, Emma recognized a kindred spirit, and for an instant she recalled how blessed she had always been. Adored and cosseted and sheltered from every unpleasantness, Emma had been totally unprepared for life itself. If Charles had lived and prospered, she might never have even known of her vulnerability. But Charles hadn't prospered, and he hadn't lived, so now she was penniless and alone and helpless the way only a woman could be helpless.

In those seconds between the moment when she first set eyes on Alice Sinclair and when Virginia pointed Emma out to her, Emma vowed that if she accomplished nothing else in her life, she would make sure that Alice Sinclair was never as helpless as she.

"This is your Aunt Emma," Virginia was saying to the little girl she held by the hand.

Alice gazed up at Emma, her cornflower-blue eyes bright with the excitement of being home again and of meeting someone new, which must always be a treat. She released her grandmother's hand, gave Emma a smile that revealed one missing front tooth, and dropped a perfectly executed curtsey.

"I'm very pleased to meet you, Aunt Emma," she piped, her yellow curls bouncing gaily as she bobbed.

"And I am very pleased to meet you, too," Emma said, descending the last step and leaning over as far as her corsets would allow so she could be more nearly on the child's level. "What happened to your tooth?"

"It fell out!" Alice informed her with the wonder of innocence. "But Mammy said a new one would grow in, and it is. Look!"

She pointed proudly to the gap where, indeed, a new tooth was just beginning to burst through the gum.

"I'm sure it will be a very pretty tooth, too," Emma assured her, thoroughly enthralled by the girl's sweetness.

"I hope so," Alice said earnestly. "I hope my teeth are as pretty as yours when I grow up. Mammy says it's important for a girl to be pretty because she might not get a husband if she isn't!"

"I don't think you'll have to worry about that," Emma said, ignoring the twinge of her own grief. She wouldn't tell Alice that a husband wasn't necessarily the answer to everything, or at least she wouldn't tell her just quite yet.

"How long are you going to stay with us?" the girl asked, plainly hoping for a nice long visit.

"I . . ." Emma began but stopped when she realized she did not want to give a definite answer, at least not with so many of Grayson's slaves standing about listening avidly to every word.

Virginia rescued her. "Aunt Emma is going to be with us for a long time," she said, stroking Alice's curls lovingly. "And if we're very nice to her, perhaps she'll stay forever."

"I'll be nice, I promise!" Alice cried, jumping up and down and clapping her hands in her excitement. "You'll be nice to her, too, won't you, Papa?" she demanded of her father who, Emma realized, had been hanging back from his daughter's encounter with Emma.

Alice rushed to him and took his hand in supplication. "Won't you, Papa? Please?"

Grayson seemed to stiffen at the question, and when he glanced up at Emma, she saw his eyes were guarded, as if he were trying to keep his feelings hidden. Of course he was, Emma thought bitterly. He didn't want his child to sense any tension between them. He wouldn't want her to know his true feelings for Emma, who felt her whole body burning with the humiliation of knowing what those true feelings were.

"Of course I'll be nice to Emma," he promised his daughter, his voice more tender than Emma had ever heard it. "What did you think? That I'd make her sleep in the quarters and take care of the chickens?"

Alice laughed at such a ridiculous prospect, and the slaves chuckled, too.

"I'll be nice to her, too," another voice promised, and Nathan stepped forward, his grin wicked as he glanced first at Emma and then at Grayson.

"Cousin Nate!" Alice cried, forgetting everything else in her joy at seeing someone who was obviously a favorite. She ran to him, blond curls streaming behind her and jumped into his arms. He caught her up in a big hug, lifted her against his chest and whirled her around.

"Don't I get a kiss, too?" he demanded when she released his neck.

Obediently and with gusto, Alice planted a smacking kiss on his cheek, and everyone laughed, Emma included.

"We're awful glad to have you back, Alice," he told her solemnly. "Didn't seem like the sun shone just right around here without you."

"That's silly," Alice insisted, although the compliment clearly pleased her.

"No, it's true," Nathan said. "I think you must take it with you when you leave."

Alice laughed, a crystal sound that Emma thought must be the distillation of pure joy, and suddenly she realized this little child was flirting with a grown man who seemed to be flirting back, just as moments ago Nathan and Virginia had seemed to be flirting, and just as Nathan had *definitely* been flirting with Emma earlier. And just like Virginia had seemed to be flirting with the riverboat captain yesterday and the captain had seemed to be flirting with Emma. Good heavens, did *everyone* in the South conduct themselves so scandalously with members of the opposite sex? Apparently so, but with one notable except: Grayson Sinclair had most certainly never flirted with Emma Winthrop, and Emma couldn't imagine an occasion when he might.

Instinctively, she glanced at him and caught him watching her with the oddest expression on his face, almost as if . . . But of course, he couldn't be lusting after her, not when he could hardly stand the sight of her. At any rate, he dropped his gaze before she could be perfectly sure of anything, although the mere suspicion of his lust had been enough to quicken Emma's heart and make her breath catch in her throat. Dear Lord, how was she ever going to live under his roof for the rest of her life if his mere glance had the power to unsettle her?

"Your grandmother said we're going to have a barbecue to welcome your Aunt Emma," Nathan was telling Alice.

"Goody, goody!" Alice exclaimed. "When, Grandma, when?"

"Very soon," Virginia assured her. "Isn't that right, Gray?"

"Yes," Grayson said, surprising Emma with an grim little smile that confused her even more. *"Very* soon."

"But . . ." she tried, about to protest again that she was in mourning, but no one seemed the least bit interested.

"Can I have a new dress for the barbecue, Papa?" Alice wanted to know as Nathan set her down.

"I shall be very disappointed if you *don't* have a new dress," Grayson said, giving his daughter the first genuine smile Emma thought she had ever seen on his face.

Alice whirled around in her delight. "Oh, Aunt Emma, I

hope you can stay forever and ever!" In her exuberance, she threw her arms around Emma's waist, and Emma hugged her back, reveling in the feel of the child's small body in her arms. She was so infinitely precious that for a moment Emma felt nothing except an overwhelming urge to protect her from every possible harm. But in the next moment she remembered how dangerous such protection could be, and she vowed anew to protect Alice in a better way: by making her strong.

"And this is the kitchen," Virginia announced as she and Emma entered the large building that sat behind the main house, separate from it and connected by a covered walkway. Emma's head was still spinning from Virginia's whirlwind tour of the house and all it's rooms. After taking leave of Grayson and Nathan and seeing Alice to her room, Virginia had suggested that Emma become acquainted with her new home. Emma had been only too happy to comply.

"This seems like a long way for your servants to carry the food," Emma remarked, wondering why the kitchen would be located so far from the house.

"It is, but this way we don't have the heat from the cooking in the house. That's very important in the summer, as you'll soon discover," Virginia assured her with a smile. "Also the danger of fire is much less."

Emma looked around and saw many of the same implements she'd had in her own kitchen back in Philadelphia, although in place of the stove was an enormous fireplace over which several black women were cooking various dishes.

" 'Morning, Miss Virginia," the oldest of the black women said, coming forward to greet her mistress. She was a tall woman but almost as broad as she was tall, although she carried her excess weight with a kind of dignity in spite of her plain, homespun clothes and bare feet. Like all the other slave women, she wore a bandana around her head. "We's real glad to have you back."

"I'm glad to *be* back," Virginia said. "Emma, this is Eliza, the best cook on the Brazos," she added, naming the river which ran past Fairview.

Eliza waved away the compliment. "Miss Virginia, she teach me everything I know."

"And Eliza taught these girls," Virginia added with obvious pride, naming each of them to Emma who smiled. Although she still found it odd to have colored servants, she was happy to note that her encounter with Chloe this morning had helped her to get over most of her discomfort.

Emma took a deep breath and asked, "Which one of you made those biscuits I had for breakfast this morning?"

All eyes went to a short, chubby girl who was turning chickens on a spit over the fire. She looked up in alarm, obviously afraid to admit to the deed.

"Well, then, I'd have to award *you* the title of 'Best Cook on the Brazos,' at least until I've tasted Eliza's biscuits," Emma told her with a smile as warm as she could muster.

The girl's astonishment was comic, and the others laughed in delight at Emma's compliment. She felt a definite change in the atmosphere, too, as if she had suddenly passed some test, although she had only done what she had been taught from childhood to do, namely compliment the servants. Appreciation for others' work was merely a mark of good breeding, something on which Emma had always prided herself. These servants's faces might be darker than those to which she had always been accustomed, but they were still servants. Obviously, the same rules applied.

"Wait 'til you taste her pie crust, Miss Emma," Eliza said. "You has to eat it real fast 'fore it floats off the plate!"

Emma laughed, as she was expected to, and then listened as Virginia explained how they could roast a whole ox in the fireplace and had done so on numerous occasions.

"We'll be fixing up a party for Miss Emma real soon," Virginia informed the cooks. "A barbecue, I think. Give you girls a chance to show her just what you can do."

"She won't be disappointed," Eliza promised.

After a few more pleasantries, Virginia and Emma took their leave.

"Did you really teach Eliza how to cook?" Emma asked, wondering what she would have done if she'd had to train her own domestic help.

"Not really," Virginia demurred. "She knew how to cook but not how to fix anything white people eat. I had to teach her my recipes, which wasn't easy since she can't read and had to memorize everything. It took years before she knew it all."

"Wouldn't it have been easier just to teach her to read?" Emma asked.

Virginia looked up in surprise, and she shrugged. "I suppose it would," she agreed with an odd little smile. "Would you like to tour the grounds and the quarters now or are you tired?"

Emma didn't feel the least bit tired. "Do we have time before dinner?"

"I think so," Virginia said. "I'll just take you through the quarters. We'll save the fields and the gardens for another day."

They stopped at the end of the walkway beside a bench which was obviously used for gardening projects. Above it hung several large-brimmed straw hats, and Virginia chose two, handing one to Emma.

"Never go out in the sun without a hat," she cautioned.

"I never do," Emma said in surprise. "It would ruin my complexion."

Virginia laughed. "I suppose it would, but here you must also be concerned with heatstroke. I don't think there's a danger today, but you aren't used to the weather yet."

The hat was shabby from much wear, but Emma judged it would do the job as she tied the frayed ribbons beneath her chin.

Virginia set a brisk pace as they started out, and for the first time Emma got a good look at the lands of Fairview. While the river side of the house was well-tended lawns, the inland side stretched away into fertile fields, now tilled and planted and sprouting a new crop in the summer sunshine. In the distance, Emma could see slaves working, although she had no idea what they might be doing. She would, she supposed, have to learn something about farming if for no other reason than not to appear ignorant in front of Grayson.

Virginia led the way down a narrow path between hedges of flowering oleander, and Emma inhaled deeply of the sweet scent. She had given no thought as to what the 'quarters' might be until they emerged at the other end of the path into a world completely different from the beautiful and gracious one in which Virginia lived.

The flowering shrubs ended abruptly where a packed earth road began. The road, if one could call such a barren plain by the name, was lined on both sides with rude cabins which ranged in size from small to tiny. Most of them, she judged, could be no more than one room in size and all of them appeared to be deserted.

Virginia had just realized that the sight of the cabins had stopped Emma in her tracks, and she stopped, too, waiting for Emma to catch up. She hurried to do so.

"What . . . ? Who lives here?" she stammered, glancing around.

"Our people live here, dear. Did you think we made them sleep on the ground?"

Emma hadn't thought at all, and if she had, she certainly wouldn't have pictured this little shanty town practically on the back doorstep of a mansion.

"All the fieldhands live here, and some of the house staff," Virginia explained, apparently oblivious to Emma's shock or else choosing to tactfully ignore it. "We encourage our people to marry, and those who do receive a cabin of their own in which they can live with their children as a family."

Each cabin had at least one window, and the larger ones had two. The chimneys appeared to be fashioned from mud and sticks, and Emma wondered why wooden chimneys didn't catch fire. At the moment, all the cabins were empty and silent.

"Where is everyone?" she asked as Virginia led her down the road between the eerily silent rows of dwellings.

"In the fields, of course," Virginia said, with a patient smile.

"The women, too?" This was even worse than Emma had imagined.

"Most of them." Virginia obviously saw nothing odd in this. "But not the children, of course."

Then Emma caught the sound of young voices, faintly at first but growing louder as she and Virginia reached the bend of the road. When they rounded the last cabin, Emma saw a building much larger than any of the others. In front of it, at least two dozen children of various ages were playing in the dusty yard, chasing each other around in circles and running and falling and tumbling together, only to jump up and run again.

Emma could not judge which were girls and which were boys because each child was clad only in a white, knee-length dress and they all had their tightly curled hair cropped short against their heads. The instant they noticed the two women, they ceased their play and descended upon them in a swarm with cries of, "Miss Virginny!"

The children closed in around Emma and peered up at her with blatant curiosity, eyes huge in their chocolate-colored faces. They were adorable, and Emma couldn't help smiling down at them as they demanded to know who she was.

"This is Miss Emma," Virginia told them. "She's my daughter-in-law, and she'll be living with us for a while. Isn't she pretty?"

A chorus of young voices agreed as tiny brown hands plucked at Emma's skirts. Self-conscious under their scrutiny, Emma glanced away, and that was when she saw the women.

Three white haired crones had emerged from the house which appeared to be some sort of common building, perhaps a dining hall of some kind. Stooped and aged, they were apparently slaves who had grown too old to work the fields, and two of them carried small brown babies which were clad only in diapers. The third stepped forward to greet them.

"It's good to have you home again, Miss Virginny," she told her mistress with much less enthusiasm than the kitchen help had shown.

"How is everything, Grace?" Virginia inquired.

"Just fine, 'cept we lost Amanda's baby. He was sickly right from the first, though. Didn't have much chance."

Virginia nodded, frowning, although she didn't seem particularly upset. It was, Emma realized with horror, as if they were talking about losing a head of livestock instead of a child.

An old man emerged from the building carrying with difficulty a large, steaming pail. "Come and get it!" he called, and the children instantly forgot about the two white women in their mad dash for a long wooden trough that sat in front of the building.

When the old man lifted the bucket and emptied it into the trough, Emma saw it contained some kind of mush, probably cornmeal, and the children fell to their knees beside the trough and began to shovel the mush into their mouths with their bare hands.

Emma gaped in horror as Virginia, apparently oblivious, and the old woman continued to discuss the physical condition of the children. The youngsters might have been little pigs gathered for their slop except that they used their fingers instead of just putting their faces down to gobble.

"Well, Emma," Virginia said when she had learned all she needed to know from the old woman, "I guess we'd better get back to the house for our own dinner."

Emma nodded numbly, hardly able to believe Virginia could have witnessed the same scene she had and been unmoved. Not only did Virginia speak of these children as if they were animals, she condoned treating them that way as well.

Virginia led her forward instead of back the way they'd come, and Emma realized the road curved around in a circle that would lead them again to the main house past more empty cabins.

When they were out of earshot of those tending the slave children, Virginia asked, "Is something wrong, dear?"

Emma hardly knew where to begin. "Those children . . . they were like hogs at a trough!"

"I guess that does look strange to you, but it's the easiest way to feed so many of them. Imagine having to wash dishes for them three times a day. We'd need two more slaves just to do that. And it's not like they suffer. They all get plenty to eat, and as you can see, they thrive. Some masters skimp on the little ones, but Gray's father always believed it was a good investment to feed your slaves well. They cost you nothing when they are born to you, and they'll be worth thousands when they're grown. A little extra food seems a small price to pay to keep them healthy and strong, don't you agree?"

Emma could only nod. "But how can you . . . ? I mean, they're human beings, after all," she stammered.

Virginia's gentle face grew grave. "No, they're not, Emma. They're not human beings at all," she said to Emma's great surprise. "They may look like us and behave like us in many ways, but you must always remember they will never be the same. Even though they grow to adulthood, Negroes will always be simple, like children. They would never be able to survive on their own. They must be cared for and provided for and protected, just the way we provide for our horses and our cattle. That is our duty in life."

"But they *aren't* horses or cattle," Emma argued. "They can talk and think and . . . and you said yourself, they marry and have families and . . ."

"Yes, they talk and think, but not the way we do. I told you, they're like children. They could never make their way in the world without help. The very thought of a Negro owning his own farm or operating a business . . ." Virginia shook her head at the absurdity of it. "And as for marrying, I'm afraid that's merely a figure of speech. When two of our people decide they want to live together, we hold a little ceremony for them and give them some gifts and a place to live, but it's not really a legal marriage, and I'm afraid *they* don't consider it particularly binding, either. If they quarrel and decide to part, they simply do so and very often take up with someone else within the week."

Emma gasped in shock, and Virginia laid a hand on her arm. "I know all this is difficult for you to understand, dear. You were raised quite differently, but you must trust me on these matters. My family has owned Negroes for generations, and we know the best way to manage them. They don't need your pity, and they don't deserve it, either. They have a far better life here than they would have had in Africa, for heaven's sake. There they would have lived like animals, running naked and sleeping in grass huts and worshiping devils. Here at least they have clothing and proper homes, and they can hear the gospel preached. I'm sure you've heard horror stories about the way Negroes are treated, and while it's true that some masters are less than kind, most of us understand our responsibilities. Why, humanity and Christian charity aside, it would simply be bad business to mistreat a slave worth several thousand dollars, now wouldn't it?"

"I suppose it would," Emma said, nearly overwhelmed by all that she had learned in so brief a time. "It's just . . . I was talking to Chloe this morning and . . ."

"I know," Virginia sympathized. "She's a very bright girl, as are most of the house servants. We choose the cleverest ones to serve there, you know, but don't be fooled. If she were turned out on her own . . . well, clever or not, I hate to think what would become of her without someone to look after her."

Emma bit back her protest. After all, she had been in the South only one short day. How could she possibly know more about slaves than Virginia did? She would simply have to trust those with more experience.

The two women walked in silence for a few minutes as Emma considered all that Virginia had told her, and then they

reached the end of the road where it curved back around to
join the path that led to the big house again. But just as they
turned the last corner, Emma saw a completely different kind
of house. This one was much larger than any of the other
cabins, although it, too, was made of logs, and it boasted a
large porch across the front . . . No, Emma mentally corrected
herself, a *gallery*. That's what porches were called in the South.
The house plainly had more than two rooms and had glass
windows and a stone chimney.

"This was our first house when we came to Texas," Virginia
explained, her voice wistful. "My husband built it with his
own hands, and Gray was born here."

Emma took a moment to admire the structure, and when
she did, she noticed that on the porch . . . no, on the *gallery*,
two small children sat playing.

Like the slave children Emma had just seen, these two wore
homespun dresses, but these children were plainly white. They
gazed at her from huge brown eyes from under shocks of light-
brown curls, their chubby, suntanned legs stretched out in front
of them as they sat to play with a set of wooden animals.

"What darling children!" Emma exclaimed. "Whose are
they?"

Before Virginia could reply, a woman stepped out onto the
porch. She wore a simple red calico dress and a kerchief over
her dark brown hair, but even the simple clothes could not
disguise her beauty. Her features were classic, and she carried
herself regally. For one long moment, her gaze met Emma's
and held, as if she were taking Emma's measure the same way
Emma was taking hers.

Emma felt a compelling urge to speak to her. After all, here
was a woman about her own age, probably the only other white
woman on the plantation besides her and Virginia, someone
who could be a friend and a companion and . . . But before
she could even open her mouth, the woman gave some silent
sign to the children who jumped up and scurried into the
house. In the next second, the woman was gone, too.

"Who was that?" Emma asked, nearly breathless with surprise.

"That was Hallie," Virginia said, and Emma was surprised again, this time by the coldness of Virginia's tone.

Virginia had begun to walk away, leaving Emma no choice but to follow. "You didn't tell me there was another white family living here," Emma scolded.

Virginia didn't even glance at her. "There isn't."

"But . . . I just saw—"

"No, you didn't. Hallie is . . . Her mother was a slave and so is she."

"But she's whiter than I am!" Emma protested.

"That may be, but it doesn't change the fact that she is a slave. Nathan bought her for us at an auction about five years ago."

They had reached the entrance to the path back to the house, and Virginia stopped there. Emma could only gape at her. "But that house," she protested. "Why does she live there if—?"

"That's the overseer's house now."

"Nathan's?"

"Yes. Hallie lives there and keeps house for him."

"But—"

"And those are the children she has borne since she has lived there with him."

Virginia's face was pinched with distaste, leaving Emma no hope that she had misunderstood the situation. She felt the blood draining from her head at the shock of it. Nathan, the devilish charmer she had met this morning in Fairview's front hall, kept a slave mistress who had borne him two children.

"That's horrible!" she cried. "How can you allow such a thing?"

"It is not my place to allow or disallow it," Virginia told her. "I am, like you, merely a guest in my son's house. He is the only one who could forbid it, and a lady would never admit to even knowing about the situation. But really, it isn't as bad as you might imagine. You are thinking how you might feel in Hallie's place, but I assure you that Negro women do not have the same sensibilities that we do. In fact, they are rather . . . uh . . . free when it comes to matters of the flesh. They don't seem to mind how many men they . . . Well, you know what I mean, and I'm sure Hallie thoroughly enjoys her position as Nathan's . . . companion."

"Enjoys it?" Emma asked incredulously.

"Of course. She doesn't have to work in the field, she has a lovely home, and she gets to raise her own children. Really, she is quite privileged, and I'm sure she appreciates that."

Emma simply didn't know what to say.

"Oh, dear, I can see this has upset you, and I'm sorry you had to learn about it on your very first day here, but perhaps that's best," Virginia said, her voice softening.

"Perhaps it is," Emma agreed, fury bringing the blood back to her head and giving her an unfamiliar urge to do something about this appalling situation.

"The peculiar institution that we call slavery has a few unpleasant aspects, but you must remember the good that we do, too. A lady has to concentrate on that and try to forget the rest. That is our duty."

Emma wasn't quite so sure. She'd been protected from unpleasantness all her life, and look how she had suffered for her ignorance. She wasn't about to suffer any more.

"Thank you for showing me the quarters," Emma said. "And thank you for explaining everything to me."

Virginia's expression softened again. "You're so welcome, dear. I know you'll be happy here once you get used to the way things are." As they strolled down the path back toward the house, she babbled on about how Emma would make many new friends at the barbecue and how she would feel perfectly at home in just a few days.

Emma made the appropriate noises of agreement, but the whole time her mind was racing as she went over and over the things Virginia had told her. And she thought of little Alice growing up amid such immorality and how she had vowed to make sure the little girl never suffered the way Emma had suffered. By the time they reached the house and disposed of their sunbonnets, Emma knew what she had to do.

"Where do you think I could find Grayson?" she asked when they stepped into the main hallway of Fairview.

"You'll see him in just a few minutes at dinner," Virginia said.

"I'd like to . . . to speak to him privately first," Emma said, already feeling the stirrings of apprehension that she would have to ignore if she were to accomplish her goal.

"You would?" Virginia asked in surprise. Apparently, it was a pleasant surprise, however, because she was smiling. "Well, this time of day, he's usually in his office." She indicated the door behind Emma, a room whose windows would overlook the fields. They had skipped this room on their tour earlier because Grayson had been working then, too. "But I'm sure be wouldn't mind a little interruption. He does hate his book-work so. Why don't you just knock? Oh, wait," she added when Emma would have turned away to do so. "Here, just let me . . ."

Hastily, Virginia smoothed some stray wisps of Emma's hair and straightened her collar. Emma couldn't imagine why she was so concerned with Emma's appearance, and Virginia didn't explain.

"There now," she said when she was satisfied. "I'll just go check on dinner. Come to the dining room when you hear the bell."

Emma waited until Virginia had left before turning to the door through which she would have to go if she wanted to confront Grayson. She pictured him on the other side of it, looking up as she entered, his dark eyes narrowed with the disapproval and contempt she always saw there.

But then she thought of those children she had seen on that porch, Nathan's children who would grow up to be slaves, too, even though they were as white as Grayson's child. And she thought of Alice and imagined her learning about what was going on in the house where her own father had been born. She could not allow such a thing, not if it was in her power to stop it.

Drawing a deep breath to still the quivering in her stomach, Emma forced her feet to carry her to the door, then forced her hand to rise and make a fist and knock.

She jumped at the sound and guiltily laid her hand over her heart in a futile effort to keep it from jumping, too.

"Come in," Grayson's voice called.

Did he sound angry? Displeased? Glad? She had no idea. All she knew was that her heart was pounding so hard, she was afraid it would break her corset stays, and she couldn't seem to get her breath. What was she doing here? She had never in her life challenged a man or confronted him on any matter. Emma had an almost overwhelming urge to gather up her skirts and flee just as fast as her feet would carry her, down the hall and up the stairs and into the room where she had awakened this morning, and Grayson would never know that she was the one who had knocked on his door.

Unless his mother told him. Unless Virginia asked him later what Emma had wanted to speak with him about, and he asked, "What do you mean?" and Virginia explained about how Emma had inquired where she might find him because she'd had something to discuss with him, and then he remembered how someone had knocked on his door and no one had answered when he'd called out and when he'd gone to check, no one had been there and—

"Come in!" he called louder, and Emma knew that no matter how much she might dread facing him, she would be even more humiliated to have him know she'd been too cowardly to face him, and so she reached for the doorknob and turned it.

Sunlight flooded the room, making Emma blink, and the lingering scent of hundreds of cigars enjoyed over many years permeated the air. When Emma was able to focus her eyes, she saw the room was actually a library, with shelves of books reaching almost up to the twelve-foot ceilings. At least, she thought inanely, she would never want for reading material while she lived here.

Grayson sat behind an enormous desk which dominated the room. He'd been working on a ledger of some sort, but now he'd laid aside his pen and was gazing up at her expectantly. He didn't look the least bit happy to see her. In fact, his handsome mouth was definitely frowning, and his dark eyes had narrowed forbiddingly.

"What can I do for you, Emma?" he asked. He didn't sound as if he wanted to do anything at all.

Emma drew a breath in one final attempt to still her clamoring heart and calm her trembling stomach, and somehow managed to get the door closed behind her. "I . . . I wanted to discuss something with you," she said, making her feet carry her across the seemingly endless expanse of ruby-red carpet to where he sat behind his desk.

For an instant Emma felt like a school girl called to the head mistress's office for a reprimand, and she had to consciously shake off the feeling of shame as she stopped before his desk.

"I hope you found your room satisfactory," Gray said, stalling for time while he gathered his wits. Why in God's name did the mere sight of Emma Winthrop have the power to scatter them? Even now, although he was making himself look at her face, he was acutely aware of all the rest of her standing there mere inches away across his desk where all he would have to do was stand up and reach out and he could touch those magnificent breasts or bury his face in their softness and lose himself forever. He really *should* be standing, of course, but he didn't dare leave his chair for fear he wouldn't be able to stop himself from fulfilling his fantasies.

"My room is lovely," she was saying.

He hardly heard her. This morning, it had been all he could do to maintain his dignity when she'd come down his stairs still pink from her bath and looking fresh and clean and sweet enough to eat. Nate had practically slavered over her, and while Gray had been furious over Nate's behavior, he hadn't been able to blame his cousin. Emma simply invited slavering.

"Uncle Sam is upstairs right now," Gray said, forcing his lascivious thoughts away, "installing a lock on the . . . uh . . . the door." Gray couldn't help wondering if he should have told Sam to nail the damn thing shut, instead. How on earth was he ever going to sleep knowing she was just on the other side of that door, lying in her bed naked or nearly so, all those lush curves warm and soft and . . .

"I know, Chloe . . . uh . . . explained everything to me. About the door, I mean. That's not why I . . . why I came."

She laid a hand on her stomach, as if she were nervous, and he suddenly realized she was, although what *she* had to be nervous about, he couldn't imagine.

Unless she was lusting after him, too.

The thought almost made him laugh out loud.

But her color was high, as if she were embarrassed about something.

"Your mother took me on a tour of the . . . the quarters," she said.

That explained her color. Probably a touch of the sun. And she smelled like sunshine, too, all fresh and new. Gray tried not to breathe too deeply.

"Yes?" he prodded when she hesitated. Dear God, why didn't she get on with whatever it was so she could go away again?

"Grayson, I don't know exactly how to say this, but . . . Well, we passed the overseer's house."

Now her color was even higher, and there could be no question that she was embarrassed. There could be no question as to why, either, if she'd passed Nate's house. What had his mother been thinking to take her there on her very first day here? But maybe his mother at least had had the sense not to tell her *everything* about that house.

Gray forced his Southern Gentleman smile, the one he always wore when he was trying to pretend things weren't really as bad as they seemed. "Did she tell you that was our first home here in Texas? We lived there nearly ten years before this house was built and—"

"She told me," Emma said stiffly, plainly uncomfortable. So uncomfortable, in fact, that Gray could no longer hope that she didn't know. "She told me some other things, too."

"Oh?" Gray wasn't going to help her. Maybe she would simply be unable to bring herself to speak of the situation. Certainly, no Southern woman of his acquaintance would even acknowledge the matter, much less consider mentioning it, not even to her own husband.

But Emma obviously lacked the gentility of all the Southern women of his acquaintance. "She told me about Hallie and . . . and her children."

Emma's face was scarlet, and Gray could feel the heat crawling up his own neck. He would, at that moment, have cheerfully strangled his mother for putting him in this position. "Emma, this is really none of your concern."

"But it *does* concern me, as it must concern every female at Fairview, including your own daughter," she insisted. Not only did her voice lack the gentle accent of a Southern woman, her personality grated as well. Perhaps the danger was less that he would bed her and more than he would murder her if she remained too long under his roof.

"And why would the females of Fairview have cause for concern?" he asked, glad to hear his voice betrayed none of the fury boiling within him.

Emma was literally wringing her hands now, so great was her distress, and every inbred instinct demanded that he relieve a lady's distress, *any* lady's distress, but Gray hardened his heart to the impulse. He wanted Emma to be unhappy here, unhappy enough to marry the first man who asked her, please God, make it soon.

"Every female must be alarmed to discover that such . . . such blatant immorality is occurring right here, practically on our doorstep." She lifted her chin, and for an instant Gray allowed himself to admire the way the sunlight glinted on her chestnut hair and the way her blue eyes sparkled like a rain-cleansed sky.

But only for an instant, because he could not ignore the stubborn set of that lovely little chin. Gray folded his hands on his desk and leaned forward in an effort to appear reasonable and hold onto his temper at the same time.

"My dear sister-in-law, you have no idea what life on a plantation is like, nor can you begin to understand the problems with which I must deal every day."

"I know this is a problem with which you should have dealt long ago!" she said, her voice annoyingly shrill. Good God, didn't Northerners teach their women *anything* about gentility?

"Do you have any idea how difficult it is to find a capable overseer for a plantation this size?"

"I—"

"Of course you don't," Gray interrupted, ruthlessly denying her any opportunity to reply. "You also do not understand how very cheap land in Texas is or how easily obtainable for any man of even reasonable ambition. Such a man can, without too much difficulty or expense, start his own farm and within a few years even own his own slaves and with a moderate amount of labor, achieve financial success. Such a man would be a fool to stay in the employ of another farmer when he could make his own fortune, and yet that is exactly the type of man I must have as my overseer to operate Fairview."

"But—"

He cut her off again. "In order to keep such a man in my employ year after year, I must allow him certain . . . certain *benefits* in addition to his salary, benefits which will make his life here pleasant and comfortable."

"Benefits that include a *mistress?*" Emma inquired, outraged.

Gray couldn't believe a gently bred female could have uttered such a word, certainly not to a man to whom she wasn't at least intimately connected. His own outrage brought him to his feet at last. "I provide him with a *housekeeper.*"

"A *housekeeper* who also happens to be a beautiful young woman who must be completely at his mercy—"

"You don't know what you're talking about!" Gray insisted, his outrage turning to plain rage as he braced his hands on the desktop to confront the unreasonable woman standing on the other side of it.

"I'm afraid I know *exactly* what I'm talking about!" Emma insisted right back, leaning over her side of his desk while he leaned over his.

"Although I am not accustomed to discussing such matters with a *female,*" he said through gritted teeth as he stood almost nose to nose with her, "I will try to forget your sex so I can tell you that things in the South have been a certain way for hundreds of years, and one shrewish Northerner is not going to change them!"

"Are you telling me that this sort of thing goes on elsewhere, on other plantations?" she demanded incredulously.

Gray held what was left of his temper with only the most desperate effort. Emma's cheeks were like spots of flame, and his own face felt as if it were about to burst. "I am telling you that where young men find themselves unable to take comfort with a wife, they will take comfort where they can."

"*You* don't have a wife!" she reminded him furiously. "Do *you* keep a slave mistress, too?"

With a roar of rage, Gray took hold of her, wanting to shake that look of righteous triumph off her beautiful face, wanting to *kiss* that look of righteous triumph off her beautiful face, to kiss her until she was gasping and helpless and as desperate as he.

But as his hands closed over the softness of her upper arms, her expression of triumph dissolved into one of shocked surprise, and her gasp of alarm shocked him in return. Dear God, what was he doing? Instantly, he released her, scrambling back so quickly he almost knocked over his chair. Emma scrambled back, too, clasping her arms around herself as if for protection.

For a long moment, they simply stared at each other across the expanse of desk, neither of them quite able to believe he had actually laid hands on her. Gray forced air back into his lungs and somehow managed to speak.

"I beg your pardon," he said stiffly, horribly aware that he was trembling with the force of suppressing the desire that raged within.

"I had hoped," she replied, as breathless as he and trembling at least as much, "to appeal to your *better nature.*" She paused, allowing him a moment to absorb the irony of her barb. And then, "I was going to remind you that you have a . . . a daughter who will, in a very short time, be old enough to understand certain . . . certain relationships. But I can see now that I was wrong to hope you would want to shield her from such immorality, so I must beg *your* pardon, Grayson. I will not overestimate your sense of honor again."

With that she turned in a rustle of skirts and sailed from the room, slamming the door with unnecessary force behind her. Frustration boiling within him, Gray picked up a book from the corner of his desk and sent it slamming to the floor.

Of all the disagreeable, unreasonable, stubborn harpies he had ever had the misfortune to encounter, Emma Winthrop led the pack! By God, if he had to give her a dowry of half his property, he'd have her out of his house by the end of the month!

Four

Emma could never recall being so furious in her entire life. Grabbing up her skirts, she flew down the hall and up the sweeping staircase, hesitating only a moment when she reached the top and realized she wasn't exactly sure which door upstairs led to her room. Making a lucky guess, she threw open one of them and ran inside, slamming this door even harder than she had the one downstairs.

"Land sakes!" a voice exclaimed in surprised, and Emma looked up, remembering what Grayson had said about someone named "Uncle Sam" being in her room putting in the lock. But she saw only Chloe who was standing over her trunk. Apparently, she'd been unpacking Emma's things. "You all right?" she asked in alarm.

Emma was far from "all right." Instinctively, she glanced over and was relieved to find that dear Uncle Sam, whoever he might be, had indeed installed a pair of substantial looking bolts at the top and bottom of the door that connected her room with Grayson's. Feeling marginally more secure, she turned back to Chloe. "I just had a . . . a disagreement with Mr. Sinclair," she admitted, violating one of the cardinal rules of domestic life which was never to air one's dirty linen in front of the help.

To Emma's surprise, Chloe smiled, laying aside the petticoat she had been folding. "Miss Lilly and him used to fight all the time. Mostly, she was in the wrong, though."

"Well, I can assure you *I* was not in the wrong!" Emma

snapped, trying in vain to get her breath. "I was always afraid that Grayson Sinclair was the most unreasonable man I knew, and now I'm *certain* of it!"

"Something he won't let you do?" Chloe asked mildly.

"No, something *he* won't do!" Emma crossed the room and flounced down on the chaise, positive that if she didn't lie down soon, she would probably faint. Chloe hurried to help her get her feet up amid the tangle of skirts and petticoats.

"You want some salts?" the girl asked solicitously.

"Not yet," Emma said, drawing deep breaths, or as deep as her corset would allow. Damn the thing. That was probably why she'd been taught all her life not to upset herself, because she wouldn't be able to get enough air into her lungs to keep from fainting. But she wouldn't use the smelling salts unless she had to.

"Mr. Gray, he pretty easy to get around if you know how," Chloe said, standing back, her arms crossed beneath her breasts. "Miss Lilly, she could do it when she remembered to keep her temper and smile real pretty and bat her eyes and—"

"I am not about to *bat my eyes* at him or any other man," Emma informed her, "particularly when I am discussing a matter of such importance!"

"And what might that be?" Chloe asked with a disturbed frown.

"The matter of . . ." Emma caught herself just in time. Talk about airing dirty linen! A lady simply did not discuss such personal matters with her servants, and Emma was certain that rule applied doubly when the servants were Negro slaves. She remembered what Virginia had told her about their being simple, too, and unable to think the way white people thought.

And if that were true, and if what Virginia had told her about the morals of the colored women were also true, Chloe wouldn't even *understand* Emma's concerns over Hallie's situation. Emma decided to find out for sure, once and for all.

"Miss Virginia took me out to see the quarters this morning," she began tentatively, watching the girl's face for reaction.

"We passed the overseer's house, and I saw the woman who lives there and her children."

Chloe's lovely brown face hardened. "Hallie," she said.

"Yes," Emma continued, still watching her closely but unable to quite identify the emotions Chloe was trying to conceal from her. "Perhaps I misunderstood her . . . her position there, but—"

"You didn't misunderstand," Chloe informed her. "She Mr. Nathan's girl. He seen her at an auction, and he buy her for hisself with Massa Gray's money. Massa Gray, he don't mind 'cause Mr. Nathan such a good overseer. He want Mr. Nathan to be happy."

Emma felt her cheeks burning with indignation, but she reminded herself of what else Virginia had told her. "But I understand that Hallie is very happy with her . . . her duties, because she doesn't have to work in the fields and—"

Chloe made a rude noise. *"Happy?* Oh, I guess she happier now than she was before. She had the most worst thing happen that can happen to a colored girl: she born pretty. 'Fore she come here, the slave dealers what had her, they used her for a whore, selling her to whoever wanted her."

Emma thought she might need the salts now, but she didn't dare interrupt Chloe's horrible tale.

"Yeah, she happier now than before, and she don't have to work in the fields, but she gots a lot harder work to do. She gots to live with a man who ain't her husband, and she gots to be afraid all the time 'bout doing something he don't like. If she do, he can sell her like that." She snapped her fingers. "If she cook the wrong thing for supper or don't iron his shirt right or say the wrong thing or even turn him down when he reach for her in the night, she gone, sold away from her younguns. Or her younguns is sold away from her, and she never see 'em again. She scared all the time, day and night, and she don't even have no friends to help her bear it, 'cause the fieldhands, they's jealous 'cause she don't have to work like they do, and the house folks, they look down on her and call her a whore."

Dear heavens, this was even worse than Emma had imagined! She had thought only of the bad influence on Alice. She hadn't even considered how difficult this was for Hallie and her children, too. "I tried to tell Grayson that he simply could not allow a situation like this to exist, but he absolutely refused to discuss the matter!" Emma informed Chloe.

Chloe shrugged one shoulder. "Maybe 'cause he gots a girl of his own."

"What?" Emma cried in horror, pushing herself upright on the chaise.

"Well, he used to, anyways, 'fore he marry Miss Lilly. They all do, all the Massas. When a boy gets to be a certain age, his daddy give him a colored girl to keep him satisfied 'til he takes hisself a wife. Sometimes the Massa, he keep the girl even after 'cause his wife, she don't like sharing her bed as much as he does. But Massa Gray, he let Opal get married herself when he did, and he took real good care of her, too. She got to stay here, and she don't work in the fields. She sews. And her boy, Massa Gray do right by him, too. Her boy, he real smart, so he work in the blacksmith shop."

"Her *boy?*" Emma asked weakly, too overwhelmed by what she was hearing to even remember to breathe.

"Yes'm, Benjamin, the boy she have when she with Massa Gray."

No wonder Grayson had been so willing to let Nathan have a mistress! Emma thought, horrified. He was just as debauched as his overseer! Emma could not imagine how such things could go on generation after generation. What had the women been doing all this time? Why had they not put a stop to it? Emma knew men's natures were coarser than women's and that it was a woman's duty to soften that nature and civilize it. Women had been doing so for centuries, at least in the societies with which Emma had always been familiar. Apparently society in the South was far different, however, and women here preferred to ignore evil instead of eradicating it. If Emma had disliked the institution of slavery before, she abhorred it now.

She heard a distant bell sounding somewhere in the depths of the house.

"Dinner ready, Miss Emma," Chloe explained at Emma's questioning look.

"I couldn't possibly eat anything," Emma said, falling back against the cushions. Dear heaven, she might never eat again, certainly not if she had to sit at the same table as Grayson Sinclair.

"You gonna hide up here?" Chloe asked, just the slightest hint of disapproval in her tone.

Emma gaped at her. She was not accustomed to having her decisions questioned by the help. But then, she wasn't accustomed to baring her soul to the help, either, nor to being instructed in the niceties of local social customs, yet that is just what Chloe had been doing. If Virginia truly thought Chloe was simple-minded, she couldn't possibly know her very well.

"You gots to go down there," Chloe continued more sternly than any maid had a right to. "You can't let him think he won or that all's he gots to do is yell at you and you'll run to your room and pout."

Of course, Grayson had done more than yell at her. Instinctively, Emma crossed her arms and ran her hands over the places where Grayson had gripped her. She would probably have bruises tomorrow, which was certainly enough reason for her to pout in her room. But did she want to do that? And did she want him to *know* she was doing that?

"But . . . what could I say to him?" she asked, completely abandoning the last lingering shreds of propriety to seek the advice of a colored maid.

"You don't gotta say nothing at all!" Chloe informed her. "Just give him the look. You know . . ." She favored Emma with a condescending glare that the Queen of England might have envied, and Emma couldn't help the yelp of laughter that escaped her.

Chloe nodded her approval. "Do that, and he won't have nothing to say to you at all. Might even get *him* hiding in *his* room!"

The girl was right, Emma knew. She couldn't let Grayson think he'd won. He'd only have one more reason to despise her. If he was going to hate her anyway, he should hate her because she stood up for herself and others, not because she was a coward.

Emma swung her feet to the floor. "How does my hair look?" she asked as she accepted Chloe's help in rising from the chaise.

Chloe's deft fingers quickly made the necessary repairs.

"Pinch your cheeks and bite your lips," she advised. "Don't want him thinking you've got a case of the vapors."

When Emma had done so and taken another moment to straighten her bodice and smooth her skirts, she lifted her chin and marched for the door. Chloe scurried ahead of her to open it so that Emma wouldn't even have to break stride, and she gave Emma a wink as she passed.

Emma was half-way down the stairs before she realized the full extent of her transgressions. Not only had she confided in a servant, she had colluded with her against the master of the house. Such things would have been unthinkable in the world from which she had come. No one had told her that different rules applied in this world, but somehow she knew they did. Nothing here was the same in this land where human beings were bought and sold like cattle and children ate at troughs like pigs and a mother had to worry that her children might one day simply disappear, never to be seen again.

This morning she had seen a white woman whom she thought might be a friend to her and had learned instead that not one thing she had assumed about the woman was true. This morning she had awakened too embarrassed to summon the brown woman who was to serve her and only a few hours later, she was gossiping and plotting with her as if they were old friends. For a moment, the irony dizzied her, but then she drew a deep breath and steadied herself on the banister.

She wasn't going to faint, and she wasn't going to cower, and she wasn't going to back down. Instead she continued down the stairs as she practiced "the look."

She found Grayson and Virginia in the dining room, an enormous room dominated by a mahogany table that could easily seat twenty people in comfort. At the moment, one end was laid with only three places, and Grayson rose as she entered. Did he look just the slightest bit uneasy? Emma hoped so.

"I'm sorry to keep you waiting," she said with her most gracious smile as she took her seat to Grayson's left.

"You didn't at all," Virginia assured her. Grayson simply took his seat once more, but Emma could feel his gaze upon her.

She glanced over at him and was pleased to note that he was watching her surreptitiously. Summoning the rage she harbored, she gave him "the look" and was gratified when his face darkened and he dropped his gaze guiltily. Chloe was so very right!

Virginia picked up the small bell to her right and rang it. The tinkling sound summoned the maid who served them their soup.

Emma would have to get used to eating her dinner at noon. Virginia had explained that because of the Southern heat, they cooked their big meal in the morning and just ate a light supper in the evening.

"Did you get to speak with Gray?" Virginia asked, making Emma jump. She had almost forgotten Virginia was there.

"Yes, I did," Emma said coldly, favoring Grayson with another look, although he didn't see it because he was pointedly not looking back.

"And did you two get everything straightened out?" Virginia prodded when neither of them offered anything more.

"Yes," said Grayson.

"No," said Emma at the same time.

This time he glared back at her, but she refused to be cowed by his anger.

"Oh, dear," Virginia said, her face wrinkling in distress. "I hope you two aren't . . . uh . . ."

Emma never learned what she had intended to say because the maid, a slim girl with ebony skin, slipped in to deliver their soup. If Emma was somewhat lax about discussing her problems in front of the servants, Virginia certainly wasn't. She smiled sweetly and thanked the girl as she set the steaming bowls of turtle soup in front of them.

As soon as the girl was gone, Grayson said, "Emma thinks she knows how to run a plantation better than people who have been doing so for generations."

Emma almost gasped in outrage. How dare he twist the truth like that?

Oblivious to Emma's fury, Virginia smiled sweetly. "Sometimes a new perspective *can* be helpful. I do hope you'll have some suggestions for how we might run the house more efficiently, Emma dear, and as I've told you, I'm counting on your help in that area."

Emma couldn't imagine how she could help Virginia run her house more efficiently, but she said, "I'll be happy to help in any way I can. I do want to earn my keep," she added with just the slightest trace of bitterness.

Grayson gave her another black look, but Virginia seemed not to notice. "And we must decide who to invite to the barbecue, Gray, and when it will be," she went on between sips of her soup. "This really is delicious, dear," she told Emma who had yet to pick up her spoon.

Chastened, Emma did so and was delighted to discover the soup was more than delicious. She only wished her stomach wasn't twisting with fury so she could truly enjoy it.

"I think we should have it next weekend," Grayson told his mother. "Can we get the invitations out that quickly?"

"That's only ten days," Virginia said in surprise.

"We'll send Ignatius out on horseback to spread the word," Grayson said, as if that settled it.

Emma didn't think anything was settled at all. "I really don't believe it would be proper for me to attend a party," she offered.

"Why not?" Virginia wanted to know.

Emma almost choked on her soup. "Because I'm in mourning," Emma reminded her impatiently, holding her temper with difficulty. Why did Grayson and his mother seem so determined to make her lose it?

"Of course you are, dear, but no one is expecting you to entertain suitors or anything, just meet your neighbors at a friendly, informal gathering. What could possibly be improper about that?"

"How informal?" she asked suspiciously. "I'm not exactly sure what a 'barbecue' is."

"Oh, it's like a picnic," Virginia explained enthusiastically. "A very *large* picnic. We'll roast an ox over a pit and then we'll eat on the lawn and afterwards we'll have some dancing."

"I couldn't possibly dance," Emma insisted

"No one will force you to, dear," Virginia assured her.

"But no one will think it improper if you do, either," Grayson added, still pointedly not looking at her.

"I would think it improper," Emma informed him.

"What Gray means is that we really don't observe the strict rules of mourning out here the way they do elsewhere in the country," Virginia hastily explained. "A good wife is such a rare and precious commodity in Texas that no lady need remain unmarried a moment longer than she wishes."

Emma was certain she had made herself clear on this point, but perhaps she was mistaken. "Virginia," Emma said slowly so there could be no misunderstanding, "I *do* wish to remain unmarried." A sentiment that was still as true as it had been the first time she had expressed it to Virginia back in Philadelphia, although her reasons had changed a great deal in the meantime. While she had once been certain no man could ever take Charles's place in her heart, she was now merely reluctant to entrust herself and her future to another man who might prove as negligent as her late husband had been.

"I felt the same way until I met Charles's father," Virginia reminded her. "You know, sometimes I find myself wondering what might have happened to all of us if I hadn't agreed to accompany my Cousin Lucretia to the shore that summer. I'd never gone to Cape May before, always to Newport, and Charles Senior had never gone on a holiday at all. If we hadn't met, I might still be a widow or perhaps I might have married someone in Texas and be living someplace else. At the very least, we never would have met you, Emma."

Grayson made a noise that might have been a grunt of disapproval, although when Emma glanced at him, his face was perfectly expressionless. She didn't have to use much imagination to know what he was thinking, though. He was thinking that if his mother had never married Charles's father, they wouldn't be saddled with Emma now, either. And probably Emma wouldn't have married Charles at all. He'd never considered taking a wife, being content to run his father's business and enjoy the simple social life provided by his father and stepmother's limited social contacts. But then his father had died, and although Virginia had intended to stay on in Philadelphia and run his household for him, Lilly had . . . Well, Lilly had died, and suddenly Virginia's own son had a greater need for her help than Charles ever would. Left alone, Charles had sought Emma's hand, and her parents, already suffering the diseases that would soon take them from her, were only too happy to give her to their dear friend.

So now, because everyone had been so intent on making sure everyone else was so well cared for, Emma was penniless and living off Grayson Sinclair's charity. Which was, she suddenly realized, even worse than living off a husband's charity because while a husband was bound by law to provide for her, Grayson was bound by nothing except his good nature, something Emma had always suspected and now knew for certain that he did not possess.

The delicious turtle soup suddenly tasted like dishwater, and Emma set her spoon aside.

Virginia chattered on gaily about her plans for the barbecue, but Emma barely heard her. And when the maid took her bowl away and brought her an absolutely scrumptious meal, Emma could only pick at it, lost in her own thoughts. But by the time the maid had served dessert, Emma's despair had once again evolved into the quiet rage that was becoming so familiar to her.

All her life, Emma had been cautioned not to express that rage or even to feel it, and until very recently, she'd had no trouble at all obeying that rule. After all, until now very little in her life had made her angry. Now, however, nearly every-thing did, especially because she understood only too well that she had no power at all to change her circumstances or anyone else's. Not unless she married again and her husband gave her that power, something that seemed highly unlikely even if she were fortunate enough to find a man she could care for.

"Would you, Emma?" Virginia asked.

Emma looked up, startled to realize she hadn't heard a word Virginia had been saying. "I'm sorry. What did you ask?"

"If you would help me write out the invitations to the bar-becue." Virginia smiled sweetly.

Emma could not refuse. She was, after all, a guest, here only at their sufferance, so whether she wanted this party or not, she had no choice. "I'd be happy to help," she lied, not one single trace of her rage evident in her voice.

"Read me another story, Aunt Emma!" Alice begged, squirm-ing in Emma's lap.

Emma looked down into those beautiful blue eyes and knew she could refuse Alice nothing, but her Mammy was not so vulnerable.

"That's enough for now," Mammy scolded. "You's gonna wear Miss Emma out."

"Just one more, *please!*" Alice pleaded.

Emma glanced at Alice's Mammy, a plump young woman who, Emma had learned in the week she had been living at Fairview, had taken care of the girl since the day she was born. The woman hardly looked old enough, but Emma knew she'd given birth to a child herself, a little girl named Rose, who was the same age as Alice and who was sitting next to her and Alice in the oversized rocking chair, her small brown body wedged in on top of Emma's skirts so she could see the pretty pictures in the book, too. Mammy's ample breasts had nursed both girls, and the two had grown up side by side, just as Lilly and Chloe had done.

"Please!" Rose echoed Alice's plea, and Emma gazed down at her sweet face that seemed too small for her enormous brown eyes.

"All right, one more," Emma agreed, turning the pages, looking for a story she hadn't read to them yet.

"Then you can play dolls with us," Alice informed her.

"Yes, yes!" Rose cried, clapping her hands.

"Miss Emma don't have time to be playing with younguns," Mammy insisted, and Emma couldn't decide if she were just giving Emma a convenient excuse to escape the nursery or if she was encouraging her to leave because she really didn't like Emma's presence here. Nothing in the woman's expression told her, either. She wore the blank look Emma had noticed that all the house servants wore, probably because they did not dare allow their masters to know their true thoughts.

Of course, Emma had nothing whatsoever to do with her time, so the prospect of playing dolls with the girls was appealing, *if* Mammy did not really resent her presence here. But how would she find out for sure?

Before she could decide, the nursery door opened and Grayson Sinclair walked in.

"Papa!" Alice cried in delight and scrambled down from

Emma's lap. Even Rose deserted her, jumping to the floor to race for her master who caught both girls up in his arms and lifted them high against his chest.

"You're getting too big for this," he complained, although his smile belied his words.

The sight of his smile caused Emma's breath to catch somewhere in her chest. She hadn't seen him smile like that since . . . since her first morning here when Alice had begged him to be nice to her. He truly smiled, it seemed, only for his daughter.

Which was probably a mercy, Emma decided as she pushed herself up out of the rocking chair, since each time he did, Emma forgot how to breathe. Of course, Grayson was handsome even when he frowned, but he was a lot easier to hate when he frowned.

"Kiss Rose, too!" Alice demanded when her father had so favored her. Obediently, he pecked the little brown girl on the cheek, making her giggle.

"And kiss Aunt Emma, too!" Alice piped gleefully.

His head jerked up, and instantly, his smile disappeared when he saw Emma standing on the other side of the room. Apparently, the mere mention of her name could take the joy from his life. She could feel the heat in her face and hated herself for betraying her humiliation so easily.

"Hello, Grayson," she said.

"I'm sorry," he replied, "I didn't know you were here."

As if to say he would not have visited his own child if he'd known he would have to see Emma, too.

"Miss Emma, she been real good with the girls," Mammy hastily explained, her plump face now set in the ingratiating smile the slaves wore when they were hoping to please. "She come near 'bout every day now. The girls, they like her stories and such."

"Of course," Grayson said, not even glancing at Mammy, his dark gaze fixed firmly on Emma whose blush had now spread over her entire body so that she felt as if she might burst into flames at the shame of his disapproval.

"Aunt Emma said she could give me lessons, Papa," Alice was telling him. "She said she could teach me how to read my own stories to myself and to Rose, too!"

"That's nice," he said absently, his gaze still locked on Emma who had just decided to surrender to her very cowardly urge to flee so she wouldn't have to endure him for another moment.

"Could she teach Rose to read, too, Papa? Could she?" Alice continued, oblivious to the tension radiating between her father and her aunt. "We could read stories to each other then!"

"We'll talk about it later," he said, finally tearing his gaze from Emma to turn back to his daughter. Emma almost sagged with relief at being released and wondered vaguely how his mere glance could have such power over her. "Now, tell me what you've been doing all day," he said to Alice as he set the girls down.

"We've been playing with our dolls! I changed my family," Alice replied, pulling her father by the hand over to the corner where her dolls resided as Rose danced along behind. "I changed Lady Lulu's name. I named her Emma instead because she has dark hair like Aunt Emma, and I made her the mama of baby Alice because I think baby Alice should have a mama who's really here and not dead like my mama is, don't you, Papa?"

Emma winced at the innocent ease with which the child asked the question, and she saw Grayson stiffen, although she could not make out his mumbled reply.

"Aunt Emma is like my mama," Alice went on, blissfully unaware of the havoc she was wreaking, "because she visits me every day just like my mama used to and reads me stories and plays with me. I hope she stays forever and ever, happily ever after, just like the stories."

Unfortunately, Emma knew only too well that "happily ever

after" only happened in stories. Her own life promised to have a less than fairy tale ending.

Too embarrassed even to take her leave, Emma began backing toward the door, determined to slip away while Alice was busy with Grayson so neither would notice her departure. Alice, she was sure, would put up an even more embarrassing fuss and Grayson would . . . Well, she didn't know what Grayson might do and she didn't want to find out.

But just as she reached the door, someone knocked. Being the closest one to it, Emma pulled it open and found one of the maids carrying a heavily laden supper tray.

" 'Evening, Miss Emma," the girl said with her practiced smile. "I's got supper for the nursery."

Emma managed to return the smile and stepped aside so the girl could carry her burden inside.

"Supper's here, girls," Mammy announced, motioning for the maid to set the tray on the table in the opposite corner of the nursery. "Now you leave Massa Gray alone. He gots his own supper to tend to."

"Don't leave yet!" Alice protested.

"I'll come back later," Grayson promised. "Give me a kiss before I go." He leaned over for Alice to plant a kiss on his cheek. When she released him, she noticed Emma still standing by the door.

"Will you come back, too, Aunt Emma?" she cried, rushing to throw her little arms around Emma's skirts.

"Of course I will. I promised I would, didn't I?"

Alice gazed up at her with eyes that sparkled with joy. "And you'll read me as many stories as I want?"

"As many as you want."

"And you'll teach me to read them myself?"

Emma glanced at Grayson who was watching them with an unreadable expression. "If your papa says it's all right."

"He will," Alice predicted without even a glance in his direction. "Oh, Aunt Emma, I love you so much! I hope you stay with us forever and ever and ever and . . ." Her face brightened even more as a new idea occurred to her. "I know! I'll ask the conjure woman for a spell to keep you here!"

The words meant nothing to Emma who had no idea what a "conjure woman" was, but she felt Grayson's fury hit them like a wave. Mammy and the maid had frozen in place, their gazes locked anxiously on Grayson.

"Who told you about the conjure woman?" he demanded sharply, making the child jump.

"Wasn't me, Massa Gray!" Mammy cried, wringing her hands in obvious terror, her eyes so wide Emma could see a rim of white all the way around. "I swear, I never told her nothing 'bout no spells! I wouldn't do that, wouldn't *nobody* do that, Massa Gray!"

"Well, *somebody* did!" Gray snapped. "Alice, who told you about the conjure woman?"

But Alice's eyes were big, now, too, as she gazed up beseechingly at Emma. "I don't 'member, Papa," she said, still clutching tightly to Emma's skirts as she looked over her shoulder at her father. "I don't, I don't! I'm sorry! I won't never talk about her again, I promise!"

Emma had instinctively wrapped her arms around the girl's shoulders. "That's all right, Alice," she assured her, patting her back.

"It is *not* all right," Grayson contradicted her. "I will not have her head filled with that nonsense." He turned to Mammy who cringed under his cold fury, "You're responsible for her, and I don't want to hear another word about spells. Do you understand?"

"Yes, sir, Massa Gray!" Mammy promised, practically cringing before him, as if she were expecting a blow.

Grayson turned back to his daughter. "And Alice, I've told you before, there's no such thing as spells or magic. It's just like . . . like . . ."

"Like the stories in the book I read you," Emma supplied when he faltered. "Remember, I explained to you how the stories were made up. Just pretend, like the stories you make up for your dolls."

Alice nodded quickly, eager to agree and end this uncomfortable discussion.

Emma made herself smile in a desperate effort to keep Alice from bursting into tears. Rose was already crying with soft, muffled sobs, into her mother's skirt. "There now, Grayson, she understands, don't you, darling?"

Alice nodded again and turned her head to look at her father again. "I understand, Papa. I won't talk about the conjure woman no more, I promise!"

Plainly, Grayson was still angry, but he managed a stiff smile. "That's a good girl. Now we'll leave you to your supper."

Emma bent and kissed Alice's forehead, keeping her smile firmly in place so the child would understand that at least *Emma* wasn't angry with her. Alice returned that smile weakly.

"Will you come back?" she asked as she released Emma.

"Yes, I will, and we can play with your dolls. I want to see which one you named after me."

"She's the prettiest one!" Alice assured her, all unpleasantness instantly forgotten. "Isn't she, Rose?"

Rose peeked out from her mother's skirts and nodded tearfully.

"I'm glad to hear it," Emma said. "Now go eat your supper, and I'll see you later."

Alice turned to face her father, and Emma was glad to see his anger had cooled.

"And I'll come back to tuck you in," he said, lifting her for one last kiss. "No more talk about spells now, you hear?"

"Yes, Papa," she said, as he set her on her feet, but Emma heard the question in her voice, the one she couldn't ask, the one that asked why this was so important. And because she couldn't ask it and would never get an answer from him, Emma knew this magic business would take on added importance in her life. Grayson's angry reaction would have the opposite ef-

•

fect from the one he'd intended . . . unless Emma could some-how undo the damage.

"Emma?"

Grayson's voice startled her. He was waiting for her to pre-cede him through the still-opened door. Emma waved at the girls who were still gazing after them apprehensively. She no-ticed the two slave women looked even more apprehensive.

She waited until Grayson had closed the nursery door be-hind them.

"What's a conjure woman?" she demanded.

"Shhh," he cautioned, drawing her away, toward the stair-way, his hand on her elbow. She shook loose of his touch, not wanting his hands on her again, and she ignored his expression of surprise.

When he judged that they were out of earshot, he said, "A conjure woman . . . well, sometimes it's a man, too . . . is one of the slaves who is . . . sort of like a magician."

"You mean like pulling rabbits out of hats and doing tricks?" Emma couldn't imagine why he would be so upset that his daughter knew about such things.

"Not exactly." His eyes were almost black, his handsome face set in a forbidding frown. "A conjure woman casts spells on people, to make them fall in love or out of love or make them do things or not do things. To make them sick or even die."

"Good heavens!" Emma exclaimed in alarm.

"It's all a bunch of superstitious nonsense, of course, but the Negroes believe it. It's something they brought over from Africa with them, and we've never been able to stop them from practicing it, not even when they become Christians."

"Why don't you just get rid of the conjure woman, then? Without her—"

"That's just it, we don't know who she is, and no one will tell. They're too afraid of her . . . even the whites who find out." Grayson's grim expression told her there was more to this story.

"You mean there are white people who believe in this . . . this magic?" she asked incredulously.

"My wife believed in it," he told her coldly.

Emma gaped at him. "Lilly?"

His smile was chilling. "They say she used a spell to get me to marry her."

"What?"

His smiled vanished. "And they say someone else used a spell to kill her."

Emma gasped, covering her mouth with both hands.

"So now you see why I don't want Alice to know about this."

He started away, but Emma wasn't finished with the conversation. She went after him, nearly running to keep up with his long, determined strides. "But don't you see, that's exactly why she *should* know about it! If all she ever hears are rumors and hints, she'll think there's something to it and maybe even start to believe in it, but if someone teaches her the truth—"

"Someone like you?" Grayson asked skeptically, stopping at the head of the stairs.

Emma's face burned at the implication that someone like her couldn't teach anyone anything, but she lifted her chin defiantly. "Yes, someone like me. I could teach her the difference between reality and superstition, the same way I could teach her to read. She's seven years old, Grayson. She should be in school—"

"There *is* no school," he reminded her.

"Then let *me* teach her."

His dark eyes seemed to burn with some inner fire, and he took her in from head to toe with one contemptuous glance. "We'll talk about it later," he dismissed her and started down the stairs.

"We'll talk about it *now!*" Emma insisted, starting after him, but in her haste she forgot to take care and, unable to see her feet for her enormous skirts, she missed her footing and stepped out into thin air. With a desperate cry, she plunged headlong toward the bottom of the twenty-foot staircase.

For one horrible, heartstopping moment, she was suspended in midair, headed helplessly to her doom. In the next, steel bands clamped around her and dragged her back to earth, up-ending her in a mad, bumping tumble of arms and legs and petticoats.

When the tumbling stopped, she was sprawled across what she very quickly realized was Grayson's body. Somehow he was beneath her, sitting on the stairs and cradling her or at least cradling the top part of her, against his chest. The bottom part of her was farther up the stairs, her legs tangled in her skirts and one foot caught between the balusters while she hung, head downward, across Grayson's body.

The steel bands were his arms which were still clamped fiercely around her as they both gasped desperately for breath. Emma heard a strange thundering and realized vaguely that it was Grayson's heart beating directly beneath her ear which was pressed against the solid wall of his chest.

She caught her breath and inhaled his heady masculine scent which seemed to engulf her in a sensual fog. She could, she realized giddily, have been content to lie against Grayson Sinclair's chest for the rest of her life.

The steel bands of his arms loosened slightly. "Are you . . . all right?" he asked between labored gasps.

Emma wasn't sure. She tried to decide if she hurt anyplace, but her brain was still whirling, as if it had fallen down the stairs without her and hadn't returned just yet.

She should, at least, try to move, she decided, seeking purchase with her downmost hand and finding it against some part of Grayson's body and pushing herself up a bit.

He gasped, or she thought he did, and when she shifted to look up at him, she was sure of it. In the next instant she was sure why because she realized one of his hands had come to rest along the side of her breast, the heel of his palm just shy of the nipple which, she also realized, had tightened into a spearpoint in reaction.

She should have flung him off or he should have flung himself off, but Emma, at least, couldn't seem to move at all, and for one long moment, *neither* of them moved as Emma stared up into the depths of his dark eyes. Eyes that were black now, smoldering with a desire she could no longer mistake, a desire that was for her and her alone, and a desire that simmered in her, too, starting at the tip of her breast where his hand caressed it and spreading quickly over her entire body, over and around and up and down and out to the very tips of her toes and the tips of her fingers. Fingers of a hand which was braced against something that moved and pulsed and *grew,* swelling beneath her palm like a living thing, and suddenly Emma knew it *was* a living thing, a part of Grayson that *shouldn't* be growing, not now, not with *her,* not under *her* touch where she shouldn't be touching at all. Dear heaven!

She snatched her hand away or tried to, but the effort sent her sprawling and sent them both sliding again. They bumped down two more steps before Grayson's frantic scrambles brought them to another halt. This time Emma's *face* was in Grayson's lap, one arm wrapped around his thigh while his was locked on her hips, one hand planted firmly on her bottom. At least she was protected by layers of petticoats. Grayson had no secrets from her at all. What she'd felt with her hand now lay rock hard beneath her cheek, and Emma could no longer have any illusions whatsoever.

"Don't move," he said thickly, and Emma wondered wildly why his voice sounded so strained. "You'll start us down again. Just do what I tell you."

Emma nodded against his lap, realizing when she heard his gasp of response that she'd made a terrible mistake. Her face felt like it was on fire, and she knew it had nothing to do with the fact that she was lying practically upside down on the stairs.

"I'm going to grab your leg," he said. He was panting as

if he'd run a mile, and Emma found her own breathing difficult in the extreme. She started to nod again and caught herself just in time.

A strong hand clamped around her ankle and pulled just as his other hand pushed, lifting her head from its unfortunate resting place. For one moment she couldn't imagine why he was spreading her legs, but then she understood she should bring her other leg down herself. Quickly, like an outraged virgin, she clamped her legs together and found herself nearly upright, her back against the balusters, her legs stretched out across one step and her skirts still a tangle everywhere except around her ankles.

She allowed herself one sigh of relief before she realized that Grayson was somewhere *below* that tangle of skirts where he could see a great deal of her legs and probably much more than that.

Frantically, she pushed and pummeled on the mountain of petticoats until she'd regained at least some semblance of modesty. Only when she had, did she allow herself to glance at Grayson who, she was relieved to note, did not seem the least bit interested in looking up her dress. Instead he was perched on the step below her, knees pulled up, elbows resting on those knees and both hands covering his face.

"Are you all right?" he asked, the sound muffled.

Now that the shock had begun to wear off, Emma was aware of twinges here and there, but still, nothing seemed to be crying out in agony. "I . . . I think so."

"Thank God." He drew a deep breath and let it out in a shuddering sigh. For a moment Emma thought . . . Of course! He was horrified at the thought of her—of *anyone*—falling because that's how Lilly had died.

And when she remembered his reaction to her, to having her in his arms just now, his *unmistakable* reaction, she realized he must care for her far more than she ever would have suspected. How could she not have known? How could she have thought he despised her when . . . ?

Instinctively, she reached out to him. "Grayson," she whispered, laying a hand on his shoulder.

He reared back as if she'd struck him, lunging to his feet with an oath, and the look he gave her could have drawn blood. "Just be more careful," he told her between gritted teeth. "I don't want to have to bury *another* stupid woman who can't even stand on her own two feet."

Mortified, Emma could only gape as he began calling for his mother and Chloe and his manservant and anyone else within earshot to come and help them. Within moments, Virginia and all the house servants were swarming and strong hands—not Grayson's—helped her to her feet and up to her room where she could loosen her stays and check herself for injuries and lie down and put a vinegar-soaked rag on her forehead.

As she lay in the semi-darkness of the canopy bed, the smell of vinegar acrid around her, Emma raged silently at Grayson Sinclair. She'd been right about one thing, he did lust after her, but she'd also been right to believe he despised her. How he could feel both for her at once, she had no idea, but she knew it just the same.

The knowledge made her cheeks burn with humiliation, and she asked Chloe for another cold cloth to cool them. She only wished she dared ask for more. One to soothe the place on her breast where Grayson's hand had rested, and another to soothe the place between her legs that burned whenever she remembered being in his arms.

Five

Using the excuse of her fall, Emma hid in her room the next day, too mortified to face Grayson no matter how many hints Chloe dropped that she was being cowardly. Chloe, of course, did not know what had passed between them there on the stairs, and Emma was not about to tell her, either. Just thinking about it, even in complete privacy, made Emma blush furiously. When she remembered how he had touched her breast and what had happened to his body beneath her hand . . . Well, she'd never even touched her husband *there*. How could she ever look Grayson in the face again?

But after trying not to think about it for an entire day, Emma finally realized that *he* should be at least as embarrassed as she was. After all, she'd only made an innocent mistake while he . . . Well, nothing that Grayson had done was *innocent*. He'd touched her intimately and let her touch him intimately without making any effort to stop it, and then he'd reacted . . . Well, perhaps he hadn't been able to stop *that* particular reaction, but he'd certainly allowed himself to be in a position to react when he hadn't needed to and . . . Well, Emma would drive herself crazy if she kept trying to figure it out.

And if she was going to live at Fairview, she would have to face Grayson sooner or later. She couldn't hide in her room forever, although she supposed the shock of nearly falling down the stairs would have given many women of her acquaintance the excuse to do so for the rest of their lives.

Emma wasn't going to, though. She had a life to live, as

empty and meaningless as it may have become, and she had a child to look after if she meant to keep the vow she had made to see that Alice never ended up like Emma. So she would have to deal with that child's father, no matter how embarrassed she might be. And, she reminded herself, Grayson had practically saved her life or at least several of her limbs. If she had fallen down those stairs . . . But of course, if he hadn't been arguing with her, she wouldn't have fallen in the first place. Did that mean she didn't really owe him any gratitude? Emma felt the frustration building in her chest and forced herself to take a few deep breaths to quell it.

"You gonna lay around all day again today?" Chloe inquired the next morning, a little too sharply for Emma's taste.

"I suffered a terrible shock," Emma reminded her.

Chloe snorted. "Miss Lilly, she fell off a horse once and went to a ball the next day, and she was just a skinny little thing."

The implication being that Emma wasn't the least bit skinny and that she hadn't even really fallen either. Grayson had managed to stop them after only about half-a-dozen steps. Chloe knew she'd suffered only a few minor bruises, too, having tended to them herself.

"Miss Virginia," Chloe went on doggedly, "she 'bout worked herself to a frazzle getting ready for this barbecue, and you laying up here like your legs was broke or something and—"

"All right!" Emma snapped, throwing off her lap robe and rising from the chaise where she had been lying. "Help me get dressed."

Chloe smiled her approval but discreetly said nothing about her triumph.

When Emma was dressed in her usual black gown and ready to venture out into the world again, Chloe asked her, "What you gonna do with these?"

She pointed to the two rag dolls Emma had fashioned while she had been languishing in her room.

"Oh," Emma said, wondering if she should trust Chloe with the information but deciding she had no other choice since she did not know how to accomplish her intentions otherwise. "They're for . . . I mean . . . I'd like to send them to the overseer's house. For the children there."

Chloe's eyes widened in surprise, but she said nothing.

"Could you see that they get delivered?" Emma prodded.

"They for Hallie's younguns?" Chloe asked, as if she wanted to make perfectly sure she'd understood.

"Yes. I didn't know if they were boys or girls—"

"One of each," Chloe said, picking up the dolls from where Emma had laid them on the dresser.

Emma had instinctively made one of each doll, too. The girl wore a dimity gown made of scraps from one of Virginia's dresses. The boy wore black serge trousers and a blue shirt, fashioned from scraps from Emma's sewing basket. "Will you see that they get the dolls then?"

Chloe stared at the dolls a moment longer, her expression grave but unreadable. "Yes'm, I will, if that's what you want."

"It *is* what I want," Emma said, then wondered if Chloe was trying to tell her something. "Unless . . . Would I be offending them?"

"No, ma'am, not offending," Chloe said, screwing her face into her fixed smile again. "I reckon they be pleased to get 'em. I'll have one of the boys take 'em over for you this morning. Now you best get downstairs and help Miss Virginia 'fore she loses her mind completely."

Emma wanted to ask Chloe why she had frowned and looked so thoughtful when she'd learned who the dolls were for, but she decided she was getting much too intimate with Chloe as it was. She'd leave the girl her own private thoughts.

Emma found Virginia on the lawn supervising the construction of a brush arbor and the digging of an enormous pit which she explained would contain the coals for roasting the steer. Although Emma had looked around carefully before leaving the house, she could see no sign of Grayson. She was, of course, relieved, but she was also worried about encountering him unexpectedly. She wanted to be ready when that moment came.

"Emma, dear," Virginia exclaimed. "Should you be up and around?"

"I'm fine, really, and I know you need some help . . . uh . . . Where's Grayson?" she added as casually as she could.

Virginia sniffed in disgust. "Wouldn't you know? He tells me to plan this party on ten days' notice, then he leaves town on business and won't be back until the night before it starts!"

Grayson was gone! Emma would have expected to feel relief, but instead she felt a curious sense of disappointment. And how odd for him to be gone when he would surely be needed so much. "When did he leave?" she asked, suddenly suspicious.

"Why, right after your . . . your accident," Virginia said, apparently reluctant to remind her of the unfortunate incident. "I'm sure it's nothing that couldn't wait until *after* the party, but you know how Gray can be when he makes up his mind. Nothing I could say would persuade him. He simply had to go."

"And he . . . he hadn't planned this trip?"

"Oh, no," Virginia said, her attention on the arbor. "You need more branches in the middle, Eustus!" she called to a slave working on the top. "We can't have the sun shining through, can we?" She turned back to Emma. "What were we talking about, dear?"

"Grayson's trip," Emma reminded her impatiently, hoping her face wasn't as red as it felt. "If he had planned it."

"Oh, no," Virginia repeated. "He hadn't said a word to me, and he always tells me ahead of time when he has to be away." She shook her head in disgust. "Sometimes I wish I could still turn him over my knee."

Emma smiled at the image of Virginia turning her grown son over for a spanking, but her mind was racing. So! Grayson had suddenly left on a business trip just after her accident—*their* accident—which mean he must have been as reluctant to face her as she was to face him! The very thought was delicious, and Emma's smile widened in appreciation. Suddenly, she couldn't wait to see him again.

Emma had planned their next encounter perfectly. She knew exactly what she was going to say and what the expression on her face would be—calm detachment—as she thanked him for saving her and hoped he'd suffered no injuries himself (she already knew he hadn't). But Emma should have known nothing ever goes as planned.

Although Grayson was supposed to be home the evening before the party, when Emma went to bed, he hadn't arrived yet. The next morning, Chloe informed her he'd gotten in late and wasn't up yet.

Guests began arriving for the barbecue by mid-morning, by which time Emma had already been at work for hours helping Virginia supervise the slaves as they put the ox on to roast and carried the plates and silverware out to the trestle tables set up in the shade on the lawn.

By nine o'clock, the morning mist had burned off in the bright sunlight, and the heat of the day began to build. Emma dearly regretted the fact that she had to wear her black serge, particularly when she saw the other women arriving in their delicate muslin and lawn gowns. They looked like enormous inverted flowers with their brightly colored hoopskirts swaying gently as they strolled the grounds under their parasols.

Emma herself sat in the shade under her broad-brimmed hat and smiled at everyone Virginia brought to meet her and tried not to let anyone know she was melting under her heavy dress.

Soon over a hundred people mingled under the trees, men and women, black and white. The colored servants moved discreetly, minding the children that ran and played among the adults or else serving the needs of their masters. Emma knew another party was going on in the slave quarters which they would visit from time to time, too. Every now and then, Emma caught sight of Alice who had gathered a bevy of children whom she kept organizing into various games and activities under the watchful eye of her Mammy. Poor Alice, Emma thought once again, she should be in school where she would have friends her own age all the time.

It was almost noon when Emma finally saw Grayson. She was still sitting under her willow tree, holding court for the Sinclair friends and neighbors as they arrived, but all the while she'd been watching out of the corner of her eye for Grayson to appear.

He was dressed in a dark suit that fit him perfectly, hugging his broad shoulders and muscular legs. He looked dapper and utterly masculine, and Emma didn't even bother to wonder why her heart quickened at the sight of him.

Still smiling and murmuring meaningless chatter to the latest group of people Virginia had brought over, she continued to watch him, preparing herself to be cool and calm when he finally came to greet her.

Except he didn't come to greet her, and after a while, Emma began to understand that he had no *intention* of coming to greet her. The perfect host, he was shaking hands and slapping backs and admiring babies and charming other women, but he wasn't coming *near* Emma.

"It's such a warm day, may I get you a lemonade, Miss Emma?" a masculine voice asked.

Emma looked up and recognized someone she'd met a few minutes ago, a gangly fellow with buck teeth. "Why thank you, Mr. Hamilton," she said, giving him her best smile.

He seemed inordinately delighted by the prospect of getting Emma some refreshment and hurried off to do so. The moment he did, Emma glanced over to see if Grayson had noticed, but he was busy discussing something with an older man Emma had met earlier but whose name she couldn't recall.

Well, if he could ignore her, she could ignore him, too. She cast around for someone with whom to ignore him and found to her surprise that she was literally surrounded by men of various ages and sizes.

"How do you like Texas, Miss Emma?" one of them asked.

"Why, it's lovely," she replied. "And everyone is so friendly."

"Where is it exactly that you live up North?" another asked.

Emma noticed he seemed to think she still lived there, and she did not correct him. "Philadelphia," she replied, and soon she was involved in a lively discussion with at least half-a-dozen gentlemen about the relative merits of the North versus the South. And they all seemed simply fascinated by her Yankee accent. Emma hadn't even known she *had* an accent.

When Mr. Hamilton brought her back her lemonade, several other gentlemen took turns fetching her refreshments of various kinds, and when the barbecue was finally served, she received no less than three plates from eager suitors. Because, as she was quickly realizing, these men really *were* suitors.

Virginia had convinced her to attend the party by assuring her no one would be courting her, but she could see that had been a bold faced lie. Every unattached male present seemed almost desperate to make her acquaintance and win her approval. They hung on her every word and competed to see who could amuse and impress her more. In fact, Emma was astonished by the competition that was developing before her as each man in turn found a way to mention how many acres he farmed and how many slaves he owned and how many bales of cotton he had shipped last year.

As the afternoon wore on, Emma almost forgot about Grayson Sinclair wandering around the grounds and giving her the widest possible berth. She was first amazed and then amused and finally overwhelmed by all the attention. Although she had been a debutante, she'd never in all her life been the belle of the ball. And, she realized, the ball itself hadn't even started.

The shadows were growing long when Virginia came to rescue her. Custom demanded that the ladies retire for a few hours to rest before the evening's festivities, and Emma was only too glad for the respite.

"I'm going to have to steal Emma away for a while," Virginia told the men who murmured their very sincere disappointment. "Don't worry, she'll be back tonight," Virginia assured them as Emma gathered her things.

"Save me a dance, Miss Emma," Mr. Hamilton begged, and they all echoed the sentiment.

Emma merely smiled. She had no intention of telling them she would not be dancing with anyone. But the thought of sitting in the Sinclair's ballroom—where Grayson would be forced to notice her—surrounded by this hoard of admirers had her eagerly awaiting the coming ball.

"You seem to be enjoying yourself, dear," Virginia observed with a sly little smile.

Emma managed a disapproving frown. "You told me I wouldn't be courted."

Virginia wasn't the least bit repentant. "If I had, would you have come out of your room?"

Emma supposed not, but she wasn't going to admit it to Virginia. "I see Grayson got back," she observed, catching a glimpse of him over by the barbecue pit.

"Oh, yes, he was very late last night."

"I hope he finished all his business."

"He didn't say," Virginia said. "At least he got back in time for the party."

"Yes," Emma said thoughtfully, anticipating the evening ahead.

Virginia left Emma to find her own way back to the house so she could finish assigning rooms to all the visiting ladies for their afternoon naps. Emma moved slowly, taking her time in case Grayson wanted to approach her, but she noticed he'd turned his back now, as if afraid of even meeting her eye. With a determined sigh, she stepped through the front door and started up the stairs.

"No, I don't want to!" she heard Alice exclaim.

It took her a moment to figure out where the child's voice had come from, and when she did, she was more puzzled than ever. Alice seemed to be in the front parlor. No one ever entered the front parlor which was reserved for company and very special occasions. Today, of course, was a special occasion, but not the kind where people would be gathered in the front parlor, and certainly Alice knew better than to go in there to play. She'd better get the child out of there before Virginia discovered her transgression.

Emma hurried back down the stairs and across the marble floor of the foyer to where the parlor door stood slightly ajar. As she pushed it open to step inside, she heard a man's voice saying, "Just one little kiss for your grandpa."

"Papa said I didn't have to if I didn't want to!" Alice insisted, her voice quivering with suppressed tears.

The room was dark, velvet drapes closed tightly against the damaging rays of the sun, but in the shadows Emma could see the man was kneeling in front of Alice. He held her arm in a grip that appeared far from gentle, and Alice was trying vainly to pull away.

"What's going on here?" Emma demanded.

They both looked up at her in surprise, and the man released Alice at once. The child ran to her and threw her arms around Emma's skirts. "Aunt Emma, he wants me to kiss him, but I don't want to!"

Emma looked up at the man in amazement. How dare he try to force a child . . . ?

"You must be Mrs. Winthrop," he was saying as he rose to his feet. Emma could see now that he was near fifty but still a fine figure of a man, tall and well made, his handsome face only enhanced by the marks of his age. His dark hair was threaded with grey, giving him a distinguished air, and he was smiling now, a perfectly charming smile. "I'm sorry we haven't met earlier. I am DeWitt Phelps . . . Alice's grandfather."

Oh, yes, Lilly's father. Emma remembered Virginia mention-

ing him the first day she'd arrived here, something about him
not being a man of his word.

"I'm very pleased to meet you, Mr. Phelps," Emma said,
managing not to sound pleased at all, although Alice apparently missed the subtlety.

"Papa said I don't have to kiss him if I don't want to!"
Alice informed her desperately, tears brimming in her eyes.

"Of course you don't, dear," Emma assured her. "No one
would think of forcing you. Affection," she added, with a
pointed glance at Mr. Phelps, "is best when given freely."

Mr. Phelps stiffened at the rebuke, but he said, "I'm afraid
you don't quite understand the situation, Mrs. Winthrop."

Emma understood Alice was upset, and that was all she
needed to know. "Where's your Mammy?" she asked the child.

"I don't know."

"Go find her," Emma said. "It's time for us all to take a
rest."

Alice nodded gratefully, and without even a backward
glance, ran from the room, leaving Emma to face Mr. Phelps.
Suddenly, she was aware that they were alone in a darkened
room.

"Mr. Phelps, I . . ." she began uneasily, but he interrupted
her.

"Mrs. Winthrop, I'm sorry we had to meet this way. I was
hoping we could be friends." He smiled, although the expression was oddly sad. "I . . . I *need* a friend in this house."

Emma blinked in surprise at the anguish in his voice. "I'm
sorry, Mr. Phelps. I don't know—"

"Lilly was my only child," he told her, stepping forward,
although she was glad to note he maintained a respectable
distance between them. "My wife passed away some years
ago, when Lilly was only five, and with her gone, too . . .
Well, Alice is all the family I have left."

"I'm terribly sorry—"

"Please understand, Mrs. Winthrop, I'm alone in the world
except for that little girl, and she . . ." His voice caught as he

struggled with the depth of his emotions. Emma did not need his pleas. She understood perfectly already. She fought the urge to reach out to him, a response that would be terribly improper since he was a virtual stranger to her, after all. "Ever since her mother . . . Well, since Lilly's terrible accident, Alice has been so strange. But perhaps you know about the nightmares."

"No," Emma said, wondering what on earth he could be talking about. "Does Alice have nightmares?"

"So I understand. And she seems to hold me somehow responsible for Lilly's death."

"Responsible?" Emma echoed incredulously.

"I know, it's ridiculous, but in her childish mind perhaps she thinks I should have protected her somehow since I'm her father. I don't know, but I *do* know that she's turned against me. She refuses to visit my home, and when I come here, she . . . Well, you saw how she was just now. I can understand that she was upset by her mother's death, but that was almost three years ago. It's time and past time for her to . . . I mean, she needs to understand that I love her and . . ."

"You're absolutely right, Mr. Phelps," Emma said when he hesitated. "But you can't *force* a child to recover from such a tragedy."

"I don't want to *force* her to do anything," Phelps insisted, taking another step toward her. "I just . . . I'm very much afraid that no one here is *encouraging* her to get over it, or at least that they aren't encouraging her to forget this . . . this aversion she's developed for me. Mrs. Winthrop, I was hoping that perhaps . . . I mean, I know you have just suffered a terrible loss yourself. A lady such as you can't help but feel what I have suffered and what I continue to suffer because I'm denied the company of my only remaining family."

"Of course!"

"Then do I dare ask that you will be my champion? That you will convince Gray and Virginia that they must help me reconcile with Alice?"

Emma saw no harm in agreeing. "I will do what I can, Mr. Phelps, but I must warn you, I will only do what I think is best for Alice."

His smile was part relief and part joy. "Then I will be eternally in your debt, dear lady."

Before she could guess his intent, he had taken her hand and raised it to his lips. Emma resisted the urge to snatch it back, and managed a gracious smile when he released it. "I can make you no promises, Mr. Phelps," she reminded him, turning to take her leave.

"I don't expect any, but you have at least given me hope."

Emma opened her mouth to warn him not to hope too much, but the words lodged in her throat when she stepped into the foyer and came face to face with Grayson Sinclair. She took small comfort in noticing he seemed as disconcerted at the encounter as she was.

"Emma," he said stiffly, drawing himself up as if for battle. And then he saw who was coming out of the parlor behind her, and his expression hardened. "DeWitt." His gaze darted back to Emma again, registering surprise, and she knew he must be wondering what she and DeWitt Phelps had been doing alone together in the parlor. "I see you've met my sister-in-law," he said icily.

"Indeed," DeWitt confirmed, his tone matching Grayson's. "I was just explaining to her that no one in this house will assist me in any way in winning back my granddaughter's affections."

"Nonsense. We have done everything possible to—"

"Everything *possible?*" he echoed sarcastically. "Like refusing to allow me to see her?"

"You have seen her regularly," Grayson insisted. "You may see her today, in fact."

"I just did," Phelps said. "She ran as if from the boogey man."

"And she will continue to run as long as you continue to

insist that she stay. She's just a child, DeWitt. She'll get over it in time."

"How *much* time?" Phelps demanded, truly angry now. "Another year? Two? Or three? Until she's grown? Or maybe even longer, until you've stolen her completely, just the way you stole Lilly—"

"Mr. Phelps!" Emma cried in alarm. His face was nearly purple with rage, and Grayson's had turned an unfortunate shade of crimson. "You are not helping your cause with Grayson or with me, either!"

Phelps glanced at her as if he'd forgotten she was there. Then, with visible effort, he brought himself back under control, although Emma noticed his hands were still curled tightly into fists. "I beg your pardon, Mrs. Winthrop. I forgot myself for a moment, but perhaps you can understand how strongly my feelings run on this matter. Please forgive my outburst." He sketched her a small bow. "I do hope you haven't changed your mind about . . . about what we discussed."

"I told you, I will do what I can," she said, although she was no longer quite as eager to help as she had been before. Still, she supposed she couldn't blame Phelps for his feelings for Grayson, especially not when she shared them.

"Thank you, dear lady. It has been a pleasure to meet you." He bowed again and then turned to Grayson. "Gray," he said, giving a curt nod, then took his leave, crossing the foyer with long, determined strides and disappearing out the front door.

Emma stared after him for a long moment, fairly breathless from the encounter.

"And what, exactly, did you agreed to do for DeWitt Phelps?" Grayson inquired with dangerous nonchalance.

Emma looked up at him in surprise. "He asked me to help him win Alice's affection."

"Did he, now? And you agreed?" His voice was no longer nonchalant, only dangerous.

"I told him I would do what I felt was best for Alice," she informed him defiantly.

"Then I will tell you once and only once that I and I alone am the one who decides what is best for my daughter. Do you understand?"

"I understand perfectly!" Emma replied, as furious as he. She could, of course, have told him she agreed with him about not forcing Alice to do anything she didn't want to do, but she didn't want to give him the satisfaction.

He looked as if he wanted to say more, but some guests had come in the front door, and he turned, greeting them enthusiastically and leaving Emma fuming in the parlor doorway.

Of all the arrogant, pigheaded . . . Emma could not even think of a name bad enough to call him! Her cheeks burning with rage, she swept across the hall and up the stairs, her chin high and her mind racing. How dare he dismiss her efforts as if she were nothing more than a . . . a brainless female! She would show him. She would put him in his place once and for all.

The instant the door of her bedroom closed behind her, Emma was calling for Chloe, but the girl was already there, waiting for her. "Land sakes, Miss Emma, what's all the fuss about?"

"We have to find something for me to wear this evening," Emma informed her, already unbuttoning her bodice.

"I thought you was gonna wear the black silk. You said—"

"I know what I said, but I changed my mind. I thought I would die from the heat in this dress today, and that ballroom will be hotter still." The dancing was to be held in Fairview's third floor ballroom.

"Besides, you want to look nice compared to them other ladies," Chloe guessed with a wise grin.

"Yes," Emma said as she stripped off her basque, not bothering to add that she wanted to look more than nice to annoy Grayson Sinclair.

"Well, now, I already pressed out this green one for you," Chloe informed her, indicating the evening gown draped across her chaise. It was her emerald green silk, the low neckline that would reveal her excellent shoulders trimmed with rich black lace. Emma had always adored the dress but had given up hope of ever wearing it again.

"That will be perfect, Chloe, and I'll need to bathe and—"

"Take a little rest first," Chloe advised. "Don't want to go to the party with big black rings under your eyes."

Emma nodded absently as the girl helped her out of her skirt and hoops, already making her plans. Before this evening was over, Grayson Sinclair would understand that whatever *his* opinion of her might be, plenty of *other* men found her worthy of their attention.

Gray actually swore aloud when he saw Emma come into the ballroom. Good God in heaven, she was beautiful, more beautiful even than he remembered her being on the day she married Charles. She fairly glowed, and her chestnut hair shone in the flickering candlelight like satin.

And that dress. What there was of it, that is. It clung faithfully to every curve of her womanly figure, or at least to every curve that it didn't expose outright. If Gray had imagined Emma's breasts as white as snow and as smooth and soft—and plump—as satin pillows, he had only guessed at half the truth. Her alabaster bosom seemed to shimmer in the artificial light.

There should be a law against women flaunting themselves like that, Gray thought as he gazed at the curve of her shoulders and the swell of her breasts above the delicate lace neckline of her gown. He imagined burying his face in the shadowed valley between them, reveling in their softness, running his tongue along her . . .

"Beautiful woman, isn't she?" Nathan inquired.

Gray started, turning on Nathan, instantly angry. "What do you mean by that?"

Nate widened his eyes in surprise. "Just making an observation, Cousin. Don't *you* think she's beautiful?"

"What I think doesn't matter a damn," Gray insisted, glancing back at Emma who had, by now, attracted the attention of every male in the room and most of the females. The women were simply nattering about her behind their fans, but the men were swooping down on her like flies drawn irresistibly by the scent of honey. Gray wanted to throttle every one of them.

"Then whose opinion of her *does* matter?" Nate asked.

"What?" Gray replied, having lost track of the conversation.

"I said, if your opinion of her doesn't matter, then whose does?"

"The man who's going to marry her," Gray said grimly, eying the crowd of snorting, slavering males now circling her.

"And who might that be?" Nate asked, genuinely curious.

"Damned if I know," Gray said, "but he'd better present himself soon or there won't be anything left of her to claim."

"What *are* you talking about?" Nathan asked in amused exasperation.

"Haven't you figured it out yet?" Gray asked impatiently. "I brought her here to marry her off. Otherwise—"

"Otherwise, she'll be living here with you for the rest of her life," Nathan finished for him. "I know, she told me she's penniless. That shouldn't deter any of the men here, though. Miss Emma's delectable person will be dowry enough, I would think."

Dowry enough and *more,* Gray thought grimly, watching as Emma moved through the crowd of her admirers, favoring each of them with a smile and a nod and a word. Living with her might be something of a challenge, with her grating accent and manner, but having all those luscious curves in his bed could help a man endure. For a moment Gray allowed himself to remember the seconds when he'd held those luscious curves in his very hands . . .

"But it seems to me you'd *want* her to live here with you for the rest of her life. How many times does a woman like that come along?" Nathan asked.

How many times indeed? For Gray, once had been more

than enough. "And what do you think makes Emma so desirable?"

Nathan gaped at him in astonishment. "Why, just look at her, man!"

Gray shook his head. "I *have* looked at her, and I've seen just what you've seen, but that's not enough, Nate. I was fooled once by a pretty face."

"She's nothing like Lilly!" Nate protested.

"She's *exactly* like Lilly in every important way. She's a fluttering, brainless little bird who'll peck a man to death if he lets her. I have no intention of letting her, which is why I plan to marry her off as quickly as possible."

"More fool you, then," Nate judged, shaking his head in mock despair. "But if that's your plan, I think I'll go over and get on her dance card while I still can."

Gray watched him go with a frown. Nate was the fool if he thought Gray would allow Emma to marry *him*. The idea of marrying her off was to get her *away* from Fairview, and having her right under his nose at Nate's house would defeat his purpose. No, Nate couldn't have her. And neither could Sherwood, Gray thought as he scanned the crowd of Emma's admirers. Sherwood drank too much, and Gray had heard rumors that Parks had beaten his first wife. Everyone knew Terrel gambled away every cent he made, and Post mistreated his slaves. Hamilton *certainly* couldn't have her. He lived too close. Emma would be visiting Virginia every week. And not Cosgrove. He was too old. Merritt was too stingy. Hill lived in a hovel. Gray had never thought much of Reinhart's politics, and O'Malley was a Catholic. And Peterson was . . . Well, he couldn't let Peterson have her either. The man was the worst horseman Gray had ever known. He couldn't let a man like that marry into his family.

But surely there was someone. Gray just hadn't thought of him yet. He would, though, and he'd give Emma Winthrop to him gladly because to be rid of her would rid him of his own torment. Dear Lord, he'd been right to worry about having her under his roof. He spent his days trying to avoid her as much as possible, hiding in his office and taking his meals at odd times when he could so he wouldn't have to sit at table with her and then actually fleeing his own house for business he didn't really have. And his nights . . . Well, he didn't even want to *think* about the nights when nothing he did could stop him from dreaming about her.

Of course, reason told him that the real Emma Winthrop would not be as wanton as she was in his dreams. No well-bred lady truly enjoyed the pleasures of the flesh. He'd learned that only too well from Lilly. But still, Gray suspected that just having Emma's flesh to pleasure would be more erotic than all the prowess a professional mistress could provide.

At times like this, he wished he'd kept Opal. The prospect of being able to go down to the quarters and slake his lust on a willing and enthusiastic partner had taken on an inordinate appeal since Emma Winthrop's arrival. And if he'd still been sixteen and able to convince himself that Opal enjoyed their trysts as much as he did, he might have been able to do it. But he was thirty now and knew better. He'd seen Opal's joy and relief when he'd told her she was free to marry a man of her own choosing and that he'd never need to use her in that way again. If he'd still had any illusions about the nature of their relationship, she had shattered them then.

And Lilly had shattered all the rest of his illusions, the ones that had deceived him into believing marriage would make him happy. So he'd been content to live without a woman, content and relieved, at least until Emma had come into his life.

The sound of her laughter came to him over the music, and he moved away, hoping distance would spare him that particular torture. She was flirting shamelessly now, working her fan the way women did, and smiling and laughing at the nonsense that her eager suitors were spouting. They looked like a bunch of curs sniffing around a bitch in heat, and Emma was doing everything in her power to encourage them. She'd even gone so far as to take a seat so that the men standing around her would have a better view of that delicious cleavage. They were probably all imagining what delights could be found by delving in that sweet, shadowy . . .

"Grayson!"

His mother's voice snapped him guilty back to reality. "Yes, Mother?" he asked, quickly schooling his expression to what he hoped was blandness.

"You have to do something with Emma, dear."

Gray almost choked. He'd just been *fantasizing* about doing something with Emma. "What did you have in mind, Mother?" he asked, certain it wasn't the same thing Gray had in mind.

"You must dance with her, dear."

Gray glanced disdainfully over at the circle of admirers. "She seems to have an abundance of possible partners already."

"That's just it," Virginia said impatiently. "All the gentlemen want to dance with her, but she's claiming she can't dance with any of them because she's in mourning. If you could get her started, though, she wouldn't be able to refuse the others."

"What do you suggest? That I drag her bodily out to the floor against her wishes?" he asked sarcastically, although he had to admit, the prospect did hold a certain amount of appeal.

His mother smiled as if he'd made a joke. "Of course not, dear. Just get her to dance somehow." Her smile turned sly. "If she doesn't, I'm afraid the gentlemen might lose interest in her, and we might never get her married off!"

She could not have said anything to motivate him more, and he knew she knew it as she sashayed off to resume her duties as hostess. Gray had been neglecting his as host, but as he glanced over at Emma again, he decided he'd better resume them at once, especially if he ever hoped to get Emma Winthrop out of his house and out of his dreams.

Emma laughed once again at a witticism one of the gentlemen had uttered for her amusement. They all seemed particularly witty this evening, perhaps because Emma seemed particularly gay. But all this gaiety was wearing her out. How on earth was she going to keep this up the entire evening?

All she'd wanted was to look her best and to have Grayson see her looking her best while other men appreciated her. But her cheeks were already aching from holding her smile, and she was bored senseless by the silly chatter.

She let her gaze wander. The ballroom was enormous, taking up almost the entire top floor of the house with tall windows that opened out to catch the evening breeze. That breeze was strong because of the cupola on top of the house. As Virginia had explained to her, the cupola served to create a draft that pulled cool, outside air in through the downstairs windows and expel the stale, inside air out through the cupola.

As a result, the ballroom was surprisingly comfortable as the evening air swept in to dissipate the heat created by over a hundred bodies and even more candles which blazed in every sconce to give the room a golden glow. Negro fiddlers stood on a small stage at one end of the room, sawing out the dance music with surprising skill, and Emma watched enviously as other couples swirled by, the brightly dressed ladies held by their soberly clad partners, hoops bobbing gracefully to reveal shapely ankles and tiny feet.

Emma was beginning to regret her decision not to dance. If she were dancing, she wouldn't have had to sit here all night making conversation with men she didn't particularly even want to know. And she wouldn't have minded showing off her own shapely ankles, either. In fact, having Grayson notice them would have been an added revenge.

But then, Grayson already knew all about her ankles. In fact, he'd actually held one right in his hand, just like he'd held other parts of her in his hand. Suddenly, the room seemed very warm, and Emma flicked open her fan in a desperate effort to cool the heat that swept over her. But that heat only increased when she looked up and saw Grayson bearing down on her.

* * *

"Excuse me, pardon me," Gray said, pushing his way to Emma's side.

She looked up at him with what could only have been alarm, her blue eyes wide with distress, her perfect, rosy mouth parted slightly in surprise. The impulse to lean down and kiss that mouth was strong, but he resisted.

"I'm sorry to interrupt," he lied somberly, "but I must speak with you a moment, Emma."

Her fan had stilled the moment she'd seen him, but now it started fluttering again, as if the prospect of speaking with him had made her feverish. "Is something wrong?" she asked.

"Just for a moment," he repeated with a small smile. "I promise to bring you right back."

"Of course," she said, her eyes still wide as she rose gracefully to her feet. She would, of course, be wondering what could have brought him to her now when he'd been avoiding her all day. He had no intention of telling her.

As they stepped away from the other gentlemen, Gray took her hand and slipped it through his arm, noticing in spite of himself how soft her skin was and how delicate her fingers were in his.

"Is it Alice?" she asked with a worried frown. "Is she—"

"Alice is fine," Gray said, not letting himself look down for fear he'd be lost in those lovely eyes or worse, in the shadow between her breasts.

She was so distressed, she didn't notice he was leading her to the dance floor until he turned and, in one swift motion, took her in his arms.

"What are you doing?" she demanded in astonishment.

"I'm waltzing," he said, proceeding to do so, "and if you don't want to be knocked over, you will do the same."

Her feet began to move, but whether she was simply responding from long habit or by conscious effort, he never knew.

"I can't dance!" she protested, her cheeks a becoming shade of rose now and her blue eyes glittering with outrage.

"On the contrary, you dance very well." Indeed, she was feather light in his arms, following him effortlessly. If only he could have led her without touching her. The warmth of her body beneath his palm and the fragility of her hand in his was heady stuff, enough to make a man forget himself completely if he wasn't careful. Gray intended to be more than careful.

"That's not what I mean!" she insisted. "I mean I can't dance because I'm in mourning!"

At last he allowed himself to look down, taking her in from head to toe in one glance. The sight was nearly breathtaking, but Gray managed to keep his breath. "I don't know much about ladies' fashions, but I do know that dress isn't black."

"It may not be black, but I'm still in mourning." Her blush had spread down her throat and was inching across her breasts. He wondered if that satiny skin would feel warm to the touch, but somehow resisted the urge to find out.

"Emma, why don't you admit defeat," he asked, not unkindly. "My mother has decreed that you will have a good time at this party, and you are powerless to resist her. We all are."

Her eyes widened again. "Virginia put you up to this!" she accused.

He merely shrugged one shoulder as he spun her around in an intricate step she had no trouble at all following.

"You lied to me! I thought something was wrong with Alice!"

"I never said anything was wrong with Alice," he reminded her. "I merely said I needed to speak with you."

She opened her mouth to say something else but apparently changed her mind and closed it again. Tightly. Pressing those sweet lips together in what Gray could only imagine was a silent challenge to him to get them opened again. He could think of several very interesting ways to accomplish that but figured Emma wouldn't allow any of them. With a sigh, he resigned himself to simply holding her for as long as the dance lasted.

Emma glared up at him, furious and having no acceptable way to express that fury. She hated Grayson Sinclair, would gladly have plunged a knife into his heart or fired a bullet into his brain, or at least she was enjoying the fantasy of doing so. In reality, she knew she could never resort to violence, not even to punish a man as dastardly as Grayson.

Of course, when she thought about it a few more seconds and asked herself what his crime was, she felt a nagging sense of shame. She wasn't angry because he'd forced her to dance. Actually, she'd been wishing she could, and now she would have no choice but to accept the other partners who had been clamoring for an opportunity, which meant she had a pleasant evening to anticipate. Oh, no, she wasn't angry over that. She was angry that he'd only asked her because Virginia had told him to. What greater insult than to be partnered just because his mother had forced him? Emma could only be thankful she *didn't* have a gun or a knife, or she might have committed the biggest breach of etiquette in Texas history.

The thought made her smile which made Grayson frown.

"You're not enjoying yourself, are you?" he asked, as if that would have been unthinkable.

"Not a bit," she replied cheerfully, "but I suddenly realized that if I glare at you the whole time, no other men will want to dance with me."

That seemed to ease his concern.

Emma tried to think of something she could say to annoy him. She settled for, "I don't see Mr. Phelps here tonight."

His response was everything she could have hoped. "I believe he left shortly after our . . . our discussion this afternoon," he told her with obvious distaste.

"He said something about Alice having nightmares ever since . . . well, since she lost her mother."

Gray's expression changed instantly at the mention of his late wife, going from irritation to icy reserve. "She did at first," he allowed. "It was only natural, I suppose, considering the circumstances of Lilly's . . . death. But she hasn't had one for months. And regardless of what he says, no one has forbidden him to see his granddaughter. He can see her as often as he likes. DeWitt was merely trying to win your sympathy."

"He said Alice refuses to visit him," Emma recalled.

"She simply prefers to stay home."

"But she spent several weeks with the McCartney's while you were away."

Grayson gave an impatient sigh. "She enjoys visiting them because they have a daughter her age. She has no playmates at the Phelps plantation."

"But—"

"Emma," he said sharply, "Alice is none of your affair. I know what is best for my daughter, and I don't need your advice."

Emma glared at him, furious and no longer worried that someone might notice. To her relief, the dance ended, and Grayson released her.

"Thank you," he said without the slightest trace of sincerity as he sketched her a small bow.

"You are most welcome," she replied just as acidly, refusing his offered arm as they made their way back to Emma's chair.

Lost in her anger, she almost didn't notice that her suitors were still waiting for her, eager smiles on their faces. Seeing her own thunderous expression, their smiles faltered a bit, but Emma caught herself just in time. Flicking open her fan, she batted her eyes as she'd observed the other women doing and smiled coquettishly at them, totally ignoring Grayson who still hovered at her elbow.

"You can't refuse a dance now, Miss Emma," Mr. Hamilton pointed out.

Emma conceded with grace. "Although my brother-in-law tricked me into breaking with tradition, I'm afraid that having done so, I must now relent. I would be honored, Mr. Hamilton." He led her to the floor for a cotillion, and Emma didn't sit down again until the musicians stopped for a rest more than an hour later.

Flushed and winded from her exertions, Emma felt an urgent need to retire to her room for a few moments to refresh herself. Begging the pardon of her gentlemen attendants, she slipped away, not even bothering to look for Grayson. She'd long since lost track of him and had been telling herself she didn't care if he saw her enjoying herself or not.

She made her way down the narrow stairway that led to the ballroom and into the hallway on the second floor. The air was noticeably cooler down here, and Emma paused to draw in a fresh breath. She was drawing another when she heard the scream.

It came from Alice's room.

Six

Emma raced for Alice's door, and just as she threw it open, the child screamed again. The room was in near darkness, lit only by a single candle, but Emma quickly made out a figure bending over the child's bed.

"Alice!" she cried and the figure straightened.

It was Mammy.

"Miss Emma, she havin' another of her dreams," the woman reported as she tried in vain to subdue the child's thrashings.

"Go fetch Miss Virginia," Emma said, hurrying to the bed. "Alice, wake up!" she commanded, sitting down on the bed and taking the child in her arms.

Alice's little body vibrated with shock, but her eyes opened at last, and she looked straight at Emma.

"Mama?" she asked, the word a hopeless plea that tore at Emma's heart.

"It's all right, dear. It was just a dream," she soothed, pulling the girl to her.

"I want my Mama," Alice cried, burying her face against Emma's bare shoulder.

Emma crooned meaningless phrases of comfort, stroking the child and patting her while she sobbed out her terror.

"Don't let him get me!" she pleaded brokenly. "Please don't let him get me!"

"I won't," Emma promised, wondering what monster had threatened the girl's dreams. "No one will hurt you, I promise."

As if to prove her promise, Emma squeezed her more tightly, cherishing the small body to her heart. Then for a moment, just for a moment, she felt so strange, as if they were not alone in the room, as if someone else were watching, and suddenly she felt as if an icy cloud had engulfed them. The cold took her breath, then just as quickly, it was gone, along with the sense that someone else was with them.

Before Emma could even consider what must have happened, Alice's body went rigid, and she screamed again. *"No! Don't let him get me!"* she shrieked in terror as she gazed horrified at something over Emma's shoulder.

Instinctively, Emma turned to look, too, and was stunned to see a man silhouetted in the doorway.

"Mama! Mama!" Alice cried hysterically, clinging desperately to Emma.

But Emma's moment of terror evaporated as she recognized the figure in the doorway as Grayson. "It's all right," she told Alice, taking her firmly by the shoulders and speaking directly into her face. "It's your Papa! Alice, it's just your Papa!"

Alice blinked, and her glazed eyes focused with difficulty, first on Emma's face and then beyond her, at the man who was coming toward them. "Papa?" she asked uncertainly.

"What's the matter, sweetheart?" Grayson's voice asked in that gentle tone Emma had only heard him use with Alice. "Did you have a bad dream?"

"The man was going to get me, Papa!" Alice informed him, unwinding her arms from Emma's neck. "Just like before!"

"There's no man here," Grayson said, sitting down on the opposite side of the bed and reaching for Alice who left Emma eagerly for the comfort her father could offer. "Only me."

"He was going to throw me off the gallery," Alice told him, her voice small and still terrified. "Just like he did Mama!"

Grayson's face might have been carved in stone as his gaze met Emma's over Alice's head. "No one is going to hurt you, darling," he promised, his large hands unbelievably gentle as he caressed the child who clung to him as desperately as she had clung to Emma moments ago.

"I want my Mama!"

Once again the anguished wail tore at Emma's heart, and she saw a spasm of pain flicker across Grayson's face as well. How horrible it must be for him to hear his child beg for a mother who was lost forever.

"There, now, darling," Grayson crooned, patting her as Emma had patted her. "Go back to sleep now. Everything is all right."

He laid her back against her pillow. She looked so small and fragile, her hair like finely spun gold clinging damply to her forehead. But her eyes were already drooping as Grayson leaned down and kissed her forehead.

"Don't leave me," she begged sleepily.

"I won't," he promised.

Suddenly, Emma was acutely aware of the fact that she and Grayson were both sitting on a bed with only inches and a small child's body separating them. Such a situation was most definitely improper, but Emma didn't move, telling herself she didn't want to startle Alice whose eyes were completely closed now.

"I couldn't find Miss Virginia nowhere!" a breathless Mammy reported as she burst in the still-opened door.

"Shhh!" Grayson cautioned, lifting a finger to his lips, and Mammy halted in her tracks. "Close the door," he added in a whisper.

Other dancers had come down the stairs, too, and were mingling in the hallway or descending to the first floor, and their chatter was growing loud. Mammy quickly shut the door, and its heavy oak muffled most of the sounds.

"How is she?" Mammy asked, coming to Emma's side of the bed and peering over her shoulder at the now-sleeping child.

"She's fine," Gray said, rising cautiously so as not to disturb his daughter.

Emma followed his lead, wishing her skirts didn't make so much noise. But Alice didn't move.

"She sleep all night now," Mammy told Emma. "Won't 'member nothin' when she wake up in the morning."

"Are you sure? I could—"

"She fine. I be right here. You go on now and have fun." Mammy shoed her away.

Reluctantly, Emma started for the door, stepping around the trundle at the foot of the bed where Rose still slept, undisturbed by all the commotion. But Grayson stopped her with a hissed warning. "This way," he said, pointing to the door that led out to the gallery onto which their bedrooms opened, too.

He was right, of course. If she used the hallway door, the noise from the other guests might disturb Alice. But still, Emma couldn't forget Alice's terrified certainty that a man had thrown her mother off that very same gallery. For an instant she imagined she felt that strange chill again and shivered.

Grayson motioned impatiently, and Emma reluctantly obeyed his summons, stepping out before him into the balmy night. The fog had crept up from the river to envelope the lawn with its shrouded mist, making it seem as if the house were completely isolated on the small island of land still visible. The gnarled oaks, draped in their moss and fog, looked like enormous monsters lurking in the shadows, ready to pounce. Had it been a night like this when Lilly had plunged to her death? Emma shivered again as the cold seemed to slither up her spine.

And then Grayson was behind her, closer than he needed to be, she was sure, and looming dangerously in the dark. She turned on him, masking her sudden fear with anger. "You said Alice wasn't having nightmares anymore!"

He stiffened under her accusation, but she couldn't make out his expression in the darkness. "I said she hadn't had one for months. I guess it was the party . . ."

"What about the party?" Emma demanded when he hesitated.

"We were having a party the night . . . the night Lilly fell."

Good heavens! No wonder the poor child was upset, and the scene with her grandfather this afternoon probably hadn't helped either. Then another, much more horrible thought occurred to her. "Did Alice see her fall? Is it possible that—"

"No, Alice did *not* see her fall," Grayson informed her curtly. "She was asleep. And she could not have seen a man throwing Lilly off because she wasn't thrown, so don't let your imagination start running wild."

"But she was so frightened!" Emma insisted. "What would make her think that if—"

"I have no idea," Grayson said coldly. "You know how imaginative children are."

"But if no one saw what happened, how can you be sure—?"

"Because she was drunk!" Grayson snapped.

Emma could tell he instantly regretted his outburst by the way he stiffened again, but she wasn't about to overlook it. "What do you mean?"

"I mean she'd had too much to drink," he admitted with obvious reluctance. "Lilly *frequently* had too much to drink, even when we *weren't* entertaining. We assume she went out on the gallery for some air and lost her balance, or else . . ."

"Or else what?" Emma prodded, needing to know the truth, as terrible as it might be.

"Or else she jumped."

Emma gasped, remembering Chloe's defense of her mistress. *"Jumped?* Why would she . . . ?"

"Because she was desperately unhappy. Lilly had been desperately unhappy most of her life and had spent her few short years in an unsuccessful quest for something, *anything,* that would stop the unhappiness. Her mother . . . Well, apparently, they were a lot alike, and her mother hanged herself when Lilly was just a child."

Emma cried out in protest, but Grayson ignored her distress.

"That was why no one was surprised to find Lilly's broken body. Everyone suspected she might someday do the same thing her mother had done, but of course Lilly wouldn't be satisfied with going quietly. She had to make a display of herself before all our friends and neighbors."

Anger and bitterness thrummed beneath his words, and a pain so deep, Emma ached for the man who had borne it for three long years. Instinctively, she reached out to him, wanting him to know she, too, had felt that pain and understood. Wanting somehow to relieve his anguish.

But when she laid her hand on his chest, her touch seemed to galvanize him. He grabbed her so roughly, she gasped, and for one awful second, she thought he was going to send her plunging to her death the same way Lilly had gone to hers. But instead of pushing her away, he pulled her close, hauling her against him with a force that took her breath and before she could catch it, his mouth closed over hers.

For a second, Emma was too stunned to react. She simply stood frozen under his assault as his mouth plundered hers ruthlessly. Vaguely, she noticed he tasted of whiskey and cigars and himself, a combination so intoxicating that her head swam, and then she realized her knees had turned to jelly and her bones were rapidly dissolving, too, melting in the blazing heat of a kiss that she was powerless to resist.

And more than powerless, she realized as she found herself clinging to the lapels of his tailcoat, because her will was gone, too. When his tongue delved between her lips to sweep the tender recesses of her mouth, she did not even *consider* resisting even though no one had ever done such a shocking thing to her before. Why, it was almost like the other thing that men did, she thought wildly, and something contracted between her legs in a spasm of desire.

Her breath seemed lodged somewhere behind her heart, and just when she thought she might faint, he lifted his mouth from hers. But she only had time to gasp once before his lips found her throat in a moist, silken caress. Down and down, his fingers there, too, stroking and fondling until he reached the swell of her breasts. But he didn't stop there, oh, no, he kept going, covering every inch of flesh with a thousand biting kisses and then soothing her feverish skin with the slick heat of his tongue.

Emma's breasts throbbed with needs she could not even name, and her nipples had tightened into tingling nubs that begged to be touched and kissed and adored. Grayson's hands caught the weight of her breasts in his palms, lifting them higher for his sensual assault, and then his torturous tongue dipped into the crevice between them, tasting and tantalizing and sending a thrill racing to her core. This time the spasm was pure lust, and it forced a cry from her throat. The cry was part anguish and part plea, and it startled Grayson into lifting his head for just a moment.

That moment saved her. Dear heaven, what was she doing? she wondered frantically. And why was she allowing Grayson to assault her like this? Had she lost her mind?

Appalled, she thrust him away or tried to. In reality, she was the one who staggered back, covering her well-kissed bosom with both hands. Beneath her fingers, her skin was still moist from his tongue, but she didn't let herself think of that. Instead she tried to think of the proper phrase to express her outrage at his conduct. She'd learned several at Miss Farnsworth's Academy, but none of them seemed quite right for the occasion. Calling Grayson a cad would hardly injure his feelings, and asking how he'd dared do such a thing to her only left her open to questions about why she'd let him.

"Are you crazy?" she demanded instead, appalled all over again at how breathless and wanton she sounded.

"I suppose I am," he replied, as breathless and wanton as she. At least he wasn't reaching for her again, because she didn't know what she would do if he did.

For a long moment they simply stood there, sobbing for breath in the darkness. Emma trembled, but whether from fear or simple reaction, she could not have said as she tried desperately to think of something to say that would make the past few minutes vanish from her memory and his.

"Now," he said at last, "you understand why you can't stay here."

"*What?*" she cried, not understanding any such thing.

"If you stay here, it is my duty to protect you, but as you have just learned, I cannot protect you from myself. That is why you must go. You must find someone to marry, and you must leave Fairview before . . . before I forget myself again. Do you understand?"

Emma could only gape at him. *Forget himself!* He'd forgotten more than *himself*. He'd forgotten her and his mother and his daughter and his dead wife and Emma's dead husband and everything else he'd ever known in his entire life. But then, she realized guiltily, so had she, at least for a moment. She swallowed down her own shame. "I understand."

He drew a ragged breath, and for a moment she thought . . . But he only nodded. "I'll see you upstairs. We'll . . . forget this ever happened."

"Yes," she said, agonizingly aware that she would never forget it as long as she lived.

He nodded again and then brushed past her, into the darkness beyond, where the door to his own bedroom lay. For a long moment, Emma simply stood there, staring into the shadows, uncertain whether she was afraid he would come back or wishing that he would.

She was certain she was alone, perfectly alone, so when she heard the faint echo of laughter, she whirled in surprise. But she saw nothing and heard nothing because no one was there. The laughter had come from somewhere else, drifting down from the ballroom above perhaps. Or from inside her own head, where a part of her could still appreciate what a fool she was. Mortified by her own conduct, she turned and ran into the sanctuary of her own room.

A single candle burned in a wall sconce, and Emma snatched up the candlestand from the nearest table and hurried over to light it. Her hand shook, but somehow she managed to touch the wick to the flame long enough to ignite it, then she carried it over to the cheval mirror. Using the feeble light, she examined her reflection with hasty thoroughness.

Remarkably, she looked exactly the same as she had the last time she had checked her reflection. Oh, perhaps her eyes were glittering a bit too brightly, but her features were unchanged. And her bosom . . . Although she examined it closely, she could detect nothing more than a decided flush on her normally flawless skin. She could show herself in the ballroom again without fear that someone would be able to guess what had passed between her and Grayson on the gallery just now.

And although she wanted nothing more than to remain here in the privacy of her room where she would not have to face anyone and pretend that nothing at all untoward had happened to her, she knew she could not. Because if she did, Grayson would know. He would know she was a coward, too ashamed to face him again. And not sophisticated enough to forget a little kiss that had, she was certain, meant nothing. Less than nothing. A kiss that Grayson had probably already forgotten, but which would haunt Emma for the rest of her life.

So Emma returned to the ballroom, a smile fixed firmly on her face and the mysterious coldness she had experienced in Alice's room settled firmly in her heart. The dancing went on until almost dawn, and she enjoyed it thoroughly. Or at least she gave the impression she enjoyed it. In reality, she felt as if she were somehow detached from everything. She smiled and laughed and bantered with her partners and allowed them to fetch her refreshments and ate and drank and danced and danced, but through it all she remained merely an observer of herself and the men whom she partnered.

And although she made a great show of ignoring him, she was acutely aware of every move Grayson made. He did not, she was surprised to note, dance more than a dozen times, partnering only his mother and some of the older ladies to whom he must have felt an obligation. Instead, he stood around and talked with the other men and imbibed rather too freely of his own liquor. By the time the musicians played their last number, Emma wondered how he was able to stand.

At least she could take comfort in knowing their encounter had disturbed him as much as it had disturbed her. It was the only comfort she was likely to get.

"Did you have a good time?" Chloe asked when Emma finally returned to her room after bidding farewell to the guests who were leaving and good night to those who were retiring.

"Yes, I had a wonderful time," she lied. "I didn't sit out a single dance."

"You sure was the prettiest lady there," Chloe remarked as she helped Emma out of her gown. "I's glad you changed your mind 'bout your dress."

Emma remembered how Grayson's tongue had played above the bodice of that dress and felt the heat coming to her face. If only she hadn't been so vain! If only she hadn't *wanted* Grayson to notice her! Pride certainly did go before a fall.

"You must be tired," Chloe observed, reminding Emma she wasn't acting at all the way a woman should be acting when she had been the belle of the ball.

Emma thought about all the reasons she had for being reticent. A lot of things had happened today, starting with her first encounter with Grayson late this afternoon and his quarrel with DeWitt Phelps and Alice's nightmare and . . .

"I should check on Alice," she said aloud.

" 'Cause of her nightmare?" Chloe said, making Emma wonder how she had known. "No need. She fine. Her mammy let us know if she ain't."

"Her grandfather said she's had those nightmares ever since her mother died," Emma remembered.

Chloe's hands stilled where she'd been untying Emma's hoops. "When was you talkin' to *him?*" she asked, her voice hard.

"This afternoon," Emma said, watching the girl closely over her shoulder. She'd seen that expression before, when Chloe was hiding strong emotion. "You don't like Mr. Phelps very much, do you?" she observed.

Chloe's expression became the mask of blandness she usually wore. "Ain't my place to like him or not," she said, as she resumed her task.

"But you certainly would have formed an opinion from growing up in his house, wouldn't you?" Emma guessed. "Did his daughter like him?"

This time Chloe didn't bother to conceal her emotions. Her dark eyes blazed with what could only have been hatred. "She had more reason than most not to, and the rest of us had enough."

"Even his wife?" Emma prodded.

" 'Specially his wife," Chloe confirmed as Emma stepped out of her hoops.

"I heard that . . . that she killed herself."

Chloe's expression hardened again. "So they say."

"You mean she didn't?" Emma exclaimed in surprise.

Chloe shrugged one shoulder. "All I know, people gots a way a dyin' 'round Mr. DeWitt, one way and another."

Emma had the unsettling feeling that Chloe was trying to tell her something, and Emma was afraid she didn't want to know what that something was. Then an even more alarming thought occurred to her. "I caught Mr. Phelps with Alice today. He had her alone in the parlor."

Chloe's head jerked up and her eyes widened. "What was he doing?"

"Trying to get her to kiss him, but she wouldn't."

"Did you make her?" Chloe asked sharply.

"Of course not! I sent her away to find her mammy."

Emma thought Chloe was relieved, although she said nothing.

"He told me Alice is afraid of him," Emma said. "That she blames him for her mother's death, and that she won't go to visit him."

"You feelin' sorry for him?" Chloe asked suspiciously.

Emma frowned. "I was until I heard the other side of the story. Mr. Phelps said that everyone at Fairview was trying to turn Alice against him, but I think they're just trying to protect Alice from . . . Well, whatever it is that frightens her."

"She don't need to visit Mr. DeWitt," Chloe said gravely. "She don't *never* need to go over there. Nothin' but misery at his place, and Miss Alice, she seen enough of that already."

"What kind of misery are you talking about?" Emma asked, still watching the girl's face, but Chloe gave nothing away.

"The kind that you don't never forget, not for as long as you live," Chloe said, her face unnaturally calm. "You'll keep Miss Alice away from him, won't you? Promise me, Miss Emma."

"Well, of course," Emma promised, puzzled by Chloe's belligerence. "I would never do anything to hurt Alice."

The assurance seemed to ease Chloe somewhat, and she finished undressing Emma and helped her into her nightdress. But when Emma sat down at her dressing table so Chloe could brush out her hair, Emma could not help remembering what else had happened tonight.

And when she recalled Grayson's fevered kisses out on the darkened gallery, she also remembered his warning: she could not stay here now. She could not take a chance that Grayson would kiss her again and that next time he might do even more than that. Somehow, someway, she must escape Fairview.

But if she did, who would protect Alice?

Emma slept very late the next day, and when she awoke, Chloe brought her breakfast in bed. Later she dressed and ventured out to find that most of the guests had already left for home. Mercifully, Grayson was making himself scarce, so Emma sought refuge in the one place she was fairly certain she would not encounter him in the middle of the day.

"Aunt Emma!" Alice greeted her joyously when she entered the nursery playroom. Rose, too, came running forward, her brown face aglow with anticipation of another story, and to Emma's surprise, another little girl had joined them. After a moment, Emma recognized her as Jane McCarthy, the daughter of the family with whom Alice had stayed while her father and grandmother were in Philadelphia.

"Jane is staying a whole week!" Alice exclaimed when they had finished with introductions. "Her mother said she could!"

"That's wonderful," Emma said, studying Alice for any signs of distress from her nightmare but finding none. "Do you think she'll like stories as much as you and Rose do?"

"Oh, she already does! Her mother reads to her all the time!" Alice assured her.

Amid much jostling for position, Emma finally settled her audience on the floor at her feet while she read, and as she did, she couldn't help but think how like a teacher she felt with her little charges staring up at her raptly.

A teacher. The word echoed in her head as she finished the story of the princess and the pea. "Would you girls like to do some lessons instead?" she asked when they begged her for another story. "I could teach you your letters."

"I already know my letters," Jane said proudly. "My mama taught them to me." A year older than Alice, Jane was a serious girl with long brown braids and large brown eyes. "I can write my name, too."

"Then you can help Rose and Alice," Emma said. "Mammy, can you find us a slate?"

Emma was surprised when she looked up to find the woman watching them with a worried frown. "Rosie don't need to learn no letters, Miss Emma," she said.

"Oh, yes, she does!" Alice protested. "She wants to, don't you, Rosie?"

Rose glanced at her mother and made not a sound, waiting for some cue as to what her answer should be. But Emma wasn't going to allow Rose to be cheated just because her mother feared what Grayson might say. "Alice, do you have a slate and some chalk?"

Alice was sure she did and even managed to find them after a few minutes of looking. While Mammy stood by, still frowning and twisting her apron in apprehension, Emma began her first lesson.

By the end of the afternoon, Alice and Rose could print their names, and Emma had not missed the fact that Rose was every bit as quick to learn as Alice. Wait until she told Virginia how wrong she had been about the slaves! Jane had proved an able assistant and was just as eager to learn more, begging Emma's help with putting the letters she already knew together to form words. They were all disappointed when the maid brought supper to the nursery, signaling the end of their first lesson.

"You'll come back tomorrow, won't you, Aunt Emma?" Alice begged.

"Aren't you tired of lessons?" Emma teased.

"No, not a bit! Please, please?"

The other two girls echoed her plea, and Emma agreed only too willingly. As she made her way back to her room to prepare for supper, she was full of plans. She'd scour Grayson's library for suitable books to use. Probably, he already owned a reader or two that would get Alice started. Emma was fairly sure she'd brought some of her old schoolbooks from home since they'd been worthless and no one had wanted to buy them in the auction. She would have to find them among her belongings that were still crated. And she'd need more supplies, another slate for Rose and . . . Suddenly, Emma remembered the children she had seen down in the quarters, the ones who spent their days in idle play and who ate from troughs like animals. Surely, they would be just as eager to learn as Rose was, and they could certainly benefit from a school. It wasn't as if Emma would be keeping them from useful work.

She was so full of plans that she forgot to be apprehensive about seeing Grayson again until she entered the dining room and found both his and Virginia's places empty.

"Miss Virginia, she say you should go ahead and eat," the

maid told her with a curtsey. "Her and Massa Gray, they be back when they can."

"Where are they?" Emma asked.

"Down at the quarters. Mammy real sick," the girl told her solemnly.

"But I was just with her a few minutes ago in the nursery, and she was fine," Emma protested.

"Oh, no, ma'am, not Miss Alice's mammy. Massa Gray's mammy. She been poorly, and now she dying."

Not knowing what else to do, Emma sat down and ate her supper in solitary splendor, although her appetite had fled. The maid had just set a piece of pie in front of her when she heard Grayson's voice in the front hall.

Without asking herself why, she got up and hurried out to find him and Virginia conferring in hushed tones. Any discomfort she might have felt at seeing Grayson again evaporated when she saw his face. It was ashen and creased with lines she had never noticed before.

As if sensing her presence, he glanced up to meet her gaze across the expanse of hallway, and for a moment Emma felt as if she'd had the breath knocked out of her. But only for a moment. In the next instant, he silently dismissed her, turning back to Virginia.

"Excuse me, Mother," he said and strode away, toward his office.

"Gray, it's a useless gesture," she pleaded. "You'll only cause discontent!"

But if he heard her, he gave no sign, disappearing into his office and closing the door behind her. Virginia sighed wearily.

"How is she?" Emma asked, going to Virginia.

"Not good," Virginia said with another sigh. "I doubt she'll last the night. I came back to make her some sassafras tea. I don't think it will help, but it was always her favorite."

Emma followed Virginia out to the kitchen where she gave orders to have the tea brewed. Then, as if just noticing Emma was there, she turned to her. "You should come with me back to the quarters. If you ever run your own plantation, you'll need to know how to nurse the sick. It's a job that always falls to the mistress."

Yesterday, Emma would have protested that she would never be mistress of her own plantation, but now she understood that both Virginia and Grayson expected her to marry and soon. As the kitchen filled with the sweet savor of the sassafras, Emma realized all that would mean to her. She would have her own home again, her own possessions, but she would have to leave Alice and all her plans to educate the girl. And if she were to marry, that meant she would have to give herself to another man. She pictured the faces of all the men she'd met at the barbecue, but she could not imagine herself with any of them.

No, when she closed her eyes, Emma could only imagine herself with *one* man, but he was the only one, it seemed, who *didn't* want her. The one who was determined to get her out of his house and out of his life as quickly as possible.

Emma felt the banked coals of her old anger flicker to life. When would this helplessness ever end? This dependence on whatever man was willing to take her in? Would she never control her own destiny?

"Come along, dear," Virginia said, interrupting her thoughts. She carried a steaming kettle containing the tea and pointed to a pie sitting on the table.

"Bring that, too," she told Emma.

"Won't that be too rich for someone as sick as—"

"It's for the family, the ones sitting up with her," Virginia explained, setting out without waiting for Emma.

The shadows were long as they made their way down the flower lined path to the quarters. Emma had not been down this path since her first day here when she had come with Virginia to simply look the place over. The buildings at the end of the path were still the same, but everything else was different tonight. While before the place had been deserted except for the children playing at the far end of the quarters, now each cabin was filled to overflowing with men and women, boys and girls. Smoke curled from each chimney and the aroma of cooking filled the air.

Children stopped in their play to watch the two white women walk by, and grown-up faces of various colors of brown peered out the windows and doorways as they passed. These were, Emma knew, the faces of the fieldhands, the workers who labored endlessly in the fields to grow Grayson's cotton and who had made him a wealthy man. The ones she saw moving in the street walked with a slow shuffle, seemingly too weary even to stand, and Emma wondered how they found the energy to prepare themselves a meal at the end of the day.

Gradually, Emma realized that a sound of which she had been dimly aware was singing. As they approached a cabin around which a small crowd had gathered, the sound clarified into a hymn whose words she recognized. One strong baritone voice led the chorus while the others hummed or crooned along, telling about the sweet journey across the Jordan River into the Promised Land. The crowd parted wordlessly for Virginia, and Emma followed in her wake, self-conscious of her finely made gown before so many in homespun and her handmade shoes before so many whose feet were bare. Ashamed, she lowered her gaze so she would not have to meet any eyes.

The cabin they entered was small but eerily neat, as if no one really lived there. Even the hard-packed dirt floor was swept clean. A few crudely made chairs stood around, but those who had been sitting on them rose when Virginia and Emma entered.

"Sit down, sit down," Virginia urged, handing the kettle to one of the women. Another took the pie from Emma with murmured thanks.

As the others sat back down, Emma saw the old woman lying on the bunk in the corner of the cabin. The bed was a wooden plank attached to two walls and covered with corn husks over which a cheap blanket had been spread. The woman lay on the blanket covered by another. She was thin and frightfully frail, the slight rise and fall of her chest the only sign of life about her, although Emma could see from the few strands of gray in her hair that she probably wasn't very old. The fact that she had been Grayson's nurse meant that she must only be about Virginia's age, but illness had shriveled her beyond her years.

A man sat beside her, holding her withered hand in his much larger one, and Emma recognized him as Thomas, Grayson's personal body servant. From the expression on his face, Emma knew he was grieving as much as Grayson was over this woman, and suddenly she realized that if what she had learned about plantation life from Chloe was always true, then Thomas must be this woman's son. She would have nursed both boys and raised them together, almost as brothers but with one crucial difference: when they were grown, one would own the other.

The woman who had taken the kettle had poured a cup of the tea and given it to Virginia who was now offering it to the woman on the bed. "Eliza brewed this special for you, Mammy," Virginia was saying as she held the woman's head and pressed the cup to her lips.

Mammy sipped weakly at the cup a few times then fell back with a sigh. "That's mighty fine," she said, her voice a thin thread of sound.

Emma heard a small disturbance outside, and then Grayson entered the cabin. Again her breath caught at the sight of him, but he didn't appear to notice her standing in the shadows. He went directly to the bed where his old mammy lay.

"I've got something for you, Mammy," he told her softly in that special voice she'd thought he only used on Alice.

"Is that my boy?" the old woman said, her eyes searching until she'd found him. Although Emma would have thought it impossible, life seemed to flow back into her for just a moment. Her eyes brightened and her thin lips formed a smile.

"Yes, Mammy, it's Gray. I brought you your freedom papers. Here they are." He took her hand and placed a piece of heavy white paper in it. Emma could see the writing on it had lots of curlicues and flourishes and a wax seal adorned the bottom. Mammy's fingers closed spasmodically around the paper. "You know what this means?" Gray asked gently. "It means you're free now."

"You hear that, Tommy?" she asked her son, gazing in wonder at the paper she held in her hand. "I's free! Praise God, I's free!"

"Yes, Mama," Thomas murmured, but Emma noticed a marked lack of enthusiasm in his response. She also noticed that instead of sharing her joy, he and Grayson were pointedly not looking at each other, as if they shared some guilty secret they might betray if they did.

"This paper," Mammy asked Grayson, "do it mean I's really free?"

"Yes, Mammy," Grayson replied patiently.

"And if 'n I show it to the pattyrollers, they let me go wherever I want?"

"Yes, Mammy, wherever you want," Grayson replied.

"An' I can go to Brazoria if I want?" she prodded, naming the nearest city on the Brazos River.

"If you like."

"And stay long as I want?"

"As long as you want."

She seemed transfixed by the paper that she barely had the strength to hold. "You's a good boy, Massa Gray, ain't he, Miss Virginia?"

"I've always thought so," Virginia agreed, and Emma saw that there were tears in Virginia's eyes. "You did a good job raising him."

For a long moment, Mammy continued to stare at the paper, drawing some kind of strength from it, but then even that strength began to ebb. Her fingers relaxed, and the paper fell to lie flat against her thin chest. "I's free," she said on a sigh.

For several minutes, no one moved or, it seemed to Emma, even breathed. Then Thomas said, "She's gone." He looked up at Grayson at last. "She was just waitin' for you to keep your promise."

Did Emma hear a hint of rebuke in his tone? She couldn't be sure and couldn't imagine why Thomas would be rebuking Grayson in the first place, so she must have been mistaken.

"We'll lay her out, Miss Virginia," one of the women said. "You go on now."

"We'll have the funeral tomorrow afternoon. Tell everyone they won't have to go into the fields after dinner," Virginia said. "I'll send a dress for her, too." She turned to her son. "Gray?"

"I'll be along," he told her. He was still looking down at the woman on the bed.

Emma could not help but feel sorry for him. He and Thomas seemed equally shattered by her death, and Emma had to resist a strong urge to offer him comfort. Grayson Sinclair, she had to remind herself, did not *deserve* her comfort.

She followed Virginia out of the house, and once again the crowd, which had grown larger, parted for them.

"She's gone," Virginia told them, and the singing took on a new poignancy that echoed into the darkening sky.

As if they'd sensed the death, the other slaves in the other cabins had grown quiet, and even the children had stopped their play. Virginia dabbed at her eyes with her handkerchief, and Emma felt the sting of tears in her own eyes, even though she hadn't known the dead woman and had no excuse for feeling any grief.

Still, one person's death diminished all of us, she reasoned, even if that person was only a slave. Certainly, even a slave could leave her mark on the world. Virginia herself had acknowledged this one's contribution to her son's life. Emma supposed generations of Southerners had been raised by women like Mammy who served without reward of any kind just because their skin happened to be dark while those who owned her were white. Her one desire had been freedom, and Grayson had granted her dying wish.

How kind of him, she couldn't help thinking, although it would have been kinder to free her when she still had some time to enjoy it. When she still might have made that trip down the Brazos and done whatever it was slaves dreamed of doing when they were free.

"What are pattyrollers?" Emma asked, remembering what Mammy had said. She and Virginia had left the quarters and were on the path back to the house.

"That's what the slaves call the patrollers, the men who patrol the roads looking for runaways," Virginia said.

"You mean slaves actually run away?" Emma asked in amazement. Where on earth could they run *to?*

"We've never had a problem," Virginia assured her, "but not everyone treats their Negroes as well as we do, and sometimes . . . Well, like I told you, they're children, really, and they think that freedom will bring them happiness. They have no idea what dangers await them, so we have the patrols to catch them and bring them back before anything happens to them."

Virginia made it sound like a kindness, but Emma had a feeling the' slaves might feel differently. She'd seen the joy on Mammy's face just now and felt sure every slave in the quarters would have reacted the same way at the prospect of freedom, no matter how brief.

"Would you like to come down for the funeral tomorrow?" Virginia asked.

"Yes, I would," Emma said, not examining her motives too closely. Her sense of duty played a large part, she knew, but another part was pure curiosity. She didn't want to know what the rest of it was.

"That's good," Virginia said, patting her arm. "It's important for us to let the darkies know we value them. Of course, we wouldn't come down for a fieldhand, but Mammy was like part of our family. Why, I can remember her chasing after those boys . . ."

Emma only half-heard her reminiscences as they walked

back to the house. After she had helped Virginia choose a
dress suitable for burying Mammy from among Virginia's cast-
offs, she retired to her room where she spent the rest of the
evening reading or trying to. She didn't make much progress
on the novel she had chosen from the library, though, because
she kept seeing Mammy's face when Grayson had handed her
the freedom paper.

Emma had no trouble at all imagining how happy the old
woman must have been because she could imagine how happy
she would be if someone handed *her* a paper and told her she
was free and would never again have to worry about whose
property she was. All during her childhood, she had belonged
to her father who had passed her along to Charles when she
was old enough to marry. Charles, in turn, had left her at
Grayson's mercy, and now Grayson was telling her she would
have to find yet another man to whom she could "sell" herself
in marriage. In some ways, she was no freer than those who
were openly called slaves.

The more she thought about her situation, the more furious
she became. How dare Grayson Sinclair inform her that she
would have to choose a husband when the last thing in the
world she wanted was to put herself at the mercy of yet another
man? How dare he dictate how she must spend the rest of her
life just because he lacked the self-control to protect the virtue
of a female who was under his protection? Emma was not to
blame for Grayson's lack of moral fiber, and she should not
be the one punished. Rather, Grayson should vow to honor her
status in his house in the future and concede to her wish to
remain single.

Of course, there was the question of Grayson's behavior toward her, but preventing another episode like the one on the
gallery last night should be relatively easy. Certainly, Emma
had no wish to repeat it and would avoid any possible recur-
rence, and if she could trust Grayson's word, he was equally
as determined. And if she was able to convince him to allow
her to complete her plans for a school for Alice and the slave

children, she would be too busy to even worry about such a thing.

Yes, that's what she would do, and she would tell Grayson her decision at the first opportunity. He couldn't possibly refuse since he couldn't force her to take a husband against her wishes and he wouldn't disgrace himself before his neighbors by denying his protection and throwing a defenseless woman out into the street. For the first time in her life, Emma realized she had the power to do what she wanted to do, and no man could stop her.

She slept soundly that night, her dreams of children and lessons, and when she awoke, she found the strangest thing on the pillow next to hers.

"What's this?" she asked Chloe when the girl came in to help Emma dress. She held up the thing she had found, which appeared to be several long strands of hair tied in an intricate loop around a small bird's feather.

"Where'd you get that?" Chloe asked in alarm, snatching the thing out of Emma's hand.

"I found it on my pillow this morning. Do you think Alice made it for me? It looks like something a child would—"

"Miss Alice don't have nothin' to do with this," Chloe explained, plainly upset. "It's a charm. A . . . a good luck charm," she added hastily.

Emma was fascinated and would have liked another look at it, but Chloe had already stuffed it into her apron pocket. "Oh, dear," Emma suddenly remembered, "Alice said she was going to ask the conjure woman for a spell to make me stay. Her father was angry and forbade her to do such a thing, but do you suppose she did it anyway? She could have snuck in here last night and left it."

"Yeah, I reckon she done that very thing," Chloe agreed eagerly. "That girl, she stubborn like her mama. You won't tell Massa Gray, will you? He be mighty mad!"

"But if he feels so strongly about it, we can't let her get

away with it. What if he finds out some other way? Or what if she does it again?" Emma pointed out.

"Don't nobody know but you and me," Chloe reminded her. "I'll tell her mammy 'bout it. She let Miss Alice know she don't never wanna do nothin' like this again!"

"I suppose that would be all right," Emma agreed reluctantly, "just so long as Alice understands it was wrong to disobey her father."

"I make sure a that," Chloe promised fervently.

Emma still felt uneasy about the situation and decided she would speak to Alice herself later, just to make sure she understood. And she supposed it wouldn't do to annoy Grayson about this when she was already planning to annoy him by refusing to obey his command to get married. She would need his approval to start her school, so she decided she wouldn't mention the charm unless Alice disobeyed him again.

She also decided to wait until after the funeral to speak to Grayson about her school. Perhaps she would even wait several days, until his grief was less so he would be more receptive to her suggestions. Meanwhile, she went to the nursery where the girls eagerly awaited their next lesson.

She was using dried beans to teach them how to count when Chloe burst into the nursery playroom.

"Miss Emma," she said, her eyes wide with alarm. "Massa Gray, he want to see you. He want to see you *right now!*"

Seven

"What does he want, Chloe?" Emma asked when she had excused herself from the nursery and stepped into the hall.

"I don't got no idea!" She was wringing her hands, though, so Emma knew this wasn't an ordinary summons.

"Do you think he found out about the charm?"

"I don't rightly see how he could've," Chloe said, "but he sure is mad 'bout somethin'! Did you do anything last night might've got him mad?"

"Certainly not! I didn't even *see* him last night except for a few moments at Mammy's cabin."

Chloe shrugged. "Then I expect the only way you'll find out is to go see what he wants."

Emma frowned, feeling the now-familiar apprehension she had experienced each time she'd come face to face with Grayson since their encounter on the gallery the night of the barbecue. She laid a hand over her stomach in an effort to quiet it.

"You stand up to him now," Chloe cautioned, seeing the gesture. "And whatever you do, don't cry. He hates for a woman to cry."

Cry? Emma had no intention of *crying* in front of Grayson Sinclair. The very idea appalled her. She lifted her chin, summoning the anger that had served her so well last night when she'd been making her plans for the future. With luck, it would give her the courage she would need now.

By the time she had reached the downstairs hallway and

stood outside Grayson's study door, Emma was livid at being summoned like an errant schoolgirl, as if she had committed some infraction for which she should be reprimanded! How dare he? In her outrage, she rapped smartly on the door.

"Come in."

Emma threw the door open and saw him sitting behind his desk, looking like a very handsome schoolmaster ready to rap her knuckles, which only made her angrier.

"You sent for me?" she asked as haughtily as she could.

"Please close the door," he said coldly.

Emma's anger turned to alarm. If she closed the door, they would be completely alone. The last time they'd been completely alone . . .

"I have no intention of molesting you, if that's what you're afraid of," he said, his disgust evident. "I simply do not want the servants to hear our conversation."

Emma didn't want him to think she'd been afraid of anything at all, and she didn't want the servants to overhear anything either. Besides, this time she was much more modestly dressed, covered from neck to feet in her usual black mourning gown, so he couldn't possibly *molest* her again, if that's what it was called. She closed the door with a decisive click and turned to face him with as much hauteur as she could muster, although she took not one step closer to where he sat. If he was on the other side of the room, he couldn't possibly touch her.

He seemed to hesitate a moment, as if gathering his thoughts. Finally, he said, "I understand you've started tutoring Alice."

"Yes, I have," she admitted with relief. Was that all? She'd been so afraid he knew about Alice giving her the charm.

"And you're also tutoring . . . Rose." It was a question.

"Yes, and I'll tutor Jane for as long as she's here. In fact, I was thinking—"

"You can't do that."

Emma blinked in surprise, certain she must have misunderstood. "What do you mean? Don't you want your daughter to learn to read and write?"

Grayson frowned, and only then did Emma notice the dark circles under his eyes and the dark shadow of beard on his jaw. He had probably not slept at all last night. She felt a stab of pity for him, but squelched it, remembering she could not afford any weakness at all.

"You may," he said, as if granting her some great favor, "continue to tutor Alice and any of her friends, but you may not tutor any of the slaves."

"What?" He couldn't be serious! Certainly, no one needed it more.

He folded his hands on his desk, as if he were trying to control their movement. "We do not teach our Negroes to read and write, Emma. I am sure someone would have told you that *if* you had bothered to consult any of us before beginning your project."

"We discussed it the other day in the nursery," she reminded him, "and you didn't raise any objections then."

"I believe we were discussing your tutoring *Alice.* I have no objection to that. As long as you are here, in this house, I'm sure my mother would be grateful for any help you can offer in that area."

Of course, he'd already told her he expected her to be *out* of this house at the first opportunity, and, Emma noticed, he didn't mention that *he* would be grateful for anything at all. Her anger was back in full force now. She strode purposefully over to his desk. "I believe Alice would do better if she were able to learn with other children, and certainly Rose has proved herself capable," she added, in case that was his objection to her teaching the slave children. "Why, in only one day, they both learned how to write their names, and Rose learned just as quickly as Alice."

Standing just on the other side of his desk, Emma could see that his eyes were red-rimmed from lack of sleep and his jaw was working as if he were holding back some strong emotion. "It's not a question of whether she's capable."

"Then what *is* it a question of?" Emma challenged, planting her hands on her hips.

"It is a question," he informed her tightly, rising slowly from his chair and bracing both hands on the desktop, "of knowing what is right and proper." His eyes were so black, she couldn't even see the pupils, and they glittered like glass. "I have tried to make allowances for you, Emma, because you were raised in a place where women are . . . well, not as gently bred—"

"What?" How dare he imply that she was less genteel than the women in the South!

"Where you were not taught," he continued, ignoring her outrage, "was in the fine distinctions that must be made in handling people of color."

"If what I have learned in my short stay here is correct, then I can only be *glad* that I never learned those distinctions," Emma replied, furious now. "Your mother informed me that the slaves are simple creatures who cannot even be trusted to care for themselves, yet I notice she trusted one of them to care for her own son, just as you trust one to care for your daughter!"

"That's a different matter—"

"How is it different?" she demanded. "Mammy has complete charge over Alice, just the way your Mammy had charge over you. Virginia told me that the woman who died last night was more of a mother to you than she was. You trust the Negroes to raise your children and tend your crops and cook your food and run your homes, and then you pretend they don't have sense enough to learn to read and write. If that's one of the *fine distinctions,* then—"

"I don't think they don't have sense enough to learn," Grayson said bitterly, surprising her into silence. "In fact, I know they do. I taught Thomas to read and write when we were boys. He learned even faster than I did."

This was more than Emma could have hoped. "Then you know I'm right! Grayson, I had this idea, and I was just waiting until the funeral was over this afternoon to tell you, but . . . Well, I was thinking I could start a school down in the quarters, for the children there. They don't have anything to do but play all day, and they're growing up so wild, like little animals. I know they could—"

"No!"

Emma jumped and gaped at him in shock.

"Are you crazy?" he demanded, his face dark with fury. "Do you know that in most Southern states, it's *against the law* to teach Negroes to read?"

"It is?" Emma asked, unable to even imagine such a thing.

"Yes, it is! And do you know why? Of course you don't know why," he said, not even waiting for her reply, "because you grew up in the North where you didn't learn a damn thing about chattel slavery because people in the North can pretend it doesn't exist and go on about their lives in self-righteous ignorance. But we in the South have to live with it every day, and while nothing makes it right, a few things make it bearable, and one of those things is keeping the slaves in ignorance."

"You *hate* slavery," Emma exclaimed, stunned by the knowledge.

"Of *course* I hate slavery! Every man worthy of the name hates it!"

"Then why do you hold slaves?" Emma demanded. "You saw how happy your Mammy was last night when you freed her. Why don't you free the rest of them and—?"

"I *didn't* free her," he said, straightening as if in defense.

"But I saw you! You gave her that paper and—"

"That paper was just a paper, nothing else. Oh, I made it look fancy and put a seal on it, but it was worthless, just a gesture to make an old woman happy before she died. No man in Texas can free a slave without an act of the legislature. And even if the legislature would see fit to allow me to free over a hundred slaves, what would become of them . . . bearing in mind that most towns in Texas have laws prohibiting free Negroes from even entering them?"

Emma gaped at him incredulously. "Well," she hedged, frantically trying to think of something, "they could stay here and work for you for wages!"

"And how would I pay them?" Grayson asked relentlessly. "The bulk of my capital, hundreds of thousands of dollars, is tied up in the slaves. Oh, if I sold them all, I'd have enough cash to pay fieldhands, but do you think I could pay them enough to work in the fields from sunup to sundown to make another man rich? And selling my people away would be worse than keeping them myself. How could I be sure they'd be well taken care of? That their new masters wouldn't beat them or starve them? That he'd keep families together and not sell children away from the parents?"

"I don't—"

"You're right, Emma, I do hate slavery," he went on relentlessly. "If I'd been given a choice, I would never have owned slaves, but no one gave me a choice. I was born owning slaves, and over a hundred people depend on me to feed and house and clothe them from the day they're born until the day they die. They are both my heritage and my curse . . . Oh, excuse me, I should have said my *responsibility,*" he added bitterly.

"But if you can't free them, you can at least make their lives a little better," Emma argued.

"By teaching them to read?" he guessed. Emma did not like the sarcasm in the question.

"Yes," she said, refusing to back down.

"So they can read the Bible and find out there's more in it than the passage about servants obeying their masters? So they can find out that God intended all men to live together as brothers?" he asked, and although his words were true, his tone was ugly enough to send Emma back a step. "So they can read books and learn about the rest of the world where slavery doesn't exist and long for something they can never have? Or perhaps you think they should read the abolitionist tracts to find out how to slaughter the whites who have been oppressing them?"

Emma glared at him. "I just think they would be better workers if they were educated. You claim to care about their welfare. Why don't you want them to better themselves?"

"Better themselves for what, Emma? So they can pick cotton faster? A slave can never hope to better himself. No matter how clever he is or how diligent, he will always be a slave, and no one wants to be a *better* slave. Why should he? If he works hard today, he gets no reward, and he will only be expected to work harder tomorrow. In fact, that's what is inherently wrong with slavery in the first place. If you've got a hired hand and he doesn't work hard enough, you fire him and hire someone who will. But if he works well, you pay him more and encourage him to do even better. A slave only works at all because he'll be punished if he doesn't. He gives only as much as he must to avoid the lash and no more. Sometimes I wonder how much cotton I could grow if I had a hundred *willing* workers in the fields, but that's something no one will ever know."

"If slavery is so . . . so inefficient, then why does it exist at all?" Emma asked.

Grayson sighed and sank wearily back down into his chair. "Because men are greedy, Emma. They saw how much the rich dark soil in America could produce, and they wanted more, but they couldn't get whites to work in their fields because a white man could go off and start his own farm, so why should he work for wages on someone else's? They needed lots of bodies who couldn't leave, so they sent ships to Africa. That's why it started, and now no one can conceive of doing it any differently."

His broad shoulders sagged, as if beneath the weight of the burden of slavery, and he braced his elbows on the desk and buried his face in his hands.

This was a Grayson Emma had never seen before. A man who was weak and vulnerable. A man who genuinely cared for those whose lives were in his hands but who was powerless to change the system that kept them in bondage. He looked so exhausted and so defeated, and he had lost so very much. Her heart went out to him, and without questioning her motives, she went to him, circling the desk so she could lay a comforting hand on his shoulder.

She had meant only to comfort, but the instant she touched him, she knew she had misjudged her own feelings. His shoulder was hard and warm beneath her palm, reminding her of his strength and his heat and the way that strength and heat had overwhelmed her the other night. But she wasn't afraid or even repulsed. Instead she felt a strange bond with him, an intimacy that gave her the right to lift her hand and place it on his neck where his raven hair curled slightly against the suntanned flesh.

His hair was soft and his skin warm, and he stiffened slightly at her touch, as if he couldn't quite believe the evidence of his own senses. Emma couldn't quite believe it either, nor could she believe the warmth spreading through her body. Her breath caught, and she inhaled his unique, musky scent. The smell triggered memories that she had suppressed, memories of his mouth on hers and his hands on her body and his kisses on her breasts.

Her nipples hardened beneath the stiff layers of her clothing, and the warmth curled inside of her into a knot of longing. She recognized that longing, although she hadn't felt it for months. She wanted a man's arms around her, holding her close, so when Grayson turned in his chair and reached for her, she went willingly.

She wrapped her arms around his neck, holding him to her bosom while his arms closed around her waist, locking the two of them together. Dear heaven, she'd forgotten how much she loved this, the closeness and the warmth and the sweetness of simply being held. No one had held her like this in so very, very long. Tears sprang unbidden to her eyes.

Grayson drew a shuddering breath that might have been a

sob, and his arms tightened around her, his hands pressing urgently against her back. When he released his breath, it came out as a agonized groan torn from deep within his soul.

Emma wanted nothing more than to ease that anguish, to absorb it, if necessary, into her very self, which is why she didn't not resist when Grayson pulled her closer still. She stroked his hair, loving its softness, loving the way it molded against his head, loving the way his hands caressed her back, loving the scent of him, loving everything about him for that one mindless moment.

And then someone rapped on the door, shattering the spell, and the door opened just as Emma and Grayson jumped guiltily apart.

"Gray, dear, I . . ." Virginia began and stopped when she saw the two of them still suspiciously close and probably looking suspiciously guilty, too.

Dear Lord, perhaps Virginia had even seen them in each other's arms! Emma thought, mortified. But if she had, she gave no indication other than mere surprise.

"I'm sorry, I thought you were alone," she said with a placid smile.

Grayson ran a hand over his face as if to smooth out his features while Emma placed a hand on her bosom where just seconds ago his head had lain. The spot still felt warm to the touch. In fact, every place he'd touched her felt warm, *too* warm, as if she might actually catch fire. Alarmed by the thought, she took another step back, putting some much needed distance between her and Grayson.

Meanwhile, he'd regained his composure, or at least most of it. His face still seemed a bit too red, but his expression was suitably blank. "We were just discussing Emma tutoring Alice."

Had they been? Emma couldn't remember. She still felt oddly breathless, although why she should be, she had no idea. Probably, it was the thought of being caught like that when what they'd been doing had been so perfectly innocent.

But if it had been so perfectly innocent, why did Emma feel so horribly guilty?

"That's very generous of you, dear," Virginia told her, coming into the room. "The poor darling should really be in school, but of course, there's no school close enough, and she's much too young to send away. Perhaps when she's older . . . At any rate, I know she would benefit greatly from anything you have to teach her."

"Uh, yes," Emma murmured, too rattled to think of something more sensible. What on earth was wrong with her? She hadn't been this disturbed the other night when Grayson had practically assaulted her!

"Did you want something, Mother?" Grayson asked rather sharply, as if he were annoyed.

"I just wondered if you were going to say anything at the grave this afternoon. I've been remembering things all morning, and if you were, I thought you might like to mention some of them, like the time Mammy nursed you through the croup. Maybe you don't remember, but—"

"If you'll excuse me, I need to get back upstairs," Emma lied with a stiff little smile.

Grayson glanced at her sharply, as if trying to see past that smile, but she didn't quite meet his eye, afraid that if she did, she might reveal something she didn't want revealed, even though she wasn't actually aware of having anything to conceal.

"Of course, dear," Virginia said. "We'll go down for the funeral right after dinner."

Emma nodded, not trusting herself to speak again, and she hurried from the room. She did not return to the nursery, however. Her mind was in too much of a muddle to deal with the children again so soon. Instead she sought the refuge of her room and was glad to see that Chloe was elsewhere.

She sank down on the chaise. Clasping her hands together in her lap, she was alarmed to notice they were trembling. In fact, the rest of her seemed to be trembling, too. But why should she be? He hadn't kissed her, hadn't even *tried* to kiss her. Perhaps he hadn't even *wanted* to kiss her!

But, Emma had to admit now that she was alone with herself, she would have *let* him kiss her if he *had* wanted to. She would have thrown back her head and opened her mouth and offered him everything. No wonder she was shaking! She had never felt so wanton about any man in her life, not even her husband.

Oh, she had always welcomed Charles's kisses, but his kisses had been nothing like Grayson's. His kisses had been soft and sweet and undemanding, just like *all* of Charles's lovemaking had been soft and sweet and undemanding. He had never even opened his mouth, and he had certainly never licked her naked bosom! The mere memory quickened her breath with outrage, or at least she was fairly sure it was outrage that quickened her breath. She didn't know *what* had caused her nipples to tighten again beneath her dress or her stomach to drop as if she'd suddenly fallen.

Instinctively, she crossed her arms over her breasts as if she could protect herself, although she knew it would take more than a gesture to protect her from Grayson. As humiliating as it was to admit, even to herself, she knew now that she really did need protection and not just from him but from her own emotions. Last night she had imagined that she would have no trouble at all avoiding another incident like the one on the gallery. Today, however, she had forgotten all her resolve and gone straight into Grayson's arms simply because he looked tired and grieved. Of course, nothing untoward had happened between them, but heaven only knew where their embrace might have led if Virginia hadn't come in when she did. The next time . . .

But of course there couldn't be a next time, not if Emma wanted to remain at Fairview, not if she wanted to help Alice and the other children, not if she wanted to remain free from another man's control. She would have to be strong and steel her self against him. She would have to forget how handsome he was and how wonderful she had felt in his arms and how his kisses had made her tremble in the night. And she would have to forget the way her own body betrayed her whenever he was near.

Oh, dear heaven, how would she ever be able to do all that when just thinking about it made her feverish with desperation?

But if she couldn't, she would have to leave Fairview. She would have to . . . to what? She would have to marry, but whom could she marry? No one had even asked her, although she was beginning to believe Virginia's assurances that someone would before too much time had passed. Practically every man she'd met at the barbecue had asked permission to call on her. But what if she didn't like the men who did ask? What if she could not bear the thought of giving herself to any of them? If she could not stay here and she could not go to another man, what on earth would she do?

She didn't know how long she sat there trying in vain to find a solution, but finally she heard the bell summoning her to the noon meal. Her heart sank when she realized she would have to face Grayson again, but at least Virginia would be there, too. He wouldn't do or say anything in front of his mother. She would be safe.

Safe? How ironic to worry about being safe from the man who was supposed to protect her!

On leaden feet, Emma made her way downstairs to the elegant dining room and was relieved to see only Virginia sitting at the table. The maid had not even laid a place for Grayson.

"Where's Grayson?" she asked as casually as she could when she had taken her seat opposite Virginia.

"He said he wasn't hungry," Virginia said, and Emma noticed that she, too, looked as if she hadn't slept much last night. Her eyes were red-rimmed, and she kept dabbing at them with her handkerchief. "He's already gone down to the quarters." She rang the little bell beside her plate to summon the first course and smiled sadly at Emma. "Poor dear, you must think we're odd to mourn so over a servant, but—"

"Oh, no," Emma assured her. "I realize that . . . that things are different here. That your slaves are more like . . . like friends than servants."

"Not *friends,*" Virginia said hastily, frowning, but before she could go on, the maid came in with their soup. Virginia waited until the girl was gone again before she said, "They aren't friends or family, either. It's hard to explain . . ." She considered the matter a moment, then said, "Did you ever have a pet, dear?"

"I had a kitten when I was a girl."

"You probably loved it very much," Virginia guessed.

"Yes, I did. I was an only child and sometimes very lonely."

Virginia smiled and nodded. "We often become quite attached to our pets. We even love them and crave their companionship. They comfort us and serve our needs, and we wouldn't be parted with them for anything. We worry over them when they are sick, and we grieve when they die as if we had lost a close family member, although," she added soberly, as if in warning, "they are not really family members or even quite human at all. Our love and loss is real but not exactly the same as it would be for a parent or a child or a spouse. Because, as I said, they are not quite human."

Emma understood that she was no longer speaking of pets. She was giving Emma another lesson in master-slave relations. But Emma knew a lot more now than she had the last time Virginia had lectured her on the subject. "Would you give a dog charge over your children, Virginia?"

Virginia blinked in surprise. "What?"

"I asked if you would put your child in the care of an animal. If you would entrust your most precious possession in the world to a pet."

Virginia stiffened, pursing her lips in disapproval. "That's not exactly the same thing."

"*Nothing* concerning slavery *is* exactly like anything else, is it? That's just the problem. You've set up all these rules, but they really don't apply, not if you think about them too closely. You tell me the slaves are all too stupid to take care of themselves in order to justify keeping them in bondage, yet you see evidence to the contrary every day of your life and simply choose to ignore it. You tell me your grief over losing Grayson's Mammy is the sorrow you'd feel over losing the family dog, yet just this morning you were reminding him how the woman had saved his life. Today you're going to bury her with the honors due a dear friend and—"

"I was afraid of this," Virginia said, pressing her handkerchief to her lips and shaking her head in silent despair, making Emma instantly regret her outburst. She hadn't meant to upset Virginia or even argue with her at all. She'd only wanted to let her know she understood, but plainly she didn't understand at all.

"I'm sorry," Emma apologized. "I'm just trying to . . . to . . . Well, you told me I might be mistress of my own plantation someday, and—"

"You mustn't judge us too harshly," Virginia said, tears gathering in her eyes. "I knew everything would seem strange to you at first, but I'd hoped that, with time, you'd come to accept our way of life."

"I know," Emma tried, but Virginia didn't seem to hear her.

"We aren't evil people, Emma. We don't beat our slaves unless we have to. We've never sold a slave unless it was his wish or unless he was simply too stubborn to work. No mother has to be afraid of losing her children, and every child knows he will always have a home here. No one ever goes hungry, and we give them good clothes to wear and comfortable homes. If a slave becomes too sick or injured to work, we still feed him and take care of him until the day he dies. Can your Northern factory workers say the same?"

Emma had no idea, but she could guess the answer was no or Virginia would not have asked the question. "Please, I—"

"All I'm asking is that you not judge us, Emma," Virginia said, dabbing at her eyes again. "At least not until you've been here longer. Would you promise me that?"

"Of course," Emma replied instantly. She would have promised anything to keep from causing Virginia further distress.

Virginia smiled and reached across the table to pat Emma's hand. "Thank you, dear." She seemed to notice that neither of them had even picked up a spoon to taste the soup. "Perhaps we should go on down to the cemetery now. We can eat when we get back."

Emma nodded, the thought of food far from appealing at the moment. Once outside, she and Virginia tied on straw bonnets to cover their heads and then strolled slowly down the path. Instead of walking through the quarters, however, they turned left and headed for another corner of the property. Emma had learned where the kitchen gardens were and where the fields began. Now she learned where the family laid their dead to rest. About half a mile from the house lay Fairview's cemetery plot. Part of it was enclosed by a wrought-iron fence and plainly contained the graves of the family. A large stone obelisk in the center, engraved with the name Sinclair, marked the final resting place of Grayson's father. Smaller stones marked the graves of Virginia's two other children who had died in infancy. Off in the far corner was a marble angel which bore the inscription "Beloved Wife," plainly Lilly's grave.

Outside the fence were many more graves, several dozen, marked only with plain wooden crosses upon which names had been written. "Henry" and "Rachel" and "William" and "Brutus." First names only and many of them now too faded to read. The forgotten ones who had been torn from their homes on the other side of the world and carried to this place against their wills. The ones who had built this plantation with their blood.

At the end of one row, a neat square hole had been dug, ready for the latest in a long line of dead.

Emma and Virginia were the first ones there, but they could

hear the others coming, their voices raised in a mournful wail. As they came closer, she could make out the words and realized they were singing a familiar hymn, although she had never heard it sung with such depth of emotion. Perhaps, she thought, she had never heard it sung by people who had *known* such depth of emotion. She had no trouble identifying that emotion either. It was despair. She had plumbed its depths herself, had felt the terror of having her whole world crumble beneath her feet and even now was facing the prospect of selling herself into an unwanted marriage, the kind of bondage white women suffered.

Her own despair might have overwhelmed her, but then she saw Grayson, walking along behind the coffin which was being borne on the shoulders of six burly colored men. The sight of him looking so solemn outraged her. How dare he grieve? What had *he* ever suffered compared to those all around him? What had *he* to fear? His word was law here, life and death to those he owned and even to those, like her, whom he only controlled.

And he did control her, she knew, because even now, hating him as she surely must, she felt the all-too-familiar flutter in the pit of her stomach and the unwanted heat stealing over her, weakening her and destroying her will. In spite of her mind which was only too aware of all the reasons she should despise Grayson Sinclair, her body longed to rush to him and take him in her arms and press herself against his strength and feel his mouth on hers again.

Her face burning with shame, she forced her gaze away from him, and saw to her surprise that a boy, one of the slaves, was staring at her. He was tall and well-made, his skin light enough to ensure some white blood in his background, and Emma judged him to be about thirteen or fourteen years old.

She had expected him to drop his gaze when she caught him staring, but he didn't. He continued to watch her intently, as if he hoped to learn something by examining her closely. Emma shrugged off the uncomfortable feeling that he had somehow sensed her lascivious thoughts about Grayson. He couldn't possibly have known such a thing, so if Emma's cheeks were burning with shame, it was only because she had a guilty conscience.

"Who is that boy?" she asked Virginia when he continued to stare.

Virginia glanced over, and the boy instantly dropped his gaze. Virginia frowned. "That's Benjamin," she said, then glanced back at Emma. "He's a fine looking boy, isn't he?" she asked.

"Yes," Emma agreed, her mind racing. *Benjamin!* That was the name of the boy Grayson had fathered with his slave mistress. Could this be . . . ? But of course he was. That would explain Virginia's frown and also her irresistible urge to brag on him. He was, after all, her grandson, no matter that she would never acknowledge the relationship aloud. That would also explain his insolence just now. Surely, he must know his heritage. She knew enough about gossip to be certain no truth so important could have been hidden from him this long.

And if he knew his heritage, did the knowledge grate on him? Did he chafe under the yoke of his bondage, knowing the master's very blood ran in his veins? Knowing that as the master's first born son, he should by rights be the master himself someday? And knowing that because of the color of his skin, he would never own anything, not even the clothes on his back?

Emma imagined a burden like that could break a person, and she had no trouble at all sensing the boy's silent rage, especially because for that one long moment he had been directing it at her. Perhaps he envied her position as an honored guest in his father's house. Perhaps he coveted her place and seethed with anger because Emma held it simply because her skin was white.

Don't envy me, she wanted to tell him.

"Aunt Emma!" Alice's sweet voice cut through her ugly thoughts, and she looked down to find the girl beside her. Her mammy had brought her and Jane down from the house. "Will you hold my hand?" she asked uncertainly, apparently overwhelmed by the situation. Beside her, Jane appeared perfectly calm, as if she'd buried many slaves in her short life.

"Of course," Emma said, taking Alice's hand in hers. Dear heaven, did Alice know about Benjamin? Would anyone have thought to protect her from the knowledge of her father's weakness? But of course, no one would dare speak of such things to his child. She would be sheltered from the truth, probably for the rest of her life, just as Emma had always been sheltered from anything remotely unpleasant. She would grow up as defenseless as Emma, believing some man would always be there to look after her and never suspecting that a man could have feet of clay.

Unless Emma taught her differently. Unless Emma made her strong. And she would. She would figure out a way that she could stay here and . . . But not right now. The singing had stopped, and Grayson was stepping forward to stand at the head of the coffin.

Grayson scanned the crowd, waiting for the house servants who had just arrived to find places. As he waited, he was acutely aware of his position, of the fact that he owned every person here, body and soul, even those whose faces were white. If he did not own his mother and his daughter and Emma outright, he owned them in every practical way. He could do with them as he pleased, treat them as cruelly or as kindly as he wished, grant or deny them food and shelter, whatever took his fancy. Every life was literally in his hands. For a moment, the burden felt heavy enough to crush him if he let himself think about it. But of course he didn't let himself think about it. He couldn't, not if he wanted to keep his sanity.

He opened the Bible he had carried with him and began to read Christ's promises of a better life to come, of mansions in heaven to those who believe. The promises his people had always offered to the slaves as a sop to make their miserable lives here on earth bearable. Serve your masters well on earth, and you will be free in the hereafter, the story went. He wondered if any of them really believed it or if they simply had no other hope.

As he listed the rewards they would receive in heaven, he was vaguely aware of the murmured affirmations from the slaves who always seemed to feel they had to respond aloud. He wondered if Mammy could hear him now, if she was smiling down on him and nodding because now she really was free or if she was cursing him because she'd discovered it was all a lie. Even the paper he'd given her and which was still in her hands to be buried with her, even that had been a lie.

When he had finished the reading, he stepped back to allow Thomas to speak. His old friend's eyes were bloodshot from weeping and lack of sleep, but he bore himself with all the dignity his mother would have required. His voice was rough with emotion as he remembered her, recalling incident after incident which proved what a good person she had been and what a faithful servant.

Gray listened with only half-an-ear to the familiar stories, wishing Thomas had a story of how his mother had broken the chains of her bondage and emerged free and strong to conquer those who had held her. Instead he had only a story of how the boy whose diapers she had changed and whose nose she had wiped had added insult to a lifetime of injury by betraying her in her final moments with a lie when he had told her she was free.

Of course Thomas didn't say that. He told everyone how Massa Gray had freed his mammy so she could go to glory no longer a slave. The other slaves praised God with shouts and wails, giving thanks that they had such a kind and generous master.

All of them except Benjamin, Gray noticed. God, the boy had grown another inch since the last time he'd seen him. He would soon be a man, but his eyes were already old. Gray could see them clearly because the boy was staring at him, a silent challenge that Gray dared not accept. Another soul whom he had betrayed. If only he'd thought . . . but of course, he'd been a boy himself then, only sixteen when his father had presented him with Opal, the beautiful mulatto girl he had purchased exclusively for his son's pleasure.

His father had congratulated him later when they'd learned Opal was with child. Gray had proved himself a man. He had never really understood the magnitude of his acts until months later when he'd seen the small baby lying on the bunk beside Opal. A real, living being whom he had created. A son but not a son. A part of him he could own but never claim. Virtually every man he knew had children in the quarters, but he had never thought about what that would mean until he had his own.

How should he treat the child? Favor him and make him the object of jealousy? Ignore him and make him bitter? Whatever he did would be wrong, and helpless to do otherwise, he had made every mistake. Now the boy hated him, which was, perhaps, inevitable. But that did not make it any easier to bear.

Yes, he might own every person here, he might have the power of life and death over all of them, but he could not make them happy. The only true power, the power to change things from what they were to what they should be, had been denied him. Cursed by the sins of his fathers, he served under a yoke of bondage, too, doomed to watch those he loved struggle and suffer and finally die. His wife, a poor miserable creature fleeing demons no one else could see. His son, doomed forever to desire what he could not possess. His daughter, haunted by a senseless tragedy.

And Emma. He didn't love her, of course. He could never love that way again. But he wanted her in every other way a man could want a woman. She tormented him by simply being, and when she offered herself to him as she had this morning, giving him the lush haven of her body in which to hide from every harsh and ugly thing in his life, he could feel the very flames of hell licking at his heels. He would not—he would *not,* God help him!—fall into that trap again.

Thomas had finished speaking. He nodded to Gray. For one awful moment, Gray couldn't recall what he had planned to say, but the flash of panic was brief, and then the words came back to him. He stepped forward. "All morning I've been trying to remember things about Mammy," he began, glad to hear his voice sounded normal, betraying no hint of his chaotic thoughts. "My mother said I should mention the time she sat up with me for three days when I had the croup, but I don't remember that. What I do remember is the licking she gave me when she caught me and Thomas skinny-dipping in the creek." He paused for the surprised gasps and the muffled chuckles. No one wanted to laugh out loud at the master, but that was exactly what Gray had intended for them to do. He smiled. "We must have been about five years old, and she told us that wasn't decent. Mammy had a strict idea of what was decent, and I learned it the hard way. Like the time Thomas and I stole some cookies from the kitchen. She marched us in and made us apologize to Eliza, and then we got switched again, didn't we, Thomas?"

Thomas nodded, his eyes wide.

"I suppose I could have pointed out to her that as the son of the house, the cookies belonged to me anyway, but I doubt that would have carried much weight with Mammy. She thought if you took something without asking, that was stealing, and she didn't want her boys to grow up to be thieves. She didn't want us to be liars or coveters or idolaters or any of the other deadly sins, either. She wanted us to know the difference between right and wrong and to always choose the right. If that meant we sometimes couldn't sit down for a week, Mammy didn't mind, so long as we learned. If I have any claim on being a good man today, it's only because of a colored woman who was father and mother and preacher and teacher and friend to me. She deserved a better life than the one she had. She deserved to live in a fine house and wear beautiful clothes and eat off China plates. What she got was far less, but if God is just, she is living in that fine house now, wearing those beautiful clothes and eating off those China plates. And she is free, as free as a dove, soaring through the heavens. I pray God gives her all that and more. No one deserves it more."

He should have spoken longer. Tomorrow he would wish that he had, but right now he just wanted to get away from all these eyes. Away to someplace dark and quiet where he could have a good stiff drink and try to forget the pain. Away to someplace where he could forget that he had added one more to the list of ghosts that haunted him.

He stepped back as the men began to lower the coffin into the ground.

Emma couldn't look at him. Grayson was, she was certain, the Devil incarnate, able to change his form and make himself appealing at will. What else could explain why sometimes she hated him and sometimes . . . ? Well, sometimes she almost felt affection for him. How could this man who spoke so lovingly of a Negro slave be the same man who had told her she would have to leave his house? The same man whose hands and mouth had taken such liberties with her? The same man who had called her insane simply because she wanted to help those less fortunate than she?

She didn't know. She only knew she didn't want to look at him because looking at him made her ache in places she didn't want to ache. In self-defense, she searched the crowd, looking for Hallie and her children. She didn't see them, although they could have been here somewhere, lurking around the fringes of the group. She didn't want to crane her neck to see behind her, and there were many people behind her. Nathan was here though, looking suitably somber in a black suit. Emma noticed no one stood near the overseer. How lonely he must be, she realized, understanding suddenly why he had needed someone like Hallie. That didn't make it right, of course, but still she could understand. Sometimes she wished for someone, too, someone to hold her in the night and . . .

She jumped when the first clods of earth struck the hollow coffin, and Alice's hand tightened in hers. Emma glanced down at the girl and saw she was looking up at her with anguished eyes.

"Will the worms eat her now?" she whispered.

"Who told you such a thing?" Emma whispered back, appalled.

"My grandpa. He said when they put you in the ground, the worms eat you until you're gone. He said they ate my mama."

Any remaining sympathy Emma might have had for DeWitt Phelps vanished.

"No, darling, when a person dies, it's like his body is sleeping, waiting for judgment day when he'll rise up again," Emma said, knowing she was breaking her own rule about sheltering Alice from the truth. But some truths were simply too ugly, and a little girl didn't need to think her mother's body was being eaten by worms, even if it was. No wonder Alice had nightmares!

"And their soul goes up to heaven?" she prodded.

"Yes," Emma confirmed. Of that, at least, she was certain.

Alice's little shoulders seemed to sag with relief, and she pressed Emma's hand against her cheek in silent gratitude. For the first time during this funeral service, Emma's eyes filled with tears. How could she ever leave this child?

When the grave was filled, Grayson and Thomas planted a small cross at the head of it on which had been written the word, "Mammy."

Then someone started singing "Rock of Ages," and the slaves began to drift away, back toward the quarters where a meal had been prepared for them.

"Can we look at my mama's grave?" Alice asked when Emma and Virginia started to lead the girls back to the house.

"Of course, dear," her grandmother said.

Emma followed her to the gate in the wrought iron fence, still holding Alice's hand. Mammy and Jane and Rose came along behind, less eager perhaps to visit another grave.

Emma felt Grayson's gaze on them as they entered the small enclosure, but she ignored it. He wasn't looking at her, anyway. He was probably looking at his daughter and wondering what she was feeling . . . Or probably he wasn't doing any such thing. The Grayson with whom she was most familiar would simply be annoyed because she was allowing Alice to dredge up memories of their tragedy. She continued to ignore him.

"That's my mama's grave," Alice informed her, pointing to the marble angel. "She's an angel now. Papa said. That's why she's got an angel on her grave."

Emma frowned, remembering what he had said about Lilly the other day. Plainly, he did not really believe Lilly was an angel.

"She used to come and kiss me every night," Alice said wistfully.

Emma noticed the dates carved into the base below the angel and automatically computed Lilly's age. Good heavens, she'd only been twenty-one when she died. Much too young to have been as unhappy as Grayson had described her.

Alice had seen enough and was already tugging at Emma's hand.

"Will you finish our lessons now, Aunt Emma?" she asked, her little face brightening as she forgot with childish ease the sadness she had felt just seconds ago. "You never came back this morning."

"If you want me to," Emma said with a smile.

"Oh, goody!" Alice cried, her blue eyes shining with pleasure. "We practiced with the beans, and we know how to count real good now!"

"I wish I lived here all the time," Jane told her with her

characteristic seriousness, "so you could give me lessons every day."

"You'd miss your family, wouldn't you?" Emma reminded her as they passed through the gate. All the slaves were gone now. Only Grayson lingered, standing over the fresh grave as he watched them.

"My mama said I'll have to go to boarding school someday anyway," Jane told her. "I'd rather be with Alice."

Boarding school. Yes, Virginia had mentioned that Alice might go away to school someday, too. It was really the only solution since the homes on the river were much too far apart to make a day school practical and private tutors were difficult to find and expensive, too. But at a boarding school, each family would pay a reasonable fee for each child, giving the teacher a respectable income and a school full of children to teach. Emma had gone to boarding school herself for a while and knew exactly how one should be run.

A boarding school. Of course! It would be the solution to all her problems! But was it possible? Could she do it? Certainly she could handle the teaching, but there would be other things involved, too. She would need a place for the school, a dormitory for the children, someone to cook and clean . . . She knew nothing about business, of course, but she was smart—no matter what Grayson might think—and she could learn. Why, she'd always had the highest grades of anyone at Miss Farnsworth's Academy.

She would have to ask someone for advice, someone who would know. She thought of Grayson and frowned. He was the most logical person, certainly, but would he simply dismiss her idea as another foolish notion because she was the one who had suggested it? Well, if he did, she would remind him that *he* was the one who wanted to get rid of her, and this was the perfect way to do it.

Yes, that was what she would do, and if he still wouldn't help her, she now knew plenty of other men she could consult. And they would be calling on her very soon.

As they walked back along the path to the house, the girls chattering away, Emma's mind was whirling with plans and questions. She would need money, too, but she had her legacy, small as it was. That would give her a start, and perhaps she could borrow some money from Grayson. He should be happy enough to see the last of her that he might even *give* her whatever she needed!

"I'll be right in," Emma told the girls when they had reached the upstairs landing. "I just want to wash up a bit."

Mammy took the children into the nursery, and Emma went to her room.

She would need books and slates and a globe and desks and . . . She should probably make a list, she thought, going to her night table to find some paper and a pencil. As she was rummaging in the drawer, something on the bed caught her eye.

Chloe had made the bed this morning, smoothing the coverlet perfectly. The object was lying right in the middle of the pillow on which Emma usually slept. It was another bird feather, this one larger and black. Tied to it with a piece of string was a scrap of lace that had been torn from something, probably a piece of underclothing. When Emma picked it up, she saw that the feather was broken, snapped neatly in half.

Eight

Emma pulled the bell cord and waited until Chloe appeared. Before Chloe could even ask what she wanted, Emma held up the broken feather. Chloe quickly closed the door behind her, her eyes wide with alarm.

"Where'd you find it?" she asked.

"On my pillow just now. How long do you suppose it's been here?"

"I made up the bed right after you went down this morning, and I ain't been back in here since. Nobody was in the house durin' the funeral. Anybody coulda put it there."

Instinctively, Emma glanced at the door that connected her room to Grayson's, and for one wild moment she pictured him slipping into her room and . . . But that was ridiculous. Besides, the door was still firmly locked.

Chloe came forward and would have taken the feather from her, but Emma refused to relinquish it.

"I haven't had a chance to speak to Alice myself yet, but—"

"Miss Alice don't have nothin' to do with this," Chloe told her grimly.

"How do you know?"

Chloe dropped her gaze, as if she were ashamed of something.

"What is it, Chloe? Tell me or . . . or I'll have to ask Miss Virginia."

The threat worked. "Please don't do that, Missy," Chloe begged. "She be real upset."

"Then tell me," Emma insisted.

Emma was sure Chloe actually paled. "That charm, it ain't . . . it ain't the kind Miss Alice wanted."

"What do you mean?"

"She want you to stay. That charm . . . and the other one . . . they's for to make you go."

Emma glanced at the broken feather. "How do you know?"

" 'Cause of the feather. It means for you to fly away. First one had your hair on it."

"My hair?" Emma echoed in amazement. She hadn't even considered the possibility.

"Yes'm. Leastways, I figure it must've been. Prob'ly got it from your hairbrush. This one . . ."

"What about it?" Emma pressed when Chloe hesitated.

"I bet that lace come from somethin' o'yourn, somethin' you wear next to your body." Emma felt a shiver stealing up her spine.

"What does the *broken* feather mean?" she asked.

Plainly, Chloe did not want to tell her. "It mean you better go or somethin' bad happen to you."

Emma couldn't believe it. Someone had gone to an awful lot of trouble to frighten her away, but who on earth wanted her gone so badly? The only person she could think of was Grayson, and he was the *last* one who would resort to using magic to accomplish his purpose. He was also the last one who needed to.

Emma shook her head, refusing to be upset. "Well, whoever sent this just might get their wish. I only hope he—or she—is willing to be a little patient."

"What you mean?" Chloe asked suspiciously.

"I mean I may be leaving Fairview very soon," Emma told her smugly.

Chloe's eyes widened with alarm. "You can't leave! Who gonna look out for Miss Alice?"

"Don't worry, if everything works out the way I hope it will, she'll be going with me."

"Where you goin'? You gonna take her up North? Someplace far away?" Chloe demanded.

But Emma wasn't ready to share her plans with anyone just yet. "No, not up North. I don't want to say anything until I'm sure, but I'll tell you soon." She glanced down at the feather she still held and smiled. "Meanwhile, maybe you could mention to the conjure woman that her spell is working and—"

"I don't know who she is," Chloe assured her, eyes wide with alarm. "They don't trust the house servants. They don't tell us so's we can't tell the massa."

"It's all right," Emma assured her, wishing she could ease Chloe's fears. "This is all a bunch of nonsense, just like Mr. Gray says. You can't really make someone do something with charms and spells."

"Miss Lilly could," Chloe insisted. "She put a love spell on Massa Gray so he marry her."

Emma frowned, remembering that Grayson had told her the same thing. "People don't fall in love because of magic. They fall in love because the other person is attractive. I've seen Lilly's picture, and certainly she was lovely enough that she didn't need magic to have men falling at her feet."

"Massa Gray, he not like other men," Chloe said solemnly.

Emma had no trouble at all believing her, but she wasn't about to say so. "Chloe, throw this thing away," she said firmly, giving her the broken feather. "I don't want to hear any more about spells and charms and magic. There's no such thing."

"You be careful now," Chloe said as Emma headed for the door.

Emma looked back over her shoulder. "I don't need to be careful," she assured the girl, and went out to find Alice and Jane for their lesson.

By the following Sunday, Emma had forgotten all about the charms. She'd been far too busy making her plans and tutoring

Alice and Jane. Rose, she had noticed, always happened to be missing when she went to the nursery, so she never had to make a decision about whether to include the little slave girl in the class.

Perhaps when she started her school, she could take Mammy and Rose with her and teach Rose privately. She would add that to the list of things she was going to tell Grayson she needed to start the school.

The list was quite long now, and Emma had begun to wonder about how much everything would cost and whether she would be able to afford it all, even with Grayson's help. Since she had never had to concern herself about money before, she really had no idea of the prices of things, and she was finding herself increasingly worried.

Which was one reason she hadn't discussed the matter with Grayson yet. She told herself she just wanted to wait until she'd had some success with actual teaching before she presumed to set herself up in the profession. And she wanted to have a practical plan to present so Grayson wouldn't simply laugh in her face.

And of course another reason she hadn't discussed it with him was because she'd seen so little of him the past few days. Sometimes she thought he was simply avoiding her, although why he would go to so much trouble, she had no idea. Still, he never seemed to be around for meals, and when he was around, he was always busy in his office or in the fields.

That was fine with Emma, too, or at least it should have been. At first she'd been relieved not to have to endure his presence, but after a few days, she found herself missing him. Well, not actually missing him, not the way you missed someone you cared about, certainly. She just found herself at loose ends sometimes, wondering where he was and what he was doing and when he was coming back. And at night she thought of him in his room, just on the other side of the door, so close that all he would have to do was turn the knob and . . . But of course the door was locked, and even if it hadn't been, Grayson would never have opened it. She was positive of that.

Sunday morning dawned brightly, the golden sun rising to burn off the river mist that clung to the ground. But it didn't stop there. It kept burning, beating relentlessly, and by the time they headed for the chapel for Sunday worship, Emma knew this was going to be the hottest day of the year so far.

Emma had thought she understood what summer was, having lived through twenty-three of them already and having endured several weeks of Texas' version, but she soon discovered she hadn't really understood, not at all. The very air seemed to shimmer with the heat, and it was only nine o'clock in the morning! By the time she had walked the short distance from the house to the chapel with Virginia and Alice, her undergarments were soaked and clinging, and she could feel the moisture running down beneath her arms and between her breasts. Her heavy black dress seemed to weigh a ton.

The chapel felt slightly cooler, perhaps because it was shaded and dark. The circuit minister had arrived the night before for his monthly visit, and he welcomed them at the door, greeting each person with a handshake, the sweat already pouring off his face. Fairview was the only plantation in the area with a chapel, and some of their near neighbors had already arrived for the service. More were coming up from the river.

Emma smiled and nodded to the people she passed as she followed Virginia and Alice up to the front of the church.

"Looks like all your admirers are here," Virginia whispered as Emma took her seat beside her.

Instinctively, Emma glanced around to confirm her statement and discovered that, indeed, almost all the men with whom she had danced at the barbecue were already here, and more were coming in every moment.

"I suppose they'll all want to stay for supper, too," Virginia said with a sigh, although her eyes were dancing with mischief.

Before Emma could even decide how she felt about that,

she sensed someone beside her and looked up to find Grayson standing at the end of the pew. Their eyes met, and for an instant Emma felt as if someone had knocked the air right out of her.

She'd forgotten how handsome he was, how tall and broad shouldered. And she'd forgotten how his eyes could seem to burn even though they were as black as night.

"Good morning," he said, sitting down beside her in the pew.

Emma hadn't seen him at all this morning. Virginia had said he'd eaten early so he would be on hand to greet their neighbors as they arrived. "Good morning," she replied, hating the way her voice sounded, so breathless and faint.

Well, how else could she sound when she was practically melting beneath the heavy layers of her clothing and when her lungs were being held in a death grip by the relentless bones of her corset? She would have to speak to Chloe about lacing her so tightly. If she hadn't known better, she might have suspected *Chloe* was the one trying to get rid of her by strangling her with her own undergarments!

Emma flipped open her fan and began to wave it frantically in a futile effort to cool the heat coursing through her.

"It'll get worse," Grayson informed her softly. "Wait until August."

She shot him a murderous glare only to find that he was smiling at Alice who was sitting on her other side. She hated it when he smiled. He looked entirely too appealing. She hated it when he was so close, too. She imagined she could actually feel the warmth of his body, although she knew that was impossible. The day was already so hot, how could she have known, in any case?

She fanned harder.

She tried not to look at him, but even when she lowered her gaze, she could see him out of the corner of her eye. His thigh beside her skirts, thick and muscular beneath the black broadcloth of his trousers. His hand, large and square and tanned, resting on that thigh. Emma tried not to remember how that hand had held her and stroked her and cupped her breast.

She fanned harder still, but she couldn't seem to cool the heat that she was certain now came from within to more than match the heat of the day. How on earth was she going to survive the service? Surely, she would melt down to nothing long before it ended.

After what seemed an interminable wait, the minister determined that everyone had arrived and took his place behind the pulpit. The chapel was simple compared to the churches back east to which Emma was accustomed. No stained glass adorned the windows, and the interior walls were crudely plastered and whitewashed instead of being covered with finely carved woods. The pews were plain benches, the pulpit a utilitarian stand, and the only ornament a simple wooden cross mounted on the wall behind it. When the minister asked them to stand and sing, they did not reach for hymnals but sang from memory songs they had known since childhood.

Emma tried to concentrate on her singing and ignore the man next to her, but when they stood, she was once again aware of his size and his strength. His elbow brushed hers, sending a shock wave through her, and she noticed he jerked away, as if he'd felt it, too. Somehow she remembered all the words to the familiar hymn, although afterwards she couldn't even recall which one they'd sung.

Then they bowed in prayer, and Emma gladly closed her eyes, shutting out the sight of him. But robbed of sight, her other senses sharpened, and she inhaled his masculine scent. Dear heaven, the heat was making her faint! For a second, she thought she might actually swoon, but then the prayer ended and she opened her eyes and resumed her seat and the weakness passed.

They sang some more, and Emma began to feel Grayson's deep baritone voice vibrating through her, as if he'd struck some kind of chord that wouldn't stop vibrating. The tremors quickened her heart and her breath and stirred other parts of

her to life, parts of her she didn't even want to *think* about in
church. She prayed fervently that no one would see the way
her nipples were making telltale bumps on the front of her
dress.

Finally, the minister began to preach. Emma hung on his
every word, desperate for the distraction, straining for meaning
and substance and a message from God that would speak to
her in a special way. But when the sermon was over, nearly
an hour later, she had no idea what it had even been about.
She did, however, know every move Grayson had made and
every breath he had taken.

Beside her, Alice had fallen asleep, her head slumped
against Emma's arm, and even though her arm had gone numb,
she hadn't even noticed until the minister asked them all to
rise for the final hymn. Gently, she laid the child down on the
pew, taking care not to wake her, and by the time she had
Alice settled, the singing had begun. Quickly, she rose, and
when she glanced up, she saw Grayson watching her, the
strangest expression in his eyes, as if . . .

Emma instantly looked away, her cheeks burning all over
again. She knew that expression, and if her body reacted one
way—heart quickening, breath catching, nipples tightening—
her mind reacted quite differently. He might lust after her, he
might long to hold her in his arms once more, but she also
knew he still despised her and wished her well away from here
and out of his life.

With any luck, she thought bitterly, she *would* be away from
here and out of his life before too much longer.

She only wished the prospect gave her more satisfaction.

When the hymn was over, the minister pronounced the bene-
diction and dismissed them. To Emma's relief, Grayson slipped
out to follow him down the aisle so he, as the host for this
week's services, could greet people along with the pastor as
they came out of the church.

Virginia was already waking Alice, telling her it was time
to go. Emma smiled at the girl's sleepy protests. After a mini-

mum of struggle, she had Alice on her feet and the three of them started down the aisle, joining the crowd moving slowly toward the door.

" 'Morning, Miss Emma," Mr. Hamilton said, smiling broadly to show both rows of his crooked teeth. "A pleasure to see you this morning."

"Thank you," Emma said sweetly.

"I hope you're planning to eat with us, Allen," Virginia said even more sweetly.

"I'd be honored," Mr. Hamilton replied, feigning surprise at the invitation.

As Emma soon discovered, virtually all the men there would be honored to join them for Sunday dinner. It was, she had to admit, a nice balm to her injured pride. Grayson Sinclair, it seemed, was the only man in Texas who *didn't* want her in his house.

"You must have something cooler to wear," Virginia whispered when they were out of the church and heading back to the house.

"Nothing black," Emma said with a frown, dabbing the moisture from her upper lip with her handkerchief.

"You'll be sick if you sit around in this heat in that dress. Of course, some men *like* women who are delicate . . ."

"All right," Emma snapped. She could just imagine Grayson's disgust if she swooned from heat prostration. Besides, she couldn't afford to faint, not with so many suitors to entertain this afternoon. As they strolled back to the house, Emma wondered if any of them knew anything about starting a boarding school.

Gray told himself it was the heat that was making him feel like he could chew nails and spit out a horseshoe. Surely, the fact that his collar was chafing his neck raw and his shirt was plastered to his back and his drawers were stuck in unmentionable places was more than enough to make him ill-tempered and mean. Watching Emma entertain her suitors had nothing whatsoever to do with his mood.

In fact, he told himself, not for the first time, he was *thrilled* to see so many gentlemen callers gathered on his veranda, buzzing around Emma like so many bees. Their enthusiasm meant that they would be competing to see who could carry Emma off first. The sooner the better, as far as Gray was concerned. After this morning, sitting next to her all during the church service . . . Well, he didn't know how he had stood having her here *this* long.

Her very presence was torture to any man with normal needs, and Gray prided himself in having *very* normal needs. Needs, he was certain, that could be met quite satisfactorily by Emma Winthrop's lush body. Even trussed up in that hideous black dress she always wore, she was a temptation, but now . . . Gray's jaw tightened as he glanced over at her again.

What in the hell had possessed her to change her clothes? And why in God's name had she changed into such an *indecent* dress? The thing was so thin, it was practically transparent. She might as well be *naked!*

Well, perhaps that was a *slight* exaggeration, he admitted reluctantly. The rose colored dress was indeed made of thin material, but she was far from naked. Gray knew perfectly well how much clothing women wore beneath such a gown, and even if the dress really had been transparent—which he even more reluctantly admitted it wasn't—only her next layer of clothing would have been visible.

Still, he didn't like the way the other men were looking at her, as if they could imagine only too easily what delights were buried beneath all those layers of bones and stays. As if they were imagining *sampling* those delights.

Gray didn't have to imagine. He knew exactly what holding Emma was like. He knew how she felt and smelled and tasted. How her softness yielded beneath his hands, how hot and wet her mouth was, how she seemed to melt against him. Dear

God, how was he going to keep his sanity if he didn't get her out of his house?

He took a long swallow of his julep, hoping its minty sweetness would help drown the memories, and gazed at Emma's bevy of suitors. Which one of them should have her? Nate, of course, was out of the question, even if he'd be willing to give up Hallie. And not Gray's former father-in-law who had also taken Sunday dinner with them today. Although Gray didn't see DeWitt hovering around Emma now, he'd been paying her court earlier, just like the others. But Gray couldn't imagine DeWitt taking another wife after all these years. He was far too old and set in his ways. Hamilton wouldn't do, either. Gray had already decided Hamilton would keep her too close to Fairview, and Gray needed some distance. Cosgrove lived the farthest away, but he was too old for her, too. Emma probably wouldn't like Parks, either; he was too fat. Terrel had bad teeth, and O'Malley's nose was too bulbous. Sherwood was too short. Gray was sure Emma didn't like short men. Reinhard was a handsome devil, but that snorting laugh of his could get on a person's nerves. Peterson was too skinny and . . .

Damn! What was he doing? He should be trying to figure out how to get Emma to *take* one of these men instead of thinking up reasons why she wouldn't! He really *must* be losing his mind. No wonder, either. He couldn't remember the last time he'd had a good night's sleep, certainly not since Emma Winthrop had been sleeping just on the other side of his bedroom wall.

Sometimes he fantasized about kicking down that door and . . . And what? Forcing himself on her? The very idea turned his julep sour in the pit of his stomach. No, he didn't want to force her. He wanted her soft and willing, clinging to him with arms and legs, as if she couldn't get enough of him. But if he kicked the door down, she wouldn't be willing.

He smiled as he tried to picture what *would* happen in such a situation. He could easily imagine Emma cowering in her bed, the covers clutched to her generous bosom, her chestnut hair spilling around her bare, white shoulders, her beautiful blue eyes wide with terror. Would she scream? Would he care?

Dear God, he really was losing his mind. He went to refill his julep.

Emma could never remember enjoying herself quite so much. Not only did she have more suitors than she could count, all of whom seemed determined to cater to her every whim and fetch her whatever she needed or might conceivably need, she had Grayson Sinclair glaring in disapproval. Plainly, he was furious, although Emma would have thought he'd be happy to see how well his plan to marry her off was working. Still, she found it gratifying, even though she knew jealousy could play no part in his anger. Probably, he was simply annoyed at having to feed so many uninvited guests, or perhaps he disapproved of how much of his liquor they were drinking.

At any rate, Emma had accomplished her own purposes admirably.

"How big is the house?" Emma asked Mr. Hill, who had just informed her he owned a place in Brazoria that might serve as a school. She had mentioned she had a friend who might be interested in starting a boarding school for young ladies in the area if such a thing were possible.

"It's only four rooms," Mr. Hill said, "but the rooms are large. The parlor could serve as a classroom, and the dining room could be the dining hall. The bedrooms upstairs could be dormitories. There's a kitchen attached, and slave quarters, of course."

"Does it have any furniture?"

"A few pieces," Mr. Hill allowed, sorry to have to admit the house wasn't completely furnished.

"I'm sure the students' families would be happy to donate furniture," Mr. Terrel offered, eager to join the conversation. No one man was allowed to dominate it for long. "Every house on the river has an attic full of things they never use."

"That's right," Mr. Parks assured her. "I could probably fill the whole place myself."

"Folks would be so grateful your friend was providing for their daughters, they'd probably give her more than she needs," Mr. Cosgrove said.

"What would I . . . I mean *she* do about books?" Emma wondered.

"We've all got books, too," Mr. Sherwood said. "Each child could bring some with her."

"And they can buy the ones they'll need for lessons," Mr. Hamilton added. "Readers and arithmetic books, things like that."

"Your friend would need to hire a cook," Mr. O'Malley decided, "but there are always plenty of Negroes put out for hire by their masters. Your friend could probably get one very cheaply."

This was even better than Emma could have imagined. If Grayson wasn't willing to loan her some slaves, she could hire her own. She would feel much better about paying wages to her servants in any case. Mentally running down the list of things she would need, Emma realized she would actually have to buy very little herself. Her meager legacy should cover any of those expenses, leaving the students' tuition to pay for the house and her salary. She had to bite her lip to keep from exclaiming her excitement.

"Miss Emma," someone whispered behind her. Emma started in surprise and looked up to see that Chloe had appeared silently. "Miss Alice needs you," she said in Emma's ear.

Fighting a surge of alarm, Emma excused herself and managed to escape her admirers by hinting that she had to relieve herself. Chloe followed her discreetly as Emma tried not to run until she was inside the house and out of sight.

"Where is she?" Emma asked as soon as she could.

"In the nursery," Chloe told her. "Mr. DeWitt, he with her."

Emma picked up her heavy skirts and fairly flew up the stairs with Chloe on her heels.

Mammy stood outside the door to the nursery playroom, wringing her hands in distress while Rose and Jane clung to her skirts, their eyes wide. "He tell me go out, Missy. I don't want to leave Miss Alice, but he say—"

"That's all right, Mammy," Emma told her, rushing past. She pushed open the door and stepped into the room.

DeWitt Phelps was down on one knee in front of Alice whom he held tightly by both arms, even though she was struggling to get away.

His head jerked up at the sound of the door opening, and he said, "I told you to stay out—" Then he saw Emma. "Oh, I'm sorry, Miss Emma," he said, pushing himself to his feet and releasing Alice in the process.

Alice ran to Emma who caught her and held her fast. The child was trembling, and her eyes were wide with fright.

"You see how they've poisoned her against me?" Phelps demanded, his face scarlet with outrage. "She won't speak to me or even look at me. She's my only grandchild, and I can't even dandle her on my knee!"

"You can't force a child to love you, Mr. Phelps," Emma tried.

"I can't when her father has filled her head with lies about me," Phelps countered. "I know what he says about me, just because I didn't want him to have Lilly, but she was too young to marry. I'll say that until the day I die. And if I'd been able to keep her from him, she'd still be alive today!"

"Mr. Phelps!" Emma chided, appalled that he was saying these things in front of Alice.

"It's true!" Phelps insisted, heedless of who might hear him. "My Lilly is dead because of him. He killed her just as surely as if—"

"Mr. Phelps!" Emma cried. "That's quite enough! Whatever arguments you have with Grayson will have to be settled with Grayson. Meanwhile, I must agree with him that your visits

4 BESTSELLING HISTORICAL ROMANCES BY YOUR FAVORITE AUTHORS CAN BE YOURS, FREE!

Kensington Choice, our newest book club now brings you historical romances by your favorite bestselling authors including Janelle Taylor, Shannon Drake, Rosanne Bittner, Jo Beverley, and Georgina Gentry, just to name a few! Each book is filled with passion, adventure and the excitement of bygone times!

To introduce you to this great new club which is part of Zebra Home Subscription Service, we'd like to send you your first 4 bestselling historical romances, absolutely free! And once you get these 4 free books to savor at home, we'll rush you the next 4 brand-new books at the lowest prices available, as soon as they are published.

The way the club works is that after your initial FREE shipment, you will get our 4 newest bestselling historical romances delivered to your doorstep each month at the preferred subscriber's rate of only $4.20 per book, a savings of up to $7.16 per month (since these titles sell in bookstores for $4.99-$5.99)! All books are sent on a 10-day free examination basis and there is no minimum number of books to buy. (And no charge for shipping.) Plus as a regular subscriber, you'll receive our FREE monthly newsletter, *Zebra/Pinnacle Romance News*, which features author profiles, contests, subscriber benefits, book previews and more!

So start today by returning the FREE BOOK CERTIFICATE provided. We'll send you 4 FREE BOOKS with no further obligation: A FREE gift offering you hours of reading pleasure with no obligation...how can you lose?

We have 4 FREE BOOKS for you
as your introduction to
KENSINGTON CHOICE!
To get your FREE BOOKS, worth
up to $23.96, mail the card below.

FREE BOOK CERTIFICATE

Yes! Please send me 4 Kensington Choice (the best of Zebra and Pinnacle Books) Historical Romances without cost or obligation (worth up to $23.96). As a Kensington Choice subscriber, I will then receive 4 brand-new romances to preview each month for 10 days FREE. I can return any books I decide not to keep and owe nothing. The publisher's prices for Kensington Choice romances range from $4.99-$5.99, but as a preferred subscriber I will get these books for only $4.20 per book or $16.80 for all four titles. There is no minimum number of books to buy and I may cancel my subscription at any time, plus there is no additional charge for postage and handling. No matter what I decide to do, my first 4 books are mine to keep, absolutely FREE!

KF0696

Name _____

Address _____ Apt. _____

City _____ State _____ Zip _____

Telephone ( ) _____

Signature _____

(If under 18, parent or guardian must sign)

Subscription subject to acceptance. Terms and prices subject to change.

4 FREE
Historical
Romances
are waiting
for you to
claim them!

(worth up to
$23.96)

See details
inside....

KENSINGTON CHOICE
Zebra Home Subscription Service, Inc.
120 Brighton Road
P.O.Box 5214
Clifton, NJ 07015-5214

upset Alice too much, especially when you try to force your attentions on her. If you will not agree to stop, then I will have to ask Grayson not to invite you here at all."

Emma had expected her threat to cow him, but Phelps simply pulled himself up taller and fixed her with the most evil look Emma had ever seen on a human face. "My daughter was the mistress of this house," he told her icily, "and *you* haven't taken her place. You've got no more right to give orders around here than one of the darkies, and you'd better remember that, Mrs. Winthrop."

Emma gasped, feeling the chill to her bones. "I think you should leave now, Mr. Phelps," she told him, matching his tone for coldness, although inside she was trembling as much as Alice.

"Don't think you can get rid of me that easily," Phelps warned. "Alice is my flesh and blood, and no one—certainly not a penniless widow living on charity—is going to keep me from her."

Stung, Emma could only stand speechless as he stormed out of the room, slamming the nursery door behind him. Only when he was gone did Alice begin to cry, as if she'd been too frightened to even make a sound when he was in the room. Emma hugged her tighter as the door flew open again and Mammy rushed in, Rose and Jane still clinging to her skirts and Chloe behind her.

"What was he doin' to her?" Chloe asked as they gathered around.

"Just talking to her," Emma said over the child's sobs, "but I don't know what he was saying. Alice seemed frightened." Emma dropped to her knees in a puddle of skirts and pushed Alice slightly away so she could look her in the face. "There now, he's gone. He won't bother you again, I promise."

Alice nodded, although she didn't stop crying, and Emma hugged her again.

"She be fine now, Missy," Mammy assured Emma. "I take care of her."

Emma didn't want to let Alice go, but after a few minutes, her sobs lessened, and when Mammy separated them, Alice went eagerly into the familiar arms of her nurse.

"Everything all right," Chloe said, helping Emma to her feet. "You done fixed it. Now you best get back to your company 'fore they come lookin' for you."

"How 'bout we get some cookies up here?" Mammy was saying to Alice who responded with a watery smile. Emma envied her resilience. She herself was still quaking from her encounter with DeWitt Phelps.

What a horrible man! No wonder his own daughter had hated him so much. Emma imagined she might resort to magic to escape such a tyrant herself.

"Come on now, Miss Emma," Chloe said. "We tell cook to send up them cookies."

"Yes, we will," Emma told Alice. Then she said to Mammy, "Call me if you need me."

Mammy nodded, and Emma stepped out into the hall. Chloe closed the door behind them.

"Thank you, Miss Emma," Chloe said, and only then did Emma notice how shaken she appeared, as if *she* had been the object of Phelps' wrath.

"Are you all right?" Emma asked in alarm.

Chloe's expression hardened. "He's a devil, that one, but he won't get that little girl. You won't let him, will you?"

"Of course not," Emma said, surprised at her vehemence, but before she could say more, Chloe headed for the back stairs.

"I go tell cook to send up them cookies," she said over her shoulder, and then she was gone.

The shadows were long when Emma stood on the veranda with Grayson and Virginia, waving goodbye to the last of her callers. She'd managed to check on Alice once again during the afternoon and found her playing happily with Rose and

Jane, as if the scene with her grandfather had never happened. Emma herself had almost recovered, too, especially when she discovered Phelps had left immediately after their encounter. She was determined to speak to Grayson about Phelps' behavior, but not today. Grayson was in too foul a mood today. Perhaps she would do so tomorrow, after she spoke to him about her school. Because she *would* speak to him tomorrow, now that she knew everything she'd hoped to accomplish was possible.

"You seemed to enjoy yourself this afternoon," Grayson remarked. He, in turn, seemed far from pleased by the knowledge.

"I did, very much," Emma said brightly, hoping to annoy him further.

He had done nothing but glare at her all day, as if he resented her popularity when she knew perfectly well he intended to marry her off at the first opportunity. Emma smiled inwardly, thinking how she was going to outwit him.

"Although," she continued, feigning distress, "I'm afraid I'm simply overwhelmed by so much attention. All those gentlemen are so kind and charming and witty, I can hardly keep up with them. And," she added, as if confessing something slightly shameful, "they all seemed determined to impress me with what wonderful husbands they would be!"

"Have you made up your mind which one you'll choose yet?" Virginia asked, lowering herself wearily into one of the wicker chairs grouped on the veranda.

From the corner of her eye, Emma saw Grayson stiffen in reaction, but she pretended not to. "Of course not," she said quite truthfully, not bothering to add that she never would. "I hardly know them. Besides," she added, flicking open her fan and waving it lazily, "I'm still in mourning."

"And you may remain in mourning as long as it suits you," Virginia agreed, her smile oddly complacent as she folded her hands in her lap and studied both Emma and Grayson through narrowed eyes.

"I can certainly understand why you went north to Cape

May for the summer," Emma told Virginia, fanning herself more vigorously as she turned to face the feeble breeze from the river. "How on earth do you bear the heat?"

"You get used to it," Grayson said grimly, shoving his hands in his pockets.

"You learn to live with it," Virginia corrected him with a small smile. "Or perhaps you can ask your next husband to send *you* North every year."

Emma laughed at that, feeling happier than she could remember being since Charles had died. "In the meantime, I'll get Chloe to draw me a cool bath. If you'll excuse me, I think I'll retire now. It's been a long day."

Grayson grunted what she took for agreement, and Virginia said, "If your room is too hot, you can sleep out on the gallery. We often do in weather like this. Chloe can fix you a pallet and—"

"Oh, I couldn't sleep *outside*," Emma said, shocked by the very idea. Really, Southerners had the strangest customs! "I'm sure I'll be fine once the sun goes down and things cool off again."

Grayson made another grunting noise, but Virginia only smiled again. "Whatever you decide. Good night, dear."

Emma wished them good night and won a grudging reply from Grayson. Honestly, what was wrong with the man? He should be *thrilled* at the way things had gone this afternoon. He must be certain her days here were numbered since she could not long resist the entreaties of so many suitors.

Well, tomorrow he would really be thrilled when she told him about her school. As she climbed the stairway to the second floor, she tried to imagine what his reaction would be. Of course, he'd be skeptical at first, figuring she would never be able to do something so complicated. He might even laugh at her, but Emma wouldn't let his scorn stop her. She had an answer for every argument he might raise, and if she didn't, she would make one up. She would wear him down until he simply had to agree, and then, the best part of all, she could be out of his house within the month.

She paused at the top of the stairs, waiting for the surge of joy that should follow the thought of her triumph. Instead, all she felt was a strangely hollow emptiness.

Hours later, Emma lay awake, staring up into the darkness and wondering how late it was. She hadn't been able to close her eyes all night. She was too hot, too restless, too full of plans and schemes, and much, much too lonely.

But she wasn't *really* lonely, she told herself over and over as she tossed and turned in the enormous bed. She didn't want a husband, didn't want a man who would control her life. She didn't want any of that, although parts of her ached for a man to share her bed, to hold her and caress her and love her in ways Charles never had. But that was ridiculous. Charles had loved her in all the ways a man loves a woman. She knew there was nothing more. There couldn't possibly be. So it must be the oppressive heat putting these wild notions in her head.

The sun had been down for ages but still the night wind drifting in through the French doors was thick and moist and suffocating. She wore only a thin cotton nightdress that was sleeveless, too, but still she felt as if she were buried under a down comforter. The very bed itself seemed to radiate heat, and when she tried turning her pillow over in search of some trace of coolness, she found the underside still damp from the last time she had turned it.

Emma laid a hand on her throat. Her skin was slick with sweat, and she remembered longingly the cool, rose-scented bath she'd taken this evening after she'd come upstairs and stripped off all the torturous layers of her clothing. The breeze had felt wonderful then, but now it simply mocked her, promising relief and offering none.

Maybe if she put some water on her wrists, she thought, pushing herself out of the feather bed. Feeling around in the dark, she found the matches on the nightstand, struck one, and lit the candle sitting there. By its light, she made her way across the cavernous room to the washstand where she poured some of the water from the pitcher into the bowl. It wasn't cool, only lukewarm, but she splashed it on her hands and throat, letting it run down over her naked breasts beneath her nightdress.

Still wet, she turned to face the breeze and felt some momentary relief as the night air evaporated the water against her skin. Drawn now by the promise, she crossed to where the French doors stood open. The breeze was stronger here but no cooler. She lifted her arms, as if she could capture it, but it eluded her.

Her body felt leaden and achy, as if she were bruised or sore. Now she understood why Virginia had suggested she sleep outside. Outside was the only place a person could breathe.

She stepped over the threshold, into the welcoming night. Overhead, the stars gleamed like a thousand jewels and the moon glowed brightly, revealing the wisps of fog clinging to the ground and the river far below that glittered back the moonlight on a thousand ripples as it flowed slowly away.

Drawn farther, Emma went to the railing, desperate to catch even the most errant breeze, and the scent of jasmine engulfed her. On the lawn, the twisted live oaks hulked, grotesque shadows in the darkness, and she felt a chill, as if something cold and wet had suddenly wrapped around her. For an instant, she thought perhaps the heat had finally broken, but then the momentary coldness was gone, and the heat closed around her again.

Her face and throat were dry now, but the fabric of her nightdress still clung damply. Her breasts felt heavy, too heavy for her body to carry, and she reached down to support them, lifting them with both hands.

She never knew what warned her. A whiff of cigar smoke.

A gasp of surprise. Whatever it was, she suddenly realized she was not alone.

"Who's there?" she demanded, quickly crossing her arms over her chest in a desperate attempt at modesty.

Like a ghost, he materialized out of the shadows, stepping reluctantly into the feeble circle of light from the candle that still burned in her room. It was Grayson, but more of Grayson than Emma had ever expected to see.

She gasped in shock, at first thinking him naked. Indeed, he was naked to the waist, his broad chest blanketed with the same raven hair that now drooped along his forehead. His bare arms hung loosely at his sides, but Emma could see their latent power in the curve of every well-defined muscle.

Slung low on his hips were a pair of cotton drawers that covered him only to mid-thigh. Below that his bare legs were even more powerfully muscled than his arms and covered with more of the dark hair. He looked so blatantly masculine, Emma couldn't seem to get her breath, and her heart was pounding like a sledge against her ribs.

"I . . . I couldn't sleep," she said inanely, knowing she should run back inside and slam the doors shut behind her. Even still, she couldn't seem to move, as if the sight of him—so *much* of him—had frozen her to the spot.

Slowly, deliberately, he raised one hand, and Emma saw he held a cheroot. He lifted it to his lips and took a drag, then tossed it away with a flick of his wrist. The cigar sailed over the railing and disappeared into the darkness. Emma imagined she could hear it hiss as it struck the dewy grass below.

He blew out the smoke on a sigh. "I couldn't sleep either," he said. His voice sounded oddly harsh, as if he were under some strain.

"I keep expecting . . . I mean, it always gets cooler when the sun goes down," she tried, knowing she shouldn't be making conversation, knowing she should run but still somehow frozen in place.

"Not here," he said, taking a step closer.

The sky flashed briefly and silently, making Emma jump, but when she looked, she saw only darkness again.

"Heat lightning," he explained. "It's storming someplace up river."

"Then the rain will cool things off," she said.

"Maybe," he replied.

Suddenly Emma was very aware that she was as naked as he except for her thin gown. Beneath her crossed arms, her breasts seemed shamefully enormous, and the humid air had sneaked under her hem to tease, sending goose bumps up the backs of her legs in spite of the heat.

"I should . . . go inside," she tried, willing her feet to move.

"Yes, you should," he told her, taking another step closer.

She could, she realized vaguely, touch him if she reached out her hand. The very thought dried her mouth with what she told herself was terror.

But why should she be afraid? Grayson wasn't going to hurt her.

"Are you . . . sleeping outside?" she asked, still unable to move. Or unwilling.

"Trying to." His face twitched slightly, as if he were holding himself very tightly in check.

"But it's too hot," she guessed, still oddly breathless.

"And I keep hearing you moan."

Heat washed over her. *"Moan?"* she echoed in an embarrassing squeak.

"Like you're lonely and don't want to be," he said, his voice simply husky now, rough with emotions that glittered in his dark eyes like the moon on the river below. "Are you lonely, Emma?"

Of course she was, but she couldn't admit it, not to him. "I . . ." she tried, but the denial wouldn't come.

"I'm lonely, too," he said, and the words sounded as if they had been torn from him. He drew a deep breath, and she watched, mesmerized as his chest rose. "Do you remember what happened the last time we were out here together?"

She could think of nothing else. She nodded, memories of his hands and lips as vivid as the very air she was trying to breathe.

"Well, it's going to happen again if you don't go inside."

She could have run then. He made no move to hold her or stop her. She could have escaped, but she didn't. She simply stood there, every nerve in her body tingling in anticipation of his touch.

The sky flashed again, and in that split second she saw him clearly, the need on his face so raw and desperate, she could not deny him. In the next second she was in his arms. His mouth found hers unerringly, and his kiss was ravenous, as if he could never get enough of her. She opened to him, surrendering her mouth and her tongue the way she wanted to surrender everything else. He tasted of cigar and bourbon and Grayson, and she could not get enough of him, either.

She wrapped her arms around his neck, reveling in the satiny smoothness of his naked shoulders. His skin felt hot, as if he burned with a fever only she could slake. She burned, too, the fire so hot something within her melted and seeped out to dew her womanhood.

His hands were everywhere, on her back and her shoulders and her hips and finally cupping her bottom to pull her into the cradle of his thighs. Separated by only the thin layers of their clothing, Emma could feel the hard evidence of his desire pressed urgently against her belly. Her own desire flared, burning an aching void deep inside her, an emptiness only he could fill.

He grabbed the braid that hung down her back and pulled, forcing her head back so that her throat was his to worship with his mouth and lips. His other hand came up to cup one breast, and he groaned deep in his chest as her nipple rose tautly beneath his thumb. Then his mouth was there, covering the nipple and caressing it until the cotton of her gown was soaked and clinging and no barrier at all.

Need raced through her, hot and molten, melting her bones until she could no longer even stand. When her knees buckled, he caught her, lifting her high against his chest. He murmured something incomprehensible as he carried her away into the darkness, but she did not question him, did not care, not so long as his arms were still around her. She had never felt like this before, and she didn't want it to end, not yet, oh, please, not yet.

He set her down on something soft, something she vaguely realized must be the pallet upon which he had been trying to sleep, but the thought was too fleeting, and besides, she didn't care. She only wanted him to kiss her again, and when she cupped his face and drew it down to hers, he groaned once more and surrendered eagerly.

Soon they were lying side by side on the pallet, his leg thrown over hers as if he needed to hold her in place, their arms wrapped tightly around each other, their hands exploring wantonly.

Emma couldn't get enough of touching him. She'd never known a man's flesh could be so soft and so hot and so intoxicating. She ran her fingers over his back and his shoulders and up his chest, burying them in the pelt of hair she found there until she could feel his heart thundering against her palms.

His hands were busy, too, tracing every inch of exposed flesh on her arms and throat and shoulders, then moving lower to caress her breasts, kneading and teasing until even she began to resent the fabric that kept him from her. She was actually relieved when his fingers started to work the tiny buttons that ran down the front of her nightdress, but in the dark under such urgency, the buttons proved beyond him. With a cry of frustration, he simply took hold of the edges and yanked. The fragile fabric gave with a tearing shriek and buttons flew everywhere, but Emma's moment of shock evaporated in the heat of his mouth as it closed over her naked flesh.

No one had ever touched her there or like that. No one had ever worshiped her lushness with lips and tongue and teeth, licking, suckling, greedy and wanton, until she was writhing with need.

She hadn't even noticed that he'd worked one hand beneath her nightdress until he caressed the burning ache between her legs. The sky flashed just as he touched her there, and she saw the triumph blazing in his eyes.

She cried out in protest, but his fingers opened her, spreading the delicate petals to find the sensitive nub she hadn't even known existed, and her cry became a moan of astonished delight.

"Yes," he breathed as she lifted herself to him, spreading her legs to grant him access

Dear heaven, what was he doing? And how was he doing it? She'd never felt such pleasure, never dreamed such pleasure. He was magic and wonder, and she adored him, worshiped him. She would have done anything he asked, anything at all if he would just keep touching her like that, so when he lifted himself over her, she didn't resist. And she didn't resist when she felt the hot shaft nudging and seeking. Instead she accepted him willingly, eagerly, filling the aching emptiness with his power and strength, filling herself with him until they were one.

Yes, yes! her mind cried as she pulled him to her, wrapping him with her arms and legs to hold him fast so they would never be parted again. Her body remembered the rhythm that only increased the searing pleasure, and they moved together as a single being, bucking and thrashing, moaning and gasping.

The sky flared again, and in that second Emma saw her own wonder reflected on his face before they plunged back into the blackness and their frantic dance of desire. The thunder cracked, splitting the night and making the house tremble beneath them, but they neither heard nor felt it as they surged toward the ultimate goal. As her body quivered and trembled with sensations she had never even imagined, Emma would have given her very soul just to know this bliss forever. At the exact moment when she knew this was true, at the exact moment when she knew she would die for him, when she knew she couldn't bear it another instant, her body convulsed in spasms of the purest ecstasy she had ever known.

Above her, Grayson cried out with his own release, and they shuddered together for what seemed forever until their bodies, sated, could take no more. For long moments they lay together, gasping, their flesh slick from passion. Then Grayson shifted his weight slightly, freeing her to breathe, although he still held her fast, his head resting on her breast.

The sky flashed again, startling Emma out of the fog of desire and back to cold consciousness again. Back to consciousness and painful, awful reality. Dear heaven, *what had she done?* she thought in horror as the thunder crashed.

The truth was only too humiliatingly plain, of course. She had given herself to Grayson Sinclair in the most wanton manner possible, without thought to right or wrong or anything else. She would never have believed herself capable of such blind lust, but then, she had never known she could *feel* such blind lust. What had come over her? Vaguely, she remembered Grayson mentioning a love spell. Could that be it? Could someone have put a spell on her? She could think of no other possible explanation as she lay there beneath him, her body spent but her mind reeling.

And what was she going to do now? What was she going to say to Grayson and what was he going to say to her and what did this mean to them both? The questions terrified her almost as much as the possible answers, and she knew she probably didn't want to know them. Still, she had to do something.

"Grayson?" she whispered, suddenly very conscious of the fact that his bare legs were entwined with hers and that his face was resting against her naked breast.

"Grayson?" she repeated when he did not respond, and then she understood: he was asleep. Sound asleep, practically in a stupor, if the limpness of his dead weight was any indication. *She* couldn't go to sleep, though. She couldn't stay here, not another second, except that she couldn't move, either, not with him practically lying on her.

She would wait a moment. Surely, he would move of his own accord soon. When he did, she would make her escape. She would flee to her own room and shut the doors and lock them and crawl back into her own bed and try to forget this ever happened. Maybe Grayson would forget, too. Maybe if she didn't ever mention it and pretended nothing had changed between them, he would think he'd dreamed it, and they could go on as before, as if everything was the same. Then she would start her school and move away, and she wouldn't ever have to see Grayson again, or at least not very often. Yes, that was what she would do. That was what they would both do. Everything would be all right. She would simply wait until Grayson moved off of her.

She could hear the rain as it arrived, pattering across the earth and pinging on the roof, and the air turned suddenly cool against her heated skin. The sound was so gentle and the coolness such a relief that she closed her eyes, just for a moment. The last thing she heard sounded very much like laughter, faint and very far away.

Nine

Emma didn't want to wake up. She was so comfortable and so warm, snuggled up to something that felt deliciously right. But someone was calling her name, insisting that she wake up, summoning her relentlessly into morning. Slowly, ever so slowly, she opened her eyes.

Where on earth was she? she wondered groggily, not seeing anything at all that looked like her bedroom, but when she tried to move to get a better look, she found she was pinned in several places. Something held her braid so she couldn't lift her head, and something else was weighing down her legs, and something else again was draped across her middle and tucked inside her nightdress to cup her breast.

"Grayson, for heaven's sake!" Virginia fairly shouted, making Emma wince. Why on earth was Virginia hollering at Grayson?

And then she heard a grunt of surprise very close, *too* close, because it had come from just behind her head. Just behind her whole body, in fact, and she suddenly realized the delicious warmth against which she had been snuggled was *Grayson,* and the weight holding down her legs was Grayson's leg, and the weight across her middle was Grayson's *arm,* and the warmth caressing her naked breast was Grayson's *hand!*

She yelped in dismay and threw off his hand and struggled up or tried to but couldn't because he was lying on her braid and had her pinned fast until he started in surprise and released her. But when she bolted up, she found that her nightdress was open to the waist and hiked up to her hips, and she didn't have enough hands to grab it closed and push it down at the same time, and when she finally had managed to do both after discovering to her horror that her nightdress had been *ripped* open—Dear Lord, had he really done that?—she finally looked up to find Virginia glaring down at them, hands planted firmly on her hips, her expression a mask of outrage.

"Grayson Sinclair!" she said, her tone even more outraged.

Emma was acutely aware that he had sat up beside her and was struggling to fasten his drawers. "Mother, I can explain," he insisted.

"I seriously doubt that," Virginia replied icily. "I would like to speak to both of you down in the parlor as soon as . . . as soon as you are both decently clothed!"

Emma's face burned with humiliation. She was an absolute idiot! How could she have imagined she could pretend this had never happened? How could she have let it happen in the first place? What had she been thinking? But of course, she hadn't been thinking at all.

"Mother, I don't think this is any of your concern," Grayson was saying, managing somehow to maintain a bit of dignity in spite of his current position.

"Then I am *making* it my concern," Virginia informed him. "I think you should retire to your room now. *Right* now," she added when he did not move.

He glanced at Emma, as if expecting her to make some protest, but Emma couldn't even look at him. She had never been so mortified in her entire life. How could she ever look at him again? Or at Virginia? Or at anyone, because they would all know. Everyone would know. She understood that something like this could never remain a secret. The house servants were probably already whispering the news to the fieldhands. She would be ruined. Utterly ruined.

Tears stung her eyes, and she covered her face with one hand while the other still held her ripped bodice together.

"Emma," Virginia said more gently, "I think you should come inside now."

Absurdly grateful for the excuse to flee, Emma scrambled up and fled, fairly running across the gallery, past Virginia to the French doors that led to her room. She heard Virginia say something to Grayson, and then she followed Emma, closing the doors behind her.

But Emma couldn't face her, not yet, at least. She took refuge behind the screen where she found the basin of water she had poured last night. Desperately, she splashed some of it on her burning cheeks.

"I'll send Chloe in," Virginia called to her, and to Emma's relief, she left.

Emma sank to the floor, covering her wet face with her wet hands and calling herself every kind of fool she could think of. She must have been insane! She had ruined herself and everything else, too. And what would Virginia do? Surely, she had reason to brand her a scarlet woman and throw her out into the street. Emma had betrayed her friend and hostess in the most despicable manner, and she deserved whatever fate befell her.

Chloe found her a few minutes later, huddled on the floor in a ball of misery.

"Miss Emma, you all right? He didn't hurt you none, did he?" she exclaimed, dropping to her knees beside Emma.

Emma looked up at her in horror. *She already knew!*

"No, I'm not . . . hurt," she managed, pushing herself up to a sitting position and trying to gather the shreds of her own dignity back around her along with her tattered nightdress.

Chloe sighed with relief, laying a hand over her heart. "You give me a fright! What you doing down here on the floor, then?" She looked at Emma more closely. "You been *crying?*" she asked in amazement.

Emma hastily swiped at her cheeks. "Certainly not!" she lied.

"You sure he didn't hurt you none? If he did—"

"No!" Emma insisted, mortified. How could Chloe be so nonchalant about it? "How did you . . . find out?" she asked.

Chloe shrugged sheepishly. "I's the one found you."

Emma groaned in dismay and covered her face again.

"I come in to wake you up, but you wasn't in your bed, so I started lookin' 'round and . . ."

"And you told Miss Virginia," Emma guessed grimly when she hesitated.

"Oh, no, ma'am!" Chloe assured her in alarm. "I wouldn't do nothing to shame you! I went lookin' for Thomas, to tell him so's he wouldn't, you know, surprise you, but Miss Virginia was in the hall, and she must've knowed something was wrong by the look on my face or something. Anyways, she wanted to know where you was, and nothin' would do her 'til she goes in your room to see for herownself." She laid a hand on Emma's arm. "I's sorry, Missy."

"So am I," Emma replied dully. Sorrier than anyone would ever know.

"I reckon you'll wanna wash up some 'fore you get dressed. I brought some hot water. Miss Virginia, she waitin' downstairs, but I reckon she'll wait as long as it takes, so no need to rush."

No need, indeed, Emma thought as she let Chloe help her to her feet. She was as anxious to see Virginia as she would have been to meet her doom. In fact, meeting Virginia *was* meeting her doom.

"Land sakes," Chloe marveled when she saw Emma's nightdress. "Massa Gray must've been in an all fired hurry."

Emma blushed crimson again, remembering that they'd *both* been in a hurry. She still couldn't believe what had happened, how she had felt and how she had lost control so completely. She had certainly never felt that way before, not with Charles, at least.

Lovemaking with Charles had always been so calm and ordinary. Once or twice a week he would ask if he could come to her room. She would be waiting for him in the dark, and he would come, clad in his nightshirt. He would kiss her and hold her for a few minutes, then he would push her nightdress up, climb on top of her and satisfy himself. She had found the process strange at first, but when she'd seen how much pleasure it gave Charles, she had been only too happy to oblige him. She had desperately wanted a child, of course, and she had enjoyed the kissing and the cuddling, too. She had even thought she enjoyed it as much as Charles enjoyed the rest. How wrong she had been if what she had experienced last night was any measure!

"Well, now, looky there," Chloe exclaimed as Emma slipped the ruined nightdress off her shoulders.

Emma glanced down and was horrified anew to see that Grayson had marked her. Her breasts were covered with red spots from where his lips had suckled.

"Won't nobody else see it," Chloe reminded her when she saw Emma's distress. "Won't nobody know but you 'n' me."

"But everyone will know what happened, won't they?" Emma said bitterly. "They probably already do."

"It's hard to keep a secret in this house," Chloe said apologetically. "Nothin' much ever happens, and when it does . . ." She shrugged again.

Emma understood only too well. "Where's that hot water?" she asked, resigned to her fate, whatever it may be. At least she would go to it looking her best.

The house seemed unnaturally still when Emma finally made her way down the stairs to the front hallway, trussed modestly into her corset and gown, her hair primly tucked and pinned. No servants were in sight, and if she'd been afraid of running into Grayson, she'd had no reason to be. She saw no sign of him or anyone else. The parlor door was shut, as it usually was, but Emma had no doubt Virginia was inside, waiting. The fact that she'd chosen the front parlor for this meeting told Emma exactly how serious the situation was. As for herself, Emma had dressed in black.

Resisting the urge to knock, she opened the door and stepped inside. Virginia was on the sofa, and Grayson stood on the other side of the room, holding a cup and saucer. He stiffened at the sight of her, but she refused to meet his eye. Simply being in the same room with him was difficult enough. Her chest felt tight, and an odd heat washed over her, making her feel cold and hot all at the same time.

Wishing her face wasn't as red as she knew it must be, she turned to Virginia, bracing herself for the older woman's scorn. To Emma's everlasting astonishment, Virginia smiled warmly.

"Come and sit down, dear," she said, patting the sofa beside her. Emma was reminded of the day the three of them had met like this in Emma's parlor. They had been discussing Emma's future then, too. This time her future seemed even more bleak, but Virginia appeared determined to make the best of it. "I think the coffee is still warm. Would you like some?"

A silver coffee service sat on the center table.

Emma took the offered seat and shook her head. She could not have swallowed anything if her life had depended upon it. Virginia ignored her refusal and poured her a cup anyway. How long had Grayson been here with her, waiting? And what had they discussed?

"I was just telling Gray," Virginia began when she had set the cup down in front of Emma, "that I think we can have things ready for the wedding by a week from Saturday. It's scandalously short notice, I know, but I don't think we dare delay much longer, do you?"

Emma stared at her blankly, hardly able to comprehend what she was saying. "Wedding?" she echoed stupidly. "Whose wedding?"

"Why, yours, dear. Yours and Gray's," Virginia said, still smiling. "Surely, you know that after . . . well, after last night," she continued after giving Grayson a sharp glance, "you *must* marry."

Marry Grayson! The thought had never even crossed her mind, and she couldn't believe it had crossed *his* either! Unless . . . Could it be true? Could last night have happened because Grayson had fallen in love with her? Could she have misjudged him all this time?

But when she looked at Grayson, she saw she had not misjudged him at all. His expression was grim, his eyes dull, like a man determined to meet a terrible fate without cringing. Her heart sank like a lead ball in her chest.

She turned to Virginia. "I can't . . . *we* can't . . . Surely, you must understand that—"

"I understand what happened between the two of you last night," Virginia informed her ruthlessly, her pale blue eyes cold. But when she saw Emma's distress, she softened again instantly. "Emma, dear, don't you *want* to stay here with us?"

Could Virginia really be so dense? "It's not that," Emma protested.

"You were going to have to marry someone anyway," Virginia argued with what she obviously believed was impeccable logic. "Why shouldn't you marry Gray?"

"But I *wasn't* going to get married at all!" Emma insisted.

"Were you planning to just stay here and live off my charity for the rest of your life?" Grayson asked acidly.

"No!" she informed him just as acidly. "I was planning to make my own way in the world!"

"Doing what?" he scoffed, and Emma would have cheerfully slapped his insolent face.

"Teaching school," she said instead. "Teaching in a boarding school for girls that I was going to start. I have everything planned." She turned to Virginia who was gaping at her as if she'd just grown another head. "Mr. Hill owns a house in Brazoria that he would rent to me. I could ask the parents of my students to donate furniture and books, and they would pay a fee for tuition and board. You said yourself that Alice should go to school but that there wasn't one close enough. Well, there would be if I started one, and lots of the planters would send their daughters. Jane would come, I know, and Alice and . . . Don't you see what a wonderful idea it is? And I'm perfectly qualified to teach. I speak French and Latin, and I know mathematics and literature and geography, and I've mastered all the skills that a young lady should know to run a household."

Now Grayson and Virginia were both gaping at her, but Emma could see they were merely surprised because it *was* a wonderful idea. And, Emma was beginning to realize, it might still offer an alternative to a marriage she didn't want.

"I can still do it!" she exclaimed, making Virginia jump. "I don't have to marry Grayson! I can move to Brazoria and start my school. We'd never have to live under the same roof again, so . . ." She gestured helplessly, unable to finish the thought, unable to say out loud what they all knew was true, that she and Grayson would never be tempted to repeat what they had done the night before.

She glanced at Grayson and was mortified to see the hope in his eyes. "We could help her, mother. I'd certainly be willing to supply anything she might need and—"

"Grayson!" Virginia snapped, her eyes steely now as she glared at her son. "You are forgetting one important thing: what happened last night is no longer a secret. The house staff surely knows by now, and in a few days, everyone on the river will know, too. Emma's reputation will be ruined, and I can't imagine any of the planters sending their daughters to a school run by a lady with a questionable reputation."

No! Emma covered her mouth to hold back the cry of protest. She hadn't thought of that! But then, she hadn't thought of anything at all except her own lust, had she? She was more than idiotic. She was an absolute fool!

"So you see, dear," Virginia went on more gently, turning to Emma, "your only choice is to marry Gray. That won't stop the gossip, of course, but if you marry, people will merely snicker about how Gray couldn't wait until he'd put the ring on your finger. The story will become just an interesting anecdote that you will laugh about in your old age. But if you don't marry . . ." Virginia shook her head in silent despair. "Well, I simply don't know what will become of you. Gray, of course, will weather the storm. Men seldom suffer in these matters, but women certainly do. I'm sure I don't have to explain myself."

She didn't, of course. Emma understood only too well. Men would congratulate Gray for seducing his sister-in-law, but they would scorn her for being seduced. The injustice of it welled in her, burning like hot bile, one more reason to hate the fact that she was a woman and so vulnerable and helpless.

"And if there was a child as a result of . . . of your indiscretion," Virginia continued, plainly uncomfortable mentioning such a delicate subject. "Well, that is why I don't think we should wait any longer than we have to before—"

"There won't be a child," Emma informed her grimly, her cheeks stinging with renewed mortification.

Virginia colored, and Emma didn't dare even glance at Grayson. "Are you saying that you didn't actually . . . ?" Virginia gestured vaguely.

"I'm saying that I'm barren, a fact you should know as well as I," Emma reminded them, feeling the dull ache of the old disappointment. "Remember I was married almost three years without ever . . . So you can put that concern out of your mind."

"I see," Virginia murmured, glancing at Grayson. Emma did not look at him herself, too humiliated already to allow him to embarrass her further. "Well, in any case, you really have no other choice. I'm sorry, dear. I had hoped that . . . I mean, I just wanted to see you settled and happy."

That was what Emma had wanted, too. She had wanted to make her own decisions and plan her own life, but now she knew that would never happen. Once again she would be at the mercy of a man, and this time she wouldn't even have the comfort of knowing he loved her. How on earth would she bear it?

"Perhaps I should leave the two of you alone now," Virginia said suddenly. "I'm sure you have a lot to say to each other."

Emma wanted to protest, wanted to beg her to stay, but what could Virginia do now? She'd already performed her duty. She had, in fact, been much more merciful than Emma had any right to expect, and she was, after all, offering Emma the opportunity of a lifetime. How many women would sell their souls for a husband like Grayson Sinclair and a home like Fairview? Too bad Emma wasn't one of them.

Only when she heard the parlor door click shut behind Virginia did Emma look up to find Grayson staring down at her. He could, she decided, at least have pretended the idea of marrying her did not completely revolt him.

For a long moment, neither of them spoke. Emma studied him, noting how haggard he looked, as if he hadn't slept as well as she knew he had last night. His dark eyes were flat, his face was pale, and his well-sculpted lips pressed into a tight, bloodless line.

What was he waiting for? Emma wondered bitterly. Did he expect her to thank him for being willing to make an honest woman out of her?

Finally, he set his coffee cup on the mantel, clasped his hands behind his back, cleared his throat and said, "First of all, I want to apologize for my behavior last night."

Emma gaped at him. Did he think that would make everything all right? Or worse, did he expect her to apologize in return? "Do you know what you've done to me?" she demanded furiously.

The color rose in his face. "Of course. I was there, remember?"

"I'm not talking about that!" she cried, jumping to her feet. "I'm talking about what you've done to my life! The last thing I wanted was another husband to control me and tell me what I can and cannot do! I was going to be free and independent. I was going to have a life of my own where I would never have to worry about pleasing some man in exchange for food and clothing and shelter, a life where I could do what *I* wanted to do!"

"What about me?" he countered, no longer pretending to be calm. "The last thing *I* wanted was another wife!"

"Oh, yes, poor Grayson," she said sarcastically. "You'll have to put up with the hardship of having a woman to cater to your every whim, who'll run your house and take care of your child and relieve you from every worry she can while never interfering in anything *you* want to do!"

"I'm afraid that hasn't been *my* experience with marriage," he replied just as sarcastically.

"I don't *want* to marry you or any other man!" Emma cried in frustration.

"I don't want to marry you either," Grayson informed her. "But what choice do we have?"

"You had a choice last night!" she reminded him bitterly.

"So did you," he reminded her right back. "Why didn't you leave when I told you to?"

She opened her mouth, but no words came out because she had no words to say. She certainly couldn't admit she hadn't gone because she hadn't wanted to, because he'd held her there with the force of his desire, a force she hadn't even wanted to resist.

Grayson stared down at her, hating her and wanting her with equal force. She was so beautiful with her face flushed and her eyes sparkling and her luscious bosom swelling. The thought of having her in his bed every night for the rest of his life was like a flame roaring inside of him, hot enough to melt his bones. But the thought of putting up with her every *day* for the rest of his life made him want to put a bullet through his brain. Dear God, he must have lost his mind completely.

"Can't you think of something?" she demanded. "Some other solution?"

"I've been trying to all morning," he snapped. Did she think he *wanted* this?

"Can't I go away somewhere?" she asked. "Someplace where no one knows what happened?"

"Where?" he challenged, wishing he knew himself. "And how would you live?"

For one awful moment, he was afraid she was going to cry. He couldn't stand to see a woman cry, and she looked so lost and defeated, he instinctively reached for her, wanting to hold her, *needing* to hold her, having thought of little else since he had awakened with her naked flesh in the palm of his hand.

She was so soft, he pulled her close and closer still, inhaling her sweet scent, and when she gasped in surprise, he caught it in his mouth in the instant before it closed over hers. Her lips yielded to his just as he had known they would, and for one blissful moment he lost himself in her.

But only for a moment. In the next, she was twisting away, frantically trying to free herself. Surprised, he released her, jerking his hands away as if she'd burned him, and the sight of her outraged expression shocked him in the second before she slapped him soundly.

"You cad!" she cried and whirled in a swish of skirts and headed for the door.

Lifting his hand to his burning cheek, he found his tongue just as she touched the doorknob. "Why didn't you slap me last night?" he demanded. "You could have saved us both a lot of misery!"

She threw open the door and fled without so much as a backward glance. Damn her! Damn her to hell. How could he feel such lust for a woman he despised? He really must be crazy.

But crazy or not, he was going to marry Emma Winthrop. He was going to take her for better or worse, to love and to cherish 'til death did them part. The only comfort he could find was that she *couldn't* be as impossible as Lilly had been.

At least Emma enjoyed sex, as he had learned at what a cost. Finally, he would be able to take some comfort in the marriage bed. Gray had never been able to figure out how the passionate little vixen who had seduced him in a field could have become such a cold wife, but after that first encounter— which Gray had finally realized Lilly had initiated—Lilly had never again expressed any interest in or enjoyment of their physical relationship. Sometimes he almost did believe that she had used some sort of magic spell on him. He had been so besotted with her in the beginning that he hadn't realized that she'd used the world's oldest trap to catch him. He hadn't even considered waiting to see if she was pregnant, either. He'd simply wanted her forever. In the end, it had only *seemed* like forever.

And now another woman had caught him the same way. Oh, maybe not exactly the same way. He knew Emma would never have initiated sex, but she'd been willing enough once he did. And maybe she'd been telling the truth about not wanting to get married—could she really have thought up that school idea all on her own? Maybe she wasn't quite as brainless as he'd believed—but Gray knew marriage was what every woman really wanted, a man to take care of her.

So Gray would take care of her, but she'd take care of him, too, at least in bed. They'd have that much, and maybe . . . Suddenly, Gray had a horrible thought. Lilly, too, had been an eager partner the first time. He understood now that she had only been pretending in order to capture him. He was sure Emma hadn't been pretending last night, but now . . .

Well, now she was furious at him and rightly so. She'd called him a cad, and he was that and more. He'd treated her abominably. Granted, he'd been justified. No one could blame him for resenting his current predicament. Still, she was in the same predicament. If they had to marry—and his mother would see to it that they did—then he should try to make the best of it.

Because if he didn't, Emma might well be as cold a bride as Lilly was.

Galvanized with horror at the thought, Gray went after her.

* * *

Emma had never been so angry in her entire life How dare he lay hands on her? How dare he think he had the right to kiss her? And how dare he think she would let him!

She picked up her skirts and headed up the stairs. She would never marry him now, not if they threw her into the street and she had to beg for her living. She'd figure out something. She'd leave here and go far away, someplace where they'd never heard of Texas at all, someplace where they'd be grateful to have an educated lady to teach their daughters. She'd get a job at a school. Maybe Miss Farnsworth would hire her. She would go back to Philadelphia and find out. And if she wouldn't—

"Aunt Emma!" Alice cried, racing out of the nursery to meet her as she reached the top of the stairs. Alice threw her arms around Emma. "Grandma said you and Papa are getting married!" she exclaimed, gazing up at Emma with her lovely blue eyes wide and her adorable face glowing with more joy than Emma had ever believed existed. "She said you're going to be my new mama and you'll stay here forever and ever and never leave me, not ever! Is it true? Is it true?"

Emma looked down at the child, her heart swelling with love, and she remembered her promise to Chloe. She'd sworn never to leave Alice unprotected. And hadn't she also vowed to herself that she would make sure Alice was never as helpless as she was? How could Emma leave her?

Before she could think of a reply to Alice's questions or her own, something caught Alice's attention, and she released Emma to run past her down the stairs.

"Papa! Papa! Are you going to marry Aunt Emma? Are you, are you?" she cried, fairly flying down the steps until her father caught her in his arms on his way up.

"Who told you that?" he asked, lifting her high against his chest. Then his dark gaze found Emma standing above them. Did he look uncertain?

"Grandma told me," Alice reported as he continued to climb, bringing them to the top step, one below where Emma stood, so that she was eye to eye with him. He stopped there, his gaze steady but unreadable. *"Are* you?" Alice asked impatiently.

Emma felt the heat blooming in her cheeks and spreading down her body, just the way it had last night when he'd touched her. He wasn't touching her now, but his gaze seemed to caress her intimately.

She forced herself to look away, to Alice whose bright eyes were so trusting and so happy.

"What does Aunt Emma say?" he asked, drawing Emma's surprised gaze again.

"She didn't say anything yet," Alice informed him, her annoyance showing. "Oh, please say it's true! Jane said she might marry somebody else and move far, far away, and I'd never get to see her, and she'd never read me stories or teach me my letters or anything ever again!"

Emma looked at this beautiful child and felt as if a steel band had tightened around her heart. If she left here now, what would become of Alice? And what would become of Emma who would never have a child of her own to love and cherish? The agony of this thought nearly took her breath, and in that instant she knew what she must do.

With difficulty, Emma smiled, praying the expression looked more natural than it felt. "Of course I'm going to marry your Papa. Your grandmother wouldn't lie, would she?"

Did Grayson look surprised? Emma couldn't be sure, although she couldn't think why he should have. He'd already known she had no other choice. In any case, Alice shrieked with joy and threw her arms around Grayson's neck and hugged him tightly, and he buried his face in her hair, concealing whatever emotions he was really feeling.

By the time Alice released him, his expression was suitably pleasant. One might even have thought him happy if one hadn't known better. Before Emma had a chance to think, Alice threw out one of her arms and wrapped it around Emma's neck, too, pulling her close. Too close, Emma instantly realized, because Alice was still in Grayson's arms, so to be hugging her was to be practically hugging Grayson, too. She was so close she could see the darker pupils in the center of his almost-black eyes, eyes that reflected back her own surprised discomfort.

"You can kiss Aunt Emma now, can't you, Papa?" Alice asked gleefully.

"I suppose I can," he allowed, although his voice sounded a bit strained.

"Kiss her then," Alice commanded, pushing their heads together until their lips touched. Fortunately, Alice seemed to think just touching lips was kiss enough and released them when they instinctively jerked apart.

Emma didn't know which of them was more disconcerted by the kiss, since Grayson looked at least as shocked as she. For her part, Emma had to curl her hands into fists to keep from lifting one of them to her lips which felt strangely hot, as if Grayson had touched them with a burning coal instead of with his own.

"I'm glad to see you've worked everything out," Virginia informed them happily as she made her way across the upstairs hallway from the nursery.

Emma stepped back, only too glad for an excuse to put some distance between her and Grayson. But Grayson took the last step to stand beside her as his mother approached, her smile sweet and smug and satisfied, as if she had accomplished something of which she was very proud.

"We haven't worked *everything* out," Emma told her grimly.

Virginia's smile didn't waver. "You will, dear," she assured her, patting her arm. "You will."

Emma completely forgot her intention to discuss DeWitt Phelps with Grayson until later that afternoon when she and Virginia were writing the invitations to the wedding. Emma would have preferred a quiet ceremony with just the immediate family—she would take little joy in the event and felt that the fewer people who witnessed it, the better—but Virginia assured her that not inviting their neighbors would cause an even bigger scandal than the gossip about their indiscretion.

"You don't want your wedding to be a little hole-in-the-corner affair, do you?" Virginia scolded. Emma decided not to admit she did.

So after she gave Alice and Jane their lessons, Emma went to the back parlor, the room the family used daily, to help Virginia with the preparations. Virginia handed her the list which was virtually the same one she had used for the barbecue, and Emma sat down at the desk to begin. She hadn't gotten very far when she noticed DeWitt Phelps' name.

"Oh, dear," she said, remembering the ugly scene with him in the nursery yesterday. Had it been only yesterday? So much had happened, Emma felt as if at least a week had passed since she had sat on the veranda surrounded by her eager suitors, secretly making plans for a life that would never be.

"What's the matter?" Virginia asked, looking up from where she was working at the table.

"I don't think we should invite Mr. Phelps."

"Whyever not?"

"I'm afraid he and I had a little . . . disagreement yesterday. About Alice."

Virginia laid her pen down. "A disagreement?" she echoed uncertainly.

"Yes, he . . . Well, he was forcing his attentions on Alice, and she was very upset. That was the second time I had caught him upsetting her like that, and I told him he must stop. He was quite rude to me, and he accused Grayson of poisoning the child's mind against him."

Virginia shook her head in disgust. "I can understand why he is so insistent about Alice. I would probably feel the same way if she refused to talk to me as she does to him, but he brings it on himself. He really is the most disagreeable man I have ever met, and believe me, I have met a few."

"I just don't think we should have him here under the circumstances." Emma wanted to add that the wedding would be difficult enough for her without having to worry about Phelps, too, but of course she didn't. Instead she added, "I wouldn't want him to ruin the day for us."

"I don't blame you a bit, dear," Virginia assured her. "It would, of course, be terrible manners to exclude him from the guest list since he is family, after all, so we will have every intention of inviting him, but somehow his invitation will be mislaid."

She smiled sweetly, and Emma felt a rush of relief. At least she wouldn't have to be worried about Alice on what promised to be the most difficult day she would ever endure. And she would also be spared having to discuss the matter with Grayson. The thought of discussing anything at all with Grayson was more than Emma could bear at the moment.

To give him credit, Grayson did make an effort to be more agreeable in the days that followed. He made polite conversation at meals and might even have been trying to charm her. Emma couldn't be perfectly certain because she was far too disturbed by his presence to judge.

That first night was the most difficult, when she lay in her bed in the dark, listening. She hadn't unlocked the connecting door, of course. She had no intention of welcoming Grayson Sinclair into her bed until she had to. When they were married, she would *have* to allow him in. That would be his right and her duty. Until then, however, she would not repeat the mistake she had made the previous night. She would not subject herself to a temptation she knew she could not resist.

But still, although the rain had broken the terrible heat, she had to leave her French doors open to keep from suffocating. All he would have to do was go outside onto the gallery and he could simply walk right into her room. If he did, Emma would be defenseless against him. He was stronger than she, and the master of this house. He could do with her whatever he wished, and when she remembered what he had done with her last night, she trembled with apprehension and ached with unfulfilled desire.

So she lay awake, listening for the slightest noise that would signal his approach. And when she dozed fitfully, she started awake at every creak and groan of the huge house. And when she awoke in the morning and realized she was alone and had been alone all night, she told herself she was relieved. She blamed her irritability on having needlessly lost so much sleep the night before.

"You don't look like a man 'bout to get hisself married," Thomas remarked as he pulled off Gray's riding boots later that day.

"What *do* I look like?" Gray challenged his old friend wearily. He'd been riding the fields all morning, but he hadn't been able to outride his troubles.

"You look like a man got a bad tooth," Thomas told him with a grin, setting the boots aside.

"I do have an ache," Gray admitted, grinning back and rubbing the spot that, in spite of his morning ride, still reminded him how much he'd wanted to visit Emma last night.

"I told you, you shoulda gone to her," Thomas reminded him. "What she gonna do? Scream for help?"

"She might have," Gray admitted, losing his smile.

"An' maybe she laying over there all mad 'cause you *don't* come," Thomas reasoned. "You think of that?"

"Yes, I did, but I also remembered the way she slapped me when I tried to kiss her yesterday. I'm afraid Miss Emma is suffering from a fit of conscience. If I try to take her now, she might end up like . . ."

He couldn't bring himself to say her name, but Thomas wasn't so delicate. "She ain't nothin' like Miss Lilly."

"Why?" Gray asked bitterly. "Because she's got breasts?"

"No," Thomas said, refusing to rise to the bait, " 'cause she good. You seen the way she is with Miss Alice. She love that chile."

"Lilly loved her, too. That doesn't mean she'll love me."

"She already do."

Gray snorted his disbelief.

"I seen you after you been with her, an' I know she done wore you out. Woman don't do a man like that 'less she love him something fierce."

Something jagged was twisting in his gut, but Gray refused to flinch, just as he refused to acknowledge the pain as a raw need that had never been met. "Lilly managed it at least once," Gray reminded him.

"Nobody say Miss Lilly don't love you. She love the best way she can. Ain't her fault she not like other folks, that she born empty inside."

Empty inside. Yes, that's what Lilly had been. A beautiful shell without a heart or a soul. But Emma wasn't like that. If anything, she had too much heart.

"So you think I ought to just break down that door and ravish Emma?" Gray asked, only half-sarcastically. They both knew perfectly well he hadn't used the door at all the first time he'd seduced her.

Thomas grinned at the image. "Uncle Sam be mighty mad if you break the door. I reckon maybe you could get her to unlock it, though."

"How?"

Thomas shrugged. "Get her a present. Womens like presents."

Gray considered. Of course! Why hadn't he thought of it himself? Because, he realized, he hadn't courted a woman in so long, he'd forgotten the rules. But they were coming back to him now. He'd been friendly to Emma, but he could be charming. He could sweep her off her feet, if he needed to. And when he remembered the way she'd clung to him out on the gallery the other night, he knew he needed to. He looked up at Thomas. "What kind of a present do you think she'd like?"

* * *

Grayson was making Emma extremely nervous. He kept smiling at her and complimenting her and generally making a nuisance of himself. He wasn't acting like a man in love, she knew. She'd been courted by a man in love, and that was completely different. No, Grayson was acting like a man with something up his sleeve. He wanted something, although Emma couldn't quite figure out what it was.

In a different situation, she would have suspected he was trying to seduce her. Grayson, however, had already seduced her, and in a matter of days he would be married to her, which would give him the right to have her whenever he wished. So she knew that couldn't be it. She also knew he cared nothing for her and even held her in contempt, so as galling as it was to admit, he couldn't possibly be hoping to win her heart, either.

Maybe his mother had simply ordered him to be nice to her, and this was the result. Or maybe he was just trying to make the best of a bad situation. Emma wished he'd leave her alone. The combination of listening for him to sneak into her room at night and wondering what he was up to during the day was taking a terrible toll. At the end of each day, she was exhausted and her head ached and her stomach threatened to rebel so that she could hardly even swallow her supper. By the time Grayson announced he would be away for a few days on business, Emma could only feel relief.

Her smile as she stood on the veranda to bid him goodbye was the first genuine one she had worn since the morning she had awakened in his arms. She waited as he kissed Alice and then his mother. When he turned finally to her, he registered surprise at her expression.

"You look awfully happy to see me go."

Emma instantly wiped the smile from her face. "I didn't mean to," she said quite honestly.

"I should hope not," he said, with a smile of his own, "but don't get your hopes up. I'll be back in time for the wedding."

Before she could respond to that outrageous statement, he leaned down and planted a kiss squarely on her mouth.

When he pulled away, his eyes were sparkling with amusement and daring her to slap him in front of Alice and Virginia and the servants who were standing around. The terrible part was she didn't *want* to slap him. She wanted to pull him back for another kiss.

Her cheeks burning with either shame or something she couldn't identify, she managed to say, "Have a safe journey."

"I will," he replied, and then he was climbing into the coach.

"Don't forget to bring me something!" Alice called as the coach pulled away, heading down to the river where it would meet the boat whose bell they had heard a few minutes ago.

Emma found herself waving wistfully at his departing figure, even though she told herself she was really *happy* he was leaving.

That night, for the first time since that *other* night, Emma slept soundly, and that night Grayson came to her. He came through the door that she'd always kept locked, and he came to her naked, his glorious body fairly shimmering in the darkness.

He was just like she remembered, warm and solid, and her body thrilled to his touch. Desire surged in her, hot and strong and infinitely sweet, and she opened herself eagerly, needing to feel him inside of her. She took his weight gladly, feeling as if she had been starved for this and would have died without it. He was life, he was joy, and Emma took it all greedily, reveling in the passion that roared inside of her, echoing like thunder and exploding like lightning until her body quaked with release.

The first spasm woke her with a start, and as her body continued to shudder, she realized to her horror that she was alone, completely alone in her bed in the dark. Dear heaven, what was happening to her? she railed as the shudders died away, leaving her sated and ashamed. Could Grayson's chaste little kiss have caused all this?

And what did it mean? Emma didn't think she wanted to

know, especially when she found herself disappointed at the memory that Grayson wasn't even in the house tonight, that he was far away and out of reach. Because if he hadn't been, Emma was very much afraid she might have unlocked that door herself and opened it and gone through.

Ten

Emma missed Grayson. She hated herself for it and she tried to deny it and she called herself a fool for doing it, but she did, nonetheless. Even the flurry of preparations for the wedding was not enough to distract her completely. She found herself looking around at odd moments as if expecting to see him, or sometimes her mind would drift in the middle of a task, and Virginia would have to summon her back with a teasing remark.

She couldn't understand what was wrong with her. She certainly wasn't in love with Grayson or anything, so why should she miss him or think about him or dream about him? Yet she did all of those things and more, things she didn't even let herself think about in the light of day.

Maybe what they said about absence making the heart grow fonder was true. Emma tried to look on the bright side: a woman *should* be thinking about the man she was going to marry. Hadn't she daydreamed about Charles?

This was different, though. Much different, and Emma didn't like it at all.

Probably she was just having trouble believing any of it. Indeed, nothing seemed quite real. She'd chosen which gown she would wear for the ceremony, and she'd consulted with the cooks about the cake and the dishes they would serve the guests and had decided how the house would be decorated, but she couldn't quite let herself believe she was really getting married. To a man she hardly knew. To a man about whom what she did know she didn't like very much. To a man who had demonstrated time and again he despised her.

And to a man who had made her feel like a woman for the first time in her life.

No wonder she had a headache by the end of every day. No wonder she crawled into bed earlier and earlier each evening, her body bone weary. And no wonder she dreamed such outrageous dreams every night.

As relieved as she had been to see Grayson go, she was even more relieved when she heard the boat's bell that summoned the carriage to the dock. He was back, and she couldn't even pretend she wasn't glad. But instead of running downstairs, she ran to her room and rang for Chloe.

The girl found her rummaging in the wardrobe. "I need to change my dress," Emma informed her, pulling out something she thought would be appropriate, a beige sprigged calico gown. Modest but becoming. Emma ignored Chloe's knowing smile as she let the girl help her out of the soiled house dress she'd been wearing all day to supervise the servants as they cleaned the ballroom.

When she was all fastened again, Emma checked her reflection in the mirror. "My hair," she cried, trying in vain to smooth it back into place.

"Sit down a minute," Chloe said. "That boat ain't even to the dock yet. You gots plenty a time."

Emma perched impatiently on her dressing table stool and allowed Chloe to make the necessary repairs.

"There now," Chloe said. "I reckon he wouldn't notice what you's wearing, though, or even if your hair stickin' straight up."

"I'm sure he'd notice *that*," Emma disagreed, stepping in front of the cheval mirror to check her appearance one last time. "Besides, I'm not doing this for *him*."

"I know, you just wanna look your best for your *pride*."

"Exactly," Emma agreed, ignoring Chloe's grin again.

Satisfied that she looked presentable, Emma swept out of

the room and down the stairs. Alice was already down in the hallway with Rose. Her friend Jane had left a few days ago. The two girls were fairly dancing with excitement.

Emma smiled and tried to keep from dancing herself.

"Papa's home!" Alice informed her happily, hurrying to take Emma's hand. "I'll bet he brought me a present. He always brings me a present!"

Virginia stepped out of the back parlor. "Ignatius already left for the dock," she reported.

"Why don't you and Rose go out on the veranda and tell us when the carriage is coming back?" Emma suggested to Alice.

The two girls eagerly ran outside. Emma placed a hand over her stomach, which suddenly felt as if it were full of butterflies.

"You look very pleased, dear," Virginia observed. "Is it possible you and Gray have . . . uh . . . reached an understanding?"

Emma was sure she didn't understand a thing about her relationship with Gray. "I'm just . . . glad he got home safely," Emma hedged, carefully schooling her features so as not to betray the excitement simmering inside of her.

"He's coming!" Alice shouted from the veranda.

"Shall we go?" Virginia asked, not waiting for Emma as she headed for the front door. Emma hesitated only a moment, just long enough to take a calming breath, before following Virginia outside.

The carriage had just started back up the hill to the house, so they had to stand there a long time. Emma tried not to fidget, but she couldn't keep from gazing at the landau as it approached, and Grayson grew clearer and clearer the closer it came.

He looked happy to be home, which was only to be expected, and much handsomer than she had remembered. She could read nothing special in his expression, certainly nothing special for her, and when he finally hopped out of the carriage, the first person he greeted was Alice. Naturally, since she had run to his arms.

If things were different, if Grayson was a normal kind of fiance, then Emma would be running to his arms, too. She would be lifting her face for his kiss and returning that kiss. Instead, she stood hugging herself, not knowing exactly what she should do as the servants emerged from the house to greet their master.

"Did you bring me a present, Papa?" Alice asked after she'd kissed him soundly.

He'd removed his hat, and the breeze was teasing his dark locks. "Of course I did," he replied, setting her back on her feet while Thomas unloaded his bags from the carriage. "I brought presents for *everyone.*"

That was when his dark gaze found Emma. He took her in from head to toe in one swift glance, and she thought she read surprised approval in his gaze in the moment before his mother distracted him.

"Welcome home, dear," she said, lifting her cheek for his kiss. "Did you finish all your business?"

"Yes," he said, giving her a peck on the cheek. Emma was pleased to notice that his gaze found her again immediately however. He watched her for a long moment, as if waiting for something.

Emma supposed he was waiting for her to welcome him home, too. She stepped forward at last, those butterflies in her stomach trying to beat themselves to death while she managed a smile. "We're glad you're home," she assured him, pleased she had found something to say that did not betray any particular emotion.

"Are you?" he inquired archly. *"How* glad?"

Emma blinked in surprise. "What?" she asked stupidly.

"Are you glad enough to give me a kiss?" His dark eyes were sparkling with mirth and challenge, daring her to refuse him when everyone standing there knew she'd already given him far more than just a kiss.

Although her cheeks were burning, Emma lifted her chin, offering a challenge of her own. "If you want one," she replied.

She saw something like admiration flicker across his face as the servants chuckled and murmured at her boldness, and then he grinned.

"Oh, I do," he assured her, and before she could blink again, he caught her around the waist and covered her mouth with his.

The kiss lasted only a moment, but when he drew away, she felt slightly stunned, so stunned that she almost didn't notice the surprise in his eyes in the second before he turned away to acknowledge the cheers from the slaves.

Emma would have stepped back, but he still held her, his arm locked around her waist so tightly that she could feel the heat from his hand right through her corset. Or at least she imagined that she could.

"Give me that bag, Thomas," Grayson was saying to his manservant. "That one has the presents in it."

Alice squealed in delight, and to Emma's relief she maneuvered herself in between them as they headed into the house so that Grayson had to release her. Still, she felt his gaze on her, and when she looked up, she saw he was studying her with great interest, as if he'd never really looked at her before. She was very glad she'd taken some pains with her appearance.

Virginia led the way into the back parlor and ordered a maid to fix Massa Gray a julep and made sure he was seated in the most comfortable chair. Alice scrambled up onto the arm so she could be almost in his lap, and his mother pulled up a chair to his left, leaving Emma to perch on the sofa to his right.

He was teasing Alice, pretending he couldn't find her present in the carpetbag, making her giggle until finally he "found" her gift, a lovely porcelain doll with blue eyes and chestnut hair and a beautiful satin gown almost exactly the color of green as the one Emma had worn to the barbecue dance. It was even trimmed with black lace.

"It's Aunt Emma!" Alice cried, hugging the doll tightly to her chest. "Oh, I love her so much! Thank you, Papa, thank you!"

"How lucky you were to find a doll with Emma's hair and eyes," Virginia remarked slyly.

"Luck had nothing to do with it," Grayson said smugly. "I had her made up special for Alice's wedding present."

Emma could only gape at him while he dug in the carpet bag for something else. Could he really have done such a thing? Could he really have told some doll maker that he wanted a doll that resembled the woman he was going to marry? Could he have stood in the shop and described Emma, picturing her in his mind, even getting the color and style of her dress right? Emma couldn't imagine Grayson even thinking of such a thing, much less actually doing it. Yet Alice was cradling the proof of it in her arms at that very moment.

"This is for you, Mother," Grayson was saying as he handed Virginia a small box.

"It's lovely!" she exclaimed as she examined the cameo brooch. Then she squinted and examined it more closely. "Does it look like Emma?"

Emma gasped, but Grayson chuckled.

"If it does, it's a coincidence," he assured her. "I didn't have a likeness of her to show."

Emma felt absurdly relieved to know he hadn't had a cameo carved of her. The doll was more than enough.

"And what's this?" he said, pretending to have discovered something unexpected in his bag.

"Is it a present for Aunt Emma?" Alice asked ingenuously.

Grayson pulled out a flat, rectangular box and shook it next to his ear, as if that could tell him. "I think it is," he told Alice with feigned surprise. "Why don't you give it to her?"

Alice scrambled down and handed the box to Emma who tried not to betray her sudden excitement. She knew what it was. She'd received enough gifts of jewelry to recognize the

shape of the box as a necklace. What could he have chosen
for her? Would she like it? And what if she didn't?

"Aren't you going to open it?" Alice inquired, making
Emma realize she'd been staring at the box too long.

"Of course," she told the child with a quick, stiff smile, and
flipped open the box. She gasped again. And gaped.

"I thought they matched your eyes," Grayson said a little
too casually, but Emma didn't see his expression. She couldn't
take her eyes off the necklace.

"Are they diamonds, Papa?" Alice asked, her young voice
filled with awe.

"No, sapphires."

The bluest, most beautiful sapphires in the world. Emma
was sure of it.

"You shouldn't have," she managed finally, still unable to
take her eyes off the glittering stones set so exquisitely in the
gold filigree.

"Why not?" Grayson asked. "You're going to be my wife,
after all. And I knew you didn't have any jewelry of your
own."

Of course she didn't. She'd sold everything of value to pay
Charles' debts.

"There are some family pieces," he went on. "Things that
belonged to Lilly, but I thought you should have something
that was yours alone."

Emma felt so many things, she could hardly sort it all out.
She loved jewels, had always loved anything that glittered, and
she loved getting presents. But this present was from Grayson,
a man who was going to be her husband but only because
convention demanded he marry her, not because either of them
would have chosen it. Was this a peace offering from him?
Was he trying to make amends for having treated her so badly?
Or was he soothing his guilty conscience? Or—the most disturbing possibility of all—was he simply trying to make her
happy?

"Put it on, dear, so we can see what it looks like," Virginia urged.

Emma's hands were trembling as she lifted the necklace from the box and draped it around her neck.

"Let me," Grayson said, getting out of his chair and stepping around behind the sofa.

His fingers brushed hers, sending a thrill over her, as he took the chain from her and fastened it. She reached up and touched the stones at her throat, just to make sure they were really there.

"It's so pretty!" Alice exclaimed, and Virginia murmured her agreement. "My doll needs a necklace, too, so you'll match!"

"I'll make one for her," Emma promised. "A green one to go with her dress."

Alice smiled happily, hugging her doll, and Virginia beamed.

Grayson laid his hand on Emma's shoulder with a familiarity that took her breath. The heat from it seemed to spread over her, reminding her of those naughty dreams she'd been having and of other things that were much more real.

Virginia rose abruptly from her chair. "Come along now, Alice, and show Mammy your doll."

"Tell Rose I brought her something, too," Grayson told his daughter. "I'll bring it up in a few minutes."

"All right!" Alice skipped out of the room, and Virginia followed after gracing them both with a beneficent smile.

Emma wished she could follow, but Grayson's hand was still on her shoulder, holding her in place. After Virginia had closed the parlor door behind her, Grayson removed his hand, but Emma's relief was short-lived because he stepped around the sofa and sat down beside her.

"I missed you," he said.

"You did?" she asked, genuinely surprised.

He smiled slightly. "You're supposed to say, 'I missed you, too.' And yes, I did miss you. Not one lady slapped my face the entire time I was away."

Emma felt the heat in her cheeks again, although she knew she had nothing whatsoever to be embarrassed about. "Is that your way of telling me you didn't misbehave while you were gone?"

"Would you be jealous if I had?" he asked, sliding his arm along the back of the sofa behind her and leaning in much too close. So close she could feel the heat from his body, or at least she felt quite warm all of a sudden.

Emma caught her breath and inhaled his musky scent. She'd forgotten how he smelled and how big he was and how his mere presence could make her heart beat like a trip hammer. It was beating that way now. "I , . ." she began but found she couldn't remember his question. She cast about frantically for something to say. "Did you . . . finish all your business?" she tried, remembering too late Virginia had already asked him this.

"Yes," he told her, his lips still quirked in that private smile. His eyes were black as midnight. "Do you know what my business was?"

Emma shook her head, not trusting her voice.

"I wanted to get you a wedding present."

"The necklace is beautiful," she said, remembering she hadn't even told him so and reaching up to touch it again. "Thank you."

He waved away her thanks. "That's just a trinket. My real gift is something else, something I think you'll appreciate much more."

Emma couldn't imagine what else he could have gotten her that she would like more.

"You know, of course, that when we marry, your property becomes mine," he went on.

For a moment, Emma didn't know what he meant. She *had* no property, only her small legacy from Charles . . . And then she understood: even that would no longer be hers. Every last trace of her brief independence would vanish, and once again she would belong completely to a man. The old anger welled up in her so fiercely that she almost didn't hear what he was saying.

"But I thought you might like to have something of your own," he continued. "I spoke with my attorney, and he drew up the papers so that the money you inherited from Charles will remain yours alone. As soon as you sign them, I'll send them to Philadelphia along with notice that you have remarried."

Emma gaped at him, hardly able to believe what she was hearing. "Why did you do this?" she asked when she could speak.

"Because I wanted to please you."

Now Emma *didn't* believe what she was hearing. "Why would you care about pleasing me?"

His smiled died. "Because you're going to be my wife. This may not have been what either of us would have chosen, Emma, but we're going to have to live together a long time. I've had one miserable marriage. I don't want to have another."

Emma didn't either. "I wasn't *planning* to make you miserable," she said.

His lips quirked into another smile. "I'm relieved to hear it."

"Although," she continued solemnly, "I would be justified."

He stiffened, and once again his smile disappeared. "I realize I wasn't very . . . gracious to you the other day when I . . . proposed."

"You *never* proposed," Emma reminded him, her face hot. Her whole body was hot, in fact. She could never remember being so mortified, not even when Virginia had found them together out on the gallery.

He actually winced, which gave Emma some little satisfaction, although not the kind she wanted.

"Then perhaps I should," he allowed without much enthusiasm, which was what she would have expected. But she didn't expect what he did next.

Taking her hand in his, he slid off the sofa down onto one

knee. "Emma, my dear, would you do me the honor of becoming my wife?"

"What are you *doing?*" Emma demanded in outrage, trying unsuccessfully to free her hand, but he was holding it much too tightly.

"I'm proposing," he informed her. "Wasn't that what you wanted?"

"Not *now!*" she cried, still trying without success to free her hand. "I wanted you to propose last week! I wanted you to at least *pretend* that the idea of marrying me didn't completely repulse you!"

"You don't repulse me," he insisted.

"Get up from there!" Emma commanded, jumping to her feet, her cheeks flaming with indignation.

He obeyed, rising up in front of her, but he still held her hand, and he was much too close, and suddenly she wished he was back on his knees.

"You *don't* repulse me," he repeated, his gaze fierce as he stared down at her.

"No, but you despise me all the same," Emma said. "You think I'm silly and stupid and boring and—"

"You're definitely not *boring!*"

"—and you can't stand the sight of me!"

"Oh, you're right there!" he said, his fingers tightening painfully on hers. "The sight of you drives me crazy. The sight of you keeps me awake at night and makes me worthless in the daylight. I've never wanted a woman the way I want you, Emma, and having you has only made it worse."

Emma gasped or would have if Grayson hadn't kissed her then, hauling her against him and devouring her mouth with his so thoroughly that she couldn't even think. She could only feel, and she felt everything. His mouth on hers, his tongue hot and insistent between her lips, his chest hard against the softness of her breasts. She ran her hands up over his shoulders to wrap her arms around his neck and bury her fingers in his hair. If she had forgotten the heat of their passion, she remembered it now as the flames scorched her, melting her defenses and her resistance and melding her to him.

So lost was she that at first she didn't even notice they were no longer alone. But after a few more moments of abandon, the sound of girlish giggles finally penetrated the fog of desire, and they broke apart, startled, to find Rose and Alice peeking at them from the doorway.

"You were kissing!" Alice informed them gleefully.

"Alice, go back upstairs!" Grayson said sharply.

The child's mouth dropped open in astonishment, and her lovely blue eyes instantly filled with tears. Emma doubted her father had ever spoken to her in that tone of voice.

"No, dear, it's all right," Emma hastily assured her, but Grayson had already repented his outburst.

"I'm sorry, sweetheart," he said, hurrying to her. His voice was gentle now, the way it usually was when he spoke to his child.

"Rose wanted to see her present," Alice explained tremulously.

"Of course she did," Grayson allowed, managing a smile for Rose who had flattened herself against the wall, her dark eyes wide with fright.

"I don't want no present now," Rose said, edging toward the door.

"Sure you do," Emma said, going to her, a reassuring smile plastered on her face even though she was still trembling in reaction to Grayson's kiss. "Just wait 'til you see what Massa Gray brought you."

"Are you mad at me, Papa?" Alice asked, the tears still trembling in her eyes.

"Why would I be mad at you?" he asked.

"You yelled at me," she reminded him.

"I didn't mean to," he said. "You just . . . surprised me."

Alice bit her lip. "Was it because you were . . . kissing Aunt Emma?"

"Yes," he said quite easily. "I like kissing Aunt Emma, and

I didn't want to stop, but that's no excuse for yelling at my favorite girl, is it?" Emma wanted to sink through the floor, but Alice melted at the compliment.

"No, it isn't," Alice agreed, showing a spark of her usual spirit. "You scared Rose, too," she scolded.

"I'm sorry, Rose," he told her solemnly. "Do you forgive me?"

Rose melted, too. "I guess," she allowed with a tiny grin.

Grayson sighed with exaggerated relief. "Well, now, how about if I show you what I brought for you?"

Rose nodded vigorously, and Grayson escorted the two little girls over to where his carpetbag still sat. Emma watched, slightly dazed, as he rummaged through it and brought out a second doll, this one made of cloth with dark brown skin and big, button eyes and a bandana tied around its head, and presented it to a delighted Rose.

Emma decided she must be dreaming. Grayson couldn't have really gone down on one knee and asked her to marry him any more than he could have given her a sapphire necklace and told her that she could keep control of her own money after they were wed. Except, she realized when she lifted her hand to her throat, the sapphire necklace was still there, cool and solid beneath her fingers. He'd wanted to please her, he'd said, and he couldn't have done anything that would have pleased her more than to let her keep her own money.

And he wanted her. More than he'd ever wanted any other woman, he'd said. It wasn't exactly a declaration of undying love and devotion, but it was something. More, certainly, than she'd ever expected. Much, much more, she thought, absently stroking the stones at her throat.

But would it be enough to ward off the misery of which he had spoken? Emma simply didn't know.

Emma slept poorly the next few nights, still listening for footsteps she never heard. If Grayson truly did want her as much as he claimed, he was doing an excellent job of restraining himself in the days before their wedding. Oh, he was pleasant enough and charming to a fault, but he made no further attempts to ravish her. Except for an occasional peck on the cheek, he didn't even kiss her. She knew she should be grateful for his self-control since it saved her from having to decide whether to once again forget every standard of decency and allow him to make love to her again. The problem was, she didn't feel grateful at all.

By the morning of her wedding, Emma was as jumpy as a cat. At least no one expected her to show her face until the ceremony, so Chloe was the only one who had to know what a wreck she was.

"You actin' just like Miss Lilly did on *her* weddin' day," Chloe finally said to her in disgust as Emma paced around the room in her dressing gown. "If'n you don't eat somethin', you faint dead away right in front of the preacher."

"How can I eat when you've laced me so tight I can't even breathe!" Emma demanded.

"Is you *scared* a marryin' Massa Gray?" Chloe asked.

Scared? Emma thought wildly. No, she was *terrified!* Certainly, she'd been nervous about marrying Charles, but this was completely different. She'd known Charles loved her and would cherish and adore her. Grayson merely wanted her, and while the thought made her blood run fast and hot with visions of what would happen between them in bed, she wanted more. She wanted *Grayson* to cherish and adore her. She wanted Grayson to be weak-kneed at the thought of her and tongue-tied and uncertain in her presence. She wanted Grayson to love her the way she loved him.

The thought stopped her in her tracks, and she glanced guiltily at Chloe, afraid for one awful moment that the girl had discerned her thoughts. But Chloe was simply staring at her with the same puzzled frown she'd been wearing a moment ago.

" 'Cause if you *is* scared of Massa Gray," Chloe continued, blissfully unaware of Emma's true fears, "you don't need to be. He likes to holler and stomp his feet, but inside he's sweet as a lamb."

"Grayson?" Emma asked incredulously.

Chloe shrugged. "Ain't you seen how he is with Miss Alice? He be that way with you, too, if you give him a chance. Now sit down here and let me do your hair."

Emma sat, although her insides still felt as if they were pacing, and Chloe set to work.

"If I didn't know better," the girl remarked after a while, "I'd think you's nervous 'bout your weddin' night."

"Don't be ridiculous," Emma said, although she could see the blush spreading over her face and bosom in her reflection. "I'm not exactly a virgin."

"Neither was Miss Lilly, but she nervous just the same," Chloe replied.

"What?" Emma gasped. "Not a . . . ? But she was only sixteen!"

Chloe's face tightened. "Yeah, but she an' Massa Gray, they . . . Well, they didn't wait for the preacher, neither. Miss Lilly, she wanted Massa Gray so bad, she do anything to get him."

"You mean she . . . ? Chloe, you make it sound like she *seduced* him," Emma marveled.

"She did," Chloe said, shocking Emma all over again. "I told you, she paid the conjure woman—the one at Massa Phelps' place—she paid her for a spell for to catch Massa Gray. Then she sends him a note, asking him to meet her one day. That's when she . . . when she let him do it. She weren't a bad girl, Missy," Chloe hastily explained, seeing Emma's horrified reaction. "She didn't even like it. She never did like it much, neither, not even after they was married. But Massa Gray, he always real patient with her and never mean like . . . Well, he never mean," she corrected herself. "So if that what you scared of—"

"I'm not scared," Emma lied, although she certainly wasn't

scared of Grayson not being patient. She didn't even *want* him to be patient. She felt her nipples tightening beneath her chemise at the thought, and she hastily closed her robe, praying Chloe wouldn't notice her involuntary reaction. "I'm just . . ." She cast about for a plausible excuse for her distress. "I'm just worried about the gossip. About people snickering behind their hands at me."

"They just jealous," Chloe said.

"Jealous?" Emma echoed in amazement.

"Yeah, the womens, they jealous 'cause you got Massa Gray, and the mens, they jealous 'cause he got you. Let 'em laugh. You be the one that's happy."

"Will I?" Emma asked, frowning at her reflection.

"Yes, you will," Chloe said. It sounded like an order.

Later, as Emma stood before the cheval mirror, she could hardly recognize the woman staring back at her as herself. She wore a sapphire blue gown of the finest silk, a dress she had never expected to wear again and which she had chosen because its color and its off-the-shoulder neckline was perfect for the necklace Grayson had given her. The jewels glittered at her throat, and her hair was swept in deep waves over each temple and pulled up into a cascade of curls on the back of her head.

Since a veil would have been inappropriate, Chloe had woven fresh flowers into her hair, and a bouquet of white rosebuds lay on the table, ready for her to carry when she went downstairs. Her cheeks were flushed, so at least she wouldn't have to worry about looking too pale, Emma thought as she studied the woman in the mirror for any imperfections. Satisfied that she looked as well as she ever would, she turned away just as someone knocked on the door.

"Are you ready, dear?" Virginia called.

"Yes, come in," Emma replied, her stomach fluttering apprehensively.

The door opened and Alice ran in. She was the one wearing white, the ruffled flounces of her skirt revealing her long pantalettes beneath. Her golden curls were bound with satin ribbons and woven with flowers, too, and she carried a basket of rose petals which she was to drop before Emma.

"Oh, Aunt Emma, you're beautiful!" Alice cried, her blue eyes glittering with admiration.

"So are you," Emma replied, smiling in spite of her tension. Alice could always cheer her up.

Virginia had come in behind Alice and very carefully closed the door behind them so no one would get a peek at the bride. Virginia was to be her matron of honor. She wore her usual black dress, but carried a bouquet of red roses. "My goodness, poor Gray will be overcome when he sees you, Emma. And I'm afraid he might have to fight a duel over you before dark!"

"That isn't funny," Emma chastised her.

"I wasn't teasing," Virginia defended herself. "When those other suitors of yours see you like this . . ." She shook her head and clucked her tongue.

Emma laid a hand on her fluttering stomach and looked heavenward for strength.

"Everyone is here," Virginia told her, "so if you're ready, I'll let them know to start the music."

"I'm as ready as I can be," Emma decided, not really anxious to begin but knowing she couldn't stand much more waiting.

"Go tell them to begin," Virginia told Alice, who took off at a run.

"Start the music!" Alice shouted as soon as she was outside the door, and Emma laughed in spite of herself. They could hear the guests down in the foyer chuckling, too, but in another moment, the fiddlers began, and Emma's heart seemed to stop.

Virginia came to her and took her hand which had gone icy. "I know you'll be very happy," she said, making Emma wish she could be as sure.

Chloe pressed the bouquet of white roses into her hand.

"Smile," she whispered, making Emma realize she felt on the verge of tears. She'd nearly cried the day she'd married Charles, too, but those had been tears of joy. She stretched her mouth into what she hoped was a convincing smile.

"Shall we go?" she asked Virginia.

Virginia nodded and led the way, throwing open the bedroom door. The upstairs landing was filled with the house servants who were privileged to witness the master's wedding. They had formed an aisle between the bedroom door and the head of the stairs for her, and when she saw their faces, so pleased and proud, Emma relaxed a bit and smiled more sincerely, nodding to acknowledge the murmurs of admiration as she passed. Virginia went first, walking slowly down the stairs, and Alice followed, under strict orders not to drop any rose petals until she was safely down the stairs so that Emma wouldn't slip and fall.

The minister waited at the far end of the downstairs hallway, so she would have to make her way through the throngs of friends and neighbors gathered there as well. She knew the instant they caught sight of her from the ripple of reaction, but she didn't look at any of them. She didn't want to risk glimpsing even the slightest hint of scorn or the barest trace of a smirk.

She descended the stairs blindly, gazing straight ahead until she reached the foot and turned and was facing the minister. Grayson stood beside him looking every inch the master in his dark suit and stiffly starched shirt. She didn't let herself look at his face until she was halfway down the hallway, and when she did, she almost stumbled.

His expression was grave, befitting a man who was entering a marriage he hadn't wanted, but his eyes were glittering with what could only be pride. Emma lifted her chin a little higher, knowing he could find no fault in her appearance or her manner. If he found fault in other areas . . . Well, she wouldn't spoil her wedding day by worrying about what those areas might be.

By the time she reached his side, her smile was genuine, and he was smiling back.

"Dearly beloved," the minister began, and before Emma was quite ready, she was promising to love and honor and obey. Then Grayson was promising to love and to cherish in return. He was lying, she knew, but seeing the way he was looking at her now, she wondered if it wasn't possible that love might come, in time. For her part, she loved him already. She loved the way he was with Alice. And the way he'd been with Lilly. Even the way he'd considered her need for independence. How many other men would have allowed their wives to keep their own inheritance? And she most certainly loved the way she felt when she was in his arms.

The next thing she knew, Grayson was slipping the ring on her finger, and she looked down in surprise to find it wasn't the plain gold band she had expected but an elaborate creation of diamonds and rubies. He winked at her gasp of surprise, bringing the color to her face, and for a long moment she was lost in the dark depths of his beautiful eyes.

"You may kiss the bride."

Emma had completely lost track of the ceremony until Grayson grinned wickedly and took her by the shoulders and planted a kiss right on her mouth. Then everyone began to cheer, and Grayson released her and took her hand and led her back down the aisle and out the front door as various guests shouted congratulations.

By the time they reached the veranda, they were both laughing, although Emma could not have said what was so funny. They stopped, positioning themselves to meet the guests as they came out to extend their best wishes, but Emma couldn't stop staring at Grayson. She'd never expected to see him smiling at her in just that way.

"You look very beautiful today, Mrs. Sinclair," he said, taking advantage of the few seconds of privacy they would have before the guests began to descend on them.

"So do you, Mr. Sinclair," she replied. "And the ring is lovely. You shouldn't have been so extravagant!"

"I married an heiress," he excused himself, but she didn't even have time to react to such a ridiculous statement before Alice and Virginia arrived to wish them well.

Emma was surprised to see that Virginia was crying, but her smile clearly showed they were tears of joy. She kissed Emma and Grayson and told them both she knew they'd be happy. Grayson, Emma noticed, did not reply. But then, neither did she.

Alice was next, and she hugged Emma fiercely. "You're my mama now, aren't you?" she asked, gazing up at Emma with those trusting blue eyes.

Emma wanted nothing more than to be Alice's mama, but she glanced at Grayson not certain exactly what she should say. They hadn't even discussed what Alice would call her.

"Yes, Emma is your mama now," Grayson confirmed, to Emma's relief.

"But you can still call me 'Aunt Emma' if you want, at least at first," Emma added hastily, not certain herself if she was really ready to be someone's mother.

"And you'll stay with us forever and ever?" Alice asked almost desperately.

Emma's heart ached for the child who had lost so much in her short life. At least she could offer her a little reassurance. "Forever and ever," she promised, glad that some good had already come out of her union with Grayson.

"I'm so glad you married Aunt Emma," Alice exclaimed, throwing herself into her father's arms. He lifted her up for a kiss.

Emma saw the tenderness on his face as he gazed at his daughter, and longing swelled within her. Perhaps someday she would see that same tenderness when he looked at his wife. Blinking at the sting of tears, she turned to greet the first guest.

Although Virginia's dire predictions of a duel were a trifle exaggerated, Emma's former suitors all let her know how disappointed they were at losing her and took full advantage of the opportunity to kiss the bride.

"You didn't waste any time claiming her for yourself," Mr. Hamilton told Grayson after he had planted a kiss on Emma's reluctant lips. Hamilton was smiling, but she had no difficulty discerning the annoyance behind his words.

Grayson smiled back, equally annoyed. "When I saw how serious the rest of you fellows were, I decided I better not give you another chance."

Grayson managed to hold his smile as each of Emma's former suitors expressed their disappointment with varying degrees of gracious acceptance, but by the time they had finished receiving all their guests, that smile was definitely strained.

Nathan, who had served as best man, was the last in line.

"Do you have a kiss left for me?" he asked Emma with a knowing grin.

"Of course," she replied, lifting her face, but after Nathan glanced at Grayson, he gave her only a chaste peck on the cheek.

He turned to Grayson and shook his hand. "I knew this was what you had in mind all along when you brought Emma here," he said. Then he added to Emma, "Didn't I say so that first day I met you?"

Emma nodded, remembering how embarrassed she'd been then at the mere suggestion that Grayson might have wanted her for himself. Of course, he hadn't, not really, and he still didn't, not exactly. Still, the way he'd been fuming over seeing other men kiss her was gratifying. He might not be jealous, not in the usual way, but he was at least possessive of her. It was a start.

"Isn't it time for you to make a toast?" Grayson asked, a slight edge to his voice.

"I believe it is," Nathan agreed cheerfully. "Come along and I'll get us some champagne."

Grayson offered Emma his arm. She looked up at him as

she took it and was surprised to see how gravely he was studying her.

"Is something wrong?" she asked.

"That's the last time any other man will ever kiss you," he said.

Emma felt a faint flush of pleasure washing over her. "You're not jealous, are you?" she teased as they followed Nathan.

He straightened a bit and something sparkled in his dark eyes. "I'm always jealous of what's mine."

The flush warmed into something much more thrilling than mere pleasure as Grayson's gaze swept over her. Desire burned low in his eyes, banked for now but still sending out an answering heat. Her breath quickened, and she felt an odd little clenching between her legs.

And then Nathan was handing them each glasses of champagne and the spell was broken, at least for the moment.

"To Gray and Emma," Nathan was saying as all the other guests lifted their glasses, too. "May they know every joy that life can bring and may they grow old together in happiness."

A hundred voices confirmed the wish, and again Emma felt the sting of tears. Would she ever know true happiness again? she wondered as she clinked her glass with Grayson's and sipped the bubbly liquid.

Fortunately, she didn't have much time for further reflection. She and Grayson had to be served their dinner so the other guests could eat, too. Some of the slaves had hunted down a wild boar which was roasting on a spit over a bed of hot coals. Roast turkey and oysters and new peas with onions and early corn and sweet potatoes and pies of every description and cornbread and biscuits and sweet butter were also among the many dishes the busy cooks had laid out for the guests.

Emma discovered that she was hungry, although her stomach still felt a bit queasy, and she was able to eat enough to satisfy her new husband who seemed unduly concerned with the matter.

After they ate, the bride and groom were expected to circulate among the guests, and Emma was soon separated from Grayson as she mingled with the ladies who all wanted to admire her ring and have a private word with her. If Emma had feared seeing a smirk or hearing a snicker, she was surprised instead to find that the other ladies were most anxious to welcome her into their society. Although they had been friendly to her before, they had treated her as a guest, not realizing she had come to Texas to stay. By marrying Grayson, she had become a permanent part of their community, however, and they all had advice to offer and plans to make and invitations to issue and gossip to share.

If anyone was jealous that she had captured Grayson, Emma saw no sign of it, but Jane McCarthy's mother expressed regret.

"I hope you'll keep your promise to teach Jane lessons when she comes to visit," Mary McCarthy said with a smile.

She was a tall, slender woman who looked to be about six months pregnant. Emma felt the old disappointment and envied her. "I certainly will, since I'll be giving Alice lessons, too."

"Perhaps you'd let me send Jane over for a visit when my time comes," she said.

"Alice would be thrilled, and so would I," Emma said, taking some satisfaction in making the decision. At least she was in charge of her life once again.

As the afternoon wore on, Emma began to understand that marrying Grayson had given her a kind of power she had never possessed before. In Philadelphia, she had managed a household with a few live-in servants. Now the lives of more than a hundred people were her responsibility. She began to understand this when Grayson appeared carrying a small burlap sack that jingled slightly.

"We need to go down to the quarters," he told her. "They're having a party of their own down there, and they'll want to see the bride and groom."

Alice accompanied them, making any intimate conversation

impossible, but Emma was glad to note that she was beginning to feel more comfortable with Grayson.

"What have you got in the bag?" she asked as they walked down the path to the quarters with Alice skipping along in front of them.

"Pennies, for the children," he explained. "The parents get a day off from work and a party."

The sound of laughter drifted up from the cabins, and Emma felt herself smiling. She remembered how appalled she had been on her first visit here. She was still appalled by the idea of slavery—that was something she would never get used to—but the slaves themselves no longer disturbed her.

They were gathered down by the big building that Emma now knew was the common dining hall. The slaves were also roasting a boar and seemed to have as much food as the guests up at the main house. For a few minutes, she got to observe them as they laughed and talked among themselves. Except for the color of their skin, they might have been any group of people she had ever seen enjoying themselves at a picnic.

Then someone caught sight of the three of them and cried out, alerting the others. Instantly, their whole demeanor changed, and they became the shuffling, obsequious servants again as they rushed forward to gather around their master and their new mistress.

"Kiss her, Massa! Kiss her!" someone shouted, and instantly others took up the chant.

Her face burning, Emma looked up at Grayson who was only too happy to obey the command. Fortunately, the kiss was brief, and Emma quickly regained her composure as she accepted the good wishes from the slaves who approached her, even though those good wishes were always for her to have lots of babies. Emma wouldn't be the only one disappointed when she and Grayson produced no children.

Grayson called for the children then, and they came rushing forward to receive their gifts. Grayson handed Emma the bag of pennies, and she and Alice distributed the coins into the small, eager hands.

They were almost finished when Emma noticed a boy who held himself back from the others. It was Benjamin, Grayson's slave son, and when she looked at him, Emma could feel his anger like a wave of heat washing out from him. His eyes fairly blazed with it, and she caught her breath when she realized it was directed at her.

He was jealous, of course, probably figuring that since Grayson had taken a new bride and would be having more children, he would become even less important to his father than he was already. If only he knew he had nothing to fear from Emma. She wanted to reach out to him, to tell him she understood his pain and felt the same pain herself.

"Alice," she said when the child had finished distributing the pennies, "Benjamin didn't get one."

Did Alice know who Benjamin was to her? If so, she gave no sign of it as she hurried over to the tall boy who, in spite of his brown skin, looked remarkably like his father.

Benjamin had stiffened at the mention of his name, and he glared fiercely at Emma, making her wish she hadn't made the effort and singled him out. He jammed his hands into his pants pockets, plainly ready to refuse her gesture. But then Alice reached him, and he looked down at her. The fading sunlight glinted off her golden curls, and she was smiling up at him beatifically as she offered the penny.

Her sweetness cracked the hard shell of his anger, and his face twisted with some spasm of inward pain. He reached out and took the coin from her with the defeated air of one who has accepted what he cannot possibly change.

But if Emma had hoped for some sign of reconciliation, he gave none. Without even glancing at her or Grayson again, he turned and strode away.

Only then did Emma realize that the crowd of slaves had fallen silent as they waited to see what would happen. The instant Benjamin disappeared behind a cabin, however, they all started talking at once, determined to pretend that nothing untoward had occurred.

If their cheer was forced, no one appeared to notice as they escorted the three of them to the edge of the quarters before returning to their party.

"You didn't have to do that," Grayson told her solemnly when the slaves were out of ear shot. "He gets enough special treatment, and he doesn't appreciate any of it."

"I don't want him to hate me," Emma replied, keeping her voice low so Alice, who was walking ahead of them, wouldn't hear.

"He'll hate you no matter what you do," he said, giving her a glimpse into the pain he, too, felt.

Emma frowned, feeling the familiar helpless frustration of not knowing what to do, and for that instant she understood the lure of the conjure woman's magic. How wonderful it would be to be able to cast a spell and make everything all right. If only such a thing were possible.

By the time they reached the path back to the house, Emma had recalled another painful situation, one she might be able to help even without magic.

"I didn't see Hallie or her children at the party," she said.

He frowned. "She doesn't . . . socialize with the others."

Of course she doesn't, Emma thought. They would hate her because of her privileged position. And she certainly wouldn't be welcome at the big house with Nathan, either.

"I'd like to go by the overseer's house and give her children their gifts," Emma said, remembering their adorable faces.

"That isn't necessary," Grayson said, still frowning.

"Yes, it is," Emma insisted. "They must be so lonely, not being able to go to either party. I just want her to know that . . . that we haven't forgotten her."

Grayson didn't move.

"Alice and I can go if you don't want to," Emma said, knowing full well that he could forbid her to do it if he chose. What would she do if he did? Defy him on her wedding day?

But Grayson went along, his disapproval still obvious even though he didn't say a thing. Emma, however, didn't care whether he approved or not. She was mistress of the plantation now, and she would do as she thought best.

The overseer's house was quiet, the door shut tightly in spite of the summer heat.

"Hallie!" Emma called. "Hallie, please come out!"

The "please" wasn't necessary, since Emma now had the authority to command Hallie to do whatever she wished. But Emma didn't want to abuse that power.

After a moment, the door opened slowly, and Hallie stepped warily out. She nodded her head in a silent greeting.

"We have something for the children," Emma told her, smiling warmly. "Would you send them out?"

Hallie did not smile back, and Emma thought she stiffened slightly in some kind of silent resistance to the request. But she could not refuse outright. She made a quick motion with her hand, and the two little ones materialized on either side of her, clinging shyly to her skirts.

"Don't be afraid," Emma told them, beckoning them forward. "We have something for you."

Emma reached into the bag and pulled out a handful of pennies. "Can you divide these between them?" she asked Alice.

Alice nodded vigorously, making her curls bounce. Taking the pennies carefully into her two cupped hands, she went to the edge of the porch. "Come on," she urged the children, who came forward only after their mother nodded her approval.

As Alice counted the pennies out into their hands, Emma stepped to the porch, too, drawn irresistibly by the children. "Aren't they beautiful?" she asked no one in particular, laying a loving hand on the smaller one's curly head. The child looked up in surprise, her chocolate eyes enormous in her small face, and seeing Emma's affectionate smile, she smiled back. Emma's heart melted.

"Say 'thank you' to the mistress," Hallie said sharply when Alice had finished counting out the coins.

"Thank you," they parroted in unison, and both of them were smiling now. Then they ran back to the shelter of their mother's skirts, greedily clutching their pennies.

"They're fine children," Emma said, needing to make Hallie's life somehow less bleak. "Any woman would be proud to have them."

Emma had expected Hallie to be pleased at the compliment. Instead her eyes widened with what Emma thought in that fleeting instant might have been terror. Then she and her children disappeared back into the house, closing the door firmly behind them.

Confused, Emma turned to Grayson for an explanation, but he only said, "We'd better get back."

She let him lead her away, but she couldn't help looking back one last time. "Did I say something wrong?" she asked him.

"No," he told her, tucking her arm in his and patting her hand reassuringly.

"I only wanted to make things better for her," Emma explained.

"You can't," Grayson said simply.

As much as she wanted to argue, she knew he was right.

Although the incident with Hallie continued to haunt her, Emma managed to enjoy the rest of the afternoon. As the sun began to set, the party moved into the upstairs ballroom, and once again the Negro musicians played for the white guests to dance.

Emma and Grayson started everyone off with a romantic waltz. Gazing up into his face, Emma could almost believe him to be a happy bridegroom who was thoroughly enjoying his wedding day. But not half as much as he would enjoy his wedding *night,* she thought, seeing the unmistakable gleam of lust deep in his eyes as he pulled her closer to him.

Emma felt an answering thrill and reminded herself that she no longer had any reason to feel guilty for her own desires. She could welcome Grayson into her bed now, and they could enjoy each other thoroughly with the full sanction of God and man. Why, then, did she still feel guilty?

Before she could answer that question, Nathan cut in, and Grayson released her with obvious reluctance. He went to claim his mother for a dance, as Nathan whirled Emma around the floor.

"You look very happy," he remarked, and Emma frowned, remembering Hallie and his children out in the quarters this afternoon. "Did I step on your foot?" he asked, seeing the sudden change in her expression.

She forced her smile back into place, knowing she couldn't possibly tell him what had disturbed her. Such things were not, she had learned, discussed in polite company, and certainly no lady would mention a man's colored mistress to him.

"I'm sorry, I was thinking about something else."

Fortunately, someone else cut in then, and Emma changed partners two more times before the dance ended. As her last partner claimed her, Emma heard laughter behind her and turned to see that Grayson had brought Alice out to the floor. He'd placed her small feet on his much larger ones, and he was waltzing her around the floor while she giggled with delight and the other guests chuckled.

Yes, Emma thought with a pang as her latest partner took her in his arms, that was the Grayson she loved.

Putting that disturbing thought away, she forced herself to be witty and bright and charming to all the men who had courted her and who now wished to claim her for a dance. She'd been dancing for a long time when she heard Alice scream.

Eleven

Emma left her partner at once and forced her way through the other couples who had also stopped dancing and turned curiously toward the center of the floor where Alice was making a scene. Emma didn't know what she expected to find, but what she did see froze her blood. Alice was struggling with DeWitt Phelps.

Phelps was smiling, although his smile was somewhat strained. "Come on now, sweetheart," he coaxed. "You danced with your father."

"Let me go!" Alice begged, her little face twisted with the effort not to cry.

Where had he come from? Emma knew he hadn't been invited, and she was certain he hadn't been here earlier. Surely, she would have noticed!

"Mr. Phelps, what are you doing here?" she demanded furiously.

"Mama! Mama!" Alice cried, breaking free of his grasp and throwing herself against Emma's skirts.

Phelps straightened, his face nearly purple with fury. *"She's not your mother!"* he cried. "Your mother is *dead!*"

"What's going on here?" Grayson demanded, breaking through the crowd. Emma noticed that the music had stopped, and now everyone was staring at them openly.

"I was just trying to dance with my granddaughter," Phelps informed him indignantly. "But as you can see, she seems to be terrified of me."

Grayson's face was nearly purple now, too. "DeWitt, I've told you before—"

"Yes, you've told me," he interrupted. "You've told me I'm not to speak to my own grandchild! It wasn't enough that you stole my daughter or that you killed her!" Everyone gasped, but Phelps didn't seem to notice. "Now you've turned Alice against me, too!"

"DeWitt, I'm afraid you've had too much to drink," Grayson said, and Emma could see how much difficulty he was having holding his temper.

"I'm not drunk!" Phelps shouted.

Alice was sobbing silently against Emma, and Emma knew she had to get the child away.

"Come with me," she whispered, pulling Alice's small arms from around her waist. Alice kept her face buried against Emma as they moved away. The crowd parted for them, murmuring sympathetically, although Emma wasn't sure for whom they were sympathetic.

She caught one woman saying, "Gray has spoiled her terribly."

And another said, "Poor DeWitt. He's a boor, but you can't blame him for loving his grandchild."

By the time she reached the ballroom door, her own cheeks were burning with fury. Virginia met them there.

"How did he get in here?" Emma demanded in a fierce whisper.

"He must have heard about the wedding," Virginia whispered back, her face pale. "I guess he figured we wouldn't turn him away, invitation or not."

And he'd been right, of course. Good manners forbade a host from being so rude, especially to someone who should, by right of his connection to the family, have been an honored guest.

"You see to Alice," Virginia said. "I'll take care of things here."

Emma led Alice down the stairs where Mammy and Chloe were waiting anxiously.

"What happened?" Chloe asked, seeing Alice still sobbing against Emma.

"Mr. Phelps is here," Emma told her grimly. "He . . . tried to get Alice to dance with him."

Chloe glanced past her, toward the stairs that led to where Phelps was, and her eyes were so full of hate, Emma gasped.

"My poor little lamb," Mammy crooned, trying to take Alice, but the girl wouldn't let go of Emma.

Which was fine with Emma. "I think we should put Alice to bed, don't you?" she asked Mammy, who nodded quickly, her expression worried.

As Emma led the child across the hall to the nursery, Alice looked up at her anxiously. "You *are* my mama now, aren't you?" she asked. "No matter what *he* says?"

"Yes, darling, yes, I am," Emma assured her. "Didn't your papa tell you so?"

" 'Course Miss Emma your mama," Mammy confirmed. "Who told you different?"

"Grandpa did," Alice said indignantly. "He said my mama is dead!"

"Poor chile," Mammy sighed, shaking her head and stroking Alice's curls lovingly.

Behind her, Emma heard Chloe mutter something. She couldn't make out the words, but she recognized rancid hatred when she heard it. When she glanced back, she saw Chloe still staring up the stairs, looking for all the world as if she could kill DeWitt Phelps with her bare hands.

Shaking off the thought, Emma hurried Alice into the nursery.

"Won't nobody bother you here, honey," Mammy assured the child, and Emma winced when she remembered that DeWitt had gone right into the nursery the last time he'd been here.

"Don't leave me!" Alice begged Emma when Mammy finally had managed to pry her little arms loose. Apparently, she remembered, too.

"I won't," Emma promised. "I'll stay with you as long as you want."

Mammy frowned, obviously thinking of the guests upstairs who would be deprived of their hostess and of how inappropriate it was for a bride to leave her own wedding reception. Although such obligations would have once weighed heavily upon her, Emma now realized that she had other, more important responsibilities. Being Alice's mother was one of those.

"Can I help you get ready for bed?" she asked the child.

Alice nodded. "Will you read me a story, too?"

"Of course," Emma promised.

Once she had dreamed of performing these same rituals with her own children, a dream that had died a painful death as she had finally accepted that she would never bear a child. But she had Alice now, and some of those dreams, at least, could come true. With loving hands, she helped Alice undress and slip into her nightdress.

Rose was already asleep on the trundle bed, so Emma snuggled close to Alice in the big bed, heedless of wrinkling her gown, and read to her softly by the light of a single candle. Then she sat with her until her eyes finally closed and her breathing settled into the steady rhythm of sleep.

Rising carefully, she smoothed the sheet over the child's small form and placed one last kiss on Alice's soft forehead. Mammy had been sitting in the rocker on the other side of the room, and now she rose to walk out with Emma.

When they were in the hall, Mammy said, "You's real good with her, Miss Emma."

"I've never been anyone's mother before," Emma said with a grateful smile. "You'll tell me if I do anything wrong, won't you?"

Mammy shook her head. "Love can't do nothin' wrong, Miss Emma. You be just fine."

Emma blinked at the sting of tears. Goodness, her emotions

were uncertain today, she thought, remembering how many other times she had been on the verge of weeping today. Then she thought of the child sleeping so peacefully in the other room, and she recalled how easily Phelps had gotten into her the last time he'd been here. "I'll have Thomas sit outside the nursery door."

"That be fine, Miss Emma," Mammy agreed eagerly.

"And send for me if Alice wakes up or has a nightmare."

"Yes'm," Mammy said.

By the time Emma returned to the party, she was angry enough to order DeWitt Phelps never to set foot on Fairview Plantation again. But DeWitt Phelps was nowhere to be seen.

Grayson, however, must have been watching for her, because he was beside her almost instantly.

"How is Alice?" he asked.

"She's asleep. I asked Thomas to sit outside the nursery door in case Mr. Phelps tries to see her again."

"He won't," Grayson assured her grimly. "He's gone."

"Are you sure?"

He frowned. "He said he was leaving. You don't think he'd try to sneak back . . ."

"He might do anything," Emma informed him. "He wasn't even invited to the wedding, but he came anyway."

"What do you mean, he wasn't invited?"

"He upset Alice the last time he was here, that Sunday after church when . . . when we had so many visitors."

Grayson's frown deepened as he recalled that those visitors had been her suitors. "How did he upset Alice?"

"He went up to the nursery, and he sent Rose and Mammy out. I don't know what he said to her, but she was crying when I got there. Then he said some very unpleasant things to me, and I had to ask him to leave."

"Why didn't you tell me?" he demanded in outrage.

"I . . ." Emma didn't want to admit her real reasons. "I didn't have much of a opportunity, and then Virginia and I were writing the invitations and I saw his name. I told her what happened, and she said we would simply forget to invite him. I would have told you, too, eventually, but I didn't think he would be here today so—"

"All right, all right," Grayson cut her off impatiently. "I can see I'm going to have to call on him and settle this once and for all."

Instinctively, Emma reached out, laying a hand on his arm as if she could stop him from doing anything foolish.

He glanced down at her hand in surprise, then looked up and smiled, all trace of his previous anger gone. "Are you worried about me, Mrs. Sinclair?" he asked.

Of course she was, but before she had time to reply, one of her former suitors approached to beg her for a dance. The rest were not far behind, and Emma found herself swept away again.

The guests seemed to have forgotten the momentary unpleasantness of Phelps' scene, but Emma could not forget. Her gaiety was forced, which was probably why she felt so exhausted a few hours later when her new husband appeared to claim her for another dance.

She went gratefully into his arms.

"You look tired," he said, studying her face.

"It's been a long day," she reminded him.

He smiled. "Maybe you should go to bed."

"I can't leave the party," she said, wondering why he would even suggest such a thing.

"No one will think it odd that the bride and groom retired early," he told her provocatively, pulling her closer. His heated gaze drifted over her bare shoulders and lower, to where her gown clung to her breasts, and she felt the glance like a caress.

"Oh." The heat washed over her, and she knew it wasn't from embarrassment.

"We can't leave together, though," he warned her. "That would attract too much attention. Why don't you sneak away first, and then I'll follow in a few minutes?"

"All right," she said. This was her wedding night, she

thought, the night she would spend in Grayson's arms, the night she had been anticipating for so long. Desire quivered within her, warm and compelling, and for the first time she began to think perhaps she hadn't made such a bad bargain after all. She had a child and a home, and she had Grayson's passion. He must feel something for her to want her as he obviously still did. Many women had been happy with far less.

If only Emma could be one of them.

When the dance ended, Emma saw that Grayson had brought them near the door. From the corner of her eye, she caught sight of several men bearing down on them, eager to claim her for the next dance.

She smiled up at Grayson. "I think I'll go check on Alice," she said loudly enough for them to hear.

"Hurry back," Grayson said, but he winked so she knew he didn't mean it.

Turning, she pretended to just notice her would-be partners. She cast them a friendly smile and a small wave, then headed for the door and went down the stairs before anyone could stop her.

A few guests mingled in the second floor hallway, engaged in quiet conversations that could not be conducted over the music upstairs. Emma swept by them with a polite smile and went directly to Alice's bedroom door. Thomas sat beside it. He rose as she approached.

"No sign of him, Missy," he reported softly.

"Is Miss Alice all right?"

"Ain't heard nary a peep out of her," he said.

"Thank you, Thomas," she said and opened the door as quietly as she could.

The room was dark, but Mammy rose from her rocker instantly the moment the door opened.

"It's me," Emma told her in a whisper. She tiptoed over to Alice's bed and was relieved to find the child sleeping soundly. After tenderly adjusting the covers, she tiptoed away again, going to where Mammy still stood beside her rocking chair.

"Thomas said he hasn't seen any sign of Mr. Phelps," Emma reported.

"Miss Alice been sleepin' real quiet. I stay right here, just in case, though."

"Thank you, Mammy. If you need me, I'll be in my room . . . uh . . . from now on," Emma added, feeling a little embarrassed even though she knew she had no reason to be.

Mammy nodded, and although it was too dark to make out her expression, Emma sensed her knowing grin.

But when Emma started for the door, she remembered the men standing in the hallway. They would see her going into her room, and they would know . . .

"You can go out on the gallery," Mammy whispered, and Emma recalled that Alice's bedroom opened onto the front gallery, too.

"Thanks," Emma whispered back and hurried to the French doors that were closed, even though the room was uncomfortably warm.

She opened them soundlessly and stepped outside, into a frigid miasma. The sudden cold took her breath, and she lifted her arms instinctively against the fog that enveloped her. But no sooner did she react than the fog and the cold evaporated, leaving her alone or so she thought. She almost screamed when a dark shape suddenly materialized from the shadows.

"Who that?" a voice challenged harshly, and Emma gasped with relief.

"It's me," Emma said, laying a hand over her racing heart. "What are you doing, Chloe?"

"Miss Emma, what for you sneaking around out here?" Chloe demanded, ignoring Emma's question.

"I'm not sneaking at all. I'm merely being quiet so I don't wake Alice, and I'm trying to get to my room without being seen. I certainly didn't expect to find my maid lurking in the darkness ready to scare the life out of me! Why are you out here?"

Chloe hesitated a moment before replying. "I's watchin' for

Massa DeWitt." The tone of her voice sent another chill over Emma.

"Surely you don't expect to find him out here," Emma said.

"I's here just in case," Chloe maintained stubbornly, and she started putting something into the pocket of her dress. Something long and thin and dangerous looking.

"What have you got there?" Emma asked in alarm.

"Nothin'," Chloe insisted, turning away as if to hide what she had from Emma.

But Emma had glimpsed the object anyway. "Is that a *knife?*" she asked, horrified. "Chloe, why do you have a knife?"

Chloe lifted her chin defiantly. "I told you, I's waitin' for Massa DeWitt. He not gonna get to Miss Alice again."

"Chloe!" Emma cried, then remembered how close they still stood to Alice's door. "Come with me," she said, grabbing her maid by her wrist and fairly dragging her down the gallery to where the doors to her own room stood open.

When they were inside, she dropped Chloe's wrist and went to the nightstand where she found the matches. She struck one, wrinkling her nose at the acrid stench of sulfur, and touched the flame to the candle wick. When she had shaken out the match, she turned to face Chloe.

"I know you hate Mr. Phelps," she began, trying to be reasonable even though her heart was thundering in her chest, "And I'm sure you have good reason, but you can't . . ." She gestured helplessly, searching for the proper words. "You can't *stab* him, for heaven's sake!"

"I will if he come after Miss Alice, again!" Chloe insisted, her chin set stubbornly.

"This is crazy!" Emma exclaimed in exasperation, wondering if she could have misjudged this girl. Could she really *be* crazy? And if she were, was she a danger to others besides Mr. Phelps?

"You don't know him, Miss Emma. You don't know nothin' 'bout that devil. If you do, you want to kill him, too!"

"Then tell me," Emma challenged, crossing her arms expectantly.

She watched Chloe's expression flicker and change as she fought some silent, inward battle with herself. Finally, her shoulders sagged, as if she'd lost that battle, but her dark eyes blazed with some inner fire when she finally said, "He like little girls."

This was hardly startling news. "Which explains why he's so desperate for Alice to like him in return."

"No, ma'am, he don't like little girls the usual way. He like them for sex."

The words were like a foreign language that Emma didn't speak, and she couldn't even comprehend their meaning. "What are you talking about?"

"Most men, they like womens. They think little girls is cute and all, but they don't want a girl 'til she's growed. You know what I mean?"

"Of course." Emma could vividly recall the frustration of being too young and immature for boys to notice her.

"Well, Massa DeWitt, he different. He don't like womens at all. He only like little girls. His wife, the mistress, she only fourteen when he marry her. A skinny little thing, just like Miss Lilly, so I reckon he could pretend she even younger than she was. But even still, he don't care much for her. He like to take his pleasure with little girls from the quarters."

Emma still could not comprehend. "Chloe, this is impossible! Men don't—"

"Massa DeWitt do," Chloe insisted.

"How do you know?" she demanded skeptically.

" 'Cause he do it to me."

Emma could only gape.

"I was real happy when Massa come down to the quarters and tell me I was gonna go live in the big house," Chloe recalled bitterly, her dark eyes fixed on something Emma could not see, some terrible scene from the distant past. "I wanted to go. I knowed I'd get pretty clothes and good food and I wouldn't have to work in the fields, not ever. My mama, she cried and cried. I reckon she knowed what he wanted with me, but there was nothin' she could do. There wasn't nothin' *anybody* could do."

"What about his wife?" Emma demanded, desperate to hear that Chloe was wrong. That such evil couldn't really exist.

"By then . . . Well, after she had Miss Lilly, he didn't never hardly even look at her again. She must've knowed what he was, but she was just a girl herself, and she belonged to him just like the rest of us. Wasn't nothin' she could do, so she took to drink. Didn't hardly ever come outa her room, which was fine with Massa DeWitt, 'cause he didn't ever wanna see her. I'd hear them fightin' sometimes, her screamin' and screamin' at him 'til he slapped her. Then she'd cry and cry until she'd drunk enough to put her to sleep. And then . . . Well, they say she hanged herself. I was too little to know for sure what happened. Anyhow, she was dead, which meant there wasn't even anybody to scream at him anymore. Not that he ever cared. By the time she died, he'd been comin' into Miss Lilly's room for years."

"Lilly's room?" Emma echoed incredulously.

"Yes'm, you recollect I told you me 'n' her, we slept together, like Rose and Alice does, her in the big bed, me in the trundle."

"And he . . . he . . ." Emma searched vainly for the words. She had no idea what a man like that might do to a child. ". . . to you, right there in his own daughter's room? In front of her?" Emma couldn't begin to imagine the horror of it.

" 'Course," Chloe said simply, as if that were only to be expected. " 'Cause he do it to her, too."

Emma stared at her, too horrified to even speak for a long moment. "To his very own child?" she finally gasped.

"Miss Lilly, she his favorite 'cause she *is* his very own chile."

Emma felt the blood rushing from her head, and she staggered. Chloe caught her and helped her over to the chaise.

Emma sat for a moment, trying to catch her breath while the room stopped spinning. When she could, she looked up at Chloe who hovered protectively, seemingly more concerned over Emma's reaction than the awful story she was telling.

"You need the salts?" Chloe asked.

"No," Emma said, not wanting to waste time with smelling salts. She had too much to think about right now. This couldn't be true, not any of it. Such things simply didn't happen, not in Emma's world. "When you said he . . . he used little girls for . . . for sex," Emma could hardly force herself to say the word, ". . . you didn't mean . . . he couldn't have . . . not . . ."

"You want to know what he done to us?" Chloe asked.

Emma couldn't believe how calm the girl was. How could she even think about such things without screaming hysterically? And Emma *didn't* want to know, of course. She didn't want to hear Chloe speak the unspeakable, but maybe, just maybe, this wasn't as bad as she thought. Maybe . . . Reluctantly, she nodded.

"He done everything," Chloe said, her voice flat, her expression closed protectively around the enormous pain Emma knew she must carry inside, the pain Emma now felt twisting inside of her, too. "Not at first, though. At first we was too little for what he really wanted. At first he just touched us and made us touch him."

She went on, telling her everything and still using that strange, emotionless voice that sounded as if she were discussing something totally ordinary when, in fact, she was describing the worst horror Emma could imagine.

"When I got bigger," she continued dry-eyed as the tears poured down Emma's face, "and started growing breasts, he didn't want me no more. Miss Lilly, though, she was like her mama, real little, and she never did grow much that way, and like I said, she was his favorite, so he just kept coming to her. That was almost worse than when he used to do it to me, too." Chloe was again staring off into the terrible past that Emma couldn't see, her lovely face twisted hideously with pain. "Just laying there and listening, so glad it wasn't me and so sorry for her I just wanted to bust inside."

With a cry of anguish, Emma reached up and clasped Chloe's hands in hers, wanting to do something, *anything,* to help her.

Chloe blinked and looked down in surprise at where Emma's hands held hers. "That was why," she said, still eerily calm, "Miss Lilly wanted to get married so bad. She wanted to get away from him, and she did. But then she had a little girl of her own, and he come sniffin' around again.'

"No!" Emma cried in renewed horror as she finally and completely understood just exactly how depraved DeWitt Phelps really was.

"Miss Lilly, she keep him away from Miss Alice, but then she . . . she die, and there ain't nobody to protect Miss Alice no more 'cept me. But now you here, Miss Emma, and you keep her safe, won't you?"

"Yes, oh, yes!" Emma assured her, squeezing her hands tightly. "Oh, Chloe, I had no idea! I never dreamed . . . But why didn't you tell someone? Virginia or Grayson or—"

"You think they gonna believe me over Massa DeWitt? Nobody believe a slave over a white man. Even if he . . . even if he done *murder* an' a slave the only one seen it, he go free, 'cause a darkie ain't allowed to testify against a white man." Chloe's face was terrible in the flickering candlelight. "So he say I lyin' 'bout him, and they won't wanna believe so they won't."

She was right, of course, as Emma had learned only too well from her few short weeks in the South. How awful for Chloe, how awful for both her and Lilly to have endured such a nightmare and then to fear for the child they both loved.

"Now you know why I have this knife," Chloe said. "If I ever see him touch Miss Alice, I kill him."

"He'll never come near her," Emma swore. "He'll never even set foot in this house again, I promise!"

"How you gonna keep him out?" Chloe asked with a frown.

"I'll . . ." Emma hesitated when she realized she wasn't really sure. Then she knew what she must do. "I'll tell Grayson what you told me. He'll believe *me.*"

Chloe stiffened. "No, he won't."

"What? Of course he will!"

"He a good man, Missy," Chloe warned. "Good mens, they don't think anybody as bad as Massa DeWitt. He think I made it all up just 'cause I don't like my old Massa."

"No, he won't," Emma insisted. "I'll *make* him believe it."

Chloe nodded stiffly, plainly unconvinced. "Sure," she said, not sure at all. "Now you best wash your face and get back to the party. Your company be wonderin' where you got to."

"Oh, dear," she said, suddenly remembering why she had come downstairs in the first place. "I'm not . . . not going back. I . . . was going to . . . retire."

Chloe nodded knowingly. "Then you better wash your face for sure. Can't have Massa Gray thinkin' you was crying on your weddin' night. Better hurry, too. He be along now directly. I expect he feelin' kinda anxious."

Emma was feeling anxious, too, but not because she was eager to welcome her new husband. Whatever stirrings of desire she had felt earlier had been thoroughly extinguished by Chloe's tale of horror. And she couldn't possibly keep such knowledge to herself, not when Alice was in danger. She would have to tell Grayson, and she would make him believe her whether he wanted to or not.

As Chloe helped her undress and wash and slip into her nightdress, she tried to think of what she would say, of what she *could* say, to him. Dear heaven, she hadn't even imagined such things really happened. She certainly had no idea how to put the horror into words she could speak to a husband she hardly knew.

"Better not say nothin' to him 'bout Massa DeWitt tonight," Chloe advised as she brushed Emma's hair out. "He be thinkin' 'bout . . . other things, and you just make him mad if you ain't thinkin' 'bout the *same* things."

But how could she? Emma wondered. How could she lie with her husband when everything he was going to do would remind her of the terrible story Chloe had told her? But she also knew Chloe was right. She would be a fool to broach this subject to Grayson tonight of all nights. He would think . . . Well, he might think she had made it up just to distract him from making love to her. Her marriage was going to be difficult enough without ruining the one thing between them that promised to bring them together.

No, she would have to save her ugly secret for later, when Grayson's mind wasn't on taking her to bed. The decision relieved her somewhat although she was still far from calm a moment later when someone rapped sharply on the door.

"Emma?"

Oh, dear, it was Grayson, knocking on the connecting door. "We forgot to unbolt it!" she whispered to Chloe, completely mortified. Would he think she'd done it on purpose? That she didn't want him to come in?

But Chloe didn't seem the least bit concerned. She just shrugged and hurried over and drew the two bolts. "I's sorry, Massa Gray," she said when she opened the door. "I plum forgot 'bout them bolts. Don't reckon we ever gonna need 'em again, now," she added with a grin.

"I hope not," he replied grinning back as he stepped into the room.

Emma didn't know what she had expected. Certainly, she hadn't expected him to be wearing only a thin silk robe. The front gaped open to reveal his naked chest, which meant he wore no nightshirt. Maybe, she found herself hoping, he had on some underdrawers, at least. Swallowing against a suddenly dry throat, she rose from her stool and, too late, realized she wore only her thin nightdress.

"I . . . Chloe hasn't braided my hair yet," she managed.

He took her in from head to toe with a long, leisurely, and

thoroughly approving glance. "Leave it loose tonight," he said, his voice husky, and Emma's throat went dry again.

"You be needin' anything else, Miss Emma?" Chloe asked.

"No, I . . . Thank you." Emma was acutely aware of her nakedness beneath the gown, and acutely aware that Grayson was acutely aware of it, too, if she could judge by the way he was looking at her.

"I wait 'til you ring for me in the mornin'," Chloe said with a wink, and then she was gone, slipping silently out the door into the hallway, leaving them alone.

Grayson smiled at her, the kind of smile women pray to see from the men they love, and Emma's heart lurched painfully in her chest. How she had longed to see such a sign from him. Why did it have to come *now*?

Gray couldn't seem to get enough of looking at Emma. If her figure was wonderful all trussed up in her corset, it was magnificent all loose and free beneath her nightdress. The skin of her throat and arms was like alabaster satin in the glow of the candlelight, and he could almost feel its softness beneath his hands. Drawn, he took a step toward her and was appalled to see her stiffen in reaction.

Dear God, was she afraid of him? She'd seemed so happy today, almost as if she were glad they had married, and certainly she already knew she had nothing to fear from him sexually. So what could have caused her to cower from him?

"Is something wrong?" he asked as gently as he could.

"What?" she asked, startled, then said quickly, "Oh, no, nothing's wrong." But she laid her hand nervously on her bosom.

"If you need more time—"

"No, really," she assured him, forcing a smile that worried him even more.

He'd been so sure that he'd made his peace with her, and she'd seemed different the past few days, as if she were at least resigned to their marriage, perhaps even anticipating it.

She hadn't unlocked the door, of course, not until tonight, but he hadn't expected miracles. But something was still wrong.

"I was very proud of you today," he tried, figuring a little flattery couldn't hurt, especially when it was true.

"You were?" She sounded surprised.

"Of course. Not only are you the most beautiful woman in the county, you are the most charming, too. I am the envy of every man I know." He smiled as his blood quickened. "If they knew how passionate you are, I would have needed armed guards to protect me today."

Her color rose deliciously. "I'm not really," she said, then seeing his surprise added, "I mean, I never was before."

Dear God, was she *trying* to drive him over the edge? With a groan he closed the short distance between them and took her in his arms. He'd meant to be gentle, to woo her slowly and patiently, but he would be lucky now to control himself until he got her in the bed.

Although he'd thought of little else these past weeks, he'd forgotten just how wonderful she felt, how soft and pliant and lusciously female. He'd forgotten how she filled his arms and how hot her mouth was and how sweet she tasted. But he'd never forget again because now she was his wife, and he could remind himself every night if he wished. He only hoped every night would be enough.

She wrapped her satiny arms around his neck and opened her mouth to him, offering herself so freely that he knew he must have been mistaken when he'd thought her reluctant. He ran his hands over her, relearning every curve and swell of her body which was so wonderfully different from his own. Breast and hip and buttocks, he filled his hands with her until that wasn't enough, until the heat of his own desire drove him beyond endurance.

She made a small sound of surprise when he lifted her into his arms, but she did not protest because she was as lost as he now. She buried her face in the crook of his neck, her breath hot against him as she clung tightly, her hair a silken fall over his shoulder. He carried her to the bed, somehow managing not to stumble even though his body throbbed with desire, and laid her down upon the coverlet.

Her hair spilled around her like a black wave, and her eyes were the color of a stormy sky as she gazed up at him in the flickering candlelight. He wanted to throw himself on her and bury himself in her softness, but he also wanted her to be equally as desperate when he finally joined his body to hers.

Using every ounce of self-restraint he possessed, he stepped back and slowly, carefully, untied his robe and shrugged it off. Her eyes widened with surprise when she saw he was naked and blatantly aroused, and she quickly looked away, embarrassed. He found her modesty exciting even as he set out to conquer it completely.

He climbed up on the bed to kneel beside her. "I've been dreaming about this night ever since the first time we were together, Emma," he told her, savoring her surprise. "I've been planning exactly what I'd do and exactly what *you'd* do."

"Me?" She looked positively mortified.

He smiled. "Don't worry. Mostly what I expect you to do is sigh with pleasure."

He thought she was blushing furiously, although he couldn't be sure because of the uncertain light. He loved it that she was so shy, so maidenly, because he knew the wanton inside of her, and he knew how to release that wanton. And this time he would release it carefully, so they could enjoy every minute. He reached for the hem of her nightdress and began to draw it up.

"The light!" she almost yelped, pointing to the candle on the bedside table.

"No, this time I want to see you," he said. "I want to see *all* of you."

As if unveiling a masterpiece, Gray took his time, drinking in the sight of her, learning her, memorizing every detail of her body, knowledge that would belong to him alone. Her delicate feet, her well-turned ankles, her shapely calves and dimpled knees. Skin white as snow and soft as satin. He paused to kiss each knee, smiling when he saw how tightly they were pressed together.

Then he revealed the white columns of her thighs, the last guardians of her womanhood, and formidable they seemed until Gray bent and traced the seam between them with his tongue, up and up and up until he reached the dark thatch of curls. Beneath them he found the bud of her desire, and he caressed it lovingly, coaxing from her a small cry.

"Yes," he said, lifting his gaze to meet hers, "that's exactly what I'd planned for you to do."

"Grayson, please," she begged, clutching handfuls of the coverlet in her distress.

"I aim to please," he replied, nudging for her to lift her hips so he could pull the gown up farther. Instinctively, she obeyed, although he supposed she might not have if she'd been thinking clearly. Or if she'd known exactly what he'd planned.

He revealed the small mound of her belly and the generous curve of her hips, then the tiny indentation of her navel. Once again he bent to her, pressing kisses across the satin of her belly, smiling when the silken flesh quivered beneath his lips. She gasped again when he dipped his tongue into her navel, and he whispered, "Oh, yes."

Then he raised his head, and with one swift motion, swung himself over her so that he was straddling her thighs. She must have thought he was going to take her then because she closed her eyes and bit her lip, but he had no intention of ending this so soon. Oh, no, not yet.

He nudged her with the tip of his shaft, finding the place he had caressed with his tongue a moment ago and settling there. Her eyes flew open but then slammed shut instantly when he began to run his hands up her body, pushing aside her nightdress as he went, over her waist and midriff and up to cup the fullness of her breasts.

But he allowed himself only a momentary indulgence before completing the task he had set for himself and lifting her nightdress up and over her head. She made a cry of protest, but she was too late, and he tossed her gown aside. Her lovely eyes wide with distress, she made a frantic effort to cover herself with her hands, but he caught her wrists and drew her hands away so he could see her.

God, she was beautiful, her lush body the essence of femininity. She could pose for a sculpture of the goddess of love except that Gray had no intention of sharing her beauty with anyone. She was his and his alone to worship and enjoy. She'd never been passionate with anyone but him, she'd said, and the knowledge thrilled him. Fate might have cheated him out of love, but at least he would have this, *they* would have this.

He bent to kiss her, lowering himself slowly until her breasts pressed against his chest and his belly rested against hers. He drank deeply of her mouth, savoring her sweetness while he tortured himself with the feel of her flesh against his. His senses were swamped with so much to see and feel and touch and savor, and he used his mouth and his hands to savor it all.

Kissing and licking and suckling, stroking and caressing, he indulged himself in an orgy of sensation, seeking out every sensitive spot on her body to tease and torment until she was gasping with a need as great as his.

When she opened herself to him, she was desperate, tugging at him with hands and legs, wrapping herself around him in a silent plea. By then he was nearly crazed with his own desire, but he took her slowly, knowing he dared not use haste for fear of losing control. He sank into her welcoming depths with a groan. Her silky heat closed tightly around him, nearly forcing him over the edge, but somehow he resisted the irresistible lure and held himself back, gasping for breath as he held himself perfectly still for the long moment until he somehow managed to ease himself back to sanity.

He kissed her then, ready to lose himself completely in the heat of her mouth and the heat of her body. As he kissed her, he began to move, slowly at first, no more than a hint of the feverish thrusting his body screamed for. But when she responded, answering his teasing thrusts with restless thrashings of her own, he could no longer hold back. He met her passionate desperation, plunging into her again and again until their bodies were slick and their breath labored and their desire was a swirling maelstrom pulling them deeper and deeper, sucking them in. Gray resisted as long as he could, straining against the beckoning oblivion, but finally he felt Emma's spasms of release rippling around him and he hurtled himself into the tide. The shudders shook him to his very soul as he spilled his seed into her, sealing once and for all the union they had made today.

His climax went on and on, as if it would never end, as if she had locked him forever into this moment of ecstasy. But of course it did end at last, the spasms eventually dying out until he lay spent and exhausted, his head resting on the sweet cushion of her breast. He never wanted to move, never wanted this moment to end, never wanted them to be farther apart than this. Then Emma tried to draw a breath, and he realized he was too heavy to stay where he was.

He shifted his weight, sliding off of her, but he took her in his arms, still unwilling to be parted from her. As he held her, the breeze from the open doors cooled their sweat-slick bodies. Gray knew that in a minute they would have to move, would have to pull down the covers and Emma would probably want to find her nightdress. But he wanted this to last as long as possible, this one sweet moment of perfect harmony when he could pretend he was happy.

He must have fallen asleep, because when he opened his eyes again, the room was dark. At first he didn't know where he was, but then he remembered this was his wedding night, and he was in Emma's bed. A smile of contentment curled his lips. Where was she? he wondered, trying to reach for her.

But his arms were under the covers someone had spread over him, and before he could free them he realized what had awakened him. It was a sound, a sound he'd never wanted to hear again, not as long as he lived. It was the sound of the woman lying beside him. She was weeping as if her heart would break.

Twelve

When Emma awoke in the light of day, she wanted to cry although she didn't, at first, know why. Then she remembered. She remembered what Chloe had told her the night before, the tale of the horror she and Lilly and how many other children had endured. And she remembered Grayson, who had come to her last night and made love to her. She'd been so distracted, she'd just wanted him to hurry up and get it over with. But he'd so been gentle and passionate, she had responded in spite of herself, in spite of the fact that every time she closed her eyes, she imagined DeWitt Phelps slaking his lust on an innocent child.

At least she'd been able to give Grayson a satisfactory wedding night, and she'd managed not to cry until later, when he was asleep and once more the guilt had overwhelmed her. Guilt for being so blessed when poor Lilly had been so miserable. But Grayson knew none of that, and he'd thoroughly enjoyed himself. She wanted him to be in a good mood and happy with her since she had such unpleasant things to discuss with him today.

And speaking of Grayson, she suddenly realized he was probably right there beside her in the bed. The thought made her body tingle with the anticipation of his touch, but the prospect of facing him now, when she was disheveled from sleep and still so upset from Chloe's story, nearly filled her with panic. *Was* he there? She listened, holding her own breath as she strained to hear his. Instead she heard nothing.

She lay facing the wall and didn't want to risk waking him by turning over, so she started probing with one foot, inching it back slowly, searching. At any moment, she expected to encounter warm flesh and braced herself for the contact. Instead she encountered nothing but empty bed. When she had extended her leg as far as it would go without finding anything, she rolled over, slowly and carefully, ever so carefully. To her relief—and disappointment—she discovered she was alone.

Dear heaven, she thought, noticing the drapes were drawn against the bright sunlight, how late had she slept? Too late, she knew at once, considering she was now mistress of the plantation. She had guests to see to and a hundred responsibilities. She scrambled up and reached for the bell pull to summon Chloe. Then she hurried to the doors and pulled back the drapes to reveal a sun high in the sky.

With a groan she started to turn away, ready to rush back and begin to wash even before Chloe could bring her hot water, but something caught her eye. It lay on the gallery just across the threshold of the still-opened French doors. At first Emma thought it was one of Alice's dolls, but when she picked it up, she realized it wasn't a doll at all, or at least not a kind of doll she'd ever seen before. It was a human figure, though, about six inches tall and fashioned crudely out of pieces of straw tied into shape with long blades of grass. A few strands of dark hair were stuck to the head, probably to indicate the figure was intended to be a female. But what Emma found most disturbing was the way someone had burned a neat round hole right where the figure's stomach should have been.

She was still puzzling over it when Chloe came into the room carrying a bucket of hot water.

" 'Morning, Miss Emma," she said, her expression as cheerful and carefree as if she'd never even heard of DeWitt Phelps. "You 'bout sleep the whole day away! Everybody downstairs is sayin' Massa Gray must've wore you out, but I say . . . What you got there?"

Emma shrugged. "I don't know. I found it outside the doors on the gallery just now."

Chloe set her bucket down and came over, taking the figure from Emma. Her eyes widened with unmistakable alarm.

"What is it?" Emma asked, but Chloe didn't seem to hear. She hurried outside and looked frantically up and down the gallery, as if she expected to see the person who had left the figure still lurking about. "What are you looking for?"

Chloe stepped back inside. "To see if there's one for Massa Gray or Miss Alice."

"Is there?"

Chloe shook her head.

"Is it another one of those charms from the conjure woman?" Emma asked, far more disturbed by Chloe's reaction than she had been by the thing itself.

"Yes'm, I reckon it is," Chloe admitted reluctantly.

"And I suppose it's another curse on me," Emma said with a sigh. Just what she needed, something else to worry about. She would have to make light of this to calm Chloe. "Let me guess, I should expect a bad case of dyspepsia."

Chloe did not reply. She was staring at the figure she still held.

"Chloe?" Emma prompted, beginning to feel some of the girl's alarm.

"I don't know for sure," Chloe began, still studying the figure, "but it bein' you and Massa Gray's weddin' night, I think it might be . . ."

"What?" Emma prompted when Chloe hesitated.

"It might be a curse so's you don't have any babies," the girl admitted reluctantly.

Emma felt the pain as if someone really *had* burned a hole in her middle. How horrible! Who could have done such an awful thing? And who could hate her so much? She thought instantly of DeWitt Phelps, but just as instantly dismissed him. He hardly seemed the type to use slave magic to achieve his purposes. But what other enemies did she have?

"I ain't sure, now," Chloe said quickly, easily reading Emma's reaction. "I ain't never seen one like this before. Maybe I's wrong."

But Emma knew she wasn't wrong. It was too logical. The person who had failed in the effort to get rid of her had decided to be satisfied with hurting her instead. Emma couldn't let Chloe know how much they had succeeded. She forced a smile. "Well, the joke is on them, in any case, since I'm already barren."

"Oh, Miss Emma!" Chloe cried.

"It's all right, really," Emma lied. "I've known for a long time now, so something like that . . ." She dismissed the charm with a wave of her hand, ". . . can't hurt me."

"You don't believe in magic anyhow," Chloe reminded her eagerly.

"That's right, I don't," Emma said. If she did, she might be tempted to find the conjure woman and seek a spell of her own to reverse nature.

Chloe frowned. "You gonna tell Massa Gray 'bout this?"

Emma considered, wondering what purpose it would serve. He would be angry, but unless he could find out who the conjure woman was, he wouldn't be able to do anything about it. No, Emma decided, the best course would be to ignore it. She didn't want whoever was responsible to think she even cared.

"No, I'm not. He's got enough on his mind. Just throw that thing in the fire. I don't ever want to see it again."

"Yes'm," Chloe said, stuffing the figure into her skirt pocket. "Now we better get you dressed 'fore folks start thinkin' you just plain lazy."

"Oh, dear, how late is it?" Emma asked, realizing she had some real things to be concerned about.

"It's gone noon, but don't worry," Chloe assured her when she groaned in dismay. "Folks don't expect a lady to be up and around first thing the day after her weddin'."

"But the guests!" Emma protested.

"They's mostly gone now. The preacher had church early, so's they could get on home. Miss Virginia, she see to everybody."

"And Grayson?" Emma wished she didn't have to know.

"He missed church, too, but that's 'bout what everybody expected. They be wonderin' what's wrong if'n the two of you come down at dawn, now won't they?" Chloe said reasonably.

Emma supposed she was right. Most newly married couples went on a honeymoon so they didn't have to worry about how late they slept or what people thought. Emma and Grayson hadn't even considered a honeymoon. Things were awkward enough between them with the distractions of everyday life. Emma couldn't imagine being completely alone with him for days at a time. Apparently, Grayson couldn't either since he hadn't suggested it.

"Come on an' wash 'fore your water gets cold," Chloe urged, and Emma obeyed. This time Chloe tactfully refrained from mentioning the passion marks Grayson had left on her body, although she did smile her approval.

"Everything go all right last night?" she asked finally as she helped Emma into her clothes—a light summer frock. Her black gowns would be packed away forever now.

"Yes," Emma said, thinking how much better their wedding night could have been if she hadn't been so upset. Grayson was a magnificent lover. The mere memory of his hands and lips on her body sent a thrill racing over her.

"You didn't say anything to him about . . . you know?" Chloe prodded when Emma offered no details.

"No," Emma assured her quickly. "I decided you were right. He has to know, though, so he doesn't put Alice in danger."

"I told you, he won't believe you," Chloe warned. "Besides, you's the one lookin' after Miss Alice now. Best if you just keep it to yourself."

But Emma didn't want to keep it to herself. She *needed* to share this horrible secret. "I'll do what I think best," she said sternly, reminding Chloe she was the mistress here.

Chloe pressed her lips together, as if she were biting back what she really wanted to say, and went about the rest of her duties in silence. When Emma was dressed, and Chloe had laboriously brushed all the tangles from her long hair and pinned it neatly up, she went back downstairs and fetched Emma a tray since she had missed both breakfast and dinner.

When Emma thought of facing Grayson in the light of day now that she was his wife and he was her husband—a much more intimate relationship than simply being lovers as they had been before—she had little appetite for the food Chloe had brought. She choked down as much of it as she could manage and, ignoring Chloe's disapproving frown, left the rest. After checking her appearance once more in the mirror and satisfying herself that she looked well, if not exactly like a glowing new bride, she left her room and made her way downstairs.

The house was quiet, and she found the rest of her new family gathered in the back parlor. Grayson sat in an armchair with Alice in his lap as he read to her, and the sight of them together made her heart leap in her chest. The child she loved and the man she . . . loved. Yes, she could no longer pretend otherwise. As foolish as she was to give her heart to a man who so obviously didn't love her in return, she could not seem to help herself.

Then they both looked up at her, and Emma's heart stopped completely.

Alice's joy' was unmistakable. "Aunt Emma! I mean, Mama!" she cried, correcting herself with only the slightest hint of embarrassment. "We thought you'd never wake up!"

Grayson was more difficult to read. He smiled, but his expression was reserved, almost uncertain. "Good morning," he said, setting Alice down and rising to his feet.

"It's afternoon, isn't it?" Emma said, managing to return his smile and wishing that her heart wasn't beating quite so quickly at the mere sight of him.

"I wasn't going to mention that," he told her, coming to

take her hands in his. He squeezed them tightly, looking as if he wanted to kiss her. For one heart-stopping moment she thought he would, *prayed* that he would, but he just looked at her, searching her face for something he obviously didn't find.

"That's very gentlemanly of you," she told him, then looked down to where Alice was tugging at her skirt.

"I told Papa to wake you up, but he wouldn't!" she reported indignantly. "All our company is gone."

Emma felt her cheeks burning as she lifted her gaze to Grayson's again. "You *should* have woken me," she told him.

"I thought you probably needed your rest," he said. His eyes were as dark as midnight, and they held a question she could not answer.

"Of course she needed her rest," Virginia said from where she still sat on the sofa. "You were probably exhausted. I know I was, and you worked twice as hard as I did getting everything ready."

At least Virginia didn't mention the *other* reason why Emma might have been exhausted. She was fairly certain their guests had been joking about it all morning though. She supposed she should be glad to have missed them.

"Papa was reading me Bible stories," Alice informed Emma. Reading anything else on Sunday would have been unseemly, of course, as would doing anything remotely like work. Even Virginia, whose hands were seldom idle, sat without her usual needlework or knitting.

"I'd like to hear your Papa reading Bible stories," Emma told her, then glanced at Grayson again. Her fingers felt so right clasped in his.

His eyes still held the question that she couldn't quite fathom, but he gave her hands one last squeeze and released them, much to her relief. She found it so hard to think straight when he was touching her. She spent the rest of the afternoon trying to think straight as she sat with Virginia and listened to Grayson's beautiful voice. Had she ever thought his accent strange? Now she could hardly imagine a more beautiful sound. How she longed to hear it speaking words of love to her in the dark as he held her in his arms.

But that, she told herself sternly, was something for which she should not hold her breath. Besides, she had much more important matters to concern her. She had to tell Grayson about DeWitt Phelps and ensure, once and for all, that Alice was safe from him.

As they sat at supper that evening, she was wondering just how soon she would have a chance to speak with Grayson alone when he turned to her and said, "Emma, perhaps you'd like to go for a walk down by the river later."

"Can I go, too?" Alice asked eagerly. She'd been allowed to join the grown-ups for this very special meal, their first as a family.

As disappointed as she was, Emma would not have had the heart to refuse her, but Virginia said, "I think your Papa wants to be alone with Emma, dear."

"Why?" Alice asked, making Emma blush.

"Because married people like to be alone sometimes," Virginia explained, a twinkle in her eyes.

"Oh," Alice said wisely, "so they can *kiss!*"

Grayson coughed suspiciously behind his napkin, and Emma didn't dare even glance at him for fear of blushing even more furiously. How ridiculous to be so embarrassed with one's own husband, she thought. Would she ever feel comfortable with him?

Although she had never actually accepted Grayson's invitation, Emma fetched a bonnet and joined him on the veranda later, when the evening shadows were growing long and the heat of the day had finally lifted. She felt oddly giddy at the prospect of a simple walk, and equally apprehensive over the subject she would have to discuss on that walk.

"I'm ready," she told Grayson as she tied the bonnet strings beneath her chin.

Gray rose to his feet, feeling oddly excited at the prospect of a simple walk. Of course, with Emma, nothing was ever really simple, not even the lust that always threatened to consume him every time he set eyes on her. She looked particularly luscious this evening, even though she was modestly covered from neck to feet. But Gray didn't need to see Emma's flesh to remember what it was like, how soft it felt or how sweet it tasted. The memories were still fresh in his mind, as was the knowledge that she was now his to sample whenever he wished.

If only he wasn't haunted by the sound of her tears in the darkness. Why had she been crying last night after they'd made love? He was positive he hadn't hurt her, and she'd certainly responded to him. Not like Lilly who had merely endured him. In spite of the fact that Lilly had seduced him into marrying her, she had hated sex, but Emma was different. Emma didn't merely endure him. So why had she been weeping the way Lilly always wept afterwards?

He wasn't sure he really wanted to know, but he also knew he couldn't bear another marriage like the one he had had. This one *must* be different. Which meant he had to find out the reason for her tears. God, why couldn't life be simple?

He offered Emma his arm and was pleased to see the way she smiled up at him. A little tentatively, but with no trace of fear or reluctance. She seemed nervous, but Gray was a little nervous himself. They walked away from the house, down the road to the river, making small talk about what a lovely evening it was.

The breeze from the river swept flower petals across their path, reminding Gray of the way Alice had scattered petals before Emma as she came down the aisle. She'd looked so beautiful.

But he'd already told her that. He'd have to think of something else to say.

"Perhaps we should have planned a honeymoon," he ventured.

"Oh, no," she said too quickly, confirming his opinion that

the idea would have been a mistake. "I mean, I know you didn't want to leave the plantation again so soon."

She was right, of course, but . . ."Yes, but I was thinking, this is a rather . . . strange way to begin a marriage. We never courted or . . ." Gray stuttered to a halt. How in the hell was he supposed to broach such a sensitive subject? ". . . or really got to know each other." They did know each other *intimately,* but they didn't know each other well. There was, Gray was beginning to appreciate, a great deal of difference.

"I thought that's why you invited me on this walk," she said, and when he glanced down, he saw she was smiling and her eyes were twinkling with amusement. "So we could get to know each other better."

"Yes, well, it was," Gray said, beginning to feel as awkward as a schoolboy reciting poetry. "I thought we could . . . talk about . . . about things that . . . we need to talk about," he finished lamely.

When he glanced at Emma again, she wasn't smiling anymore. "Yes," she agreed, "we do need to talk."

Gray knew a moment of relief, but then he realized he didn't have the slightest idea how to begin.

"You seemed . . . unhappy last night," he tried.

"I was very upset," she agreed easily. "But not over anything *you* did," she added quickly, seeing his horrified expression.

"What were you upset about? Did someone say something to you? One of those fellows who thought he was going to marry you?" Gray demanded, thinking he would call the fellow out and take great pleasure in shooting him.

"No, nothing like that," she assured him, her lovely blue eyes clouded. "It was . . . something Chloe told me."

"Chloe?" Gray asked uneasily. He should have known better than to assign Lilly's maid to Emma. He should have known she would be trouble. He should have sold her away years ago, gotten rid of every last trace of his first wife. But it was too late now.

"Yes, she told me . . . oh, Grayson, I don't know how to say this, it's so awful." She turned her head away so that her hat brim shielded her face, but not before Gray saw the tears shimmering in her eyes.

Dear Lord, what could Chloe have said? Gray considered a myriad of possibilities, including blaming him for Lilly's death. If she had . . . But Gray somehow managed to hold onto his temper. "Perhaps you should just say it, no matter how horrible," he suggested grimly.

She nodded, or at least the brim of her hat bobbed. Then she turned back to him, her face set against the tears that still threatened. "She told me about . . . about Mr. Phelps."

This time Gray's relief was complete. This wasn't about him at all! "His behavior last night was abominable," Gray agreed quickly. "And I told you, I'm going to call on him and have it out with him. He can't go on frightening Alice—"

"There's more," Emma said, interrupting him. "Things you don't know. Terrible things." They'd stopped walking. Her face was pale, and she looked so distressed, Gray wanted to take her in his arms.

He settled for patting her hand where it rested on his arm. "I don't know what Chloe told you, but nothing is that bad," he assured her.

"This is," she assured him right back. "Chloe said he . . . that he . . . that he uses little girls for . . . for his pleasure."

"What?" Gray knew he must have misunderstood.

The color came to Emma's pale cheeks. "He uses little girls like . . . like a man uses his wife."

This was the most preposterous thing Gray had ever heard. *"Chloe* told you this?"

Emma nodded. "She said he takes the little girls from the quarters and . . . and . . ."

"Emma," he said, holding his temper with difficulty. He didn't want to upset Emma any further. "You must understand something about slaves. They never have anything good to say about their masters."

"But Chloe—"

"I know," he said, cutting her off. "Chloe hates DeWitt. Lilly hated him, too. He was a terrible father and a worse master. He should probably be shot, which is why Chloe says such terrible things about him. But you mustn't believe them."

"But she said—"

"I'm sure she said many things," Gray said firmly. "But you weren't raised with slavery, so you don't understand. Every slave complains about his former master and even his current one, no matter how humane and kind and generous that master might be. I daresay, my own slaves vilify me thoroughly when my back is turned, even though I have always done everything in my power to make their lives as pleasant as possible. They hate me simply because I *am* their master."

"But this is different!" Emma insisted.

"Yes, it is," Gray agreed. "If a good master is vilified, then an evil master suffers far worse. While I know DeWitt is cruel—his beatings are legendary—his slaves would never content themselves with simply telling the truth about him. They would invent tales about him that would curdle your blood to make him sound even worse than he was. You wouldn't believe the stories I've heard slaves tell, about beatings and chains and punishments no human would even imagine, much less inflict."

"*Someone* could imagine them," Emma pointed out sharply, "or you wouldn't have heard about them."

Gray wasn't accustomed to being challenged, but he bit back his annoyance. His purpose was to mend fences with Emma, not tear them down. "My point," he continued doggedly, "is that you cannot believe everything a slave tells you, particularly about a previous master."

"But this wasn't just a 'tale,' " she insisted stubbornly. Gray decided that was the trait he liked least about her, that and her penchant for argument. "Chloe *knows!* She was one of the little girls he . . . he abused."

"So she says," Gray pointed out reasonably. "And I suppose

she told you in great detail everything he did to her when she was a child."

"Yes," she replied, surprising him. "She told me *everything* he did to her. He *used* her like a . . . a . . ."

"Which *proves* it didn't happen," Gray said, growing impatient with this distasteful subject. "Men don't . . . Emma, do you know what you're saying? That a man would even want to . . . with a *child?* The very idea . . . It's unthinkable!"

"She said you wouldn't believe me," Emma said, frowning.

"Of course I won't! *No one* would believe such a thing, because such things simply don't happen!"

"She said you wouldn't believe me because you're a good man, and good men don't do things like that, but DeWitt Phelps is *not* a good man, Grayson. You said yourself he's cruel, that he beats his slaves unmercifully. Why, he even drove his own wife to suicide!"

"She was a drunk!" Grayson snapped, suddenly panicked at the thought of exploring the subject of drunken, suicidal wives. He forced himself to remain calm. "Emma, listen to me, I am your husband, and I know best about this. Chloe is only trying to win your sympathy—"

"My *sympathy?*" she cried. "Is that what you think? Well, you're completely wrong! She doesn't want my sympathy or anyone else's either! She's only trying to protect Alice!"

"Protect her from *what?*" Gray demanded in exasperation.

"From DeWitt Phelps!"

At first Gray couldn't make the connection, and when he did, rage swelled in him. "He's her *grandfather,* for God's sake! Even if he did use slave girls—which I don't believe for a moment—he couldn't possibly—"

"He was Lilly's *father,* but that didn't stop him from using *her!* Chloe said she was his *favorite!*"

"My God!" Gray exclaimed in horror, grabbing her by the shoulders and jerking her around to face him. "Do you know what you're saying?"

"I know *exactly* what I'm saying!" Her eyes were terrible

as she gazed up at him, frightened yet blazing with determination. "DeWitt Phelps is the devil incarnate!"

"And Chloe is a *lying little bitch!*" He fairly shouted into her face. He saw her shock, but he didn't allow himself regret. "Come on, I'll prove it to you," he said, releasing her shoulders and taking her arm. He jerked her forward, and she almost stumbled, but he caught and held her steady, never slackening his pace as he marched her back up the hill to the house, fury driving him with every pace.

He didn't allow himself so much as a glance at her for fear she would be crying and her tears would melt his anger. This was for Emma's own good, after all It was his duty to protect her from being taken in by every darkie on the place, and he could let nothing shake his resolve.

When they reached the veranda, he thrust her ahead of him through the front door, and she managed to wrench free of his grip. But he had her where he wanted her now, so he made no attempt to hold her again.

"*Chloe!*" he shouted. "Get down here!"

In a moment, Chloe appeared, leaning over the railing on the upstairs landing. Her eyes were so wide, he could see white all the way around her pupils, and seeing him, she hurried around and down the stairs, wringing her hands nervously as she came.

"Yes, Massa?" she asked, glancing fearfully at Emma, but he gave her no time to get any moral support.

"Miss Emma told me what you said about Mr. Phelps," he informed her furiously. He could have sworn her light brown face went one shade lighter, and she literally began to tremble. "You tell her it isn't true, that you made the whole thing up."

"What on earth?" Virginia said, coming out of the back parlor, but Gray silenced her with a gesture.

"*Tell* her, Chloe," he commanded, taking a threatening step toward her.

She cringed. "Yessir, whatever you say, Massa!" she said,

cowering before him. "It all a lie, Miss Emma, every word! I swear! I sorry, Massa Gray! I never meant no harm!"

"No harm!" Gray echoed incredulously. "Do you know how much you upset Miss Emma? I ought to sell you back to Mr. Phelps!"

"Oh, no, please, Massa!" Chloe cried, dropping to her knees in abject terror and clasping her hands before her in supplication. "Please don't sell me, please! I do anything! You can beat me and put me to work in the fields, anything at all, just please don't sell me to Massa DeWitt! Please, Massa, please!"

"Stop this!" Emma cried, startling Gray. "Stop it this instant! Nobody's going to sell you to anybody, Chloe, and nobody's going to beat you either. Get up from there this instant." She went to the girl, and tried to help her up, but Chloe was shaking so badly, she couldn't move.

"Stay out of this, Emma," Gray told her. "This is none of your concern."

"It most certainly *is* my concern!" she insisted, startling him again with her vehemence. "I'm the mistress of this plantation now, and Chloe is *my* maid, and *I* will be the one who says what happens to her!"

Gray opened his mouth to put her right back in her place, but when he saw the fury glittering fiercely in her eyes, he was so shocked, he forgot what he was going to say.

"Stop crying," Emma told the girl who was sobbing now, so terrified she probably didn't even realize Emma had saved her. "Get up. Come on now," she added gently, easing Chloe to her feet. "Everything is fine. Nobody's going to hurt you." Her words were soft for Chloe's ears, but the glance she gave Gray would have cut glass.

But Gray had no intention of harming the girl now that he'd gotten what he wanted. He had done his duty and taught Emma a lesson she wouldn't soon forget. "We won't speak of this again, Emma," he told her sternly.

He saw her shoulders stiffen, but she refused to meet his gaze. Instead she helped Chloe start back up the stairs. But

Gray didn't need to hear her surrender. He would allow her what was left of her pride. He could afford to be generous since he had won.

Emma had never seen anyone this frightened. Chloe was shaking so badly, she could hardly walk as Emma helped her up the stairs and into her bedroom. And Emma had never been so angry at anyone as she was at Grayson. How could she ever have thought him kind or gentle? How could she ever have thought she *loved* a man so cruel and heartless and unreasonable?

Chloe was still sobbing when Emma closed the bedroom door behind them, and she led the girl over to the chaise and sat her down. When Chloe realized where she was, she tried to get up, muttering, "Oh, no, Missy," but Emma planted her hands firmly on the girl's shoulders until she was sure Chloe would stay. Then she hurried over to the washstand where she wet a washcloth in the cold water in the pitcher and carried it back over to Chloe.

"Here, put this on your eyes. You're going to be all right now," Emma promised. "I won't let him do anything to you. You're going to stay right here with me, and no one's going to lay a hand on you."

Chloe looked up at her with reddened eyes. "I's sorry, Missy."

"For what?" Emma asked.

"He mad at you, too, now. I never mean to make no trouble for you."

"Of course you didn't!" Emma assured her.

"An' I's sorry I told you all that stuff 'bout Massa DeWitt. I know you think I lied, but—"

"Why would I think you lied?" Emma asked in surprise.

Chloe blinked at her in confusion. " 'Cause I just said I did."

Emma couldn't believe it. "I know you only said that because you were afraid of Grayson."

"You do?"

"Of course I do! I had no idea how . . . how much power a master has over his slaves until I saw you on your knees just now. And if I'd doubted what you said about Mr. Phelps, seeing how terrified you were of going back to him would have convinced me. Oh, Chloe, if anyone deserves a beating, it's Grayson!"

Chloe's eyes were like saucers as she stared up at Emma.

"I should have taken your advice," Emma went on, shocking her even more, "and not told him at all. You said he wouldn't believe me, and he didn't. Just like you thought, he can't imagine anyone . . . Well, neither can I, come to that, and if you hadn't told me what you did, I probably wouldn't have believed it either." She patted Chloe's shoulder. "But *we* know it's true, and we can protect Miss Alice."

Chloe nodded eagerly. "Yes'm, we can. An' now you best go and make up with Massa Gray. He won't be mad long, 'specially if you tells him you's sorry—"

"What?" Emma exclaimed in outrage. "Why should *I* apologize when *he's* the one in the wrong?"

Chloe shrugged. " 'Cause he the Massa."

She was right, of course. Grayson was Emma's master just as he was master of everyone else at Fairview. And Chloe was also right that all Emma would have to do was grovel at his feet and beg his forgiveness and things would be well between them again.

Except things *wouldn't* be well with Emma, not if she had to humiliate herself like that. The old Emma probably would have done so without a thought. In fact, she was sure she *had* apologized to Charles more than once when he was wrong but too stubborn to admit it, just to make peace. And what had such spinelessness ever gotten her? Not one single thing. Instead, she had lost everything she had ever held dear. She had nothing left except her pride, and she would be damned if she would lose it, too.

And, she thought, not only was she not going to apologize to Grayson, she was going to show him in no uncertain terms how she really felt. She only had one weapon to use against him, but she was pretty sure it would be effective. She strode over to the door connecting his room to hers and shoved home the bolts with two decisive clicks.

"Miss Emma, what you doin'?" Chloe asked, appalled.

"Asserting my independence," Emma replied.

Emma never came back downstairs. Gray could have predicted that she would be pouting in her room. Lilly could pout for days, so Gray was used to it. He had no intention of *staying* used to it, though. He had wanted this marriage to be different, and by God, it would be.

After he had undressed that night, he noticed Thomas was turning down his bed.

"Don't bother with that," Gray told him with a sly grin as he slipped on his robe.

Thomas frowned. "You think she gonna let you in?"

Gray frowned back. "Why shouldn't she?"

" 'Cause she mad at you is why." Thomas seemed a little put out himself, probably because he'd always had a soft spot for Chloe, although God knew why since she'd never paid him the slightest bit of attention.

"She won't be mad at me for long," Gray predicted. "I know exactly how to calm her down."

"You sure 'bout that?" Thomas asked skeptically.

Gray ignored him and strode confidently to the door that led to her room. The knob turned easily enough, but when he pushed, the door didn't budge. He pushed again, harder. It still didn't budge.

"Somethin' wrong?" Thomas asked innocently.

Gray tried again, twisting the knob harder. The door didn't move.

"Uncle Sam, he put them locks on good 'n' tight," Thomas remarked.

Gray stepped back, glaring at the door incredulously. He couldn't believe it. Damn her to hell, she'd locked him out!

"Want me to see if her gallery doors is open?" Thomas asked. "You could maybe sneak in that way."

Gray was getting sick of Thomas' sarcasm. "Shut up!"

"You gonna sell me away to Mr. Phelps, too?" he asked, no longer bothering to conceal his own anger.

"I told you, I was only trying to frighten the girl," Gray reminded him, exasperated. His father would have told him that was what he got for becoming too familiar with a servant. "You know I've never sold anyone off this plantation."

"I don't reckon that made much difference to *her.* For all she knowed, she be the first." He made a show of turning the bed down, pointedly reminding Grayson of the locked door.

Gray turned back to glare at it again. Damn her to hell and back! Thomas was right about the gallery doors, of course, although if Emma was stubborn enough to lock this one, she might have locked those, too, regardless of the heat, and be lying in her bed sweltering in spite. Gray wasn't going to humiliate himself by going out there to find out, though.

"I told you, your new wife ain't like the old one," Thomas said.

"Only because there were no locks on this door when Lilly was alive," Gray said bitterly.

"No, 'cause she ain't pouting in there to get her own way like Miss Lilly always done. She just plain mad 'cause you acted like a fool today."

"Damn you, Thomas," Grayson exclaimed furiously, but Thomas was unmoved.

"Somebody gots to tell you, and ain't nobody brave enough but me. You can sell me off the place if you want, but 'til you do, I keep tellin' you."

Gray planted his hands on his hips. "Will you quit talking about selling you? You know I'd never do that, no matter how mad you make me!"

"Just like you'd never sell Chloe, 'cept she don't know that. Don't any of us know it for sure, 'cause *you* don't know it for sure. The price of cotton go down, you might get too poor to keep us."

Gray had no answer for that, because it was only too true. The specter of such poverty haunted him every day of his life. "I had to frighten the girl," he defended himself, taking the conversation back to safer territory. "You don't know the things she told Emma. I can't have her terrifying my wife, and Emma needs to understand she can't believe everything the servants tell her."

"You could've told her some other way," Thomas pointed out. "Private, just the two a you. Now she just plain mad."

Once again, Thomas was right. Gray was even sicker of this than of his sarcasm. "You can go now," he snapped.

"That temper of your'n get you in more trouble if you don't look out," Thomas said, ignoring Gray's command. "Miss Emma, she ain't scared a you like Miss Lilly was, and you can't just sweet talk her back into bein' happy again. You gonna have to make up with her on her own terms."

"Damnit, Thomas, get out of here!"

For a long moment, Thomas didn't move, as if he wanted to say more. Gray hoped to hell he didn't. He'd never struck Thomas in anger, but if the man didn't get out of here soon, he wasn't sure he'd be able to control himself. Finally, Thomas left, giving Gray one last, silent warning before letting himself out.

Gray swore aloud when the door had closed behind him and resisted the urge to smash something or put his fist through the wall. He hadn't thrown a tantrum in a very long time, and he didn't want to start now. Besides, Emma would hear the noise and be sure she'd won. Damn her, she was *not* going to win.

Gray might have been a bit high-handed in the way he'd gotten the confession out of Chloe, but he had still done the right thing, never mind what Thomas thought about it. He couldn't let the girl get away with something like that. Imagine telling Emma such a horrible story. Lilly and her father . . . Gray shuddered at the thought.

He shouldn't have been surprised, though. The slaves had wonderful imaginations when it came to their own sufferings. He really should have told Emma some of the tales he'd heard through the years. Perhaps the one about the pregnant woman who was staked out on the ground with her swollen stomach in a hole so that when she was beaten, the unborn child would be protected. Or the one about being beaten with a hand saw. Or the contraptions the slaves claimed some masters welded onto captured runaways to prevent further escapes. Gray shook his head. If he believed half of what he'd heard, he would lose all faith in mankind.

Not that he blamed the slaves for lying about their ill treatment, though. They should be excused just about any attempt to make their lives easier. In their place, Gray supposed he would do the same and try to win sympathy from whoever would listen. Gray was not in their place, however, and *his* place was to discriminate between real problems and those invented to fool a trusting soul. As his wife and mistress of Fairview, Emma could not afford to be too trusting.

Gray took a puff of his cigar, then realized with a start that he had no memory of lighting it. Dear God, he had better get hold of himself, he thought. He'd only had a fight with his wife, nothing to get so upset about.

True, the fight had occurred on the first day of their marriage, and true, it had been over something utterly unspeakable, but still, it was only an argument. Emma was naturally angry and upset, but she would get over it. He would give her a day or two. He could hold out that long. He'd held out much longer with Lilly many times, and he'd wanted Lilly just as much as he wanted Emma. He was sure he had.

Of course, no woman he had ever known was like Emma. No other woman was as lush and beautiful and desirable. No other woman was as passionate, meeting his need with one as powerful as his own.

He rubbed his growing erection, willing it to subside, and thought about the gallery doors again. Surely, they weren't closed, not in this heat . . .

But no, he wouldn't stoop that low. If Emma didn't want him in her bed, he wouldn't force her. Good God, she'd probably accuse him of being worse than DeWitt Phelps if he tried. So he would be as stubborn as she. And before too long she would unlock that door again.

Or else, he thought grimly, he would have to break it down.

Thirteen

Emma had decided she was a fool. Locking that door had been silly and childish. She should have left it open so Grayson could come in and she could face him and settle their argument once and for all. Instead she had locked him out without a word, figuring, she supposed, that he would confront her about it and demand an explanation and she could then get things settled between them. But he hadn't confronted her. He hadn't mentioned it at all. As far as Emma knew, he hadn't even *tried* to open the door and didn't even know she'd locked it in the first place!

That was silly, of course, because he surely must know by now. Nearly three weeks had passed, and she couldn't imagine a man like Grayson Sinclair remaining celibate that long when he had a wife in the next room. So he must have *tried* to open the door and found it locked and realized what she had done and surely he would know why she had done it. Which meant he didn't care.

He didn't care that his new bride had shut him out of her bed. Emma couldn't believe it, especially not when *she* cared so very much. Which was what made her a fool. Only a fool would lie awake night after night aching for a man to touch her when all she had to do was get up and throw two little bolts and turn one little doorknob, and he would be right there to touch her and kiss her and hold her and make love to her until she cried out with ecstasy.

But she couldn't do that. She couldn't open that door *now,* not until he . . . Well, not until he did *something*. The problem was, Emma didn't know exactly what she wanted him to do. She'd thought and thought about it, but she still didn't know, so she couldn't even explain to him the terms under which she would welcome him back into her bed.

She wanted him to apologize for scaring Chloe, of course, and for not believing her story and for making her say she had lied when she hadn't. But that would mean he would have to believe the story himself, and Emma had come to realize during these long, lonely weeks without him that he couldn't do that. He simply couldn't believe *anyone*—certainly not his own wife—had suffered such unspeakable torment.

So Emma was stuck. Stuck in a sham of a marriage that wasn't a marriage at all. She and Grayson might have been brother and sister. They spoke courteously to each other at meals and when they encountered each other in the hallways, but the warmth that had begun between them had gone just as cold as their marriage bed.

Virginia noticed it, Emma was sure, but all she did was frown worriedly when she was with them both. Did she know they didn't sleep together? Emma hoped not, at the same time she hoped she did. If she did know, Emma could have asked her for her advice on how to solve this problem. But if she did know, Emma would also have been too humiliated to even raise the subject with her. So Emma just went plodding on, pretending everything was fine.

Fortunately, her new duties kept her so busy, she didn't have a lot of time to brood, at least during the daylight hours. Emma had not realized how much Virginia did each day, and now she understood why she had been so eager to have Emma to share the work load. When Emma had been merely a guest, Virginia had shielded her, but now Emma was the mistress, and Virginia only too happily taught her everything.

In addition to giving Alice her lessons each day, Emma planned the meals and supervised the cooks and gave the servants their orders and made sure they were obeyed, checked the house daily for necessary cleaning and repairs, oversaw the laundry and the mending, kept the household accounts, supervised the distribution of food and clothing and household items to the slaves, and tended the sick, taking care to make sure they really *were* sick and not just trying to get out of a day's work.

She soon learned to do Alice's lessons first thing in the morning because by mid-afternoon, she was exhausted, and in the evening she had to retire to her room right after supper. Most nights she was asleep even before the sun went down. Perhaps she should be glad Grayson wasn't coming to her. She would have probably been too tired to receive him.

"Things were much harder in the early days," Virginia told her as they walked down to the slave quarters one afternoon, carrying the huge baskets of the remedies they would use to treat the sick and injured. The heat was making Emma feel nauseated. "Back then we couldn't get ready-made clothes or even cloth. We had to spin our own cotton and make every stitch that went on their backs and our own. And we only ate what we grew ourselves, too. That first year, we ran out of flour and didn't have any bread until the next harvest."

Emma nodded, trying to imagine being so isolated. She was having a hard enough time getting used to having to send away for everything she needed instead of simply telling a servant to run out and buy it.

They stopped by several of the slave cabins where a few of the workers were laid up with complaints of one kind or another. Today was a test of sorts for Emma who had been learning the various remedies so she could serve as nurse without Virginia's guidance. She did fairly well, dosing one with chamomile tea for a stomach ache and applying an ointment made from elderberry flowers and lard to a rash which was probably poison ivy. A bad burn was treated with clarified honey and wrapped in linen rags. Another underwent a miraculous cure when confronted with the prospect of downing a dose of the hated bitters and fairly ran out to the fields to join his fellows.

A few of the children had jiggers which they had contracted while playing in long grass, and Emma gladly rubbed the elderberry salve on their little brown legs, too. They were still shy around her, although they were beginning to warm, and she worked hard to get them to smile. A few of them actually did.

Emma couldn't remember what to do for a toothache and had to consult Virginia's journal. Most plantation mistresses kept such books which contained recipes, household hints and remedies. Finding the correct entry, she applied oil of cloves to the young woman's tooth.

"If that doesn't work," Virginia warned the girl, "you'll have to have it out."

"Yes'm," the girl replied, plainly terrified at the prospect.

Emma was terrified, too. "Will _I_ have to pull the tooth?" she asked in a whisper when they had left the house.

"Oh, no, the blacksmith does that," Virginia assured her, to Emma's relief.

They were heading back to the house when someone called out to them. They turned to see a woman coming toward them, dragging a reluctant young man in her wake. After a moment, Emma recognized the boy as Benjamin, Grayson's son.

"What is it, Opal?" Virginia asked. Emma's heart did a little leap in her chest. This was Grayson's slave mistress, Benjamin's mother.

"Benjamin ain't eatin' right," Opal told them when she had managed to haul her son up to them. "Just picks at his food. Says he ain't hungry, but when did you ever see a boy who ain't hungry?" she demanded.

She had been, Emma could see, a lovely young woman. Her eyes were still beautiful, dark and deep, and the delicate curve of her face was still evident. Her skin was the shade they called "high yellow," although Emma would have called it golden brown, but the years had not been kind to her. At thirty, she was middle-aged, with fine lines creasing her eyes and her mouth, and her once slender body had thickened.

"I told you that you weren't too old for the spring tonic," Virginia scolded the boy. Emma had learned that in the spring, each child, both black and white, was given a dose of "spring tonic" to purify their blood. Apparently, Benjamin had refused his. "Now I'll have to make you up some special." Virginia didn't act as if she minded the extra effort, though. She was looking the boy over with obvious pride. "He doesn't seem to be suffering much, though," she told his mother. "He's growing like a bad weed. Gets taller every time I see him."

"I've had to take them pants down twice since winter," Opal informed her with a pride of her own. "He doin' real good in the blacksmith shop, too. Uncle Sam, he say he ain't never seen a boy learn so fast."

"Do you like your work there?" Virginia asked him. Plainly, her interest was more than mere curiosity. She truly cared about the boy, although he didn't seem to notice.

"It's better'n workin' in the fields," he replied sourly. "An' don't make me up no tonic, 'cause I don't need it. Nothin' wrong with me."

"A boy with no appetite?" Virginia scoffed. "I think you'll need a double dose."

"Tell Massa Gray give me my freedom, I eat plenty," Benjamin said.

Virginia and Emma gasped, and Opal swatted her son. "What you thinkin' to say a thing like that to Miss Virginny?" she demanded furiously. "He don't mean nothin'," she assured the two white women hastily. "He just talkin'. He hears things, and you know how childrens is, don't have a lick a sense."

"Who has been talking to you about freedom?" Virginia asked him sternly, her face pale although she was trying not to reveal how upset she truly was.

"Nobody," the boy said defiantly. "I been talkin' to myownself, ever since Massa freed his old mammy. He could free me, too, if he wanted."

"Hush up now, you hear?" his mother cried in outrage, swatting him again, but he hardly blinked.

Instead, he turned his defiant gaze on Emma. "You tell him," he said to her. "You tell him what I said."

"I's sorry, Miss Virginia," Opal said, assuming that cringing posture that Emma had grown to recognize, as if she feared a blow. Perhaps she did. "He just a boy. He don't know what he sayin'. Don't tell Massa Gray, will you? He just be upset, and ain't no need for him to be upset. Benjamin, he don't mean nothin'." She had turned her plea to Emma, who quickly nodded her agreement. Even if she and Gray had a normal marriage, she probably would not have raised this issue. As things now stood between them, she couldn't even consider discussing his illegitimate son with him.

Apologizing again, Opal backed away, pulling her son with her, although Emma noticed he still did not appear the least bit repentant. Her heart ached for him, for *all* of them who yearned for a freedom they could never have.

Virginia took Emma's arm to lead her away, but not before Emma caught a glimpse of someone who had been lurking in the shadows of a nearby cabin, watching the entire scene. Looking again, she saw no one, as if the person had simply vanished into thin air. But Emma had recognized her even from that brief glimpse. The only thing she couldn't figure out was why Hallie would have been spying on them like that.

"I don't know what we're going to do with that boy," Virginia said with a sigh as they strolled back up the path to the house. "He's always been sort of a . . . a favorite with Gray," she explained, skirting the issue delicately. For a moment Emma wondered if she should admit she knew all about Benjamin, but then Virginia said, "He probably needs a beating, but Gray won't hear of it. He won't raise a hand to the boy and never would. And you see the result, don't you? 'Spare the rod and spoil the child.' That's doubly true with slaves."

"Do you really think a beating would make him happy with his lot in life?" Emma asked, horrified.

"It would make him more . . . resigned," Virginia said tightly. Then she shook her head. "I told Gray he'd cause trouble if he gave Mammy that paper and let her think she was free. Now all our people are stirred up."

"Are you going to tell Grayson what he said?" Emma asked.

"I don't think he needs to be bothered just now, do you?" Virginia asked with a conspiratorial smile. "He worries about that boy enough already, and now he's got a new bride and . . . Well, let's just let this work itself out, shall we?" she added, patting Emma's shoulder.

Emma wasn't exactly sure this *could* work *itself* out, but she was only too happy to agree. She reconsidered for a moment that evening when she saw Grayson at supper, but couldn't imagine how she would bring up the subject of his slave son to him, especially considering their currently strained relationship, so she didn't.

The days went by in a blur as Emma continued to learn the inner workings of the plantation and her duties as mistress, but nothing changed with Grayson. He was unfailingly polite to her, sometimes even charming, but never more than that.

"Unlock the door," Chloe told her time and again as she sat in her room staring at the drawn bolts.

But Emma was afraid to unlock it. What if she did and he *still* didn't come to her? So she left it locked and waited. For what, she did not know.

No wonder she felt so awful all the time, especially in the evening when bedtime approached and she knew she would have to go upstairs and lie alone all night in that huge bed. Her head ached and her stomach churned, and sometimes she could barely choke down enough of her supper to keep from earning one of Virginia's worried frowns. She even searched the remedy book for a tonic for nerves but found none.

So she took what joy she could in little Alice's unbridled adoration and what pride she could in Alice's swift progress in her lessons and continued training herself to be the best mistress any plantation ever had.

Which was why she could no longer ignore something very disturbing which she had discovered in the course of her duties. As much as she dreaded the confrontation, she knew she would have to bring the matter to Grayson's attention. After putting it off for several more days, she finally called herself a fool and marched to his office door one afternoon, clutching a ledger book to her bosom as if for protection.

"Come in," he called when she knocked.

Taking a deep breath and calling herself a fool once more for being so nervous—the man was her *husband* after all, as little as she might feel like his wife—she opened the door.

Grayson was rubbing his eyes wearily when she stepped into the room, closing the door behind her because she didn't want anyone to overhear this conversation. He didn't look up for a moment, and when he did, he seemed surprised.

"Emma," he said. Did he sound happy to see her? Not exactly, although she was relieved to hear no trace of annoyance in his voice, either.

"I'm sorry to interrupt," she said, forcing herself to approach his desk. The sunlight made speckled patterns on the carpet through the lace curtains, and she walked through them.

"Don't be sorry," he said, leaning back in his chair and rubbing the bridge of his nose with his thumb and forefinger as if he had a headache. "I'm glad for any excuse to get me away from these books."

She saw that he, too, had been working over a ledger. "Is something wrong?" She didn't want to bring him bad news if he already had serious problems.

"Something is *always* wrong when I'm trying to balance the accounts," he told her with a small smile. "You see, I can't ever seem to get them to *balance.*"

She liked that smile. It seemed almost friendly. The knot of tension in her stomach loosened a bit. "Let me see," she said, no longer feeling quite as shy or awkward. She laid her own ledger on the corner of his desk and reached for the book open before him. "What's the matter?"

His smile was tolerant now, as if he were indulging a child. "There," he said, turning the book toward her and pointing to the rebellious column of figures.

Conscious that he was watching her with amused expectation, she ignored the heat in her cheeks and forced herself to concentrate on the numbers.

"Oh, I see the problem," she said after a moment. "You just added it up wrong. This should be a nine instead of an eight."

"What? Where?" he demanded in surprise, grabbing the ledger and turning it back toward himself again.

"There," she said, reaching down to touch the page.

He grabbed her hand, holding it away while he silently re-totaled the figures in his head. He seemed unaware that he still held her hand, but Emma was desperately aware of it: His grip was strong and sure, his hand warm and slightly calloused, just the way she remembered it. The memory made her slightly weak, or maybe she was just having one of her spells, she told herself sternly. And if she didn't make herself breathe, she was going to faint, too.

Drawing a breath, she studied his face. His attention was on the numbers, his lips moving slightly as he did the arithmetic in his head, so Emma could watch him at leisure, something she had not done for many weeks. He looked tired and drawn. Could he be having as much trouble sleeping as she was? She told herself not to think about such things, but she couldn't seem to help it, probably because he still held her hand so tightly, almost as if he didn't want to let her go.

"Good God, you're right!" he exclaimed, as if he could hardly fathom such a thing. Whatever concern she had felt for him evaporated, and she jerked her hand out of his, annoyed.

"Of course I'm right," she told him pulling her hand to her waist and cradling it with her other, as if it had been injured.

"How did you do that?" he asked, his eyes narrowing suspiciously.

"I added them up."

"I know," he said impatiently. "I mean, how did you add them up so *quickly?*"

Emma shrugged. "I just did. I . . . I've always been good with figures," she said, telling herself she didn't have to feel defensive.

He leaned back in his chair again, studying her as if he'd never seen her before.

"Which is why," she hurried on self-consciously, "I discovered something I think you should know." She laid her hand on the account book she'd brought in with her. "I was doing an inventory of the storehouses. I know, it's not the right time of year, but I just wanted to get an idea of what we have on hand and . . ." She faltered when she saw how intensely he was staring at her, but forced herself to go on. "Then I compared what I found with what the household accounts say we *should* have and . . . well, I hate to say this, Grayson, but I'm afraid your slaves are stealing from you."

She clasped her hands in front of her again and braced herself for his reaction.

For a long second he didn't have one, as if he hadn't understood what she'd said. Then, to her astonishment, he smiled. Broadly.

"Of course they're stealing from me," he said. "They always do."

Emma gaped at him. "What do you mean?"

"I mean that slaves always steal from their masters. It's a tradition." He leaned forward in his chair again, resting his arms on the desk and folding his hands. "And it's only natural. Think about it. What is a man's duty to his family?"

Emma blinked at the sudden change of topic. "Why, to . . . to provide for them," she said after a moment, thinking how poorly Charles had done his duty to her.

"That's right," he said, nodding his approval, "and a man is judged by how *well* he provides for his family. A man who gives them a comfortable place to live and adequate food and warm clothing is considered good, while a man who does not is considered evil or at least worthless and is scorned by his neighbors."

"Yes, but what does this have to do with—?"

"Our slaves have families, too," he pointed out. "They also want to provide for those families, but they have no means of doing so. They cannot improve their lot by working harder, and they cannot even be sure their master will provide enough food and clothes or adequate shelter for them even if they do. So how can a man prove he is doing his duty to his family under those circumstances?"

Emma frowned. "By *stealing?*"

"Exactly. A male slave who can steal can give his family meat when the others have none. He can give them an extra piece of clothing or make his home a little nicer than the others. They don't feel guilty because they feel the master owes them more than he gives them. It is the slave's version of successful business."

"But that . . . that's terrible!"

"Why?" he asked, as if he really didn't know.

"Because it encourages immorality!"

"Emma, slavery itself is immoral. We buy and sell them as if they were cattle. Then we put them together to breed, hoping they will give us children that will increase our wealth. Some masters don't even bother with any kind of wedding ceremony, but even those of us who do know that slave marriages aren't binding. Stealing is the least of the immorality in a slave's life."

Emma thought of all the aspects of slavery she had discovered and learned to hate, one of them more than the rest. "And some masters breed with the women themselves," Emma said, startling herself with her boldness. She covered her mouth quickly, wanting to call the words back, but there they were between them just the same.

Grayson stiffened as if she'd struck him, but if she'd expected anger, she got none. Instead he paled. "Yes," he said hoarsely, agreeing with her. "And the children are doubly cursed, neither white nor black. They must bear their fathers' sins."

But Emma could clearly see that Grayson still bore at least some of the burden for his own transgressions. As she must bear some guilt for reminding him of his private pain. "I'm sorry," she said, wishing she could say something to make this right but knowing it was far too late for this to ever be right.

He pulled his lips back into the semblance of a smile, although his eyes were still shadowed. "And I'm sorry, too, that you won't ever be able to make the household accounts come out right. Maybe you'd like to try your hand at balancing these," he said, gesturing to his own ledger, "since you are obviously so good at it."

But Emma knew perfectly well what Grayson's opinion of her intelligence was, so she also knew he was being sarcastic. Stung, she snatched up her ledger book. "I wouldn't dream of usurping your authority," she told him. "I'm sorry to have interrupted you."

She turned to go, eager to escape, but he stopped her.

"Emma?"

She turned back warily.

He was smiling for real now, or trying to, stretching his Southern charm over his true emotions. "Was there something else? Something besides the accounts that you wanted to . . . to talk with me about?"

She thought of the locked door and the apology she wanted for Chloe and herself and the way she missed his touch and wanted a real marriage, not this hollow mockery. She thought of all that and more with a hunger that made her knees feel weak.

But when she looked at him sitting behind his desk, his powerful hands folded expectantly, his dark eyes daring her to strip her soul bare before him, she said, "No," and walked out of the room.

By suppertime, Emma had a pounding headache. She told herself it was the result of a trip to the quarters in the afternoon sun. She'd withdrawn to her room and removed her corsets and lain down with a vinegar soaked rag on her forehead, but nothing seemed to help. Probably because she kept thinking over and over again what she should have said to Grayson downstairs this afternoon and berating herself for not saying it. Why hadn't she been braver? Why hadn't she spoken up when he'd given her the perfect opportunity? When he probably was praying she would say something, *anything,* to set things right between them? She was worse than a fool. She was a complete idiot.

She heard the click of the door opening and looked up from under her vinegar rag to see Chloe tiptoeing in. She carried a covered tray. "Miss Virginia, she say you should try and eat somethin'," Chloe reported softly.

The very thought made Emma's stomach clench in resistance. "I couldn't."

But Chloe brought the tray over to the bed anyway. "Cook, she fixed this special for you," she urged, pulling the cloth off the tray to reveal a selection of delicacies artfully arranged on a china plate.

The delicious aroma wafted up, and that was the last straw. Emma's stomach rebelled completely. Before she could even call for a basin, she felt the gorge rising in her throat. Desperate, she flung the tray away, leaned over the side of the bed and vomited.

Distantly, she heard Chloe scream and the crash of the tray and dishes hitting the floor, but all she really knew was gratitude that Chloe somehow got a basin under her head before she vomited again.

She heaved until her stomach was empty and then she heaved some more, until she collapsed back on the bed in exhaustion. She lay there gasping when the door flew open and Virginia burst in. "What on earth?" she demanded, and a second later, Emma heard Grayson asking, "What the hell—?"

"Miss Emma, she just through bein' sick," Chloe explained hastily as Emma covered her face and tried to sink out of sight

among the bedclothes. Just what she wanted, to have Grayson
see her like this. How mortifying! "Everythin' be fine now,"
Chloe was assuring them both.

"I thought she just had a headache," Grayson was protesting
as Chloe tried to shoo them out.

"I'll send someone up to help you clean this up," Virginia
said.

"Yes'm, you do that," Chloe replied and somehow succeeded in getting them both out before Emma died of humiliation.

A little while later, Emma lay on her chaise feeling amazingly better. Chloe and another maid had cleaned up the mess
and sprinkled rose water around to get rid of the stench. Emma
had washed her face and brushed her teeth and wrapped herself
in a clean robe. Now she filled her lungs with the fresh, hot
air that blew in from the gallery through the French doors.
She had just realized that her headache was almost gone and
that she was actually hungry when her bedroom door opened.

For some reason, she expected to see Grayson, or perhaps
she only hoped she would see him. He'd seemed so concerned
earlier when he'd come roaring into the room, but then, maybe
he'd only been annoyed. She couldn't really trust her senses
at that awful moment, so she couldn't be sure. But her visitor
wasn't Grayson.

"How are you, dear?" Virginia asked, twisting her hands
anxiously as she made her way across the room to where
Emma lay by the French doors.

"I'm better, thank you. I don't know what came over me,"
she said, embarrassed to have caused such a commotion.

"Do you feel up to seeing Alice? She's terribly upset, and
she won't believe us when we tell her that you're really fine.
She heard the crash and she thinks . . . Well, heaven only
knows what she thinks, poor dear, but—"

"Of course I'll see her," Emma exclaimed. "Have her come
right in. Chloe? Will you fetch her?"

"Yes'm." Chloe hurried out.

Virginia pulled up a chair next to the chaise and sat down. "You haven't felt well for several days, have you?" Virginia asked solicitously.

More like several weeks, Emma thought, but she didn't want to worry Virginia. "It's probably the heat. I'm still not used to it yet. I probably shouldn't have walked down to the quarters this afternoon, but I wanted to check on—"

The door flew open and Alice ran in. "Mama, Mama!" she cried, racing across the room to fling herself on Emma. *Mama,* Emma had long since decided, was the most beautiful word in the world.

"Careful, dear!" Virginia cried, trying to catch her, but Emma didn't need protection from Alice's love.

"They said you were sick!" Alice cried, her lovely face pinched with distress as she clung to Emma.

"I'm a little sick but not much," Emma admitted, pulling the girl up to sit beside her on the chaise.

"I heard a big crash and a scream," Alice reported, her cornflower eyes huge. "Just like when my other mama, when she . . ." Tears flooded those eyes, and Emma hugged her close.

"That was my supper tray," she hastily explained. "I knocked it out of Chloe's hand when I threw up, and I guess she was the one who screamed. That's all you heard." Dear heaven, had she really heard Lilly's fatal fall? How awful! No wonder she had nightmares.

"Don't die, please, don't die!" Alice begged, clinging desperately to Emma's neck.

"Of course she won't die," Grayson's voice said, and Emma looked up to see him standing in the open doorway. He looked so tall and handsome, her heart did a little flip in her chest even as her cheeks colored in humiliation over their previous meeting. He came in tentatively, as if uncertain of his welcome, but something in Emma's expression must have reassured him. By the time he reached her side, he was almost smiling. Emma couldn't seem to take her eyes off him. "You aren't going to die, are you, Emma?"

Was it a question or a plea? She could almost imagine . . .

"Don't be silly, Gray," Virginia scolded. "Everyone dies."

Alice cried out in protest.

"But Emma isn't going to die for a long, long time, not until she's a very, very old lady," Virginia corrected herself hastily. "Isn't that right?"

"Of course it is," Emma assured the child. "I'm not going to leave you."

"Promise?"

"I promise," Emma said, although she couldn't help glancing up at Grayson. To her dismay, he was frowning.

But he might have just been concerned because he said, "Are you all right?"

"I'm fine, really," Emma assured him. She tried to read his expression. He seemed worried, but perhaps he was just annoyed with her for causing him trouble.

"Just a touch of the sun," Virginia added. "She went down to the quarters this afternoon. I should have told you to wait until evening."

"I needed to check on Henry's burn," Emma reminded her. "It was festering and—"

"But she hasn't felt well for several days," Virginia told Grayson.

"I'm sure it's just the heat," Emma said. "I'm not used to it."

"Maybe we should send you to Galveston for a while," Grayson suggested, his expression unreadable. "There's a sea breeze and—"

"No, don't go away!" Alice cried, hugging Emma more tightly. "You said you wouldn't leave!"

"Just for a week or two," Grayson coaxed. "Until she feels better."

Alice looked up at Emma beseechingly, her eyes filling with tears again. "You promised!"

As tempting as a sea breeze seemed at the moment, Emma knew she couldn't leave Alice. "I don't think that will be necessary," she told Grayson, hazarding another glance at him. He was still frowning. She could almost believe he really cared what happened to her, but probably he was just hoping she would head off to Galveston where she wouldn't be a bother to him. "I'm sure I'll be fine. I'll just be more careful about going out in the heat of the day."

But Grayson was still frowning. "Maybe we should at least send for the doctor."

"Don't be silly," Emma said, frowning back. "All that expense, and he'll just tell me to be more careful. Really, I'm fine!" she insisted.

"If you're sure," he said. She wished she knew what he was thinking, why his eyes were so shadowed and his frown was so deep. If she thought for one moment he really cared about her . . .

"I'm sure," she replied. "In fact, I'm feeling so much better, I was even thinking about sending Chloe down for another supper tray."

"It's not a good idea to eat so quickly after . . . after being ill," Virginia warned.

"But I'm starving," Emma argued. And oddly enough, she was.

"Well, something light then," Virginia reluctantly agreed. Tea and toast, perhaps. I'll tell Cook. Come along, Alice. Emma needs her rest."

Alice had just begun to perk up, but her face fell at her grandmother's command.

"I'm not too sick to read to you," Emma told her. "Why don't you fetch one of your books."

"No, *I* can read to *you!*" Alice exclaimed, instantly happy. She scrambled down from the chaise and took off at a run.

"Slower!" her grandmother cautioned, and Alice obediently slowed, but not by much. "I'll send you a tray, dear," she told

Emma, rising and reaching down to pat her shoulder before turning to go.

Emma looked up, expecting Grayson to follow his mother, but instead he merely watched her, waiting until she was out of the room before turning back to Emma. His eyes were still shadowed with that expression she could not identify, and suddenly she felt hot, as if someone had lit a fire in the already warm room. She was acutely aware that they were alone together in her bedroom for the first time in weeks.

He looked as if he wanted to say something, something very important. He lifted his hand beseechingly, then quickly closed it into a fist and dropped it back to his side again. After what seemed an eternity during which Emma couldn't make herself breathe, he said, "I still think I should send for the doctor."

She let out the breath she had been holding in a disappointed sigh. "I said there's no need."

"I don't care about the expense, Emma. There's no reason for you to suffer if—"

"I'm not suffering!" she insisted impatiently, wishing she dared tell him the real reason she was ill. Wishing she could tell him she would be fine if he would just come to her bed again. She took a deep breath and pushed such thoughts from her mind. "I'm just a pampered Eastern lady who isn't used to doing quite as much work as Southern ladies are expected to do," she explained with a smile she hoped was reassuring.

Apparently it wasn't. "Dear God, I didn't intend to work you to death," he exclaimed, obviously horrified at the thought. "You're not a slave here, Emma. If we expect too much from you, all you have to do is say so and—"

"You don't expect too much from me," Emma said, appalled. She couldn't let him think she was even more worthless than he already suspected. "And no one is working me to death. As I said, I'm just not used to the heat, and I'll be more careful in the future."

His mouth settled into a grim line as he stared down at her, his eyes dark and glittering in a way that took her breath. Once again, she couldn't seem to breathe and once again, his hand reached out to her. "Emma," he whispered, the word holding more emotion than she'd heard from him in weeks.

But before he could say more, Alice burst into the room again. "Wait 'til you see how good I can read this," she announced happily, blissfully unaware of how unwelcome she was at this moment.

Emma gazed up at Grayson with dismay, silently begging him not to leave so she could find out what he had been about to say to her. But he had straightened again, and whatever emotions she had glimpsed were now safely tucked away out of sight again.

"I . . . You'll let me know if you need anything," he said stiffly.

"Yes," she replied, not knowing what else to say. She watched him until he was gone, closing the door behind him as Alice climbed up onto the chaise beside her.

"What story would you like to hear?" she asked Emma very seriously, in exactly the tone of voice Emma always used with her.

In spite of herself, Emma smiled. Thank heaven for this child or she might lose her mind completely.

Gray was losing his mind, he decided as he sat behind his desk, his face buried in his hands. He'd had the perfect opportunity to confront Emma, and what had he done? Not a damn thing except make things between them even worse.

Although how they could be worse, he had no idea. He hadn't touched her in weeks, not since their wedding night almost two months ago. He hadn't wanted a marriage like the one before, and he'd gotten his wish. Instead of having a wife who despised sex, he had a wife who refused it completely, and there didn't seem to be a damn thing he could do about it.

He was too much the Southern gentleman, that was the problem. Too concerned with manners and propriety. He *should* have kicked down the door that first night, before he'd had time to think about it. After he'd thought about it, of course, he'd realized an act of such violence was virtually guaranteed to make Emma hate him for life. Since then, he'd considered a variety of other possible solutions, from a stern confrontation all the way to begging her on bended knee. He'd rejected each in turn as too cowardly or too idiotic. And now she was sick.

Lilly hadn't been above feigning illness to escape her marital duties, but Emma certainly wasn't faking. So how was he supposed to inform an ill woman that he was tired of sleeping alone and expected her to pleasure him?

Muttering a curse, he hardly heard the door opening. When he did, he looked up expectantly, hoping against hope that . . . But of course, it wasn't Emma.

"Gray, dear, I'm sorry to disturb you." His mother looked genuinely distressed, more upset even than she had a few minutes ago when they'd been so worried about Emma.

Emma. Fear brought him up out of his chair. "Is Emma ill again? What—?"

"Oh, no, dear," she assured him hastily, although her expression didn't lighten. "She seems just fine now. I . . . I have to show you something."

Only then did he notice that she was holding a small bundle wrapped in a dirty rag.

"What is it?"

Virginia set the bundle down on his desk and unwrapped the rag to reveal a curious assortment of items. Feathers and straw figures and . . . "What's this?"

"Chloe told me something very disturbing," she said gravely.

Chloe again, Gray thought bitterly. He should have known.

"She said someone has been leaving these charms in Emma's room."

"Charms?" He glanced down at the items again, his suspicions growing. "What do you mean, *charms?*"

"You know, from the conjure woman," Virginia explained impatiently. "Someone has cast a spell on her."

Gray swore, then quickly apologized to his mother for his outburst.

"I know you don't believe in these things, dear," Virginia went on as if she hadn't heard, "but look at them. These feathers are simply to make her go away, of course. Chloe said they came first, before . . . well, before you and Emma married. But this one," she held up a crude straw figure with a hole burned out of its middle, "came the morning after your wedding, and this one," she held up another figure, this one with holes burned in the stomach and head, too, "came a few days ago when Emma started feeling really ill. Chloe found the second figure, and she didn't even tell Emma about it. She simply buried them all at midnight in the dark of the new moon in an effort to break the spell, but Grayson—"

Gray was so angry he could hardly speak. This was just what he needed on top of everything else. *"Mother,"* Gray said sternly, silencing her ranting, "this is all nonsense."

Virginia pulled herself up to her full height and favored him with her best motherly glare. "You can scoff all you want, Gray, but this is a religion, a religion that the Africans have practiced for centuries. They may worship devils, but devils have power in this world, too. Someone has called those devils up to make Emma ill, and Emma *is* ill!"

Gray glared right back, holding his temper with difficulty. "A few bits of straw can't hurt Emma."

"Something is hurting Emma!" Virginia cried, and Gray could see she was even more upset by this than he had imagined.

"Yes, something is, but it's not magic," he said grimly.

"What do you mean?"

Gray glanced down at the curious assortment of objects, then raised his gaze to his mother again. "I don't think for a minute that magic made Emma sick, but maybe . . ."

"Maybe what?" Virginia prodded when he hesitated.

He could hardly make himself say the words. "Maybe whoever is doing this is so anxious to prove her power that . . . that she's *poisoning* Emma."

Fourteen

Emma was in the nursery with Alice, going over her lessons, when Grayson summoned her a few days later. Chloe brought the message, and although she didn't look frightened, she did look very upset.

"What's the matter?" Emma asked her when they were out in the hallway.

"I don't know. Massa Gray, he say to find you and tell you to come. He say it real important. He gots something to tell you."

Hating the knot of apprehension that immediately formed in her stomach, Emma hurried down the stairs. What on earth could he want? Emma could only imagine one subject Grayson would need to discuss with her, although why he had suddenly decided, after two months, that it was a matter of urgency, she couldn't imagine.

Well, she welcomed this confrontation. She was sick of living like a nun when she was a bride, and no matter how unpleasant the confrontation was, if it ended with Grayson returning to her bed, she would have no regrets. Not even, she admitted reluctantly, if it meant she had to swallow her pride.

The office door was open, but to Emma's surprise, both Grayson and Virginia were inside. Grayson was half-sitting on the near edge of his desk, arms braced tensely on either side of him, while Virginia paced around the room, wringing her hands. Grayson straightened the instant he saw her, and Virginia stopped in her tracks.

"Oh, my dear, how are you feeling?" Virginia asked, coming to her instantly.

So much for her hopes that this would be an opportunity to settle things with Grayson. "I keep telling you, I'm fine," Emma lied. At least she was fine for the moment. Morning was always her best time. Only she and Chloe knew that in the week since Emma had first thrown up, she had been sick almost every evening, and Chloe was sworn to secrecy. Emma couldn't bear the thought of everyone in the household doting on her even more than they already did.

"Why don't you sit down, dear?" Virginia suggested. "We . . . we have something to discuss with you," she said after a quick glance at Grayson.

Had they put their heads together and decided to send her to Galveston against her will? Or worse, to some Northern city where she wouldn't even be able to keep an eye on Alice? If they tried, she would—

"What is this about?" she demanded, sick of being treated as if she weren't strong enough to bear even the slightest strain.

"Chloe showed us these," Grayson said wearily, turning to pick something up from his desk.

For a moment, Emma couldn't imagine what he could have in such a filthy rag, and then he opened it to reveal the charms she had found in her room.

Oh, dear, did they think Alice had something to do with this? Surely, Chloe had told them—

"Do you know what they mean, dear?" Virginia asked.

"Yes, Chloe explained them." Why didn't they get to the point?

"The slaves and . . ." Grayson cast his mother a withering glance, *"some* whites take these things very seriously," he said. "They really believe a spell can make someone sick or well or make them do things they wouldn't normally do."

"Well, I don't," Emma snapped, her patience at an end. "I told Chloe to burn those things. I didn't want whoever sent them to think I paid them any attention at all."

"You don't have to pay them attention for them to work, dear," Virginia informed her anxiously. "And you *have* been ill . . ."

"Mother, please," Grayson said, sounding a little impatient himself. "Emma, I've been trying to find out who's responsible for this."

"I told you, it doesn't matter—"

"It matters very much," Grayson insisted. "I can't have the slaves casting spells on their mistress. Besides . . ."

Emma looked at him curiously when he hesitated, trying unsuccessfully to read his expression.

"Gray thinks they might be doing more than simply casting spells," Virginia reluctantly admitted when he did not go on.

"What do you mean?"

"I think someone may have . . . may have given you something to make sure you got sick," Grayson said grimly, "so the slaves would think the spells truly have power."

Emma gaped at him. "You think someone is trying to *poison* me?"

"It's possible," he said.

Emma could only stare in horror. Her one comfort was the knowledge that Grayson seemed as upset about the possibility as she.

"Nathan sent me word that he's found out who the conjure woman is. He's bringing her here."

Emma had a dozen questions, but before she could ask any of them, a disturbance in the hallway outside distracted her. They heard a man's rough tones and a woman's lighter ones, pleading and sobbing.

As their footsteps approached the office door, Emma instinctively backed up a step, and she was surprised to encounter something solid. Looking up, she saw that Grayson had come up behind her, almost as if he were protecting her in some way. He laid his hand on her shoulder, and she felt the warmth of it course through her body. For one instant, she felt safe and secure and cherished, but then Nathan and his companion appeared in the doorway, and all other thoughts vanished.

He had been practically dragging the woman by the arm, and now he furiously thrust her into the room ahead of him. She stumbled and fell to her knees, her face buried in her hands as her shoulders shook with wrenching sobs.

Her dark hair was loose and fell in silken waves around her, and her bare arms were the color of ivory. For a moment, Emma thought there must be some mistake. Surely, this woman was white . . . And then she knew. *"Hallie?"* she cried in horror.

Hallie's head jerked up. Her beautiful face was streaked with tears, her eyes wide with terror as she gazed at her accusers.

Grayson's hand tightened on her shoulder as the shock registered with him, too. Hallie was the conjure woman.

How humiliating for Nathan, who had harbored the traitor in his own bed. Emma glanced at him and was shocked to see his face was ashen. He was more than angry and embarrassed, she realized instantly. He had been betrayed. Betrayed by a woman who was far more to him than a mere mistress.

"I found where she keeps all her . . . her things," Nathan reported hoarsely. "The things for her magic. They were under the floorboards in the . . . the children's bedroom." The words sounded as if they had been ripped from his soul.

"Oh, please, Massa Gray, please don't sell me away from my babies! Please, oh, please, I never do no magic again, I swear!" Hallie pleaded, her hands clasped in supplication, just the way Chloe's had been that day when she had begged Gray not to sell her back to DeWitt Phelps. Hallie's terror was even more stark than Chloe's had been, and it tore at Emma's heart.

"Who asked you to put a spell on Miss Emma?" Gray demanded, his fury more terrible than Nathan's because he was holding it so tightly in check.

"Nobody, Massa, I did it myownself," Hallie admitted, her whole body cringing as fresh tears poured down her face.

"Why?" Emma cried, wondering what she could have done to Hallie to make her hate her so much.

Hallie's wild gaze shifted to Emma. Plainly, she didn't want to say, but Nathan cuffed her on the shoulder. "Tell her!"

Emma winced at the blow, but Hallie hardly seemed to feel it. Her eyes were like two holes burned into her face as she lifted them to Emma again. "I's scared you take Massa Nate away from me."

Emma gasped and so did all the other whites in the room. "You were *jealous?*" Emma could hardly believe it.

"He talk 'bout you all the time," Hallie explained frantically. " 'Bout how pretty you is and such a fine lady. If he marry you, he don't need me no more!"

"Hallie!" Nathan cried in an anguished voice that was like a lash to Emma's sensitive heart.

But Hallie didn't even glance at him. She was focused on Emma now, as if sensing her sympathy. "I don't want to harm you none," she wailed. "I just want you to go away!"

How horrible! Emma could actually feel the terror Hallie must have felt at the prospect of being cast aside, possibly even sold, and what about her children, those precious little children?

"That doesn't explain *this,*" Grayson said, snatching up one of the straw figures from his desk and holding it up. Emma realized she'd never seen that one before and was horrified to see the hole burned right through the head. She couldn't help thinking about the headaches she'd been suffering for weeks and instinctively raised her hand to her temple. "It came after Miss Emma and I were married. Surely, you didn't still think she was going to take Nathan away from you then."

"I . . . I . . ." Hallie looked wildly around, as if seeking some form of escape, but all she saw was a ring of accusing faces. "I was scared she wanted my babies," she finally admitted in a hoarse whisper.

"What?" Nathan fairly shouted.

Hallie cringed again, and Emma saw that all the color had

drained from her face. She swayed on her knees, as if she were going to faint, but Nathan grabbed her by the arm and held her upright, forcing her to look at him.

"What are you talking about?" he demanded fiercely, his own face scarlet with rage.

"She barren!" Hallie cried. "She can't have no babies of her own, but I seen the way she look at *my* babies. *My* babies which is white as Miss Alice. She always comin' around, giving them presents, and then she say right to my face that she want them! That when I . . ." She caught herself and turned to Emma. "Oh, please, Missy, you can have my babies, only please, please, don't sell me away! I work in the fields, I do anything you say, only please, just let me stay where they are so I can know they all right!"

Emma felt the tears running down her own cheeks, but she made no move to wipe them away. "When did I say I wanted your babies?" she asked, mystified.

"The day you marry Massa Gray," she reminded her urgently. "You come to the house, and you say any woman be proud to have my childrens."

Emma's mind was whirling as she tried to recall exactly what had happened that day, how she had inadvertently caused such panic, but then she realized it was useless. Regardless of what Emma had really said, Hallie had simply heard what she had most feared.

"And how," Gray asked, his voice like molten steel, "did you know Miss Emma was barren?"

Hallie's eyes widened even farther with renewed panic, and she glanced fearfully at Virginia who cried out in protest, then clamped her hand over her lips, as if to call it back.

"Mother?" Gray asked, fury trembling beneath the word.

"Oh, Gray, I'm so sorry!" Virginia said, her face as ashen as Nathan's had been a moment ago. "Emma, dear, I was only trying . . . I mean, I know how much you . . ."

"You *went* to this woman?" Gray asked incredulously. "You bought a *spell* from her like some superstitious darkie?"

"I didn't know who she was!" Virginia insisted, her eyes filling with tears. "I sent Beulah. She . . . Oh, Emma, I was only trying to help! I know you don't believe in magic, neither of you, but I thought if you had a child, you'd . . . you'd come to love each other in time, so I . . ."

Emma closed her eyes, unable to witness Virginia's anguish another moment. Unable, too, to bear her own anguish.

Grayson's hand still rested on her shoulder, and now it tightened again, as if he were giving her comfort. As if . . .

But then he said, "And so, Hallie, you put something in Miss Emma's food to make *sure* your spell worked. To make sure she got sick and even died."

"Oh, no, Massa!" Hallie cried, her horror too complete to be feigned. "I never done nothin' like that! My spells, they work on they own! I don't need to do nothin' else!"

"How *could* she have, Gray?" Virginia asked reasonably, although Emma noticed her voice still quivered with emotion. "She had no access to the kitchens."

"Maybe she bribed someone—or frightened them—into helping her," he guessed.

"I don't even *know* them girls in the kitchen, Massa!" Hallie swore in renewed panic. "They never even speaks to me! You ask 'em if they help me! They tell you! I never done nothin' to Miss Emma 'cept them spells, I swear!"

"If you're lying, Hallie, I'll see you hanged," Gray told her. His tone send a chill up Emma's spine and practically petrified poor Hallie.

"On my babies' lives, I swear it, Massa Gray!" she cried, fresh tears spilling down her face. "If Miss Emma really sick, I make a spell to get her better again!"

"No more spells!" Nathan shouted, jerking her arm so hard, Emma was afraid he would break it.

Hallie cried out in pain, and then fell silent. For a long moment, no one else spoke either, and then Nathan asked raggedly, "What shall I do with her?"

Beside her, Emma felt Grayson stiffen. "We can't keep her here, not after this."

"*No!*" Hallie's wail turned Emma's blood cold. Hallie grabbed Nathan's leg, clinging to him desperately. "You *promised!*" she cried, her face twisted with a terror Emma couldn't even begin to understand. "You swore to me you'd never sell me away! You swore I'd never leave my babies! You *promised* me, Nathan!" she sobbed.

"*Stop it!*" Nathan tried, but his voice lacked force, and Emma saw at once that he was weeping, too. His face was white except for a spot of color on each cheek, and his eyes were wretched with despair. "Stop it, Hallie!" he rasped again, trying in vain to loosen her hold on his leg.

"You swore it on your *soul!*" Hallie screamed hysterically. "You said you'd die and burn in hell before you'd let me go!"

Nathan grabbed her shoulders and gave her a sharp shake which silenced her instantly. "Don't you see?" he said desperately into her upturned face. "I don't have any choice!"

"Well, *I* do," Emma said, stepping forward, out from under Grayson's protective hand. She felt his surprise, but she didn't even glance at him or at Virginia or Nathan, either, for fear they would try to stop her. She only looked at Hallie who was looking back with such abject terror that Emma's blood seemed to stop in her veins.

"Hallie," she began, speaking gently, "I never wanted your babies. They *are* beautiful, the kind of children any mother would be proud of, but I would never dream of taking them away from you. I never wanted Nathan, either, and I'm also pretty sure he never wanted me. How could he when he obviously loves you so much?"

She felt the shock rippling through the room and saw it register plainly on Hallie's tear ravaged face, but she ignored it, focusing only on what she had to do. "It's true, isn't it, Nathan?" she asked him without lifting her gaze from Hallie's. "You do love her, don't you?"

For a long second, she thought he wouldn't reply, but finally he whispered, "Yes." The word was broken but unmistakable.

Hallie's eyes closed as she shuddered with an agony Emma knew she could never comprehend.

"Yes, I love her," Nathan said more firmly, his words filled with bitterness, "but that doesn't matter, does it, Gray?"

"No, it doesn't," Grayson agreed, and Emma turned on him in surprise. "Emma, she tried to kill you."

"She put a *spell* on me!" Emma reminded him in exasperation. "Because she was afraid of me, afraid I'd take her children away from her, and I can't blame her for that. I probably would have done the same thing in her place. From what I understand, slaves have been putting spells on their masters for hundreds of years. How many of them have died of it?"

"That's not the point," Gray insisted angrily.

"Then what *is* the point?"

"The point is you really are sick, dear," Virginia offered.

"Which means," Gray continued grimly, "that she must have done more than simply put a spell on you."

"You can't really think she tried to poison me," Emma said as Hallie cried out in protest again. "You heard her when you accused her, and I think she's telling the truth about the girls in the kitchen not being willing to help her. None of the house servants will even look at her. But why don't you ask them yourself? Your methods of interrogation are so effective, I'm sure they couldn't hide the truth from you for long, particularly when they find out the conjure woman is no longer a threat to them," she added sarcastically.

"As usual, you don't understand any of this," Grayson informed her angrily, finished with trying to reason with her. "Even if she didn't try to poison you—and I most certainly *will* question the kitchen help to find out—Nathan is the overseer here. If he can't keep his own household in order, how can we expect the rest of the slaves to respect him?"

"They don't respect him *now!*" Emma informed him, just as angry as he. "For heaven's sake, they know he's been sleeping with the conjure woman for years! They only fear him, just the way they fear all white people. And they'll fear him even more now because he's taken all the power away from their conjure woman."

She looked around, gratified to see the shock on their faces because they knew she was right. When her gaze touched Hallie, she saw not only shock but the beginnings of hope deep in her eyes.

"Get up from there, Hallie," Emma said, suddenly annoyed to have her cowering on her knees like that. "No one is going to sell you or your babies, not as long as I'm mistress of this plantation."

But Grayson was still master. "She *has* to be punished." His voice was like steel.

"Yes, Massa," Hallie agreed obsequiously as Nathan helped her to her feet. "You's right. I—"

"Stop that!" Nathan snapped, startling them all. "Stop that slave talk. You know I hate it."

Hallie's eyes widened with distress as her gaze darted from Nathan to Grayson and back again. Obviously, Nathan had taught her to speak proper English, but she didn't dare do so to Grayson.

"What kind of punishment did you have in mind?" Emma inquired, saving Hallie the trouble of having to decide what to do.

Grayson's face tightened with obvious distaste. "If we don't sell her away, we have to give her a . . . a beating."

Emma's stomach twisted in horror, but she lifted her chin defiantly. "And who will give this beating?" she challenged, knowing she had to put an end to all this nonsense once and for all. "Nathan, who loves her?" A glance at Nathan's chalk white face provided more than adequate answer to that. "Or the master whose wife she tried to kill?"

Emma could easily see that Grayson had no stomach for such a deed. "It's Nathan's job as overseer to . . . to discipline the slaves," he said righteously.

"I won't do it," Nathan told him flatly. "You can fire me if you want to, but I won't hurt her."

"But she's got to be punished," Grayson insisted.

"Then *I'll* do it," Emma said, not too angry to be amused by their shocked expressions.

"Emma, you don't—"

"I said I'll do it, and I meant it," she told Grayson. "I'm the one she tried to kill. I think it's only fitting, don't you? And then the other slaves will be afraid of *me,* too!"

"Emma, dear," Virginia tried, her hands twisting in distress, "you have no idea . . ."

"Then tell me. What do you beat the slaves with? A whip?" she asked. "Where do you keep it?"

When no one replied, she turned to Hallie. "Where does Nathan keep his whip?"

"He gots . . ." She glanced at Nathan and corrected herself. "He's got one at the house."

"Good, I'll send for it." She brushed past them to go to the door, intending to summon a servant, but she found all the house staff hovering in the hallway, blatantly eavesdropping, their eyes wide with disbelief. "Go fetch me Massa Nathan's whip," she told the nearest one.

He darted away, leaving the others staring at her dumbfounded.

"Bring her out here, and tell me how this is done," Emma commanded. "Do you have a whipping post?"

"Emma, this has gone far enough," Grayson informed her, although she noticed much of his normal confidence seemed to have vanished.

"No, it hasn't," she replied. "You're always telling me I don't understand how to run a plantation, so I'm going to learn. You think Hallie needs to be beaten and neither you nor Nathan have the stomach for it, so I'm going to do it. Bring her out here!"

Something in her expression must have convinced Nathan that she meant business, because he brought Hallie out into the hallway. Oddly enough, she no longer looked frightened, although Emma was beginning to feel a twinge of fear herself. Had she gone too far?

But one glance at Grayson's disapproving frown told her she hadn't gone far enough. She would have to see this through. Figuring it was useless to seek instruction from him, she turned and found Chloe among the wide-eyed servants.

"Tell me what to do," she commanded.

Chloe hesitated, studying Emma's face for a long moment, and then she said, "You ties her to a tree, arms around like this." She circled her arms as if she were hugging a big tree trunk. "Take down her dress and whip her on her back."

"How many times?" Emma asked, and she could have sworn the servants flinched as a unit.

"I'd say ten," Chloe guessed, plainly offering the minimum punishment.

But Emma didn't care. One lash was too many. "Outside," she told Nathan. "Find a tree."

Nathan glanced at Grayson, but Emma was not going to be overruled. "Take her outside," she told the servants, and eager hands grabbed Hallie and dragged her away. Finally they would get revenge on this woman who had kept them in fear for so long.

"Emma, I should let you go through with this," Grayson said, his expression grimmer than she had ever seen it, his dark eyes more confused.

"Yes, you should," she told him. "It will teach me a lesson."

Without bothering to wait for a reply, she strode out after the slaves. When she reached the veranda, she saw the slaves were tying Hallie to one of the trees in the yard. They'd stripped her dress down to her waist, and her skin shone pearly white in the morning sunlight.

The slave she had sent for the whip was racing across the yard, and he skidded to a halt in front of her and handed her the most hideous object Emma had ever seen. She had imagined a long whip like teamsters used, but this was a short one, with a single handle and several tails.

Nathan had come up beside her. "You don't know what you're doing," he told her anxiously. "You might really hurt her. You might hurt *yourself*."

"I know exactly what I'm doing," Emma informed him, stalking over to where Hallie was now tied to the tree.

"Gray, you can't let her do this!" Nathan pleaded.

"Emma, stop this right now!" Grayson commanded, but Emma didn't even break stride. *"Emma!"*

He caught her arm and wrenched her around to face him, but whatever he saw on her face startled him so much, he released her at once. Certain now that she must do this thing, she turned and headed for the tree.

When she reached Hallie, she saw that the girl was trembling slightly, but when she turned her head, Emma also saw a calm acceptance in her eyes. For a second Emma felt tears choking in her own throat as she realized Hallie would have endured any punishment at all if it meant she wouldn't lose her children. Emma only hoped she had chosen the right one.

The house servants were all gathered around, watching with the same baffled amazement they had displayed in the hallway. She wished the fieldhands could be here, too, but she couldn't wait for them or she would lose her nerve. They would hear the story, in any case. Generations to come would hear *this* story, she thought grimly.

"You all know what Hallie did, don't you?" she asked the dark faces watching her. A few heads nodded, but most seemed frozen in place. "She put a spell on me, because she's the conjure woman, and she thought she could do me harm. She thought she could make me sick. Chloe," she called, finding the girl in the crowd. "Have I been sick?"

Chloe had started at the sound of her name, and for a moment Emma was afraid she wouldn't back up Emma's lie. After what seemed an eternity, she said, "No, ma'am, you ain't been sick. I never seen a lady so healthy in all my days."

Emma lifted her chin as haughtily as she could. "Your conjure woman has lost her power. Her spells don't work anymore, and I'm going to show you just how important I think it is that she tried to put one of her silly little spells on me."

Emma lifted the hideous whip. Hallie tensed, her smooth, white back braced for the blow, and Emma brought the whip down with a snap.

"One," she counted as the crowd gasped.

She raised the whip again. *Snap.*

"Two," Emma said through clenched teeth.

Three.

Four

Five.

They gasped each time, but Emma didn't dare look at them for fear she would falter.

Six.

Seven.

Would Grayson stop her? Would he save her? But no, she didn't want that, wouldn't allow that.

Eight.

The whip was so heavy, she could hardly lift it.

Nine.

Dear heaven, only one more. Please give me strength.

She lifted the whip one last time and brought it down with a final snap against the petticoated fullness of her own skirts.

"Ten." Only then did she look up.

Beside her Hallie sagged against her ropes, her beautiful, pearly white back as smooth and unmarked as it had been. The slaves were still staring, some in fear, some in admiration, some in simple confusion. She would have to explain to them one more time.

"You see," she told them patiently, forcing her voice not to shake, "A silly little spell that doesn't work doesn't even deserve a beating. I've taken all her power away, and Hallie isn't a conjure woman any more."

She threw the horrible whip down and started back to the

house. Grayson and Virginia still stood on the veranda, their expressions stunned, but Nathan ran forward to meet her.

"Oh, Emma, how can I ever—?"

How odd, his voice sounded so distant. "Just take her home, Nathan," Emma said, her own voice sounding distant, too. "And for God's sake, be good to her."

"I will," he promised, but Emma hadn't waited for his reply. She needed to get into the house, needed to be away from so many prying eyes because whatever hidden strength had carried her through that awful scene was rapidly evaporating.

The sunlight seemed foggy, somehow, as if her eyes were full of tears, but when she blinked, they didn't clear.

Something was wrong with Grayson. He was angry, of course. He didn't like to be defied, but this was more than simple anger. His eyes were so strange as she approached him, but she couldn't stop to figure out why. She couldn't stop for anything, not if she wanted to maintain the fiction that she wasn't ill.

"Emma," Grayson said, his voice husky and full of questions, but she didn't stop. She swept by him, into the house. *Oh, please,* she prayed, *let me make it to my room before . . .*

Behind her and very far away, she heard Virginia saying, "Oh, dear. Grayson, do something . . ."

But she didn't stop. The stairs were ahead, just a few feet away, but they were so tall, so many stairs, and her head was spinning now. But she couldn't faint, not yet, not here, not where they could see her. They would know she'd been lying, that Hallie's spell really had worked, and she was sick and was going to die.

Frantically, she grasped the railing, not letting herself think about the steps and how many there were and how she couldn't fall, not yet, not yet. Lift her foot, yes, that's it, another and another.

"Emma, wait!" Grayson called, but he was too far away to help her, and she couldn't wait for him to come because she had to get upstairs and out of sight. But the room was growing dark, so dark, and she couldn't see the stairs anymore. She grabbed for the railing, but it wasn't there, and she plunged into the black abyss.

Gray caught her as she fell. "Mother, close the door so they don't see her," he whispered fiercely, and Virginia hurried to do his bidding.

"Did they see?" he asked when the door was shut.

"I don't think so," Virginia reported. "They were all watching Nathan cut Hallie down."

Gray looked at Emma's beautiful face, so pale now, her long, dark lashes brushing her delicate cheeks. He lifted her into his arms. "I'll take her upstairs," he told his mother. "Send Chloe up, but don't alarm anyone. Don't let them know that—"

"Of course, dear, of course!" she called back impatiently. "Just hurry. Get her out of sight before they come back! And loosen her stays!"

By the time he reached the top of the stairs, Gray was panting. Emma alone was an armload, but her heavy skirts and petticoats nearly doubled her weight. He reached her door and somehow managed to open it without dropping her. When they were inside, he kicked it shut behind him and lurched for the bed.

Although his arms were trembling and his breath came in labored gasps, he laid her down gently, tenderly, and then stood back to look at her once again. Dear God, was this the same woman who had come here only three short months ago? he marveled as something twisted painfully inside of him. Had he once thought her a worthless, spineless, brainless ninny? Had he once believed her selfish and spoiled? Gray did not think he had ever known a smarter, braver, more selfless person in his entire life.

When he thought of how she'd stood up to him downstairs, refusing to let him sell Hallie, he . . . Well, he was furious, of course. No one ever questioned him. No one.

No one, of course, except Emma, who had not only questioned him but convinced him he was wrong. No, not just wrong but a fool into the bargain. And then she had shown him up, out mastered the master by refusing to whip a slave who deserved much worse than whipping and thereby punishing her more thoroughly than the lash ever would have.

She was, he understood in that one instant of clarity, the woman for whom he had been waiting his entire life.

Emma's breath rasped in her throat, reminding him that he had more important things to worry about than his own feelings. What had his mother said? Oh, yes, loosen her stays.

Quickly, he began to unbutton her bodice, painfully aware of how much he'd longed to do just that for months now but under much different circumstances. His fingers were clumsy in his haste, but somehow he managed the task at last. Where in the hell was Chloe anyway?

Then he opened her bodice, and thoughts of Chloe vanished. All he could think about was Emma, beautiful Emma, and the alabaster swell of her breasts above the lacy edge of her chemise. His body quickened instantly in response, and he cursed himself for his weakness. Emma didn't need his lust now.

Carefully, steeling himself against the feel of her, he reached down and grasped the top edge of the corset beneath the luscious fullness of her breasts. Forcing himself not to think about the way her tender curves yielded to him, he unfastened the first hook of the corset. After that, it was easier, and in moments he had the whole thing undone and was rewarded by seeing Emma take a deep, shuddering breath.

He grabbed her hand and began to chafe her wrist, conscious of the silkiness of her skin as he drank in the sight of her femininity. How he'd longed for just a glimpse of her. How he'd burned with desire, night after lonely night, thinking of her lying just where she was now. How he'd yearned for the chance, just once more, to lay his head upon those breasts and taste again her satiny heat. But he had never, not once, wanted to love her. Which was why he could hardly believe that now, right now, when he could feast his eyes on all her physical charms, the flame in his heart burned even hotter than the flame in his loins.

Humbled at last, Gray lifted her limp hand to his lips and kissed it fiercely.

Behind him the door opened abruptly, and he heard Chloe whisper, "Dear Lord Almighty!"

He turned and saw his mother had followed her in, closing the door carefully behind her.

"Did you ever see such a thing in all your life?" Virginia demanded, still whispering so no servants would overhear. "When she took that whip, I thought my heart would stop!"

But Gray wasn't even listening. He was too busy looking at Emma. His Emma, the woman he had almost dismissed as unworthy of anything beyond his desire. The woman he loved.

Chloe had climbed up on the opposite side of the bed to kneel beside her and was breaking open the bottle of smelling salts. Gray wrinkled his nose against the acrid smell, but he didn't let go of Emma's hand. Chloe passed the bottle under her nose, and Emma stirred, shaking her head, trying to escape the odor, and finally opened her eyes.

"Miss Emma, can you hear me?" Chloe asked.

"Yes," Emma snapped, irritated. "What on earth . . . ?"

She looked around slowly, taking in the scene of Gray, Virginia and Chloe hovering over her. "What happened?" she asked after a puzzled moment.

Gray couldn't help his smile. "Don't you remember? You whipped Hallie. Or didn't whip her, I should say."

Her lovely blue eyes widened as the memories returned. "Did I really? Did I . . . ?"

"You most certainly did," he informed her, delighted at the color that rose in her cheeks, delighted by every single thing about her. God, what a woman. And she could even balance his ledger books!

"How is Hallie? Is she—?"

"She fine," Chloe reported, sitting back on her heels,

"though I expect she feelin' a little faint herself about now. You done scared her and everybody else near to death!"

Emma's gaze found Gray. Her eyes were troubled, but he saw no regret in them. "I had to do it," she told him. "I had to do *something* so you wouldn't sell her. How could I live with myself if I separated her from her children? Oh, dear, did I tear my dress with that whip?" she wondered with a delightfully worried frown.

She looked down, trying to see, but instead noticed how her bodice was hanging open. "Oh, dear," she cried and tried to clasp it shut, but she only had use of one of her hands because Gray still held the other, and he wasn't about to let it go. That seemed to alarm her more than finding her bodice open, but before she could say anything, Chloe spoke.

"They all sayin' you took Hallie's powers, Missy," she reported gleefully. "They sayin' *you* the conjure woman now!"

"That's ridiculous," Emma insisted, struggling to hold the two sides of her bodice with one hand while Gray caressed the other. "You tell them it isn't true!" she commanded with another puzzled glance at Gray who only smiled benignly back at her.

"They believe what they wanna believe, Missy," Chloe said. She didn't seem too concerned, and Gray couldn't blame her. Chloe was probably delighted to have the other slaves think her mistress was so powerful.

"We were all very proud of you today," Virginia said, and Gray saw the surprise flicker in Emma's eyes.

"Proud?" she echoed incredulously.

"Yes," Gray confirmed, shocking her thoroughly. "Proud." He pressed his lips to her hand again and savored the surprised confusion that creased her beautiful forehead.

He had thoroughly botched things with her, but he could change. He could win her back because he *had* to win her back, and he would make her so happy she would never even remember how awful he had been to her. He could even, please God, make her love him in return.

"But," Virginia was saying, her face clouded with worry,

"you can't be sick anymore. If you are . . . Well, they'll know you lied, and . . . oh, dear, they'll think Hallie has more power than ever!"

He watched Emma's expression harden with resolve. "Then I won't be sick."

In that moment, Gray almost believed she could heal herself by the simple force of her will. Perhaps the slaves were right. Perhaps she *had* stolen Hallie's power.

"Now you folks get out of here and let me get Miss Emma fixed up so she can show herself in public again. We paint a little color into her cheeks and—"

"Paint?" Emma exclaimed in outrage.

"Lots a ladies paint they faces, Missy, and we can't have you lookin' like a ghost, not if'n you wanna make folks think you feelin' fine."

"Chloe's right," Virginia said. "But if you don't feel well enough to join us for dinner today, naturally everyone would understand, after what happened—"

"I'll be there," Emma said with more determination than Gray had ever imagined she possessed. But then, he'd never imagined she would defy his orders and whip a slave or not whip a slave in front of the entire house staff, either.

"I'll be waiting," he told her, hoping she could see the anticipation shining in his eyes.

She saw *something* there, something that confused and perhaps alarmed her, but that was all right. Practically everything he planned to do from now on would confuse her. Just to confuse her once more, he kissed her hand again before returning it to her.

"Come on, Mother, let's let Emma get herself put back together."

Virginia was reluctant to leave, but he took her arm and led her out. When they had closed the bedroom door behind them, she looked up at him with wonder. "I don't know what surprised me more today, Emma's behavior or your reaction to it."

"What did you find so surprising?" he asked, amused.

Virginia shook her head. "Probably the fact that you didn't simply murder Emma outright for defying you the way she did. Instead you seemed . . . I don't know, impressed somehow. And just now, the way you kept kissing her hand, I could almost believe you really cared about her."

"She's my wife," he reminded her.

"So was Lilly," she reminded him right back. "And so has Emma been for over two months now, but I've never seen you quite so . . . affectionate with her before."

"Mother," he said in warning, not quite ready yet to discuss such a sensitive topic with anyone.

"All right," she said, acquiescing with a knowing smile. "But I must say I'm very glad to see it finally happening."

"To see *what* finally happening?" he asked, knowing he would probably regret asking.

Virginia's smile broadened. "To see you falling in love with Emma. I've known since the first moment I met her that she would be the perfect wife for you, and it's a relief to see you've finally realized it, too."

Chloe tried to convince Emma not to go downstairs for dinner, but Emma knew she couldn't hide in her room. If she did, rumors would start and . . . Well, she wanted everyone to see that she was hale and hearty and not languishing in her room like some vaporous female. Besides, she always felt better in the daytime, regardless of her faint, and she knew she would probably have to retire to her room after supper in any case. Better to show herself now.

She did feel surprisingly well, too, all things considered. As long as she didn't think about Hallie's bare back and that horrible whip, she would be just fine. Facing Grayson would be trial enough.

Or would it? For the life of her, she couldn't make sense of his behavior just now. He'd been furious with her, she knew, and then she'd humiliated him by defying him in front of the servants. She was probably lucky he didn't tie *her* to a tree, but instead he had seemed almost pleased when he'd stood beside her bed and held her hand and kissed it . . .

Emma found herself cradling that hand and gazing at it in wonder. Grayson had actually kissed her hand! The knowledge filled her with warmth, and when she remembered the way he had looked at her, that heat turned to liquid fire. Or at least she *thought* he'd been looking at her in that very special way, as if he wanted to take her in his arms and make love to her until they were both exhausted. She'd been so scattered, she couldn't be perfectly sure, and all things considered, it hardly seemed possible.

Was it possible? Could she have won his heart by doing everything common sense told her should have alienated him completely? There was, she decided as she made her way downstairs, only one way to find out.

All her lingering doubts vanished when she entered the dining room and saw Grayson's face. He rose from the table and came toward her, his dark eyes shining with what could only be pleasure.

"Are you all right?" he asked softly, for her ears alone.

Instead of feeling annoyed at being asked that question for the one thousandth time, she found herself oddly touched. "Yes, I'm fine," she assured him with a smile.

But she noticed he took her arm anyway as he led her to the table. But perhaps he only wanted an excuse to touch her. For her part, she was very glad he did, and she felt a sense of loss when he had seated her in her chair and stepped away.

Virginia smiled at her from across the table and rang the bell to signal the maid to serve them their soup. The maid couldn't seem to keep her eyes off Emma who found herself coloring under the unusual scrutiny. She supposed she would have to get used to it. The slaves had probably never had a mistress quite like her.

As soon as the maid was gone, Emma picked up her spoon,

but before she could dip it into the bowl, Grayson reached over and took it.

She looked up in surprise to see he was switching their bowls.

"Just in case," he told her with a smile.

Emma stared at him for a long moment, her heart swelling with happiness. She hadn't believed for a moment that anyone was trying to poison her, but Grayson had. His gesture was more than polite concern or even duty. He was literally risking his life for her. She had to blink at the sting of tears.

"Oh, Grayson," she began, not knowing exactly what to say.

"Better eat your soup before it gets cold," he advised with a warm smile. A cherishing smile that Emma held close to her heart.

Amazingly, Emma went about her duties for the rest of the day without any ill effects. For the first time in weeks, she even managed to join the family in the parlor after supper—a supper during which Grayson once again ate the food that had been served to her—instead of retiring, exhausted, to her room as she had been wont to do. Grayson was charming and thoughtful and, yes, loving, in his attentions to her.

So loving, in fact, that as soon as she did retire to her room that night, she drew back the bolts on the connecting door. Surely, tonight he would come.

But Grayson didn't come to her that night or the next, even though he continued to treat her in this new and very exciting way. Emma was beginning to wonder if she would have to open the door herself and go into *his* room, when she heard him outside on the gallery just as she came into her room that evening to prepare for bed.

He was talking to Thomas, telling him he could go, and as Emma hurried to the French doors that stood open to the evening breeze, she caught a whiff of cigar smoke. Without allowing herself to think about what she was doing for fear she wouldn't be able to do it, she stepped out into the twilight shadows of the gallery.

For a moment that strange chill engulfed her, like a breath of icy wind that seemed to hang in the air even on the hottest days. Emma had finally decided it was some oddity of the house that caught the river breeze and held it in pockets.

She shivered, and Grayson looked over. He seemed very pleased to see her.

Suddenly, she was nervous, not certain exactly what to say. "That's so strange, the way the air out here is cold in certain places," she observed as the cold dissipated.

"What do you mean?" he asked, turning to face her. He held a cheroot in his hand.

"Haven't you noticed? Sometimes you come out here and the air feels positively icy, even if the day has been very hot, but just for a moment, and then it's gone."

"No, I've never noticed," he said with a smile. "Maybe that's something that only happens to conjure women."

She gave him a mock glare. "I warned you about that. Not everyone knows you're joking."

"What makes you think I'm joking?" he teased, leaning lazily against one of the posts supporting the roof. He looked very appealing in his shirtsleeves with the cuffs rolled up to expose his muscular forearms. The breeze from the river ruffled his hair.

Emma remembered how it felt to have those arms wrapped around her, and she instinctively stepped closer to him.

His smile warmed several degrees, and he tossed the cheroot over the railing. "You look very beautiful tonight, Mrs. Sinclair. One might almost say your color is blooming."

Emma self-consciously touched her cheek, aware that her color was always high when she was around Grayson. "It isn't paint, either. I've been . . . feeling remarkably well the past few days."

Indeed, her theory that Grayson's ill temper was making her ill had proven oddly true. The malaise that had gripped her for so many weeks had lifted completely, leaving her feeling more vibrant than she could ever remember.

Something flickered in his eyes, something very like desire, and Emma took another step closer. She wanted him to kiss her, she wanted it desperately, but she had no idea how to let him know. Perhaps if she touched him . . .

The breeze ruffled his hair again, and she reached up to brush it off his forehead. He caught her hand and held it for a long moment while he searched her eyes for the answer to some vital question. She didn't know what he wanted to see, but her heart was full of love, and she could only pray he could see that shining in her eyes.

After what seemed an eternity, he turned his face and pressed his lips into her palm. A thrill raced up her arm, tightening her nipples and shortening her breath. Her heart pattered in her chest as her hand caressed his cheek, glorying in the roughness of his day's growth of beard against the satin of his skin.

Slowly, ever so slowly, he released her wrist and lifted both of his hands to her face, cupping it as if he found her so infinitely precious he could not believe he actually held her. And then he lowered his lips to hers. His kiss was tentative at first, until he felt her eager response. With a groan, he enfolded her in his arms, hauling her against his chest and devouring her mouth, claiming her with a passion both primitive and exalting.

Emma clung to him, answering him with lips and tongue and arms and hands, relearning every inch of him she could reach as he, too, explored nearly forgotten territory. When they were breathless, he bent her back over his arm so he could cover her throat with kisses while one hand took the weight of her breast in a breath-stealing caress.

"Perhaps," he said between kisses, "you could . . . unlock the door . . . tonight . . ."

The request registered slowly in Emma's passion fogged brain, but finally she managed to gasp, "I already did! Days ago!"

He froze, his hand still on her breast, and he lifted his face so he could see her. *"Days* ago?" he echoed incredulously.

She nodded, breathless from the intensity of his gaze.

With another groan, he crushed her to him, covering her mouth with his in a soul searing kiss. She was sure her bones were actually melting when she heard someone calling Grayson.

"Massa! Massa!" Thomas's voice cut through their passion like a knife.

They broke apart as Thomas burst out through the doors to Grayson's room.

"Thomas, this better be important," Grayson warned through gritted teeth, still holding Emma with one arm.

But Thomas didn't smile. His face was ashen. "It's Benjamin, Massa. He gone."

Fifteen

Emma had to run to keep up with Grayson as he fairly flew down the stairs to where an anxious group of people waited for him in the foyer. Nathan's was the only white face looking up at them as they descended the stairs. Virginia, apparently, had already retired for the night, and no one had roused her. Among the others, Emma saw Opal, Benjamin's mother. She had obviously been weeping hysterically, although she was calmer now. A tall man with coffee-colored skin had his arm around her and was offering what comfort he could. He was, Emma thought absently, probably her husband. The others looked vaguely familiar, although Emma couldn't put names to them just then.

"I've already sent for the patrollers," Nathan told Grayson as he reached the bottom of the stairs. "They'll bring their dogs."

Opal cried out in anguish, covering her face with both her hands.

"They won't hurt him," Grayson assured her, his voice husky with emotions Emma could only imagine. "We just need the dogs to track him."

"He hasn't been gone too long," Nathan reported. "We should be able to pick up his scent without any trouble."

"When did he leave?" Grayson asked Opal.

Opal shook her head frantically. "I don't know! He didn't tell me he was leavin' 'cause he knowed I wouldn't let him go!"

"When was the last time you saw him?" Gray prodded, and

Emma noticed that his knuckles had whitened where he gripped the railing.

"This mornin', early, before I goed to work. He was just fixin' to leave for the blacksmith shop." Her voice broke and her husband pulled her back against his side, burying her face against his chest.

"Did he work with Uncle Sam today?" Gray asked Nathan.

Nathan shook his head. "Sam said he's been kind of lazy these past few weeks, going off fishing sometimes instead of coming into the shop, which was why he didn't think anything of it when the boy didn't show up this morning."

"Did he take anything with him?" Gray asked.

"Near as we can figure, just his spare clothes and a blanket," Opal's husband reported grimly.

"Could he have gotten any food?"

No one replied, but Emma knew what they were all thinking, that he could have easily stolen whatever he needed from the storehouse.

"Go on back to the quarters, now," Grayson told the slaves. The command was as gentle as he could make it under the circumstances. "We'll send word as soon as we hear anything, Opal. I promise."

She raised her eyes to meet his gaze, and for a long moment she simply stared at him, as if trying to judge the truth of his promise. Emma tried to imagine how she must feel, about Grayson and about losing her son by him, but she knew she could never begin to understand. She did know how she would feel if Alice were out there alone in the dark, however.

"We'll find him," Emma promised, drawing Opal's startled gaze.

"He just wanted to be free, that's all," Opal reminded her pitifully.

"Come on," her husband said gruffly, and he led her away. The others followed, leaving only Nathan.

Grayson turned to where Emma stood above him on the steps. "What did she mean?"

Emma almost winced at the pain she saw in his dark eyes. She hated to cause him even more, but she had no choice. "He asked me . . . Virginia and I saw Benjamin down in the quarters one day. He asked us to tell you that he wanted you to free him like you did your old Mammy."

This time his whole face twisted with agony, and Emma instinctively reached out to him. But he was beyond her comfort now. He turned to Nathan.

"Do you think anyone helped him?"

Nathan shrugged. "He didn't have any really close friends in the quarters. He . . . held himself aloof."

"Any girls?" Grayson pressed.

"I don't think so. I think he'd just been planning it for a while, real careful. He's a smart boy, and he probably asked questions about what he'd need to do. Opal said he's been talking about being free and acting moody. He must've purposely taken those days off at the shop so Uncle Sam wouldn't raise the alarm on him when he really did run."

He was so clever, so smart, Emma thought grimly. Blood will tell.

Grayson turned back to Emma. "You might as well go on to bed. We probably won't know anything until morning anyway."

"I'll stay with you for a while," she said, knowing she wouldn't be able to sleep in any case, and the thought of being up in her room alone, waiting, was intolerable. Besides, Grayson needed her.

"I'll be in my office," Grayson told Nathan. "Call me when the patrollers get here."

He stood aside and let Emma precede him down the stairs, then followed her into his office. She took a seat on the settee that stood along one wall, and Grayson went immediately to his liquor cabinet and poured himself a drink.

"Would you like some sherry?" he asked her.

She shook her head. She didn't need any stimulants. She

watched for a few minutes as Grayson paced restlessly, wondering what on earth she could say to him. Finally, she decided.

"Why don't you just let him go?"

He stopped so abruptly, the whiskey sloshed over the edge of his glass. *"What?"* he asked, apparently unable to believe what he had heard.

"Let him go," she repeated, knowing she was right. "You can't *give* him his freedom, but you can let him escape. He can start a new life and—"

"As usual, you don't understand," Grayson snapped, his fury overwhelming his grief as he glared down at her. "He *can't* escape."

"But he already did!"

"He escaped from Fairview and the people who love him and care about him, but where can he go? North? They sometimes head north because they know there's no slavery in the North, but they have no concept of how far away it is or the fact that you have to pass through a lot of dangerous territory to get there. Sometimes they go South, though, to Mexico, which is closer but no easier to get to. And sometimes they actually make it, the ones who are smart and who know where they're going, but not the children, Emma, and Benjamin is just a child. He won't make it. He'll be caught, and do you know what will happen to him then, if we aren't the ones who catch him?"

Emma shook her head, not trusting herself to speak.

"He'll be sold to the highest bidder," Grayson informed her, his voice rising with his anger. "A boy like him, strong and healthy, might bring as much as two thousand dollars, and nobody will mind if his ownership papers aren't exactly legal. And they'll put him in the fields and they'll work him until he drops and then they'll beat him and make him work some more! But that's only if he's lucky enough to get caught," he continued, his face almost ugly with bitter fury. "If he's *not* lucky, he'll simply starve to death or fall in a hole and break his leg and lie there helpless while the vultures come to pick out his eyes—"

"Stop!" Emma cried, clamping her hands over her ears so she wouldn't have to hear any more. "Oh, Grayson, I'm sorry, I didn't know!"

But he hardly seemed to hear her. He took a long swallow of the whiskey, then drew back his arm and threw the glass at the fireplace where it smashed into a thousand pieces.

His violence frightened her, but when Emma sprang to her feet, she didn't run away. Instead she ran to him, taking him in her arms. "Don't!" she cried, pulling his stiff body to hers. "Don't blame yourself!"

"Who else can I blame?" he demanded bitterly, resisting her embrace, but she didn't let him escape. She wrapped her arms around his waist and held him fast.

"You can blame whoever started this terrible slavery business in the first place," she told him frantically, gazing up at him with every ounce of her love shining on her face. "You can blame me for not telling you he wanted his freedom so badly. You can blame Uncle Sam for not reporting that he was missing, or you can blame Nathan for not controlling the slaves better."

"That's ridiculous!" he snapped, trying in vain to loosen her hold on him.

"No more ridiculous than blaming yourself!" she pointed out, clinging desperately and hoping, *praying,* that reason would finally pierce the armor of guilt he had wrapped around himself.

"I was his *father!"* he cried savagely, taking her shoulders in a bruising grip that made her wince.

"And you did all you could to make his life better!" Emma reminded him just as savagely. "But you couldn't free him and keep him safe! No one could do that, so you did what you could. No man could have done more!"

"I could have not made him in the first place!" he fairly shouted into her upturned face, finally stripping his agony naked before her.

"You didn't know!" she cried. "You didn't know the price

you would pay, and no one thought to warn you, but you've suffered for that sin every day since, and you'll suffer every day until you die. Isn't that enough?"

His eyes were like bottomless pits of despair. "Not if he dies for the freedom I couldn't give him."

With a sob, Emma wrapped her arms around his neck and pulled him to her, burying his tortured face in the curve of her neck while she wept over him. He shuddered and went still, clinging to her as if his life depended upon it. She was whispering a desperate prayer for Benjamin when Nathan opened the office door.

"The patrollers are here," he reported as they drew apart.

Grayson scrubbed his hands over his face and pulled himself up straight, squaring his shoulders. But when he would have gone, she took his hand, reminding him that he was not alone. The glance he gave her was too quick to read, but she thought she saw at least a touch of gratitude.

When they reached the front door, he gently disengaged his hand, patting hers reassuringly before releasing it, then turned and stepped out onto the veranda. Emma followed him silently.

The men carried torches which, Emma tried to tell herself later, was what made them look so sinister. Still, she couldn't recall ever seeing a more disreputable lot of men. There were four of them, some toothless, all wearing scraggly, tobacco stained beards. Their clothes were filthy and tattered, their boots worn and muddy, and each of them had a dog on a makeshift leash. The dogs were sad faced bloodhounds who circled restlessly, as if they sensed the urgency and did not quite understand why no one had given them a command.

Nathan was filling them in on the situation. They asked gruff questions about what the boy looked like, how long he'd been gone, if he'd ever run away before. When they were satisfied, one of the men asked, "Do you want us to sic the dogs on him when we find him? Make him an example?"

Emma couldn't help the cry of protest that escaped her lips, and she saw Grayson stiffen with fury. "No," he told them as coldly as she had ever heard him speak. "You are not to harm him in any way. If I see so much as a bruise—"

"Whatever you say, Mr. Sinclair," one of the men assured him quickly, nervously, and the others exchanged knowing glances.

Emma wondered what they thought they knew, but of course she didn't ask.

"We'll get him back for you," another of the men promised eagerly. "These younguns, they don't know nothin' about hiding out. We'll pick up his trail in no time at all and have him back before you know it."

"There'll be a bonus if he's unharmed," Grayson told them, and Emma saw their eyes light up greedily.

The men took their leave, going with Nathan down to the quarters for something of Benjamin's that they could use to get his scent. When they had disappeared into the darkness, Grayson turned back to her.

"You might as well go on to bed," he told her.

"Are you going to wait up?" she asked.

"For a while," he said, and she knew he wouldn't sleep until Benjamin was found, no matter how long that took.

"Then so will I. I'll get us some coffee."

He could have protested, could have ordered her to bed, so Emma knew how much he must want her there not to offer the slightest argument. She had the maid bring them coffee and, later, sandwiches, and she filled the dark empty silence with chatter. She told him about her childhood and her school years and even the trips she and Charles had taken, every interesting anecdote she could think of, talking until her voice went hoarse, just so Grayson wouldn't have to think about why they were waiting or what those awful men might find when—and if— they located Benjamin.

Finally, she couldn't talk anymore, so she laid her head on the arm of the settee, just to rest for a few moments, and when she opened her eyes again, the pale gray light of dawn was seeping through the windows.

She sat up with a start and saw that Grayson was asleep, too, his head resting on his arms as he slumped over his desk. Poor darling, she would have Thomas come down to take him upstairs. They weren't helping Benjamin by denying themselves the comfort of a bed.

But before she could move, she heard a noise outside and realized that was what must have disturbed her. It was the sound of distant shouting. The shouts were not happy sounds. Feeling the first stirrings of alarm, she jumped up and ran to the window.

"What is it?" Grayson asked, startling her.

"I don't know," she lied, terrified that she knew exactly. The patrollers were back, and they were leading a horse that carried a suspicious looking burden.

Grayson was beside her in a minute, and when he saw what she had seen, he cursed and ran, out the door and out of the house and across the fields.

Emma was right behind him, holding her skirts with both hands but still unable to keep up. By the time she reached them, they had untied the bundle on the horse's back and lowered it to the ground. Grayson's cry of anguish was like a knife in her heart.

"He was dead when we found him," one of the patrollers was saying, his voice shaking from apprehension. "You can see how his leg is all swolled up. Must've stepped on a rattler. We found him down by the river, just a couple miles from here. Never would've found him at all if we hadn't seen the vultures. I mean," he hurried on when he saw Grayson's expression. "He was real clever. Filled his socks with pepper so the dogs lost the scent right away. We just kept on, making sweeps, hoping they'd pick it up again. Then we saw the . . . Well, we found him then."

Emma had to clamp both hands over her mouth to keep from sobbing aloud. Benjamin looked so horrible with his clouded eyes staring blankly at the sky and his lips curled back from his teeth in an obscene rictus of death. His leg was indeed swollen, almost twice its normal size, and he'd torn the seam of his pant leg to accommodate it before he . . . The tears streamed down her face as she thought of what Grayson had said last night about him dying alone and helpless.

"We done everything we could, Mr. Sinclair," another of the patrollers was saying anxiously when Grayson made no reply. "He was cold when we found him. They wasn't nothin' we coulda done."

But Grayson didn't reply, didn't even glance at them. "Pay them off," he told Nathan, and then he took his son in his arms and rose stiffly to his feet, cradling the limp body to his chest. "I'll take him to his mother."

The others stepped back, making room for him, and Emma took a step to follow, but he turned on her, his eyes blazing with an emotion she had never seen before.

"Stay here," he told her, his voice like the sound of breaking glass.

How could she let him bear this alone? "But—"

"Please," he begged, and while she would have defied a command, she was powerless against his plea.

She nodded dumbly and watched him go. Her whole body ached for his grief and his guilt and his pain. And for his courage, too. He could have simply sent the boy's body to his mother, but he had chosen instead to take it himself, to face her anguish and share it.

She watched until Grayson had disappeared down the path, then turned back to the house. Virginia was standing in the doorway, her hand over her mouth. She must have just heard or perhaps she didn't know the worst of it yet. If Grayson could face Opal, she could handle Virginia. She took a deep breath and quickened her step.

"You gonna be sick now for sure," Chloe scolded later when Emma finally retired to her room. "Sittin' up all night, what was you thinkin'?"

"I was thinking my husband needed me," Emma told her with a sad smile. She'd wanted the night to be so different. When Grayson had taken her in his arms out on the gallery and kissed her, finally, she'd been so certain that they would make love at last. Instead they'd spent a night of horror that had somehow brought them even closer than physical lovemaking ever could.

She'd wanted to share the rest with him, too, but he hadn't returned from the quarters yet, and Chloe and Virginia had insisted that she get some sleep. Indeed, she was bone tired, as much from the emotional stress as from the sleepless night. Wearily, she allowed Chloe to undress her, and she slipped into her nightdress.

When she had braided Emma's hair, Chloe drew the drapes against the morning sunlight, but even when Emma was alone in the silent room, her exhausted body stretched out on the soft bed, sleep eluded her. Every time she closed her eyes, she saw Benjamin's twisted face, and she had to open them again.

She didn't know how long she had been lying there, staring up at her canopy, when she heard a crash from Grayson's room. Her heart pounding with terror, she bolted from the bed, ran to the connecting door, and threw it open.

Grayson was there, standing at his washstand. The mirror above it was smashed, and his hand was still raised in a fist. Blood seeped from it.

"Grayson, what have you done?" she demanded, running to him.

He hardly seemed to notice her. He was still staring at the broken mirror until she took his bleeding hand and wrapped a towel around it. She was glad to see it wasn't cut very badly. She dipped the end of the towel into the pitcher and began to dab at the cuts.

"How can you stand to look at me?" he asked. "I can't even stand to look at myself!"

"You didn't kill him," Emma reminded him. "And you didn't make him run away. That was his choice."

"I could have stopped him," Grayson argued as she led him to the bed and forced him to sit down.

"How? What could you have done?" she challenged, still dabbing at the cut. The bleeding had already stopped.

"I could have freed him. I could have—"

"And then he would have run off just the same!" Emma pointed out. "Do you think he would have stayed if he didn't have to? And if he was free, you couldn't have stopped him. No one could have stopped him."

The bedroom door opened, and Thomas stepped in, his eyes wide with alarm, but when he saw Emma, he hesitated.

"It's all right," she told him, and he nodded once, stepping back out as silently as he had entered.

Grayson didn't even seem to realize he had been there. He was still staring off into space, his bloodshot eyes bleak, his unshaven face haggard by more than just a lack of sleep.

"I never heard a woman cry like that," he said, his voice broken as he remembered Opal's reaction to her son's death. "Like someone was tearing the heart right out of her. I'll never forget that sound as long as I live."

Emma remembered the sound Grayson had made when he saw Benjamin's body, and she knew she would never forget it either. She put her arms around him and pulled him to her, cradling his head against the fullness of her breasts. With a groan, he embraced her, running his hands hungrily over her body through the fragile barrier of her nightdress.

Soon she realized his shoulders were shaking, and she knew he was weeping, grieving for the son he had never been able to properly love. His tears were all the more terrible because they were silent, as if the love he had not been able to openly acknowledge must be mourned in private, too. She held him fast, tears streaming down her own cheeks as well, until at long last he shuddered and went still.

She started to draw away, but he locked his arms around her and lifted his ravaged face.

"Don't leave me, Emma."

"Of course I won't leave you," she assured him, brushing the hair back from his forehead. "Where would I go?"

"No, I mean now. Don't leave me now. Stay with me, Emma. Stay with me and pretend . . . pretend you love me."

The broken plea tore at her heart, and she cupped his face tenderly in her hands. "I *do* love you, Grayson. I love you so very much."

For one long moment she watched the knowledge register deep in his dark eyes, and she saw the tiny glow that might have been the beginning of hope. And then she saw nothing at all because she was on her back on the bed, and Grayson was kissing her as if his very life depended upon the sweetness he drank from her lips.

Her body responded instantly to his, as if every nerve had been yearning for this precise moment in which to surge to life. Frantically, they stripped away the clothes that separated them until they lay with no barriers between them, flesh to flesh and heart to heart. Hands stroked feverishly, searing and kneading. Legs tangled wildly, catching and holding. Need roared in her, the need to hold and to keep and to love, the need to be held and cherished and worshiped.

Grayson did all of that and more, driving her nearly insane with his fingers and lips, stoking the fire within until it raged, until she begged him to take her.

"Love me, love me," she pleaded mindlessly.

"I do," he gasped as his fiery hardness filled her. "I do!"

The confession sent the fire out of control until it filled her, turning her blood molten and her bones to liquid fire. She surged with him, meeting him thrust for thrust, greedy and wanton and nearly insane with the desire that only he could quench. The flames licked higher and hotter, building and building until she could no longer control it, until she no longer wanted to control it, until she no longer had any thought at all, and her body exploded into a million blazing pieces.

The sparks of her soared out into the void, and it seemed a long time until they fell back to earth again, one by one by one, and she was herself again and whole. When she finally opened her eyes again and drew a steady breath, she was almost surprised to find herself still in Grayson's sunlit bed. Somehow she had half-expected to have been transported to some exotic locale. And then she realized Grayson's bed *was* an exotic locale: the place where he had finally confessed his love to her.

At first she thought he was asleep. He lay so still, with his head upon her breast and his legs still tangled with hers, and she was content simply to hold him, knowing that he was hers now, truly and completely. Then he stirred slightly and lifted his head so he could see her face.

He still looked exhausted and inexpressibly sad, but she saw the hope in his eyes, blazing brightly now, and the love.

"Did I hurt you?" he asked, his voice husky as he pushed himself up so his face was even with hers.

"No," she assured him, feeling the color rising in her face. She smiled wickedly. "Did *I* hurt *you?*"

His smiled flickered, then died again. "I don't know," he said. "Is it true? Do you really love me?"

"Yes, oh, yes," she cried, reaching up to caress his whisker roughened cheek.

He closed his eyes as a tremor shook him, and when he opened them again, she thought she saw as much relief as joy there. "I can't imagine why you should," he said, "but I'm not going to argue with you. I need you too much. I had no idea *how* much until last night."

Emma waited, hoping he would say more, needing him to say the words when he wasn't in the throes of passion. When he didn't, she said, "And do you love me, too?"

"Yes, oh, God, yes," he swore, pulling her to him for a fierce hug. Then he pulled back, until he could see her face again. "I love you, Emma," he told her solemnly.

Her eyes filled with tears.

"Oh, God, don't cry!" he begged in dismay. "Please, don't cry!"

"I can't seem to help it," Emma said, blinking but only succeeding in dislodging the tears to run down her face. "I'm not unhappy, really, I'm not! It's just that . . . I thought you hated me."

"I never *hated* you," he objected, almost comically outraged by the mere suggestion.

"Well, despised me, then," she demurred. "At the very least you didn't like me very much."

"I was a fool," he informed her. "No, not a fool, an idiot. An arrogant, selfish idiot."

"Then it's true? You really didn't like me?" Knowing was one thing. Hearing from his own lips was something else again, and fresh tears formed in her eyes.

"I didn't know you," he defended himself. "I didn't *want* to know you, either. I already desired you more than I'd ever desired any other woman in my life, and—"

"You did?" she exclaimed in genuine surprise.

"Of course I did! How could I help it?" he asked, running a hand provocatively down her naked side to rest on her bare hip.

Renewed desire tingled over her, but she resolutely ignored it.

"And when did you, uh, stop disliking me?" she prodded.

He smiled slowly. "Well, now, let me think. I guess it started the first time you lectured me on the evils of slavery."

"No!" she protested, certain he was teasing her.

"I swear! And then I saw how you were with Alice and, of course, knowing that every other man in the county wanted you, too, helped a lot, but you really won my heart once and for all when you showed me why my ledger wouldn't balance."

Emma gaped at him. "You mean it wasn't when we . . . that night we . . . out on the gallery?"

"Well, that was very nice," he assured her with a wicked grin, running his hand over the swell of her bottom and sending delicious ripples all over her, "but not what made me fall in love with you."

"You mean, all this time . . . oh, Grayson, I've been such a fool!"

"We both have, but that's over," he promised. "From now on, no matter what happens, we'll have each other." His eyes had darkened with the remembered pain, and Emma wrapped her arms around him again.

This time their lovemaking was slow and languorous, and they savored every kiss and touch and caress until tenderness was no longer enough, and they both cried out in soul shattering release. Afterwards they slept in each other's arms.

Later, when they awoke, they dressed and went down to the quarters hand in hand to see Benjamin laid out and to mourn for a boy whose life had hardly even begun.

That night as Emma lay in Grayson's arms again, he whispered, "I wouldn't be able to get through this without you."

And Emma knew she had finally found her place.

Grayson and Emma hardly had time to either grieve or rejoice, however, because the harvest began just a few days later. From dawn until full dark, the slaves worked in the fields, harvesting the cotton and the corn while the kitchen help went about preserving the abundance of the vegetable garden.

Emma was sure she had never seen so much food in any one place in her life, and for the first time she understood the phrase "the land of milk and honey." But that food had to be properly stored or it would be lost, so Emma spent her days supervising in the kitchen and the storehouses while Grayson spent his riding the fields to help Nathan supervise the picking.

At night they were sometimes even too tired to make love, but still Grayson slept with her every night, holding her until the morning light summoned them to another full day's labors. And if Grayson still grieved for his lost son, he could bear it because of Emma's love. And if Emma sometimes felt overwhelmed by the demands of being a plantation mistress, she would endure because of Grayson's love.

By the time the harvest was complete, Emma was certain no woman had ever been happier than she. She had everything she had ever wanted and more, a loving husband, a beautiful daughter and role to fill. For her the harvest celebration was much more than a mere party to mark the end of hard work for the season and give thanks for a bountiful crop. For Emma, it was a private thanksgiving that her life finally had true meaning.

The Sinclairs gave the first harvest party of the season, and all their neighbors came, as they would go to theirs in turn. Emma and Virginia laid out their bounty of red, ripe tomatoes and potatoes, white and sweet, and juicy watermelons and cantaloupes and sweet roasting caro. Their own slaves and those from other plantations engaged in a corn shucking contest with the winners receiving a gold coin. Afterwards, everyone danced under the stars on a wooden platform built in the yard for that purpose as the slave musicians played their ragtag instruments. Corn shuck torches lighted the festivities, and corn squeezings enlivened them.

Emma had to smile when slave women from other plantations brought their babies for her to touch. They didn't say they wanted her blessing or in any way indicate *why* they had sought her out, but Emma knew it was her reputation for having stolen Hallie's powers that made her so popular. And she was glad to see that Hallie was at the party this time, too.

Of course, she didn't mingle with the whites, or even with Nathan, but she no longer seemed to be an outcast among her own either. If only . . . But Emma wouldn't wish for large miracles. She would content herself with the small ones.

Or at least she thought she would until Nathan found her and Grayson just after the dancing began.

"You've done a fine job," Grayson told him happily, shaking his hand. "I'm afraid I'm going to have to double your usual bonus this year."

"Gray, I don't know how to tell you this . . ." he began, looking oddly uncomfortable for one who had been receiving accolades all day.

"Is something wrong?" Emma asked in alarm, and Grayson's smile disappeared, too.

"Not wrong, exactly, although you might disagree . . . Oh, shoot, I guess there's nothing for it but to tell you right out. I'm afraid this will be my last summer with you."

"You're leaving?" Grayson confirmed, hardly able to believe it.

"I'm sorry to say I am," Nathan admitted with a wan smile. "It's past time. My father's debts were paid long ago, and I've saved up quite a bit, more than enough to give me a start on my own place."

"But where will you go?" Emma asked, and then she remembered an even greater concern. "And what about Hallie and the children? Surely, you can't—"

"That's really why I'm leaving," he said, all trace of humor gone from his face. "It's past time for that, too. I . . . Well, I was hoping you'd let me buy Hallie and the children from you. I'd like to take them with me."

At least Nathan wasn't going to simply leave them behind, as if they had meant no more to him than the house Grayson had given him to live in. But still . . . "Nathan, what about the children? What will become of them? And Hallie, too?"

Nathan's eyes were grave when he looked at Emma. "I know what I *hope* will become of them, which is why I plan to marry Hallie. We can't stay here in Texas, of course, or anywhere in the South, but I was thinking we could go to Kansas. It's a free state, and I've heard the farmland is good there. No one would know us, and we can start a new life together. No one will ever have to know Hallie was a slave."

"Oh, Nathan!" Emma cried, impulsively hugging him.

"Look how happy she is for you, Nathan," Grayson groused. "She doesn't seem to realize that I've just lost the best overseer in Texas."

"You'll find someone else," Nathan said, his smile back in place when Emma released him.

"Not likely, not anyone as good as you," Gray protested.

"But I wish you all the best, and just to prove it, I'll give you Hallie and the children as a gift. Can't have you starting your new life short of funds, can I?"

"Oh, Grayson!" Emma cried, throwing her arms around her husband this time.

"Gray, I don't know what to say! That's too much! I can't accept!" Nathan protested.

"Of course you can," Gray told him over Emma's shoulder as he held her fast. "Now go find Hallie and tell her the good news. I want to kiss my wife."

He did, too, until Emma had to push him away and remind him sternly that they had company, and he should mind his manners. Grayson promised to mind more than his manners the next time he got her alone. Emma couldn't imagine a better end to what had been a perfect day, and she seemed to float as Grayson led her to the dance floor.

She was still floating hours later as she strolled around the edges of the party, checking to see that everything was going well. The dancing promised to go on all night, and Emma was pleased to see the food promised to hold out as well. Should she send someone for another jug of whiskey? she was wondering when she heard Chloe calling her name.

Emma's heart lurched in her chest when she saw Chloe racing across the lawn as if the devils of hell were after her. Dear Lord, it couldn't be, she told herself, but she picked up her skirts and ran toward Chloe, praying that she was wrong.

Sixteen

"He here, Missy," Chloe gasped.

"He can't be!" Emma protested. They had pointedly *not* invited DeWitt Phelps to the celebration.

"I seen him sneaking up the back stairs. He knocked me down, and I played dead 'til he gone, then I come runnin'!"

"Are you all right?" Emma asked, turning her so the light from the nearest torch fell on her bruised face.

"Don't worry 'bout me," Chloe cried, impatiently shaking off Emma's hands. "Go find Miss Alice!"

"Get Grayson," Emma called as she picked up her skirts again. "Tell him I need him upstairs!" And then she ran as she had never run before.

By the time she reached the house, she was sobbing for breath and cursing the corsets that were threatening to cut her in half, but she didn't stop when she reached the stairs. Her breath rasping in her throat and dark spots dancing before her eyes, she took them two at a time, hauling herself up by the railing when her legs threatened to fail her.

When she reached the top, she literally fell to her knees, unable to go another step until the spots cleared and she was able to force some air into her beleaguered lungs.

Alice! her mind screamed, but it was several more moments before her body could respond. Staggering to her feet, still gasping, she ran to Alice's bedroom door, but when she tried to open it, it wouldn't budge. Dear heaven, he'd blocked it somehow, she realized in renewed panic. She thought of the playroom which connected to the bedroom, but he had probably blocked that door, too. Then she remembered the door to the gallery. Even if he'd locked it, she could break the glass and—

She was already running, into her own bedroom and out the French doors and down the gallery. The air around the nursery doors was so cold, Emma thought she might be able to see her breath, and it swirled strangely, sending chills racing over her. But she barely had time to register the strange phenomenon as she threw her weight against the doors. They gave easily and burst open. Emma went stumbling into the room, and what she saw stopped her heart.

DeWitt Phelps was sitting on Alice's bed, reaching out to the child who was huddled with the covers pulled up to her chin, staring at him with eyes wide with absolute terror in the light of the single candle he had lit.

He looked up at Emma, surprise and rage twisting his strangely handsome face. "Get out!" he snarled, jumping to his feet.

"*You* are the one who isn't welcome here," she cried.

"Because I didn't get an invitation?" he taunted. "You didn't invite me to your wedding, either, but that didn't keep me away. You'll never keep me away from Alice. She's mine!"

Spittle flew from his mouth, and his eyes glittered strangely, and for the first time Emma began to doubt even his sanity. Surely, he knew he must obey her authority here. All she had to do was call for help, and the room would be filled with servants and . . . or would it? All the house servants were at the party. Even Mammy seemed to have deserted her post, and little Rose's bed was empty, too. Grayson was coming, of course, but only *if* Chloe could find him. And would he come in time?

"I'm going to have to ask you to leave," she tried, assuming her haughtiest expression, but Phelps simply sneered at her.

"And what if I don't? Are you going to throw me out?" he asked menacingly, starting toward her. "In front of all your friends and neighbors? And what do you think they'll say about that Yankee bitch who wouldn't even let poor old DeWitt see his own grandchild?"

"They'll say I was right when I tell them what you did to your own *daughter!*" Emma cried, instinctively backing away.

But he laughed, throwing back his head and making a sound that curdled Emma's blood. "They won't believe you. *No one* will believe you!"

"But Chloe knows! She was *there!*"

"And you think anybody'd believe a nigger? A nigger and a Yankee bitch?"

Fear coiled in her as he kept coming, closer and closer, the madness shining unmistakably in his eyes. "If you lay a hand on me, I'll scream!" she threatened.

"No!" Alice shrieked from where she huddled on the bed. "Don't hurt my Mama! Don't throw her over the gallery!"

Phelps' face twisted with rage, but before Emma could decide at whom his rage was directed, the sound of running feet outside the door distracted them both.

"Emma! Alice!" Grayson's voice shouted.

"Papa! Papa!" Alice cried, her voice shrill with terror. "Don't let him throw my Mama over the gallery again! Hurry, Papa, hurry! Don't let him hurt her again!"

Dear heaven! Emma thought wildly, seeing Phelps' fury transform into abject terror. Was Phelps even more than a defiler of children? Could he also have murdered his own daughter?

She heard Grayson slamming his weight against the nursery door, trying to force it open. Phelps had braced a chair beneath the handle, and it trembled now under the force of Grayson's assault.

"You killed Lilly, didn't you?" Emma accused, certain she was right even before she saw the rage contorting Phelps' face again. "You pushed your own child to her death, and Alice saw it, and that's why she's been frightened of you ever since!"

The chair splintered with a horrendous sound, and the door

flew open. Grayson burst in, stumbling to a halt while his gaze swept the room.

But Emma had no more than registered that fact when Phelps grabbed her, clamping his arm around her neck and dragging her in front of him as if to shield himself from Grayson.

"What the hell is going on here?" Grayson demanded as Alice screamed again.

"Don't hurt her! Don't hurt her!"

Fighting for breath, Emma was only vaguely aware that Phelps had wrestled her over to where the candle sat on Alice's dresser. He snatched it up and held it out like a weapon.

"Stay where you are, Sinclair," he snarled viciously, "Or I'll set her on fire!"

Grayson gasped with horror at the very real threat, and Emma would have if she could have gotten the breath to gasp. Her gown, she knew, would go up like a torch, trapping her in the deadly flames until she died in screaming agony.

She clawed frantically at the arm that held her throat, but he didn't even seem to feel it.

Blow out the candle! her mind screamed as the fragile flame danced before her, but she couldn't even draw a breath. Dark spots danced before her eyes, and the sounds of Alice's screams began to fade.

"Are you out of your mind?" Grayson was shouting. "Why would you want to hurt Emma? They'll hang you, DeWitt! You'll never get away with this! Just let her go, man!"

"He killed Miss Lilly," another voice said, this one cold and hard and seeming to come from nowhere, and then Chloe stepped into the wavering light from the trembling candle. "That night she died, he up here trying to get to Miss Alice, but she catched him, and she tell him she gonna ruin him so he pick her up and throw her over the railing."

"Liar!" Phelps cried, nearly hysterical. Emma could feel him shaking and smell the stench of his terror. His grip on her slackened for just a moment, just long enough for her to

suck in one single life sustaining breath before he tightened it again. "She's lying! Nobody'll believe a nigger girl! She can't even testify against me in a court of law!"

Emma saw the horror register on Grayson's face as he realized the truth at last. "You killed Lilly! You killed your own child!"

"Stay back!" Phelps shouted in panic, brandishing the candle as Grayson instinctively started for him. "I won't hurt her if you stay back. I'm leaving now," he told them, fighting to keep his voice steady. "I'm going out on the gallery, and I'm going to climb down the trellis, and you aren't going to stop me, and then I'm going away and you won't ever find me, so don't even try, Sinclair. Do you hear me, don't even try!"

He was dragging Emma backward now, and even though she refused to help, refused to move her feet and even went limp in his arms, his strength was no match for hers. She could see Grayson, his beautiful face contorted with rage, his hands clenched into fists as he watched, helpless, unable to risk her life because he loved her so very much. And dear little Alice who was still screaming, her voice shrill and thin and hysterical as she begged Phelps not to kill her mama again. And Chloe, her dark eyes glittering with an anguish Emma could only imagine.

They had reached the French doors now, and Phelps dragged her through them. Instantly the frigid air engulfed them, swirling wildly around them and taking what little breath she had left.

"What the hell?" she heard Phelps mutter, and she imagined she felt an icy wind tearing at them. Could a storm have blown up so suddenly? she wondered wildly.

But she didn't have time to wonder more because Phelps was hauling her across the gallery, and Alice's screams increased to a frenzy. Grayson and Chloe surged forward, no longer able to resist the overwhelming urge to aid her, but Phelps' cry stopped them in their tracks.

"I'm warning you!" he shouted, brandishing the candle. The

frigid wind roared in her ears, but miraculously, the candle flame barely flickered. "Don't come any closer or I'll burn her!"

Didn't any of their guests see them now? The grounds were swarming with people, but they were far away, over by the dance floor where the music would drown out any sounds they made.

"If you hurt her, I'll hunt you down and kill you with my own hands!" Grayson shouted, but Phelps laughed or tried to. The freezing wind was so loud now, it swallowed the sound, although the candle flame still burned brightly.

They were almost to the railing now, and Emma increased her struggles, arching her back, clawing at his arm, twisting violently.

And then, suddenly, she was free. She paused an instant to suck in a desperate breath. As if from a distance, she heard Grayson's cry, a sound of anguish that seemed torn from his soul, but she was turning to see what had become of Phelps. If she could stop him, if they could catch him . . .

But the wind was roiling and churning and so cold her blood felt frozen in her veins, and she couldn't move as the wind rose up between her and Phelps like a miasma, twisting and turning until it actually took shape. The shape of a woman all white and ghastly and shimmering in the light that seemed to be growing brighter somehow although the candle was gone now, a light that flickered around Emma and warmed the frigid air with a blast of intense heat. The woman lifted her hand and pointed at Phelps and opened her mouth, that horrible mouth that was just a black hole in her terrible face, and she wailed the wail of the damned.

Phelps was frozen, one leg over the gallery, as he stared transfixed at the apparition. Then *his* mouth opened, a horrible black hole in a horribly twisted face, and he cried out, *"Lilly!"*

Like a man pursued by the very demons of hell, he leaped onto the railing and jumped, flinging himself out into the blackness with a desperation born of simple, mindless terror. His scream seemed to fill the night.

But Emma registered the horror for only an instant before Grayson threw her down and began beating on her with his coat. Then Chloe was there with a blanket torn from Alice's bed, and they were both on her in a frantic effort to smother the flames that Phelps had started on her skirts to ensure that they would be too busy to pursue him until he'd had a chance to escape.

By the time she had registered the terror that she was on fire, the fire was out. Chloe had run for water and was emptying the pitcher from her bedroom over Emma's skirts just to make sure as Grayson literally ripped the fabric from her body.

When he had dragged her free of the sodden mass, he took her in his arms. From down on the lawn she could hear the shouts of her guests who had heard Phelps' scream and were coming to see what had happened.

"Are you all right?" Grayson asked. "Are you burned? Did he hurt you?"

Her throat ached, and she still couldn't properly get her breath because her corsets were binding her so very tightly, and she didn't know if she was burned or not, but she didn't think of any of that. "Did you see her? Lilly, she was here! She—"

"Yes, yes," Grayson said, stroking the hair back from her face. "It's all right now." He turned to where Chloe hovered anxiously. "Go get my mother and the doctor and for God's sake, find Mammy and get her up here to calm Alice down!"

The child was still screaming, probably certain that Emma had been murdered just as Lilly had.

"Bring her here," Emma said or thought she did, because she really couldn't get her breath and the night was suddenly much, much darker and Grayson's face was wavering. But she wasn't cold anymore, she realized vaguely as she slipped into unconsciousness. And that strange storm was over.

* * *

Grayson paced restlessly outside Emma's bedroom. The doctor was with her, and Virginia, but they'd sent him out while the doctor examined her.

How could this be happening? he asked himself over and over, still unable to make any sense at all out of what he had witnessed this evening.

DeWitt had killed Lilly. Of that much he had no doubt. Both Alice and Chloe had borne witness, and Phelps' own reaction to the charge had proven it. Poor Alice, his poor baby, having to see her own mother murdered before her eyes and then to see Emma attacked by the same man and set on fire . . .

Grayson shuddered as he recalled the longest moment in his life, from the instant he had seen DeWitt touch the flame to Emma's skirt to when he finally reached her to smother the fire. Logically, he knew only seconds had passed, but he had relived his whole life in those seconds, and he had known he didn't want to live another minute without Emma beside him.

And now she lay in there, possibly injured, possibly dying, and there wasn't a single thing he could do for her. Dear God, why had he wasted so many precious months? Why had he been so determined to deny himself happiness that he had turned away from the one woman who could give it to him? They'd only had a few short weeks in which to even begin to love each other. How could he bear to go on without her now?

If only he'd believed her when she'd first told him about DeWitt. If only he'd trusted her and not been so damn arrogant and sure that he was right . . .

A door opened, but when he looked up, he saw it was the nursery door. Chloe stepped out.

"Alice?" he asked. His poor baby had been completely hysterical, certain Emma was dead no matter how they had tried to convince her otherwise. Mammy had managed to calm her down, but she had still been inconsolable. The only way to truly comfort her would be to take her in to see an Emma who was completely recovered, but at the moment, Emma wasn't completely recovered.

"Miss Alice doin' better," Chloe reported. "She wanna see Miss Emma, though. Is she—?"

"I haven't heard anything yet," Gray reported in frustration.

Chloe nodded, her dark eyes full of emotions he couldn't even begin to understand. She had suffered so much, even more than mere slavery could inflict, and Gray had only made her suffering worse by refusing to believe her.

"I'm sorry, Chloe," he said, figuring his father would be turning in his grave to hear him apologizing to a slave but knowing he couldn't live with himself if he didn't.

She looked surprised. "For what, Massa Gray?"

"For not believing you about DeWitt and . . . and what he did to you and . . . to Lilly." Even now, the admission nearly stuck in his throat.

"Didn't nobody ever believe 'cept Miss Emma," she told him. "I don't reckon folks *could* believe a thing like that, or leastways, they don't want to."

"And he . . ." Gray didn't really want to know for sure, but he also knew he couldn't live with himself until he'd heard her say it right out. "He did those things to Lilly, too?"

She nodded solemnly, and Gray felt the agony of it twisting in his gut.

"That why she never like for you to touch her, Massa," Chloe said quickly, as if she needed for him to know this. "She love you, but she can't stand for no man to touch her after . . . after what *he* done. She try 'cause she want to be a good wife to you, but she just can't."

Gray nodded, unspeakably grateful to understand at last just how tortured his Lilly had been. For a moment he wished that DeWitt Phelps had survived the fall from the gallery so he could kill him with his bare hands.

But DeWitt was beyond vengeance. And Lilly was beyond help. All Gray could do now was put the pieces of his family back together and go on. If, please God, he was given the chance.

The door to Emma's room opened, and Virginia stepped out.

Her face was haggard, but she was smiling. "She's awake, and she wants to see you."

Gray brushed past her, not wanting to waste a minute on questions.

The doctor was putting his things back into his bag, and when he looked up, he too was smiling.

Then Gray saw Emma, and he forgot everything else. She looked so beautiful with her dark hair falling around her shoulders, and her face so white and perfect. She held out her hand, and he went to her, sitting down on the bed beside her, careful not to jar her. He took her hand in both of his and lifted it to his lips for a fierce kiss. Dear God, she looked so small and frail in the big bed, propped up by so many pillows.

"What . . . how is she?" he asked the doctor.

"I'll let her tell you," he said, then to Emma, "Remember what I said."

She nodded, and he left, but Gray hardly even noticed. He had eyes only for Emma.

"How is Alice?" she asked before he could question her.

"She's calmer, but she wants to see you."

"We'll send for her in a minute, after I tell you . . . Oh, Gray, did you see what happened out on the gallery? Lilly was there! She really was!"

Gray patted her hand, glad to see at least that her color was coming back. "So you said."

"You mean you didn't see her? Well, it wasn't her exactly, of course, but her ghost or her spirit or something. Remember I told you how I always felt a chill when I went out on the gallery? I sometimes felt like someone was watching me, too, and it must have been Lilly. Her spirit must have been lingering there, just waiting, maybe even looking after Alice or trying to protect her somehow. Anyway, she finally materialized just as Mr. Phelps was getting ready to climb down from the gallery."

"I'm afraid I didn't see anything except those flames licking up your skirt," Gray said grimly, remembering that awful sight and how helpless he had felt and how frightened.

"Mr. Phelps saw her," Emma insisted. "He called her name before he . . . Well, he didn't exactly fall, did he? It was almost like he . . . like he *jumped* off."

Gray didn't want to talk about DeWitt Phelps or even about the ghost of his dead wife. If Lilly had risen from the dead to avenge her own death, Gray could only be grateful to her.

"What do you have to tell me?" he prodded, not sure he wanted to hear but needing to know even the worst. "Are you burned? Are you—?"

"I'm not burned," she told him, shaking her head in wonder. "I guess my petticoats were so thick, they shielded me from the fire, and you got to me so quickly . . ."

Gray shuddered and pressed her hand to his lips again, uttering a silent prayer of gratitude that he'd been as quick as he had. But when he looked at her again, he saw where the bruises were forming on her throat. "He hurt you," Gray guessed, anger roiling in him again, along with a renewed urge to execute DeWitt Phelps.

"No," she assured him quickly, lifting her free hand to her abused neck. "Except for a few bruises, I'm fine."

"But there's something else, isn't there?" he prodded, nearly desperate now as terror gripped him.

"Yes but . . . it's not anything to do with what happened tonight. It . . . it has to do with when I was sick before. Remember when I threw up and—"

"Yes, yes," he agreed, willing her to hurry and tell him the worst.

"I was sicker then than I let you know. I was ill almost every night. Not always throwing up, but just weak and tired and—"

"But you're better now," he argued, desperate to prove her wrong. He wasn't going to lose her now to some mysterious ailment when he had just snatched her back from the very fires of hell. "You've been fine these past weeks and—"

"I still have what made me sick before," she told him, her fingers tightening on his. "But it isn't bad. At least I don't think it is, and I hope you won't think so either because—"

"What is it?" he demanded, angry now, furious at the forces that seemed determined to drive them apart now that they had finally found each other.

Emma bit her lip, obviously reluctant, but finally she said, "I'm going to have a baby."

"A baby?" he echoed stupidly.

"Yes, a baby," she confirmed, her eyes suddenly brighter than he had ever seen them. "When I was sick, that was morning sickness, only Dr. Evans says it sometimes comes at night, which was why we didn't realize what it was, and besides I thought I *couldn't* have a baby so naturally, I never realized and neither did Chloe, I guess, and Dr. Evans said he thought maybe Charles just didn't try as hard as you did to give me a baby, but you haven't really been trying at all, not until lately, and by then it was already started. It probably got started on our wedding night, or maybe even that very first time on the gallery, so I guess it *is* a good thing Virginia made us get married so quickly and—"

"A baby?" Gray repeated incredulously. "That's all that's wrong with you?"

"Not *wrong* exactly," Emma insisted, "although Dr. Evans said that's probably why I fainted tonight and probably why I fainted the day I didn't whip Hallie, too, but if I stop wearing my corsets, he said I'll be fine and—"

Gray stopped her with a kiss, covering her mouth with his because he needed to be joined to her some way. He took her gently in his arms, terrified of hurting her but desperate to feel her softness and her heart beating against his. After a long time, he lifted his mouth from hers and, still cradling her in his arms, gazed down at her. He had not, he was certain, ever loved her more than he did at that moment.

"Then you don't mind?" she asked a little breathlessly.

"Mind? About what?"

"The baby," she reminded him uncertainly.

He felt the smile forming on his face, a big, goofy smile of unutterable joy. "I thought nothing could make me happier than simply knowing you were all right, but I was wrong. I love you, Emma. I love you more than life itself, and I'll love our baby just as much."

"Oh, Grayson, I love you, too. I don't think I knew how much until tonight. I would have been perfectly happy to have just you and Alice in my life, but now—oh, my goodness, we should send for Alice so she can see I'm all right!" she remembered anxiously.

"We will," Gray said. "But just let me hold you for another minute first."

He drew Emma to him, tucking her head into the curve of his shoulder so he could press his lips to the tender skin on her temple. He closed his eyes, savoring the pure joy of the moment, and when he opened them again, he saw Lilly.

She was standing in the gallery doorway, a shimmering wraith against the black night beyond. As he stared in stunned disbelief, she lifted one vaporous hand to her lips and blew him a kiss, and then, waving, she slowly disappeared.

Author's Note

I hope you enjoyed Emma and Grayson's story. For years I had hesitated to write a book set on a plantation in the pre-Civil War South. One reason for this was because I couldn't quite figure out how to make a slave owner a sympathetic character. After I researched the time period, however, I learned that many otherwise good people owned slaves and that they had developed elaborate methods for justifying themselves. Virginia expresses many of those justifications, while Grayson reveals the frustrations of a reluctant slave owner.

The other reason I didn't want to set a book in the pre-Civil War South was because I knew I would have to leave the characters just starting a new life together when in a few short years the Civil War would tear their world apart. But Emma kept demanding that I write her story, so finally I had no choice. Because I would worry about her, though, and because I knew my readers would wonder what happened to Fairview and its people after the war, I researched not only the great plantations of Texas but also what became of them after the war ended.

As I had expected, most planters were ruined by the war when the main source of their wealth, their slaves, were freed. They no longer had a work force for the enormous task of running their plantations, and most of them had to sell their land for taxes to profiteers who divided the farms up into small plots and leased them to sharecroppers. Others were able to make the transition to cattle ranching which finally came into its own in the years after the war.

I wanted a happier ending for Gray and Emma, however, and I finally found one. A certain Texas planter had just shipped his cotton crop to the mills in England when the Civil War broke out. The shipment arrived safely, but the mill owners were unable to transfer the payment to the planter because of the war, so the funds languished in an English bank for nearly five years. When the war finally ended, the planter who had been virtually penniless during the war discovered that he had over two hundred thousand dollars waiting for him. While his neighbors went bankrupt, he prospered in the New South, and although he was never quite as wealthy as he had been in the golden years of the old South, his descendants still live in the house he built. I decided that this is what happened to Emma and Grayson and Alice and the children Emma bore. I hope my decision pleases you, too.

I love to hear from my readers. Please write and let me know how you liked this book. Enclose a long self-addressed stamped envelope and I will send you a newsletter letting you know when my next book is coming out. Write to me at:

Victoria Thompson
c/o Cornerstone Communications
5416 Sixth Ave., Suite 128
Altoona, PA 16602

Taylor-made Romance from Zebra Books